The yellowbacks... classics of popular fiction

The yellowjackets or yellowbacks were a great series of bestselling adventure and crime thrillers that had its origins in the mid to late 19th century following on from the 'penny dreadfuls'. They virtually began the mass market revolution of the early 20th century with a clear standard format and imprint/series livery (what would today be called branding). Hodder & Stoughton published the yellowjackets in two main series with series run dates of: 1923-1939 and later 1949-1957.

As the tagline ('where thrillers really began') on the back cover implies, the imprint and series focused on thrillers that were the bestsellers of their time. This current reissue or retro revival if you will, brings back many of these masterpieces, now classics in their own way and extends it further by including key titles from that period that were either great crime or thriller or even general commercial fiction (including sub-genres of noir, horror, gothic, romance, westerns, etc.) influences of their time. There are some perennial favourites and many rarities either lost or not easily available being revived in the current series. Writers and characters ranged from adventure heroes like Bulldog Drummond, Allan Quatermain, Richard Hannay or the Saint through thriller grandmasters Edgar Wallace and E. Phillips Oppenheim, crime and mystery maestros like Patricia Wentworth, GK Chesterton, Agatha Christie and the Detection club, to western and swashbucklers like Zane Grey, Max Brand, Captain Blood and even romance or general fiction classics like Hermina Black, Denise Robins, Marie Corelli or Stella Morton. These were books that had storytelling at their heart and always entertained.

The yellowbacks had both hardback (with varying design elements) and paperback (which built the series look) versions with the latter still carrying the imprint 'yellowjacket'. The current reissues pay tribute to both and use an amalgam of elements from both editions while retaining the complete yellow (or 'mustard-plaster') livery with the author's name in blue beveled type with a 'simulated emboss' effect and a white outer 'outline', and the book title in black. These reissues retain the distinctive size of the original mass market paperback and follow the three main category variations—the thrillers (crime, westerns, mystery, adventure) had blue lettering for the author's name, while Romance and softer general fiction had red; and other categories like humour had green.

For more detail and a full list of titles visit https://www.hachetteindia.com/home/yellowbacks

THE COMPLETE
JUST MEN OMNIBUS

VOLUME 2

THE COMPLETE JUST MEN OMNIBUS

Richard Horatio Edgar Wallace was a British writer who virtually invented the thriller market and was the first to introduce police characters as leading protagonists rather than amateur sleuths.

Born into poverty as an illegitimate child in London, Wallace left school at the age of 12. He joined the army at age 21 and was a war correspondent during the Second Boer War for Reuters and the Daily Mail. Struggling with debt (he had a weakness for the horses), he left South Africa, returned to London and began writing thrillers to raise income, publishing books including *The Four Just Men*. Drawing on his time as a reporter in the Congo, Wallace serialised short stories in magazines and published adventure stories featuring his first series character Sanders of the River. He signed with Hodder and Stoughton in 1921 and became an internationally recognized author.

Wallace was such a prolific writer that it was claimed that one of every four books published in England were written by him. Apart from his reportage, Wallace wrote screen plays, poetry, historical non-fiction, 18 stage plays, 957 short stories and over 170 novels, 12 in 1929 alone. Over 160 films have been made from Wallace's work and his story-screenplay for the Hollywood classic *King Kong*.

THE
COMPLETE
JUST MEN OMNIBUS

Edgar Wallace

VOLUME 2

The Three Just Men
Again the Three

The Complete Just Men Omnibus

The Three Just Men first published in 1924; and *Again the Three* first in 1928 -- both by Hodder & Stoughton, London..

This Hodder Yellowback edition © Hachette India 2023
(Registered Name: Hachette Book Publishing India Pvt. Ltd.)
An Hachette UK Company www.hachetteindia.com

1

All rights reserved. No part of the publication may be reproduced, stored in a retrieval system (including but not limited to computers, disks, external drives, electronic or digital devices, e-readers, websites), or transmitted in any form or by any means (including but not limited to cyclostyling, photocopying, docutech or other reprographic reproductions, mechanical, recording, electronic, digital versions) without the prior written permission of the publisher, nor be otherwise circulated in any form of binding or cover other than that in which it is published and without a similar condition being imposed on the subsequent purchaser.

The texts in these editions in most cases have been reprinted as is, with minimal editorial changes and by and large no bowdlerizing for political correctness; though in some editions, a few words and phrases considered archaic, or those considered offensive now, along with archaic punctuation may have been modified in places to make the text more accessible to today's readers. The narratives, language, beliefs, social mores and/or cultural depictions, in these volumes are a reflection of their times and must be viewed as such. They may also contain certain cultural, racial and gender prejudices and stereotypes that may be outdated or clearly wrong then and wrong today; but their removal would be tantamount to claiming these prejudices never existed. The Publisher does not endorse or support those depictions or stereotypes; and these books have been made available for a discerning audience that will read it for entertainment value and a chronicle/record of popular fiction of past times.

Cover design by Priya Singh adapted from the original classic yellowjacket by Hodder & Stoughton.

Cover illustration by Hodder original.

Series note: Some of the books in the series (unless otherwise credited) may have cover or inside illustrations from the original yellowbacks or early editions, and while full restoration has been attempted, some images may be grainy or faded due to the condition of the original material. The end notes or bonus material or blurb details may have been sourced from the public domain or free use publications such as Wikipedia and attribution is hereby made also allowing similar free use reproduction from here. Sources requiring further specific attribution may write in and further detailing and/or corrections shall be made in subsequent printings/editions.

Reprint specifications may be subject to change including but not limited to finishes, paper, colour sections.

ISBN: 978-93-5731-172-4

Hachette Book Publishing India Pvt. Ltd.
4th & 5th Floors, Corporate Centre,
Plot No. 94, Sector 44, Gurugram - 122 003, India

Typeset in Electra LT STD 10/12.5 pt by Manipal Technologies Limited, Manipal

Printed and bound in India by Manipal Technologies Limited, Manipal

CONTENTS

1. The Three Just Men 1
2. Again the Three 319

THE THREE JUST MEN

CONTENTS

1.	The Firm of Oberzohn	5
2.	The Three Men of Curzon Street	16
3.	The Vendetta	25
4.	The Snake Strikes	31
5.	The Golden Woman	37
6.	In Chester Square	46
7.	"Moral Suasion"	54
8.	The House of Oberzohn	62
9.	Before the Lights Went Out	70
10.	When the Lights Went Out	74
11.	Gurther	82
12.	Leon Theorizes	88
13.	Mirabelle Goes Home	97
14.	The Pedlar	106
15.	Two "Accidents"	118
16.	Rath Hall	129
17.	Written in Braille	148
18.	The Story of Mont D'or	157
19.	At Heavytree Farm	165
20.	Gurther Reports	177
21.	The Account Book	183
22.	In the Store Cellar	195
23.	The Courier	202

CONTENTS

24.	On the Night Mail	210
25.	Gurther Returns	219
26.	In Captivity	225
27.	Mr Newton's Dilemma	235
28.	At Prater's	248
29.	Work for Gurther	254
30.	Joan a Prisoner	267
31.	The Things in the Box	279
32.	The Search	288
33.	The Siege	299
34.	The Death Tube	315

1

THE FIRM OF OBERZOHN

"£520 p.a. Wanted at once, Laboratory Secretary (lady). Young; no previous experience required, but must have passed recognized examination which included physics and inorganic (elementary) chemistry. Preference will be given to one whose family has some record in the world of science. Apply by letter, Box 9754, *Daily Megaphone*. If applicant is asked to interview advertiser, fare will be paid from any station within a hundred and fifty miles of London."

A good friend sent one of the issues containing this advertisement to Heavytree Farm and circled the announcement with a blue pencil. Mirabelle Leicester found the newspaper on the hall settee when she came in from feeding the chickens, and thought that it had been sent by the Alington land agent who was so constantly calling her attention to the advertisers who wished to buy cheap farms. It was a practice of his. She had the feeling that he resented her presence in the country, and was anxious to replace her with a proprietor less poverty-stricken. Splitting the wrapper with a dusty thumb, she turned naturally to the advertisement pages, having the agent in mind. Her eyes went rapidly down the "Wanted to

Buy" column. There were several "gentlemen requiring small farm in good district," but none that made any appeal to her, and she was wondering why the parsimonious man had spent tuppence-ha'penny on postage and paper when the circled paragraph caught her eye. "Glory!" said Mirabelle, her red lips parted in excited wonder. Aunt Alma looked up from her press-cutting book, startled as Mirabelle dashed in. "Me!" she said dramatically, and pointed a finger at the advertisement. "I am young—I have no experience—I have my higher certificate—and daddy was something in the world of science. And, Alma, we are exactly a hundred and forty miles from London town!"

"Dear me!" said Aunt Alma, a lady whose gaunt and terrifying appearance was the terror of tradesmen and farm hands, although a milder woman never knitted stockings.

"Isn't it wonderful? This solves all our problems. We leave the farm to Mark, open the flat in Bloomsbury... we can afford one or even two theatres a week..."

Alma read the announcement for the second time.

"It seems good," she said with conventional caution, "though I don't like the idea of your working, my dear. Your dear father..."

"Would have whisked me up to town and I should have had the job by tonight," said Mirabelle definitely.

But Alma wasn't sure. London was full of pitfalls and villainy untold lurked in its alleys and dark passages. She herself never went to London except under protest.

"I was there years ago when those horrible Four Just Men were about, my dear," she said, and Mirabelle, who loved her, listened to the oft-told story. "They terrorized London. One couldn't go out at night with the certainty that one would come back again alive... and to think that they have had a free pardon! It is simply encouraging crime."

"My dear," said Mirabelle (and this was her inevitable rejoinder), "they weren't criminals at all. They were very rich men who gave up their lives to punishing those whom the law let slip through its greasy old fingers. And they were pardoned for the intelligence work they did in the war—one worked for three months in the German War Office—and there aren't four at all: there are only three. I'd love to meet them—they must be dears!"

When Aunt Alma made a grimace, she was hideous. Mirabelle averted her eyes.

"Anyway, they are not in London now, darling," she said, "and you will be able to sleep soundly at nights."

"What about the snake?" asked Miss Alma Goddard ominously.

Now if there was one thing which no person contemplating a visit to London wished to be reminded about, it was the snake. Six million people rose from their beds every morning, opened their newspapers and looked for news of the snake. Eighteen daily newspapers never passed a day without telling their readers that the scare was childish and a shocking commentary on the neurotic tendencies of the age; they also published, at regular intervals, intimate particulars of the black mamba, its habits and its peculiar deadliness, and maintained quite a large staff of earnest reporters to "work on the story."

The black mamba, most deadly of all the African snakes, had escaped from the Zoo one cold and foggy night in March. And there should have been the end of him—a three-line paragraph, followed the next day by another three-line paragraph detailing how the snake was found dead on the frozen ground—no mamba could live under a temperature of 75 Fahrenheit. But the second paragraph never appeared. On the 2nd of April a policeman found a man huddled up in a doorway in Orme Place. He proved to be a well-known and apparently wealthy stockbroker, named Emmett. He was dead. In his swollen face were found two tiny punctured wounds, and the eminent scientist who was called into consultation gave his opinion that the man had died from snake-bite: an especially deadly snake. The night was chilly; the man had been to a theatre alone. His chauffeur stated that he had left his master in the best of spirits on the doorstep. The key found in the dead man's hand showed that he was struck before the car had turned. When his affairs were investigated he was found to be hopelessly insolvent. Huge sums drawn from his bank six months before had disappeared.

London had scarcely recovered from this shocking surprise when the snake struck again. This time in the crowded street, and choosing a humble victim, though by no means a blameless one. An ex-convict named Sirk, a homeless down-and-out, was seen to fall by a park-keeper near the Achilles statue in Hyde Park. By the time the keeper reached him he was dead. There was no sign of a snake—nobody was near him. This time the snake had made his mark on the wrist—two little punctured wounds near together.

A month later the third man fell a victim. He was a clerk of the Bank of England, a reputable man who was seen to fall forward in a subway train, and, on being removed to hospital, was discovered to have died—again from snake-bite.

So that the snake became a daily figure of fear, and its sinister fame spread even so far afield as Heavytree Farm.

"Stuff!" said Mirabelle, yet with a shiver. "Alma, I wish you wouldn't keep these horrors in your scrapbook."

"They are Life," said Alma soberly, and then: "When d'you take up your appointment?" she asked, and the girl laughed.

"We will make a beginning right away—by applying for the job," she said practically. "And you needn't start packing your boxes for a very long time!"

An hour later she intercepted the village postman and handed him a letter.

And that was the beginning of the adventure which involved so many lives and fortunes, which brought the Three Just Men to the verge of dissolution, and one day was to turn the heart of London into a battlefield.

Two days after the letter was dispatched came the answer, typewritten, surprisingly personal, and in places curiously worded. There was an excuse for that, for the heading on the note-paper was

OBERZOHN & SMITTS, MERCHANTS AND EXPORTERS.

On the third day Mirabelle Leicester stepped down from a bus in the City Road and entered the unimposing door of Romance, and an inquisitive chauffeur who saw her enter followed and overtook her in the lobby.

"Excuse me, madame—are you Mrs Carter?"

Mirabelle did not look like Mrs Anybody.

"No," she said, and gave her name.

"But you're the lady from Hereford... you live with your mother at Telford Park... ?"

The man was so agitated that she was not annoyed by his insistence. Evidently he had instructions to meet a stranger and was fearful of missing her.

"You have made a mistake—I live at Heavytree Farm, Daynham—with my aunt."

"Is she called Carter?"

She laughed.

"Miss Alma Goddard—now are you satisfied?"

"Then you're not the lady, miss; I'm waiting to pick her up."

The chauffeur withdrew apologetically.

The girl waited in the ornate ante-room for ten minutes before the pale youth with the stiff, upstanding hair and the huge rimless spectacles returned. His face was large, expressionless, unhealthy. Mirabelle had noted as a curious circumstance that every man she had seen in the office was of the same type. Big heavy men who gave the impression that they had been called away from some very urgent work to deal with the triviality of her inquiries. They were speechless men who glared solemnly at her through thick lenses and nodded or shook their heads according to the requirements of the moment. She expected to meet foreigners in the offices of Oberzohn & Smitts; German, she imagined, and was surprised later to discover that both principals and staff were in the main Swedish.

The pale youth, true to the traditions of the house, said nothing: he beckoned her with a little jerk of his head, and she went into a larger room, where half a dozen men were sitting at half a dozen desks and writing furiously, their noses glued short-sightedly to the books and papers which engaged their attention. Nobody looked up as she passed through the waist-high gate which separated the caller from the staff. Hanging upon the wall between two windows was a map of Africa with great green patches. In one corner of the room were stacked a dozen massive ivory tusks, each bearing a hanging label. There was the model of a steamship in a case on a window-ledge, and on another a crudely carved wooden idol of native origin.

The youth stopped before a heavy rosewood door and knocked. When a deep voice answered, he pushed open the door and stood aside to let her pass. It was a gigantic room— that was the word which occurred to her as most fitting, and the vast space of it was emphasized by the almost complete lack of furniture. A very small ebony writing-table, two very small chairs and a long and narrow black cupboard fitted into a recess were all the furnishings she could see. The high walls were covered with a golden paper. Four bright-red rafters ran across the black ceiling—the floor was completely covered with a deep purple carpet. It seemed that there was a rolled map above the fireplace—a long thin cord came down from the cornice and ended in a tassel within reach.

The room, with its lack of appointments, was so unexpected a vision that the girl stood staring from walls to roof, until she observed her guide making urgent signs, and then she advanced towards the man who stood with his back to the tiny fire that burnt in the silver fireplace.

He was tall and grey; her first impression was of an enormously high forehead. The sallow face was long, and nearer at hand, she saw, covered by innumerable lines and furrows. She judged him to be about fifty until he spoke, and then she realized that he was much older.

"Miss Mirabelle Leicester?"

His English was not altogether perfect; the delivery was queerly deliberate and he lisped slightly.

"Pray be seated. I am Dr Eruc Oberzohn. I am not German. I admire the Germans, but I am Swedish. You are convinced?"

She laughed, and when Mirabelle Leicester laughed, less susceptible men than Dr Eruc Oberzohn had forgotten all other business. She was not very tall—her slimness and her symmetrical figure made her appear so. She had in her face and in her clear grey eyes something of the countryside; she belonged to the orchards where the apple-blossom lay like heavy snow upon the bare branches; to the cold brooks that ran noisily under hawthorn hedges. The April sunlight was in her eyes and the springy velvet of meadows everlastingly under her feet.

To Dr Oberzohn she was a girl in a blue tailor-made costume. He saw that she wore a little hat with a straight brim that framed her face just above the lift of her curved eyebrows. A German would have seen these things, being a hopeless sentimentalist. The doctor was not German; he loathed their sentimentality.

"Will you be seated? You have a scientific training?"

Mirabelle shook her head.

"I haven't," she confessed ruefully, "but I've passed in the subjects you mentioned in your advertisement."

"But your father—he was a scientist?"

She nodded gravely.

"But not a great scientist," he stated. "England and America do not produce such men. Ah, tell me not of your Kelvins, Edisons, and Newtons! They were incomplete, dull men, ponderous men—the fire was not there."

She was somewhat taken aback, but she was amused as well. His calm dismissal of men who were honoured in the scientific world was so obviously sincere.

"Now talk to me of yourself." He seated himself in the hard, straight-backed chair by the little desk.

"I'm afraid there is very little I can tell you, Dr Oberzohn. I live with my aunt at Heavytree Farm in Gloucester, and we have a flat in Doughty Court. My aunt and I have a small income—and I think that is all."

"Go on, please," he commanded. "Tell me of your sensations when you had my letter—I desire to know your mind. That is how I form all opinions; that is how I made my immense fortune. By the analysis of the mind."

She had expected many tests; an examination in elementary science; a typewriting test possibly (she dreaded this most); but she never for one moment dreamt that the flowery letter asking her to call at the City Road offices of Oberzohn & Smitts would lead to an experiment in psycho-analysis.

"I can only tell you that I was surprised," she said, and the tightening line of her mouth would have told him a great deal if he were the student of human nature he claimed to be. "Naturally the salary appeals to me—ten pounds a week is such a high rate of pay that I cannot think I am qualified—"

"You are qualified." His harsh voice grew more strident as he impressed this upon her. "I need a laboratory secretary. You are qualified"—he hesitated, and then went on—"by reason of distinguished parentage. Also"—he hesitated again for a fraction of a second—"also because of general education. Your duties shall commence soon!" He waved a long, thin hand to the door in the corner of the room. "You will take your position at once," he said.

The long face, the grotesquely high forehead, the bulbous nose and wide, crooked mouth all seemed to work together when he spoke. At one moment the forehead was full of pleats and furrows—at the next, comparatively smooth. The point of his nose dipped up and down at every word, only his small, deep-set eyes remained steadfast, unwinking. She had seen eyes like those before, brown and pathetic. Of what did they remind her? His last words brought her to the verge of panic.

"Oh, I could not possibly start today," she said in trepidation.

"Today, or it shall be never," he said with an air of finality.

She had to face a crisis. The salary was more than desirable; it was necessary. The farm scarcely paid its way, for Alma was not the best of managers. And the income grew more and more attenuated. Last year the company in which her meagre fortune was invested had passed a dividend and she had to give up her Swiss holiday.

"I'll start now." She had to set her teeth to make this resolve.

"Very good; that is my wish."

He was still addressing her as though she were a public meeting. Rising from his chair, he opened the little door and she went into a smaller room. She had seen laboratories, but none quite so beautifully fitted as this—shelf upon shelf of white porcelain jars, of cut-glass bottles, their contents engraved in frosted letters; a bench that ran the length of the room, on which apparatus of every kind was arranged in order. In the centre of the room ran a long, glass-topped table, and here, in dustproof glass, were delicate instruments, ranging from scales which she knew could be influenced by a grain of dust, to electrical machines, so complicated that her heart sank at the sight of them.

"What must I do?" she asked dismally.

Everything was so beautifully new; she was sure she would drop one of those lovely jars... all the science of the school laboratory had suddenly drained out of her mind, leaving it a blank.

"You will do." Remarkably enough, the doctor for the moment seemed as much at a loss as the girl. "First—quantities. In every jar or bottle there is a quantity. How much? Who knows? The last secretary was careless, stupid. She kept no book. Sometimes I go for something—it is not there! All gone. That is very regrettable."

"You wish me to take stock?" she asked, her hopes reviving at the simplicity of her task.

There were measures and scales enough. The latter stood in a line like a platoon of soldiers ranged according to their size. Everything was very new, very neat. There was a smell of drying enamel in the room as though the place had been newly painted.

"That is all," said the long-faced man. He put his hand in the pocket of his frock-coat and took out a large wallet. From this he withdrew two crisp notes.

"Ten pounds," he said briefly. "We pay already in advance. There is one more thing I desire to know," he said. "It is of the aunt. She is in London?"

Mirabelle shook her head.

"No, she is in the country. I expected to go back this afternoon, and if I was—successful, we were coming to town tomorrow."

He pursed his thickish lips; she gazed fascinated at his long forehead rippled in thought.

"It will be a nervous matter for her if you stay in London tonight—no?"

She smiled and shook her head.

"No. I will stay at the flat; I have often stayed there alone, but even that will not be necessary. I will wire asking her to come up by the first train."

"Wait." He raised a pompous hand and darted back to his room. He returned with a packet of telegraph forms. "Write your telegram," he commanded. "A clerk shall dispatch it at once."

Gratefully she took the blanks and wrote her news and request.

"Thank you," she said.

Mr Oberzohn bowed, went to the door, bowed again, and the door closed behind him.

Fortunately for her peace of mind, Mirabelle Leicester had no occasion to consult her employer or attempt to open the door. Had she done so, she would have discovered that it was locked. As for the telegram she had written, that was a curl of black ash in his fire.

2

THE THREE MEN OF CURZON STREET

No. 233, Curzon Street, was a small house. Even the most enthusiastic of agents would not, if he had any regard to his soul's salvation, describe its dimensions with any enthusiasm. He might enlarge upon its bijou beauties, refer reverently its historical association, speak truthfully of its central heating and electric installation, but he would, being an honest man, convey the impression that No. 233 was on the small side.

The house was flanked by two modern mansions, stone-fronted, with metal and glass doors that gave out a blur of light by night. Both overtopped the modest roof of their neighbour by many stories—No. 233 had the appearance of a little man crushed in a crowd and unable to escape, and there was in its mild frontage the illusion of patient resignation and humility.

To that section of Curzon Street wherein it had its place, the house was an offence and was, in every but a legal sense, a nuisance. A learned Chancery judge to whom application had been made on behalf of neighbouring property owners, ground landlords and the like, had refused to grant the injunction for which they had pleaded, "prohibiting the said George Manfred from carrying on a business, to wit the Triangle Detective Agency, situate at the aforesaid number two hundred and thirty-three Curzon Street in the City of Westminster in the County of Middlesex."

In a judgment which occupied a third of a column of The Times he laid down the dictum that a private detective might be a professional rather than a business man—a dictum which has been, and will be, disputed to the end of time.

So the little silver triangle remained fixed to the door and he continued to interview his clients—few in number, for he was most careful to accept only those who offered scope for his genius.

A tall, strikingly handsome man, with the face of a patrician and the shoulders of an athlete, Curzon Street—or such of the street as took the slightest notice of anything—observed him to be extremely well dressed on all occasions. He was a walking advertisement for a Hanover Street tailor who was so fashionable that he would have died with horror at the very thought of advertising at all. Car folk held up at busy crossings glanced into his limousine, saw the clean-cut profile and the tanned, virile face, and guessed him for a Harley Street specialist. Very few people knew him socially. Dr Elver, the Scotland Yard surgeon, used to come up to Curzon Street at times and give his fantastic views on the snake and its appearances, George Manfred and his friends listening in silence and offering no help. But apart from Elver and an Assistant Commissioner of Police, a secretive man, who dropped in at odd moments to smoke a pipe and talk of old times, the social callers were few and far between.

His chauffeur-footman was really better known than he. At the mews where he garaged his car, they called him "Lightning," and it was generally agreed that this thin-faced, eager-eyed man would sooner or later meet the end which inevitably awaits all chauffeurs who take sharp corners on two wheels at sixty miles an hour: some of the critics had met the big Spanz on the road and had reproached him afterwards, gently or violently, according to the degree of their scare.

Few knew Mr Manfred's butler, a dark-browed foreigner, rather stout and somewhat saturnine. He was a man who talked very little even to the cook and the two housemaids who came every morning at eight and left the house punctually at six, for Mr Manfred dined out most nights.

He advertised only in the more exclusive newspapers, and not in his own name; no interviews were granted except by appointment, so that the arrival of Mr Sam Barberton was in every sense an irregularity.

He knocked at the door just as the maids were leaving, and since they knew little about Manfred and his ways except that he liked poached eggs and spinach for breakfast, the stranger was allowed to drift into the hall, and here the taciturn butler, hastily summoned from his room, found him.

The visitor was a stubby, thick-set man with a brick-red face and a head that was both grey and bald. His dress and his speech were equally rough. The butler saw that he was no ordinary artisan because his boots were of a kind known as veldtschoons. They were of undressed leather, patchily bleached by the sun.

"I want to see the boss of this Triangle," he said in a loud voice, and, diving into his waistcoat pocket, brought out a soiled newspaper cutting.

The butler took it from him without a word. It was the Cape Times—he would have known by the type and the spacing even if on the back there had not been printed the notice of a church bazaar at Wynberg. The butler studied such things.

"I am afraid that you cannot see Mr Manfred without an appointment," he said. His voice and manner were most expectedly gentle in such a forbidding man.

"I've got to see him, if I sit here all night," said the man stubbornly, and symbolized his immovability by squatting down in the hall chair.

Not a muscle of the servant's face moved. It was impossible to tell whether he was angry or amused.

"I got this cutting out of a paper I found on the Benguella— she docked at Tilbury this afternoon—and I came straight here. I should never have dreamt of coming at all, only I want fair play for all concerned. That Portuguese feller with a name like a cigar—Villa, that's it!—he said, 'What's the good of going to London when we can settle everything on board ship?' But half-breed Portuguese! My God, I'd rather deal with bushmen! Bushmen are civilized—look here."

Before the butler realized what the man was doing, he had slipped off one of his ugly shoes. He wore no sock or stocking underneath, and he upturned the sole of his bare foot for inspection. The flesh was seamed and puckered into red weals, and the butler knew the cause.

"Portuguese," said the visitor tersely as he resumed his shoe. "Not niggers—Portugooses—half-bred, I'll admit. They burnt me to make me talk, and they'd have killed me only one of those hell-fire American traders came along—full of fight and fire-water. He brought me into the town."

"Where was this?" asked the butler.

"Mosamades: I went ashore to look round, like a fool. I was on a Woerman boat that was going up to Boma. The skipper was a Hun, but white—he warned me."

"And what did they want to know from you?"

The caller shot a suspicious glance at his interrogator.

"Are you the boss?" he demanded.

"No—I'm Mr Manfred's butler. What name shall I tell him?"

"Barberton—Mister Samuel Barberton. Tell him I want certain things found out. The address of a young lady by the name of Miss Mirabelle Leicester. And I'll tell your governor something too. This Portugoose got drunk one night, and spilled it about the fort they've got in England. Looks like a house but it's a fort: he went there..."

No, he was not drunk; stooping to pick up an imaginary match-stalk, the butler's head had come near the visitor; there was a strong aroma of tobacco but not of drink.

"Would you very kindly wait?" he asked, and disappeared up the stairs.

He was not gone long before he returned to the first landing and beckoned Mr Barberton to come. The visitor was ushered into a room at the front of the house, a small room, which was made smaller by the long grey velvet curtains that hung behind the empire desk where Manfred was standing.

"This is Mr Barberton, sir," said the butler, bowed, and went out, closing the door.

"Sit down, Mr Barberton." He indicated a chair and seated himself. "My butler tells me you have quite an exciting story to tell me—you are from the Cape?"

"No, I'm not," said Mr Barberton. "I've never been at the Cape in my life."

The man behind the desk nodded.

"Now, if you will tell me—"

"I'm not going to tell you much," was the surprisingly blunt reply. "It's not likely that I'm going to tell a stranger what I wouldn't even tell Elijah Washington—and he saved my life!"

Manfred betrayed no resentment at this cautious attitude. In that room he had met many clients who had shown the same reluctance to accept him as their confidant. Yet he had at the back of his mind the feeling that this man, unlike the rest, might remain adamant to the end: he was curious to discover the real object of the visit.

Barberton drew his chair nearer the writing-table and rested his elbows on the edge.

"It's like this, Mr What's-your-name. There's a certain secret which doesn't belong to me, and yet does in a way. It is worth a lot of money. Mr Elijah Washington knew that and tried to pump me, and Villa got a gang of Kroomen to burn my feet, but I've not told yet. What I want you to do is to find Miss Mirabelle Leicester; and I want to get her quick, because there's only about two weeks, if you understand me, before this other crowd gets busy—Villa is certain to have cabled 'em, and according to him they're hot!"

Mr Manfred leant back in his padded chair, the glint of an amused smile in his grey eyes.

"I take it that what you want us to find Miss Leicester?"

The man nodded energetically.

"Have you the slightest idea as to where she is to be found? Has she any relations in England?"

"I don't know," interrupted the man. "All I know is that she lives here somewhere, and that her father died three years ago, on the twenty-ninth of May—make a note of that: he died in England on the twenty-ninth of May."

That was an important piece of information, and it made the search easy, thought Manfred.

"And you're going to tell me about the fort, aren't you?" he said, as he looked up from his notes.

Barberton hesitated.

"I was," he admitted, "but I'm not so sure that I will now, until I've found this young lady. And don't forget,"—he rapped the table to emphasize his words—"that crowd is hot!"

"Which crowd?" asked Manfred good-humouredly. He knew many "crowds," and wondered if it was about one which was in his mind that the caller was speaking.

"The crowd I'm talking about," said Mr Barberton, who spoke with great deliberation and was evidently weighing every word he uttered for fear that he should involuntarily betray his secret.

That seemed to be an end of his requirements, for he rose and stood a little awkwardly, fumbling in his inside pocket.

"There is nothing to pay," said Manfred, guessing his intention. "Perhaps, when we have located your Miss Mirabelle Leicester, we shall ask you to refund our out-of-pocket expenses."

"I can afford to pay—" began the man.

"And we can afford to wait." Again the gleam of amusement in the deep eyes.

Still Mr Barberton did not move.

"There's another thing I meant to ask you. You know all that's happening in this country?"

"Not quite everything," said the other with perfect gravity.

"Have you ever heard of the Four Just Men?"

It was a surprising question. Manfred bent forward as though he had not heard aright.

"The Four—?"

"The Four Just Men—three, as a matter of fact. I'd like to get in touch with those birds."

Manfred nodded.

"I think I have heard of them," he said.

"They're in England now somewhere. They've got a pardon: I saw that in the Cape Times—the bit I tore the advertisement from."

"The last I heard of them, they were in Spain," said Manfred, and walked round the table and opened the door. "Why do you wish to get in touch with them?"

"Because," said Mr Barberton impressively, "the crowd are scared of 'em—that's why."

Manfred walked with his visitor to the landing.

"You have omitted one important piece of information," he said with a smile, "but I did not intend your going until you told me. What is your address?"

"Petworth Hotel, Norfolk Street."

Barberton went down the stairs; the butler was waiting in the hall to show him out, and Mr Barberton, having a vague idea that something of the sort was usual in the houses of the aristocracy, slipped a silver coin in his hand. The dark-faced man murmured his thanks: his bow was perhaps a little lower, his attitude just a trifle more deferential.

He closed and locked the front door and went slowly up the stairs to the office room. Manfred was sitting on the empire table, lighting a cigarette. The chauffeur-valet had come through the grey curtains to take the chair which had been vacated by Mr Barberton.

"He gave me half a crown—generous fellow," said Poiccart, the butler. "I like him, George."

"I wish I could have seen his feet," said the chauffeur, whose veritable name was Leon Gonsalez. He spoke with regret. "He comes from West Sussex, and there is insanity in his family. The left parietal is slightly recessed and the face is asymmetrical."

"Poor soul!" murmured Manfred, blowing a cloud of smoke to the ceiling. "It's a great trial introducing one's friends to you, Leon."

"Fortunately, you have no friends," said Leon, reaching out and taking a cigarette from the open gold case on the table. "Well, what do you think of our Mr Barberton's mystery?"

George Manfred shook his head.

"He was vague, and, in his desire to be diplomatic, incoherent. What about your own mystery, Leon? You have been out all day... have you found a solution?"

Gonsalez nodded.

"Barberton is afraid of something," said Poiccart, a slow and sure analyst. "He carried a gun between his trousers and his waistcoat—you saw that?" George nodded.

"The question is, who or which is the crowd? Question two is, where and who is Miss Mirabelle Leicester? Question three is, why did they burn Barberton's feet?... and I think that is all."

The keen face of Gonsalez was thrust forward through a cloud of smoke.

"I will answer most of them and propound two more," he said. "Mirabelle Leicester took a job today at Oberzohn's— laboratory secretary!"

George Manfred frowned.

"Laboratory? I didn't know that he had one."

"He hadn't till three days ago—it was fitted in seventy-two hours by experts who worked day and night; the cost of its installation was sixteen hundred pounds—and it came into existence to give Oberzohn an excuse for engaging Mirabelle Leicester. You sent me out to clear up that queer advertisement which puzzled us all on Monday—I have cleared it up. It was designed to bring our Miss Leicester into the Oberzohn establishment. We all agreed when we discovered who was the advertiser, that Oberzohn was working for something—I watched his office for two days, and she was the only applicant for the job—hers the only letter they answered. Oberzohn lunched with her at the Ritz-Carlton—she sleeps tonight in Chester Square."

There was a silence which was broken by Poiccart.

"And what is the question you have to propound?" he asked mildly.

"I think I know," said Manfred, and nodded. "The question is: how long has Mr Samuel Barberton to live?"

"Exactly," said Gonsalez with satisfaction. "You are beginning to understand the mentality of Oberzohn!"

3

THE VENDETTA

The man who that morning walked without announcement into Dr Oberzohn's office might have stepped from the pages of a catalogue of men's fashions. He was, to the initiated eye, painfully new. His lemon gloves, his dazzling shoes, the splendour of his silk hat, the very correctness of his handkerchief display, would have been remarkable even in the Ascot paddock on Cup day. He was good-looking, smooth, if a trifle plump, of face, and he wore a tawny little moustache and a monocle. People who did not like Captain Monty Newton — and their names were many — said of him that he aimed at achieving the housemaid's conception of a guardsman. They did not say this openly, because he was a man to be propitiated rather than offended. He had money, a place in the country, a house in Chester Square, and an assortment of cars. He was a member of several good clubs, the committees of which never discussed him without offering the excuse of wartime courtesies for his election. Nobody knew how he made his money, or, if it were inherited, whose heir he was. He gave extravagant parties, played cards well, and enjoyed exceptional luck, especially when he was the host and held the bank after one of the splendid dinners he gave in his Chester Square mansion.

"Good morning, Oberzohn—how is Smitts?" It was his favourite jest, for there was no Smitts, and had been no Smitts in the firm since '96.

The doctor, peering down at the telegram he was writing, looked up.

"Good morning, Captain Newton," he said precisely. Newton passed to the back of him and read the message he was writing. It was addressed to "Miss Alma Goddard, Heavytree Farm, Daynham, Gloucester," and the wire ran:

> "HAVE GOT THE FINE SITUATION. CANNOT
> EXPEDITIOUSLY RETURN TONIGHT. I AM
> SLEEPING AT OUR PRETTY FLAT IN DOUGHTY
> COURT. DO NOT COME UP UNTIL I SEND FOR
> YOU.—MISS MIRABELLE LEICESTER."

"She's here, is she?" Captain Newton glanced at the laboratory door. "You're not going to send that wire? 'Miss Mirabelle Leicester!' 'Expeditiously return!' She'd tumble it in a minute. Who is Alma Goddard?"

"The aunt," said Oberzohn. "I did not intend the dispatching until you had seen it. My English is too correct."

He made way for Captain Newton, who, having taken a sheet of paper from the rack on which to deposit with great care his silk hat, and having stripped his gloves and deposited them in his hat, sat down in the chair from which the older man had risen, pulled up the knees of his immaculate trousers, tore off the top telegraph form, and wrote under the address:

> "HAVE GOT THE JOB. HOORAY! DON'T BOTHER
> TO COME UP, DARLING, UNTIL I AM SETTLED.
> SHALL SLEEP AT THE FLAT AS USUAL. TOO
> BUSY TO WRITE. KEEP MY LETTERS.—
> MIRABELLE."

"That's real," said Captain Newton, surveying his work with satisfaction. "Push it off."

He got up and straddled his legs before the fire.

"The hard part of the job may be to persuade the lady to come to Chester Square," he said.

"My own little house—" began Oberzohn.

"Would scare her to death," said Newton with a loud laugh. "That dog-kennel! No, it is Chester Square or nothing. I'll get Joan or one of the girls to drop in this afternoon and chum up with her. When does the Benguella arrive?"

"This afternoon: the person has booked rooms by radio at the Petworth Hotel."

"Norfolk Street... humph! One of your men can pick him up and keep an eye on him. Lisa? So much the better. That kind of trash will talk for a woman. I don't suppose he has seen a white woman in years. You ought to fire Villa—crude beast! Naturally the man is on his guard now."

"Villa is the best of my men on the coast," barked Oberzohn fiercely. Nothing so quickly touched the raw places of his amazing vanity as a reflection upon his organizing qualities.

"How is trade?" Captain Newton took a long ebony holder from his tail pocket, flicked out a thin platinum case and lit a cigarette in one uninterrupted motion.

"Bat!" When Dr Oberzohn was annoyed the purity of his pronunciation suffered. "There is nothing but expense!"

Oberzohn & Smitts had once made an enormous income from the sale of synthetic alcohol. They were, amongst other things, coast traders. They bought rubber and ivory, paving in cloth and liquor. They sold arms secretly, organized tribal wars for their greater profit, and had financed at least two Portuguese revolutions nearer at home. And with the growth of their fortune, the activities of the firm had extended. Guns and more guns went out of Belgian and French workshops. To Kurdish insurrectionaries, to ambitious Chinese generals, to South American politicians, planning, to carry their convictions into more active fields. There was no country in the world that did not act as host to an O.&S. agent—and agents can be very expensive. Just now the world was alarmingly peaceful. A revolution had failed most dismally in Venezuela, and Oberzohn & Smitts had not been paid for two shiploads of lethal weapons ordered by a general who, two days after the armaments were landed, had been placed against an adobe wall and incontinently shot to rags by the soldiers of the Government against which he was in rebellion. "But that shall not matter." Oberzohn waved bad trade from the considerable factors of life. "This shall succeed: and then I shall be free to well punish—"

"To punish well," corrected the purist, stroking his moustache. "Don't split your infinitives, Eruc—it's silly. You're thinking of Manfred and Gonsalez and Poiccart? Leave them alone. They are nothing!"

"Nothing!" roared the doctor, his sallow face instantly distorted with fury. "To leave them alone, is it? Of my brother what? Of my brother in heaven, sainted martyr... !"

He spun round, gripped the silken tassel of the cord above the fireplace, and pulled down, not a map, but a picture. It had been painted from a photograph by an artist who specialized in the gaudy banners which hang before every booth at every country fair. In this setting the daub was a shrieking incongruity; yet to Dr Oberzohn it surpassed in beauty the masterpieces of the Prado. A full-length portrait of a man in a frock-coat. He leaned on a pedestal in the attitude which cheap photographers believe is the acme of grace. His big face, idealized as it was by the artist, was brutal and stupid. The carmine lips were parted in a simper. In one hand he held a scroll of paper, in the other a Derby hat which was considerably out of drawing.

"My brother!" Dr Oberzohn choked. "My sainted Adolph... murdered! By the so-called Three Just Men... my brother!"

"Very interesting," murmured Captain Newton, who had not even troubled to look up. He flicked the ash from his cigarette into the fireplace and said no more. Adolph Oberzohn had certainly been shot dead by Leon Gonsalez: there was no disputing the fact. That Adolph, at the moment of his death, was attempting to earn the generous profits which come to those who engage in a certain obnoxious trade between Europe and the South American states, was less open to question. There was a girl in it: Leon followed his man to Porto Rico, and in the Café of the Seven Virtues they had met. Adolph was by training a gunman and drew first—and died first. That was the story of Adolph Oberzohn: the story of a girl whom Leon Gonsalez smuggled back to Europe belongs elsewhere. She fell in love with her rescuer and frightened him sick.

Dr Oberzohn let the portrait roll up with a snap, blew his nose vigorously, and blinked the tears from his pale eyes.

"Yes, very sad, very sad," said the captain cheerfully. "Now what about this girl? There is to be nothing rough or raw, you understand, Eruc? I want the thing done sweetly. Get that bug of the Just Men out of your mind—they are out of business. When a man lowers himself to run a detective agency he's a back number. If they start anything we'll deal with them scientifically, eh? Scientifically!"

He chuckled with laughter at this good joke. It was obvious that Captain Newton was no dependant on the firm of Oberzohn & Smitts. If he was not the dominant partner, he dominated that branch which he had once served in a minor capacity. He owed much to the death of Adolph—he never regretted the passing of that unsavoury man.

"I'll get one of the girls to look her over this afternoon—where is your telephone pad—the one you write messages received?"

The doctor opened a drawer of his desk and took out a little memo pad, and Newton found a pencil and wrote:

"To Mirabelle Leicester, care Oberzohn (Phone) London. Sorry I can't come up tonight. Don't sleep at flat alone. Have wired Joan Newton to put you up for night. She will call—ALMA."

"There you are," said the gallant captain, handing the pad to the other. "That message came this afternoon. All telegrams to Oberzohn come by 'phone—never forget it!"

"Ingenious creature!" Dr Oberzohn's admiration was almost reverential.

"Take her out to lunch... after lunch, the message. At four o'clock, Joan or one of the girls. A select dinner. Tomorrow the office... gently, gently. Bull-rush these schemes and your plans die the death of a dog."

He glanced at the door once more.

"She won't come out, I suppose?" he suggested.

"Deuced awkward if she came out and saw Miss Newton's brother!"

"I have locked the door," said Dr Oberzohn proudly.

Captain Newton's attitude changed: his face went red with sudden fury.

"Then you're a—you're a fool. Unlock the door when I've gone—and keep it unlocked! Want to frighten her?"

"It was my idea to risk nothing," pleaded the long-faced Swede.

"Do as I tell you."

Captain Newton brushed his speckless coat with the tips of his fingers. He pulled on his gloves, fitted his hat with the aid of a small pocket-mirror he took from his inside pocket, took up his clouded cane and strolled from the room.

"Ingenious creature," murmured Dr Oberzohn again, and went in to offer the startled Mirabelle an invitation to lunch.

4

THE SNAKE STRIKES

The great restaurant, with its atmosphere of luxury and wealth, had been a little overpowering. The crowded tables, the soft lights, the very capability and nonchalance of the waiters, were impressive. When her new employer had told her that it was his practice to take the laboratory secretary to lunch, "for I have not other time to speak of business things," she accepted uncomfortably. She knew little of office routine, but she felt that it was not customary for principals to drive their secretaries from the City Road to the Ritz-Carlton to lunch expensively at that resort of fashion and the epicure. It added nothing to her self-possession that her companion was an object of interest to all who saw him. The gay luncheon parties forgot their dishes and twisted round to stare at the extraordinary-looking man with the high forehead.

At a little table alone she saw a man whose face was tantalizingly familiar. A keen, thin face with eager, amused eyes. Where had she seen him before? Then she remembered: the chauffeur had such a face—the man who had followed her into Oberzohn's when she arrived that morning. It was absurd, of course; this man was one of the leisured class, to whom lunching at the Ritz-Carlton was a normal event. And yet the likeness was extraordinary.

She was glad when the meal was over. Dr Oberzohn did not talk of "business things." He did not talk at all, but spent his time shovelling incredible quantities of food through his wide slit of a mouth. He ate intently, noisily—Mirabelle was glad the band was playing, and she went red with suppressed laughter at the whimsical thought; and after that she felt less embarrassed.

No word was spoken as the big car sped citywards. The doctor had his thoughts and ignored her presence. The only reference he made to the lunch was as they were leaving the hotel, when he had condescended to grunt a bitter complaint about the quality of English-made coffee. He allowed her to go back to her weighing and measuring without displaying the slightest interest in her progress.

And then came the crowning surprise of the afternoon—it followed the arrival of a puzzling telegram from her aunt. She was weighing an evil-smelling mass of powder when the door opened and there floated into the room a delicate-looking girl, beautifully dressed. A small face framed in a mass of little golden-brown curls smiled a greeting. "You're Mirabelle Leicester, aren't you? I'm Joan Newton—your aunt wired me to call on you."

"Do you know my aunt?" asked Mirabelle in astonishment. She had never heard Alma speak of the Newtons, but then, Aunt Alma had queer reticences. Mirabelle had expected a middle-aged dowd—it was amazing that her unprepossessing relative could claim acquaintance with this society butterfly.

"Oh yes—we know Alma very well," replied the visitor. "Of course, I haven't seen her since I was quite a little girl—she's a dear."

She looked round the laboratory with curious interest.

"What a nasty-smelling place!" she said, her nose up-turned. "And how do you like old—er—Mr Oberzohn?"

"Do you know him?" asked Mirabelle, astounded at the possibility of this coincidence.

"My brother knows him—we live together, my brother and I, and he knows everybody. A man about town has to, hasn't he, dear?"

"Man about town" was an expression that grated a little; Mirabelle was not of the "dearing" kind. The combination of errors in taste made her scrutinize the caller more closely. Joan Newton was dressed beautifully but not well. There was something... Had Mirabelle a larger knowledge of life, she might have thought that the girl had been dressed to play the part of a lady by somebody who wasn't quite sure of the constituents of the part. Captain Newton she did not know at the time, or she would have guessed the dress authority.

"I'm going to take you back to Chester Square after Mr Oberzohn—such a funny name, isn't it?—has done with you. Monty insisted upon my bringing the Rolls. Monty is my brother; he's rather classical."

Mirabelle wondered whether this indicated a love of the Greek poets or a passion for the less tuneful operas. Joan (which was her real name) meant no more than classy: it was a favourite word of hers; another was "morbid."

Half an hour later the inquisitive chauffeur put his foot on the starter and sent his car on the trail of the Rolls, wondering what Mirabelle Leicester had in common with Joan Alice Murphy, who had brought so many rich young men to the green board in Captain Newton's beautiful drawing-room, where stakes ran high and the captain played with such phenomenal luck,

"And there you are," said Gonsalez complacently. "I've done a very good day's work. Oberzohn has gone back to his rabbit-hutch to think up new revolutions—Miss Mirabelle Leicester is to be found at 307, Chester Square. Now the point is, what do we do to save the valuable life of Mr Sam Barberton?"

Manfred looked grave. "I hardly like the thought of the girl spending the night in Newton's house," he said.

"Why allow her to remain there?" asked Poiccart in his heavy way.

"Exactly!" Leon nodded.

George Manfred looked at his watch.

"Obviously the first person to see is friend Barberton," he said, "If we can prevail on him to spend the evening with us, the rest is a simple matter—"

The telephone bell rang shrilly and Leon Gonsalez monopolized the instrument.

"Gloucester? Yes." He covered the receiver with his hand. "I took the liberty of asking Miss Alma Goddard to ring me up... her address I discovered very early in the day: Heavytree Farm, Daynham, near Gloucester... yes, yes, it is Mr Johnson speaking. I wanted to ask you if you would take a message to Miss Leicester... oh, she isn't at home?" Leon listened attentively, and, after a few minutes: "Thank you very much. She is staying at Doughty Court? She wired you... oh, nothing very important. I—er—am her old science master and I saw an advertisement... oh, she has seen it, has she?"

He hung up the receiver.

"Nothing to go on," he said. "The girl has wired to say she is delighted with her job. The aunt is not to come up until she is settled, and Mirabelle is sleeping at Doughty Court."

"And a very excellent place too," said Manfred. "When we've seen Mr Barberton I shouldn't be surprised if she didn't sleep there after all."

Petworth Hotel in Norfolk Street was a sedate residential hostel, greatly favoured by overseas visitors, especially South Africans. The reception clerk thought Mr Barberton was out: the hall porter was sure.

"He went down to the Embankment—he said he'd like to see the river before it was dark," said that confidant of so many visitors.

Manfred stepped into the car by Leon's side—Poiccart seldom went abroad, but sat at home piecing together the little jigsaw puzzles of life that came to Curzon Street for solution. He was the greatest of all the strategists: even Scotland Yard brought some of its problems for his inspection.

"On the Embankment?" Manfred looked up at the blue and pink sky. The sun had gone down, but the light of day remained. "If it were darker I should be worried... stop, there's Dr Elver."

The little police surgeon who had passed them with a cheery wave of his hand turned and walked back.

"Well, Children of the Law"—he was inclined to be dramatic—"on what dread errand of vengeance are you bound?"

"We are looking for a man named Barberton to ask him to dinner," said Manfred, shaking hands.

"Sounds tame to me: has he any peculiarities which would appeal to me?"

"Burnt feet," said Leon promptly. "If you would like to learn how the coastal intelligence department extract information from unwilling victims, come along."

Elver hesitated. He was a man burnt up by the Indian suns, wizened like a dried yellow apple, and he had no interest in the world beyond his work.

"I'll go with you," he said, stepping into the car. "And if your Barberton man fails you, you can have me as a guest. I like to hear you talking. One cannot know too much of the criminal mind! And life is dull since the snake stopped biting!"

The car made towards Blackfriars Bridge, and Manfred kept watch of the sidewalk. There was no sign of Barberton, and he signalled Leon to turn and come back. This brought the machine to the Embankment side of the broad boulevard. They had passed under Waterloo Bridge and were nearing Cleopatra's Needle when Gonsalez saw the man they were seeking.

He was leaning against the parapet, his elbows on the coping and his head sunk forward as though he were studying the rush of the tide below. The car pulled up near a policeman who was observing the lounger thoughtfully. The officer recognized the police surgeon and saluted.

"Can't understand that bird, sir," he said. "He's been standing there for ten minutes. I'm keepin' an eye on him, because he looks to me like a suicide who's thinkin' it over!"

Manfred approached the man, and suddenly, with a shock, saw his face. It was set in a grin—the eyes were wide open, the skin a coppery red.

"Elver! Leon!"

As Leon sprang from the car, Manfred touched the man's shoulder and he fell limply to the ground. In a second the doctor was on his knees by the side of the still figure.

"Dead," he said laconically, and then: "Good God!"

He pointed to the neck, where a red patch showed.

"What is that?" asked Manfred steadily.

"The snake!" said the doctor.

5

THE GOLDEN WOMAN

BARBERTON had been stricken down in the heart of London, under the very eyes of the policeman, it proved.

"Yes, sir, I've had him under observation for a quarter of an hour. I saw him walking along the Embankment, admiring the view, long before he stopped here."

"Did anybody go near him to speak to him?" asked Dr Elver, looking up.

"No, sir, he stood by himself. I'll swear that nobody was within two yards of him. Of course, people have been passing to and fro, but I have been looking at him all the time, and I've not seen man or woman within yards of him, and my eyes were never off him."

A second policeman had appeared on the scene, and he was sent across to Scotland Yard in Manfred's car for the ambulance and the police reserves necessary to clear and keep in circulation the gathering crowd. These returned simultaneously, and the two friends watched the pitiable thing lifted into a stretcher, and waited until the white-bodied vehicle had disappeared with its sad load before they returned to their machine.

Gonsalez took his place at the wheel; George got in by his side. No word was spoken until they were back at Curzon Street. Manfred went in alone, whilst his companion drove the machine to the garage. When he returned, he found Poiccart and George deep in discussion.

"You were right, Raymond." Leon Gonsalez stripped his thin coat and threw it on a chair. "The accuracy of your forecasts is almost depressing. I am waiting all the time for the inevitable mistake, and I am irritated when this doesn't occur. You said the snake would reappear, and the snake has reappeared. Prophesy now for me, O seer!"

Poiccart's heavy face was gloomy; his dark eyes almost hidden under the frown that brought his bushy eyebrows lower.

"One hasn't to be a seer to know that our association with Barberton will send the snake wriggling towards Curzon Street," he said. "Was it Gurther or Pfeiffer?"

Manfred considered.

"Pfeiffer, I think. He is the steadier of the two. Gurther has brain-storms; he is on the neurotic side. And that nine-thonged whip of yours, Leon, cannot have added to his mental stability. No, it was Pfeiffer, I'm sure."

"I suppose the whip unbalanced him a little," said Leon. He thought over this aspect as though it were one worth consideration. "Gurther is a sort of Jekyll and Hyde, except that there is no virtue to him at all. It is difficult to believe, seeing him dropping languidly into his seat at the opera, that this exquisite young man in his private moments would not change his linen more often than once a month, and would shudder at the sound of a running bath-tap! That almost sounds as though he were a morphia fiend. I remember a case in '99... but I am interrupting you?"

"What precautions shall you take, Leon?" asked George Manfred.

"Against the snake?" Leon shrugged his shoulders. "The old military precaution against Zeppelin raids; the precaution the farmer takes against a plague of wasps. You cannot kneel on the chest of the vespa vulgaris and extract his sting with an anaesthetic. You destroy his nest—you bomb his hangar. Personally, I have never feared dissolution in any form, but I have a childish objection to being bitten by a snake."

Poiccart's saturnine face creased for a moment in a smile. "You've no objection to stealing my theories," he said drily, and the other doubled up in silent laughter.

Manfred was pacing the little room, his hands behind him, a thick Egyptian cigarette between his lips.

"There's a train leaves Paddington for Gloucester at ten forty-five," he said. "Will you telegraph to Miss Goddard, Heavytree Farm, and ask her to meet the train with a cab? After that I shall want two men to patrol the vicinity of the farm day and night."

Poiccart pulled open a drawer of the desk, took out a small book and ran his finger down the index.

"I can get this service in Gloucester," he said. "Gordon, Williams, Thompson and Elfred—they're reliable people and have worked for us before."

Manfred nodded.

"Send them the usual instructions by letter. I wonder who will be in charge of this Barberton case? If it's Meadows, I can work with him. On the other hand, if it's Arbuthnot, we shall have to get our information by subterranean methods."

"Call Elver," suggested Leon, and George pulled the telephone towards him.

It was some time before he could get into touch with Dr Elver, and then he learnt, to his relief, that the redoubtable Inspector Meadows had complete charge.

"He's coming up to see you," said Elver. "As a matter of fact, the chief was here when I arrived at the Yard, and he particularly asked Meadows to consult with you. There's going to be an awful kick at the Home Secretary's office about this murder. We had practically assured the Home Office that there would be no repetition of the mysterious deaths and that the snake had gone dead for good."

Manfred asked a few questions and then hung up.

"They are worried about the public—you never know what masses will do in given circumstances. But you can gamble that the English mass does the same thing—Governments hate intelligent crowds. This may cost the Home Secretary his job, poor soul! And he's doing his best."

A strident shout in the street made him turn his head with a smile.

"The late editions have got it—naturally. It might have been committed on their doorstep."

"But why?" asked Poiccart "What was Barberton's offence?"

"His first offence," said Leon promptly, without waiting for Manfred to reply, "was to go in search of Miss Mirabelle Leicester. His second and greatest was to consult with us. He was a dead man when he left the house."

The faint sound of a bell ringing sent Poiccart down to the hall to admit an unobtrusive, middle-aged man, who might have been anything but what he was: one of the cleverest trackers of criminals that Scotland Yard had known in thirty years. A sandy-haired, thin-faced man, who wore pince-nez and looked like an actor, he had been a visitor to Curzon Street before, and now received a warm welcome. With little preliminary he came to the object of his call, and Manfred told him briefly what had happened, and the gist of his conversation with Barberton.

"Miss Mirabelle Leicester is—" began Manfred.

"Employed by Oberzohn—I know," was the surprising reply. "She came up to London this morning and took a job as laboratory assistant. I had no idea that Oberzohn & Smitts had a laboratory on the premises."

"They hadn't until a couple of days ago," interrupted Leon. "The laboratory was staged especially for her."

Meadows nodded, then turned to Manfred.

"He didn't give you any idea at all why he wanted to meet Miss Leicester?"

George shook his head.

"No, he was very mysterious indeed on that subject," he said.

"He arrived by the Benguella, eh?" said Meadows, making a note. "We ought to get something from the ship before they pay off their stewards. If a man isn't communicative on board ship, he'll never talk at all! And we may find something in his belongings. Would you like to come along, Manfred?"

"I'll come with pleasure," said George gravely. "I may help you a little—you will not object to my making my own interpretation of what we see?"

Meadows smiled.

"You will be allowed your private mystery," he said.

A taxi set them down at the Petworth Hotel in Norfolk Street, and they were immediately shown up to the room which the dead man had hired but had not as yet occupied. His trunk, still strapped and locked, stood on a small wooden trestle, his overcoat was hanging behind the door; in one corner of the room was a thick hold-all, tightly strapped, and containing, as they subsequently discovered, a weather-stained mackintosh, two well-worn blankets and an air pillow, together with a collapsible canvas chair, also showing considerable signs of usage. This was the object of their preliminary search.

The lock of the trunk yielded to the third key which the detective tried. Beyond changes of linen and two suits, one of which was practically new and bore the tab of a store in St. Paul de Loanda, there was very little to enlighten them. They found an envelope full of papers, and sorted them out one by one on the bed. Barberton was evidently a careful man; he had preserved his hotel bills, writing on their backs brief but pungent comments about the accommodation he had enjoyed or suffered. There was an hotel in Lobuo which was full of vermin; there was one at Mossamedes of which he had written: "Rats ate one boot. Landlord made no allowance. Took three towels and pillow-slip."

"One of the Four Just Men in embryo," said Meadows dryly. Manfred smiled.

On the back of one bill were closely written columns of figures: "126, 1315, 107, 1712, about 24," etc. Against a number of these figures the word "about" appeared, and Manfred observed that invariably this qualification marked one of the higher numbers. Against the 107 was a thick pencil mark.

There were amongst the papers several other receipts. In St. Paul he had bought a "pistol automatic of precision" and ammunition for the same. The "pistol automatic of precision" was not in the trunk.

"We found it in his pocket," said Meadows briefly. "That fellow was expecting trouble, and was entitled to, if it is true that they tortured him at Mosamodes."

"Moss-AM-o-dees," Manfred corrected the mispronunciation. It almost amounted to a fad in him that to hear a place miscalled gave him a little pain.

Meadows was reading a letter, turning the pages slowly.

"This is from his sister: she lives at Brightlingsea, and there's nothing in it except..." He read a portion of the letter aloud:

> "... thank you for the books. The children will appreciate them. It must have been like old times writing them — but I can understand how it helped pass the time. Mr Lee came over and asked if I had heard from you. He is wonderful."

The letter was in an educated hand.

"He didn't strike me as a man who wrote books," said Meadows, and continued his search.

Presently he unfolded a dilapidated map, evidently of Angola. It was rather on the small scale, so much so that it took in a portion of the Kalahari Desert in the south, and showed in the north the undulations of the rolling Congo.

"No marks of any kind," said Meadows, carrying the chart to the window to examine it more carefully. "And that, I think, is about all—unless this is something."

"This" was wrapped in a piece of cloth, and was fastened to the bottom and the sides of the trunk by two improvised canvas straps. Meadows tried to pull it loose and whistled.

"Gold," he said. "Nothing else can weigh quite as heavily as this."

He lifted out the bundle eventually, unwrapped the covering, and gazed in amazement on the object that lay under his eyes. It was an African bete, a nude, squat idol, rudely shaped, the figure of a native woman.

"Gold?" said Manfred incredulously, and tried to lift it with his finger and thumb. He took a firmer grip and examined the discovery closely.

There was no doubt that it was gold, and fine gold. His thumb-nail made a deep scratch in the base of the statuette. He could see the marks where the knife of the inartistic sculptor had sliced and carved.

Meadows knew the coast fairly well: he had made many trips to Africa and had stopped off at various ports en route.

"I've never seen anything exactly like it before," he said, "and it isn't recent workmanship either. When you see this"—he pointed to a physical peculiarity of the figure—"you can bet that you've got something that's been made at least a couple of hundred years, and probably before then. The natives of West and Central Africa have not worn toe-rings, for example, since the days of the Caesars."

He weighed the idol in his hand.

"Roughly ten pounds," he said. "In other words, eight hundred pounds' worth of gold."

He was examining the cloth in which the idol had been wrapped, and uttered an exclamation.

"Look at this," he said.

Written on one corner, in indelible pencil, were the words: "Second shelf up left Gods lobby sixth."

Suddenly Manfred remembered.

"Would you have this figure put on the scales right away?" he said. "I'm curious to know the exact weight."

"Why?" asked Meadows in surprise, as he rang the bell.

The proprietor himself, who was aware that a police search was in progress, answered the call, and, at the detective's request, hurried down to the kitchen and returned in a few minutes with a pair of scales, which he placed on the table. He was obviously curious to know the purpose for which they were intended, but Inspector Meadows did not enlighten him, standing pointedly by the door until the gentleman had gone.

The figure was taken from under the cloth where it had been hidden whilst the scales were being placed, and put in one shallow pan on the machine.

"Ten pounds seven ounces," nodded Manfred triumphantly. "I thought that was the one!"

"One what?" asked the puzzled Meadows.

"Look at this list."

Manfred found the hotel bill with the rows of figures and pointed to the one which had a black cross against it.

"107," he said. "That is our little fellow, and the explanation is fairly plain. Barberton found some treasure-house filled with these statues. He took away the lightest. Look at the figures! He weighed them with a spring balance, one of those which register up to 21 lb. Above that he had to guess—he puts 'about 24,' 'about 22.'"

Meadows looked at his companion blankly, but Manfred was not deceived. That clever brain of the detective was working.

"Not for robbery—the trunk is untouched. They did not even burn his feet to find the idol or the treasure house: they must have known nothing of that. It was easy to rob him—or, if they knew of his gold idol, they considered it too small loot to bother with."

He looked slowly round the apartment. On the mantelshelf was a slip of brown paper like a pipe-spill. He picked it up, looked at both sides, and, finding the paper blank, put it back where he had found it. Manfred took it down and absently drew the strip between his sensitive finger-tips.

"The thing to do," said Meadows, taking one final look round, "is to find Miss Leicester."

Manfred nodded.

"That is one of the things," he said slowly. "The other, of course, is to find Johnny."

"Johnny?" Meadows frowned suspiciously. "Who is Johnny?" he asked.

"Johnny is my private mystery." George Manfred was smiling. "You promised me that I might have one!"

6

IN CHESTER SQUARE

WHEN Mirabelle Leicester went to Chester Square, her emotions were a curious discord of wonder, curiosity and embarrassment. The latter was founded on the extraordinary effusiveness of her companion, who had suddenly, and with no justification, assumed the position of dearest friend and lifelong acquaintance. Mirabelle thought the girl was an actress: a profession in which sudden and violent friendships are not a rare occurrence. She wondered why Aunt Alma had not made an effort to come to town, and wondered more that she had known of Alma's friendship with the Newtons. That the elder woman had her secrets was true, but there was no reason why she should have refrained from speaking of a family who were close enough friends to be asked to chaperon her in town.

She had time for thought, for Joan Newton chattered away all the time, and if she asked a question, she either did not wait for approval, or the question was answered to her satisfaction before it was put.

Chester Square, that dignified patch of Belgravia, is an imposing quarter. The big house into which the girl was admitted by a footman had that air of luxurious comfort which would have appealed to a character less responsive to refinement than Mirabelle Leicester's. She was ushered into

IN CHESTER SQUARE

a big drawing-room which ran from the front to the back of the house, and did not terminate even there, for a large, cool conservatory, bright with flowers, extended a considerable distance.

"Monty isn't back from the City yet," Joan rattled on. "My dear! He's awfully busy just now, what with stocks and shares and things like that."

She spoke as though "stocks and shares and things like that" were phenomena which had come into existence the day before yesterday for the occupation of Monty Newton.

"Is there a boom?" asked Mirabelle with a smile, and the term seemed to puzzle the girl.

"Ye-es, I suppose there is. You know what the Stock Exchange is, my dear? Everybody connected with it is wealthy beyond the dreams of avarice. The money they make is simply wicked! And they can give a girl an awfully good time—theatres, parties, dresses, pearls—why, Monty would think nothing of giving a string of pearls to a girl if he took a liking to her!"

In truth Joan was walking on very uncertain ground. Her instructions had been simple and to the point. "Get her to Chester Gardens, make friends with her, and don't mention the fact that I know Oberzohn." What was the object of bringing Mirabelle Leicester to the house, what was behind this move of Monty's, she did not know. She was merely playing for safety, baiting the ground, as it were, with her talk of good times and vast riches, in case that was required of her. For she, no less than many of her friends, entertained a wholesome dread of Monty Newton's disapproval, which usually took a definite unpleasant shape.

Mirabelle was laughing softly.

"I didn't know that stockbrokers were so rich," she said dryly, "and I can assure you that some of them aren't!"

She passed tactfully over the gaucherie of the pearls that Monty would give to any girl who took his fancy. By this time she had placed Joan: knew something of her upbringing, guessed pretty well the extent of her intelligence, and marvelled a little that a man of the unknown Mr Newton's position should have allowed his sister to come through the world without the benefit of a reasonably good education.

"Come up to your room, my dear," said Joan. "We've got a perfectly topping little suite for you, and I'm sure you'll be comfortable. It's at the front of the house, and if you can get used to the milkmen yowling about the streets before they're aired, you'll have a perfectly topping time."

When Mirabelle inspected the apartment she was enchanted. It fulfilled Joan's vague description. Here was luxury beyond her wildest dreams. She admired the silver bed and the thick blue carpet, the silken panelled walls, the exquisite fittings, and stood in rapture before the entrance of a little bathroom, with its silver and glass, its shaded lights and marble walls.

"I'll have a cup of tea sent up to you, my dear. You'll want to rest after your horrible day at that perfectly terrible factory, and I wonder you can stand Oberzohn, though they tell me he's quite a nice man..."

She seemed anxious to go, and Mirabelle was no less desirous of being alone.

"Come down when you feel like it," said Joan at parting, and ran down the stairs, reaching the hall in time to meet Mr Newton, who was handing his hat and gloves to his valet.

"Well, is she here?"

"She's here all right," said Joan, who was not at all embarrassed by the presence of the footman. "Monty, isn't she a bit of a fool? She couldn't say boo to a goose. What is the general scheme?"

He was brushing his hair delicately in the mirror above the hall-stand.

"What's what scheme?" he asked, after the servant had gone, as he strolled into the drawing-room before her.

"Bringing her here—is she sitting into a game?"

"Don't be stupid," said Monty without heat, as he dropped wearily to a low divan and drew a silken cushion behind him. "Nor inquisitive," he added. "You haven't scared her, have you?"

"I like that!" she said indignantly.

She was one of those ladies who speak more volubly and with the most assurance when there is a mirror in view, and she had her eyes fixed upon herself all the time she was talking, patting a strand of hair here and there, twisting her head this way and that to get a better effect, and never once looking at the man until he drew attention to himself.

"Scared! I'll bet she's never been to such a beautiful house in her life! What is she, Monty? A typist or something? I don't understand her."

"She's a lady," said Monty offensively. "That's the type that'll always seem like a foreign language to you."

She lifted one shoulder delicately.

"I don't pretend to be a lady, and what I am, you've made me," she said, and the reproach was mechanical. He had heard it before, not only from her, but from others similarly placed. "I don't think it's very kind to throw my education up in my face, considering the money I've made for you."

"And for yourself." He yawned. "Get me some tea."

"You might say 'please' now and again," she said resentfully, and he smiled as he took up the evening paper, paying her no more attention, until she had rung the bell with a vicious jerk and the silver tray came in and was deposited on a table near him.

"Where are you going tonight?"

His interest in her movements was unusual, and she was flattered.

"You know very well, Monty, where I'm going tonight," she said reproachfully. "You promised to take me, too. I think you'd look wonderful as a Crusader—one of them—those old knights in armour."

He nodded, but not to her comment.

"I remember, of course—the Arts Ball."

His surprise was so well simulated that she was deceived.

"Fancy your forgetting! I'm going as Cinderella, and Minnie Gray is going as a pierrette—"

"Minnie Gray isn't going as anything," said Monty, sipping his tea. "I've already telephoned to her to say that the engagement is off. Miss Leicester is going with you."

"But, Monty—" protested the girl.

"Don't 'but Monty' me," he ordered. "I'm telling you! Go up and see this girl, and put it to her that you've got a ticket for the dance."

"But her costume, Monty! The girl hasn't got a fancy dress. And Minnie—"

"Forget Minnie, will you? Mirabelle Leicester is going to the Arts Ball tonight." He tapped the tray before him to emphasize every word. "You have a ticket to spare, and you simply can't go alone because I have a very important business engagement and your friend has failed you. Her dress will be here in a few minutes: it is a bright green domino with a bright red hood."

"How perfectly hideous!" She forgot for the moment her disappointment in this outrage. "Bright green! Nobody has a complexion to stand that!"

Yet he ignored her.

"You will explain to Miss Leicester that the dress came from a friend who, through illness or any cause you like to invent, is unable to go to the dance—she'll jump at the chance. It is one of the events of the year and tickets are selling at a premium."

She asked him what that meant, and he explained patiently.

"Maybe she'll want to spend a quiet evening—have one of those headaches," he went on. "If that is so, you can tell her that I've got a party coming to the house tonight, and they will be a little noisy. Did she want to know anything about me?"

"No, she didn't," snapped Joan promptly. "She didn't want to know about anything. I couldn't get her to talk. She's like a dumb oyster."

Mirabelle was sitting by the window, looking down into the square, when there was a gentle tap at the door and Joan came in.

"I've got wonderful news for you," she said.

"For me?" said Mirabelle in surprise.

Joan ran across the room, giving what she deemed to be a surprisingly life-like representation of a young thing full of innocent joy.

"I've got an extra ticket for the Arts Ball tonight. They're selling at a—they're very expensive. Aren't you a lucky girl!"

"I?" said Mirabelle in surprise. "Why am I the lucky one?"

Joan rose from the bed and drew back from her reproachfully.

"You surely will come with me? If you don't, I shan't able to go at all. Lady Mary and I were going together... now she's sick!"

Mirabelle opened her eyes wider.

"But I can't go, surely. It is a fancy dress ball, isn't it? I read something about it in the papers. And I'm awfully tired tonight."

Joan pouted prettily.

"My dear, if you lay down for an hour you'd be fit. Besides, you couldn't sleep here early tonight: Monty's having one of his men parties, and they're a noisy lot of people—though thoroughly respectable," she added hastily.

Poor Joan had a mission outside her usual range.

"I'd love to go,"—Mirabelle was anxious not to be a killjoy—"if I could get a dress."

"I've got one," said the girl promptly, and ran out of the room.

She returned very quickly, and threw the domino on the bed.

"It's not pretty to look at, but it's got this advantage, that you can wear almost anything underneath."

"What time does the ball start?" Mirabelle, examining her mind, found that she was not averse to going; she was very human, and a fancy dress ball would be a new experience.

"Ten o'clock," said Joan. "We can have dinner before Monty's friends arrive. You'd like to see Monty, wouldn't you? He's downstairs—such a gentleman, my dear!"

The girl could have laughed.

A little later she was introduced to the redoubtable Monty, and found his suave and easy manner a relief after the jerky efforts of the girl to be entertaining. Monty had seen most parts of the world and could talk entertainingly about them all. Mirabelle rather liked him, though she thought he was something of a fop, yet was not sorry when she learned that, so far from having friends to dinner, he did not expect them to arrive until after she and Joan had left.

The meal put her more at her ease. He was a polished man of the world, courteous to the point of pomposity; he neither said nor suggested one thing that could offend her; they were half-way through dinner when the cry of a newsboy was heard in the street. Through the dining-room window she saw the footman go down the steps and buy a newspaper. He glanced at the stop-press space and came back slowly up the stairs reading. A little later he came into the room, and must have signalled to her host, for Monty went out immediately and she heard their voices in the passage. Joan was uneasy.

"I wonder what's the matter?" she asked, a little irritably. "It's very bad manners to leave ladies in the middle of dinner—"

At that moment Monty came back. Was it imagination on her part, or had he gone suddenly pale? Joan saw it, and her brows met, but she was too wise to make a comment upon his appearance.

Mr Newton seated himself in his place with a word of apology and poured out a glass of champagne. Only for a second did his hand tremble, and then, with a smile, he was his old self.

"What is wrong, Monty?"

"Wrong? Nothing," he said curtly, and took up the topic of conversation where he had laid it down before leaving the room.

"It isn't that old snake, is it?" asked Joan with a shiver. "Lord! That unnerves me! I never go to bed at night without looking under, or turning the clothes right down to the foot! They ought to have found it months ago if the police—"

At this point she caught Monty Newton's eye, cold, menacing, malevolent, and the rest of her speech died on her lips.

Mirabelle went upstairs to dress, and Joan would have followed but the man beckoned her.

"You're a little too talkative, Joan," he said, more mildly than she had expected. "The snake is not a subject we wish to discuss at dinner. And listen!" He walked into the passage and looked round, then came back and closed the door. "Keep that girl near you."

"Who is going to dance with me?" she asked petulantly. "I like having a hell of a lively night!"

"Benton will be there to look after you, and one of the 'Old Guard'—"

He saw the frightened look in her face and chuckled. "What's the matter, you fool?" he asked good-humouredly. "He'll dance with the girl."

"I wish those fellows weren't going to be there," she said uneasily, but he went on, without noticing her:

"I shall arrive at half-past eleven. You had better meet me near the entrance to the American bar. My party didn't turn up, you understand. You'll get back here at midnight."

"So soon?" she said in dismay. "Why, it doesn't end till—"

"You'll be back here at midnight," he said evenly. "Go into her room, clear up everything she may have left behind. You understand? Nothing is to be left."

"But when she comes back she'll—"

"She'll not come back," said Monty Newton, and the girl's blood ran cold.

7

"MORAL SUASION"

"There's a man wants to see you, governor."

It was a quarter-past nine. The girls had been gone ten minutes, and Montague Newton had settled himself down to pass the hours of waiting before he had to dress. He put down the patience cards he was shuffling.

"A man to see me? Who is he, Fred?"

"I don't know: I've never seen him before. Looks to me like a 'busy.'"

A detective! Monty's eyebrows rose, but not in trepidation. He had met many detectives in the course of his chequered career and had long since lost his awe of them.

"Show him in," he said with a nod.

The slim man in evening dress who came softly into the room was a stranger to Monty, who knew most of the prominent figures in the world of criminal detection. And yet his face was in some way familiar.

"Captain Newton?" he asked.

"That is my name." Newton rose with a smile.

The visitor looked slowly round towards the door through which the footman had gone.

"Do your servants always listen at the keyhole?" he asked, in a quiet, measured tone, and Newton's face went a dusky red.

In two strides he was at the door and had flung it open, just in time to see the disappearing heels of the footman.

"Here, you!" He called the man back, a scowl on his face. "If you want to know anything, will you come in and ask?" he roared. "If I catch you listening at my door, I'll murder you!"

The man with a muttered excuse made a hurried escape.

"How did you know?" growled Newton, as he came back into the room and slammed the door behind him.

"I have an instinct for espionage," said the stranger, and went on, without a break: "I have called for Miss Mirabelle Leicester."

Newton's eyes narrowed.

"Oh, you have, have you?" he said softly. "Miss Leicester is not in the house. She left a quarter of an hour ago."

"I did not see her come out of the house."

"No, the fact is, she went out by way of the mews. My—er" —he was going to say "sister" but thought better of it—"my young friend—"

"Flash Jane Smith," said the stranger. "Yes?"

Newton's colour deepened. He was rapidly reaching the point when his sang-froid, nine-tenths of his moral assets, was in danger of deserting him.

"Who are you, anyway?" he asked.

The stranger wetted his lips with the tip of his tongue, a curiously irritating action of his, for some inexplicable reason.

"My name is Leon Gonsalez," he said simply.

Instinctively the man drew back. Of course! Now he remembered, and the colour had left his cheeks, leaving him grey. With an effort he forced a smile.

"One of the redoubtable Four Just Men? What extraordinary birds you are!" he said. "I remember ten-fifteen years ago, being scared out of my life by the very mention of your name—you came to punish where the law failed, eh?"

"You must put that in your reminiscences," said Leon gently. "For the moment I am not in an autobiographical mood."

But Newton could not be silenced.

"I know a man"—he was speaking slowly, with quiet vehemence—"who will one day cause you a great deal of inconvenience, Mr Leon Gonsalez: a man who never forgets you in his prayers. I won't tell you who he is."

"It is unnecessary. You are referring to the admirable Oberzohn. Did I not kill his brother... ? Yes, I thought I was right. He was the man with the oxycephalic head and the queerly prognathic jaw. An interesting case: I would like to have had his measurements, but I was in rather a hurry."

He spoke almost apologetically for his haste.

"But we're getting away from the subject, Mr Newton. You say this young lady has left your house by the mews, and you were about to suggest she left in the care of Miss—I don't know what you call her. Why did she leave that way?"

Leon Gonsalez had something more than an instinct for espionage: he had an instinct for truth, and he knew two things immediately: first, that Newton was not lying when he said the girl had left the house; secondly, that there was an excellent, but not necessarily a sinister, reason for the furtive departure.

"Where has she gone?"

"Home," said the other laconically. "Where else should she go?"

"She came to dinner... intending to stay the night?"

"Look here, Gonsalez," interrupted Monty Newton savagely. "You and your gang were wonderful people twenty years ago, but a lot has happened since then—and we don't shiver at the name of the Three Just Men. I'm not a child—do you get that? And you're not so very terrible at close range. If you want to complain to the police—"

"Meadows is outside. I persuaded him to let me see you first," said Leon, and Newton started.

"Outside?" incredulously.

In two strides he was at the window and had pulled aside the blind. On the other side of the street a man was standing on the edge of the sidewalk, intently surveying the gutter. He knew him at once.

"Well, bring him in," he said.

"Where has this young lady gone? That is all I want to know."

"She has gone home, I tell you."

Leon went to the door and beckoned Meadows; they spoke together in low tones, and then Meadows entered the room and was greeted with a stiff nod from the owner of the house.

"What's the idea of this, Meadows—sending this bird to cross-examine me?"

"This bird came on his own," said Meadows coldly, "if you mean Mr Gonsalez? I have no right to prevent any person from cross-examining you. Where is the young lady?"

"I tell you, she has gone home. If you don't believe me, search the house—either of you."

He was not bluffing: Leon was sure of that. He turned to the detective.

"I personally have no wish to trouble this gentleman any more."

He was leaving the room when, from over his shoulder: "That snake is busy again, Newton."

"What snake are you talking about?"

"He killed a man tonight on the Thames Embankment. I hope it will not spoil Lisa Marthon's evening."

Meadows, watching the man, saw him change colour.

"I don't know what you mean," he said loudly.

"You arranged with Lisa to pick up Barberton tonight and get him talking. And there she is, poor girl, all dressed to kill, and only a dead man to vamp—only a murdered man." He turned suddenly, and his voice grew hard. "That is a good word, isn't it, Newton—murder?"

"I didn't know anything about it."

As Newton's hand came towards the bell: "We can show ourselves out," said Leon.

He shut the door behind him, and presently there was a slam of the outer door, Monty got to the window too late to see his unwelcome guests depart, and went up to his room to change, more than a little perturbed in mind.

The footman called him from the hall.

"I'm sorry about that affair, sir. I thought it was a 'busy'."

"You think too much, Fred"—Newton threw the words down at his servitor with a snarl. "Go back to your place—which is the servants' hall. I'll ring you if I want you."

He resumed his progress up the stairs and the man turned sullenly away.

He opened the door of his room, switched on the light, had closed the door and was half-way to his dressing-table, when an arm like steel closed round his neck, he was jerked suddenly backward on to the floor, and looked up into the inscrutable face of Gonsalez.

"Shout and you die!" whispered a voice in his ear.

Newton lay quiet.

"I'll fix you for this," he stammered.

The other shook his head.

"I think not, if by 'fixing' me you mean you're going to complain to the police. You've been under my watchful eye for quite a long time, Monty Newton, and you'll be amazed to learn that I've made several visits to your house. There is a little wall safe behind that curtain"—he nodded towards the corner of the room—"would you be surprised to learn that I've had the door open and every one of its documentary contents photographed?"

He saw the fear in the man's eyes as he snapped a pair of aluminium handcuffs of curious design about Monty's wrists. With hardly an effort he lifted him, heavy as he was, threw him on the bed, and, having locked the door, returned, and, sitting on the bed, proceeded first to strap his ankles and then leisurely to take off his prisoner's shoes.

"What are you going to do?" asked Monty in alarm.

"I intend finding out where Miss Leicester has been taken," said Gonsalez, who had stripped one shoe and, pulling off the silken sock, was examining the man's bare foot critically. "Ordinary and strictly legal inquiries take time and fail at the end—unfortunately for you, I have not a minute to spare."

"I tell you she's gone home."

Leon did not reply. He pulled open a drawer of the bureau, searched for some time, and presently found what he sought: a thin silken scarf. This, despite the struggles of the man on the bed, he fastened about his mouth.

"In Mosamodes," he said—"and if you ever say that before my friend George Manfred, be careful to give its correct pronunciation: he is rather touchy on the point—some friends of yours took a man named Barberton, whom they subsequently murdered, and tried to make him talk by burning his feet. He was a hero. I'm going to see how heroic you are."

"For God's sake don't do it!" said the muffled voice of Newton.

Gonsalez was holding a flat metal case which he had taken from his pocket, and the prisoner watched him, fascinated, as he removed the lid, and snapped a cigar-lighter close to its blackened surface. A blue flame rose and swayed in the draught.

"The police force is a most excellent institution," said Leon. He had found a silver shoe-horn on the table and was calmly heating it in the light of the flame, holding the rapidly warming hook with a silk handkerchief. "But unfortunately, when you are dealing with crimes of violence, moral suasion and gentle treatment produce nothing more poignant in the bosom of your adversary than a sensation of amused and derisive contempt.

The English, who make a god of the law, gave up imprisoning thugs and flogged them, and there are few thugs left. When the Russian gunmen came to London, the authorities did the only intelligent thing—they held back the police and brought up the artillery, having only one desire, which was to kill the gunmen at any expense. Violence fears violence. The gunman lives in the terror of the gun—by the way, I understand the old guard is back in full strength?"

When Leon started in this strain he could continue for hours.

"I don't know what you mean," mumbled Monty.

"You wouldn't." The intruder lifted the blackened, smoking shoe-horn, brought it as near to his face as he dared.

"Yes, I think that will do," he said, and came slowly towards the bed.

The man drew up his feet in anticipation of pain, but a long hand caught him by the ankles and drew them straight again.

"They've gone to the Arts Ball." Even through the handkerchief the voice sounded hoarse.

"The Arts Ball?" Gonsalez looked down at him, and then, throwing the hot shoe-horn into the fire-place, he removed the gag. "Why have they gone to the Arts Ball?"

"I wanted them out of the way tonight."

"Is Oberzohn likely to be at the Arts Ball?"

"Oberzohn?" The man's laugh bordered on the hysteric.

"Or Gurther?"

This time Mr Newton did not laugh.

"I don't know who you mean," he said.

"We'll go into that later," replied Leon lightly, pulling the knot of the handkerchief about the ankles. "You may get up now. What time do you expect them back?"

"I don't know. I told Joan not to hurry, as I was meeting somebody here tonight."

Which sounded plausible. Leon remembered that the Arts Ball was a fancy dress affair, and there was some reason for the departure from the mews instead of from the front of the house. As though he were reading his thoughts, Newton said:

"It was Miss Leicester's idea, going through the back. She was rather shy... she was wearing a domino."

"Colour?"

"Green, with a reddish hood."

Leon looked at him quickly.

"Rather distinctive. Was that the idea?"

"I don't know what the idea was," growled Newton, sitting on the edge of the bed and pulling on a sock. "But I do know this, Gonsalez," he said, with an outburst of anger which was half fear; "that you'll be sorry you did this to me!"

Leon walked to the door, turned the key and opened it.

"I only hope that you will not be sorry I did not kill you," he said, and was gone.

Monty Newton waited until from his raised window he saw the slim figure pass along the sidewalk and disappear round a corner, and then he hurried down, with one shoe on and one off, to call New Cross 93.

8

THE HOUSE OF OBERZOHN

In a triangle, two sides of which were expressed by the viaducts of converging railroads and the base by the dark and sluggish waters of the Grand Surrey Canal, stood the gaunt ruins of a store in which had once been housed the merchandise of the O.&S. Company. A Zeppelin in passing had dropped an incendiary bomb at random, and torn a great ugly gap in the roof. The fire that followed left the iron frames of the windows twisted and split; the roof by some miracle remained untouched except for the blackened edges about the hole through which the flames had rushed to the height of a hundred feet.

The store was flush with the canal towing-path; barges had moored here, discharging rubber in bales, palm nut, nitrates even, and had restocked with Manchester cloth and case upon case of Birmingham-made geegaws of brass and lacquer.

Mr Oberzohn invariably shipped his spirituous cargoes from Hamburg, since Germany is the home of synthesis. In the centre of the triangle was a red-brick villa, more unlovely than the factory, missing as it did that ineffable grandeur, made up of tragedy and pathos, attaching to a burnt-out building, however ugly it may have been in its prime.

The villa was built from a design in Mr Oberzohn's possession, and was the exact replica of the house in Sweden where he was born. It had high, gabled ends at odd and unexpected places. The roof was shingled with grey tiles; there were glass panels in the curious-looking door, and iron ornaments in the shape of cranes and dogs flanking the narrow path through the rank nettle and dock which constituted his garden.

Here he dwelt, in solitude, yet not in solitude, for two men lived in the house, and there was a stout Swedish cook and a very plain Danish maid, a girl of vacant countenance, who worked from sun-up to midnight without complaint, who seldom spoke and never smiled. The two men were somewhere in the region of thirty. They occupied the turret rooms at each end of the building, and had little community of interest. They sometimes played cards together with an old and greasy pack, but neither spoke more than was necessary. They were lean, hollow-faced men, with a certain physiognomical resemblance. Both had thin, straight lips; both had round, staring, dark eyes filled with a bright but terrifying curiosity.

"They look," reported Leon Gonsalez, when he went to examine the ground, "as if they are watching pigs being killed and enjoying every minute of it. Iwan Pfeiffer is one, Sven Gurther is the other. Both have escaped the gallows or the axe in Germany; both have convictions against them. They are typical German-trained criminals, as pitiless as wolves. Dehumanized."

The "Three," as was usual, set the machinery of the law in motion, and found that the hands of the police were tied. Only by stretching the law could the men be deported, and the law is difficult to stretch. To all appearance they offended in no respect. A woman, by no means the most desirable of citizens, laid a complaint against one. There was an investigation—proof was absent; the very character of the complainant precluded a conviction, and the matter was dropped—by the police.

Somebody else moved swiftly.

One morning, just before daybreak, a policeman patrolling the tow-path heard a savage snarl and looked round for the dog. He found instead, up one of those narrow entries leading to the canal bank, a man. He was tied to the stout sleeper fence, and his bare back showed marks of a whip. Somebody had held him up at night as he prowled the bank in search of amusement, had tied and flogged him. Twenty-five lashes: an expert thought the whip used was the official cat-o'-nine-tails.

Scotland Yard, curious, suspicious, sought out the Three Just Men. They had alibis so complete as to be unbreakable. Sven Gurther went unavenged — but he kept from the tow-path thereafter.

In this house of his there were rooms which only Dr Oberzohn visited. The Danish maid complained to the cook that when she had passed the door of one as the doctor came out, a blast of warm, tainted air had rushed out and made her cough for an hour. There was another room in which from time to time the doctor had installed a hotchpotch of apparatus. Vulcanizing machines, electrical machines (older and more used than Mirabelle had seen in her brief stay in the City Road), a liquid air plant, not the most up-to-date but serviceable.

He was not, curiously enough, a doctor in the medical sense. He was not even a doctor of chemistry. His doctorate was in Literature and Law. These experiments of his were hobbies — hobbies that he had pursued from his childhood.

On this evening he was sitting in his stuffy parlour reading close-printed and closer-reasoned volume of German philosophy, and thinking of something else. Though the sun had only just set, the blinds and curtains were drawn; a wood fire crackled in the grate, and the bright lights of three half-watt lamps made glaring radiance.

An interruption came in the shape of a telephone call. He listened, grunting replies.

"So!" he said at last, and spoke a dozen words in his strange English.

Putting aside his book, he hobbled in his velvet slippers across the room and pressed twice upon the bell-push by the side of the fire-place. Gurther came in noiselessly and stood waiting.

He was grimy, unshaven. The pointed chin and short upper lip were blue. The V of his shirt visible above the waistcoat was soiled and almost black at the edges. He stood at attention, smiling vacantly, his eyes fixed at a point above the doctor's head.

Dr Oberzohn lifted his eyes from his book.

"I wish you to be a gentleman of club manner tonight," he said. He spoke in that hard North-German tongue which the Swede so readily acquires.

"Ja, Herr Doktor!"

The man melted from the room.

Dr Oberzohn for some reason hated Germans. So, for the matter of that, did Gurther and Pfeiffer, the latter being Polish by extraction and Russian by birth. Gurther hated Germans because they stormed the little jail at Altostadt to kill him after the dogs found Frau Siedlitz's body. He would have died then but for the green police, who scented a Communist rising, scattered the crowd and sent Gurther by road to the nearest big town under escort. The two escorting policemen were never seen again. Gurther reappeared mysteriously in England two years after, bearing a veritable passport. There was no proof even that he was Gurther — Leon knew, Manfred knew, Poiccart knew.

There had been an alternative to the whipping.

"It would be a simple matter to hold his head under water until he was drowned," said Leon.

They debated the matter, decided against this for no sentimental or moral reason — none save expediency. Gurther had his whipping and never knew how near to the black and greasy water of the canal he had been.

Dr Oberzohn resumed his book—a fascinating book that was all about the human soul and immortality and time. He was in the very heart of an analysis of eternity when Gurther reappeared dressed in the "gentleman-club manner." The dress-coat fitted perfectly; shirt and waistcoat were exactly the right cut. The snowy shirt, the braided trousers, the butterfly bow, and winged collar...

"That is good." Dr Oberzohn went slowly over the figure. "But the studs should be pearl—not enamel. And the watch-chain is demode—it is not worn. The gentleman-club manner does not allow of visible ornament. Also I think a moustache... ?"

"Ja, Herr Doktor!"

Gurther, who was once an actor, disappeared again. When he returned the enamel studs had gone: there were small pearls in their place, and his white waistcoat had no chain across. And on his upper lip had sprouted a small brown moustache, so natural that even Oberzohn, scrutinizing closely, could find no fault with it. The doctor took a case from his pocket, fingered out three crisp notes.

"Your hands, please?"

Gurther took three paces to the old man, halted, clicked his heels and held out his hands for inspection.

"Good! You know Leon Gonsalez? He will be at the Arts Ball. He wears no fancy dress. He was the man who whipped you."

"He was the man who whipped me," said Gurther without heat.

There was a silence, Dr Oberzohn pursing his lips.

"Also, he did that which brands him as an infamous assassin... I think... yes, I think my dear Gurther... there will be a girl also, but the men of my police will be there to arrange such matters. Benton will give you instructions. For you, only Gonsalez."

Gurther bowed stiffly.

"I have implored the order," he said, bowed again and withdrew. Later, Dr Oberzohn heard the drone of the little car as it bumped and slithered across the grass to the road. He resumed his book: this matter of eternity was fascinating.

The Arts Ball at the Corinthian Hall was one of the events of the season, and the tickets, issued exclusively to the members of three clubs, were eagerly sought by society people who could not be remotely associated with any but the art of living.

When the girl came into the crowded hall, she looked around in wonder. The balconies, outlined in soft lights and half-hidden with flowers, had been converted into boxes; the roof had been draped with blue and gold tissue; at one end of the big hall was a veritable bower of roses, behind which one of the two bands was playing. Masks in every conceivable guise were swinging rhythmically across the polished floor. To the blasé, there was little difference between the Indians, the pierrots and the cavaliers to be seen here and those they had seen a hundred times on a hundred different floors.

As the girl gazed round in wonder and delight, forgetting all her misgivings, two men, one in evening dress, the other in the costume of a brigand, came from under the shadow of the balcony towards them.

"Here are our partners," said Joan, with sudden vivacity. "'Mirabelle, I want you to know Lord Evington."

The man in evening dress stroked his little moustache, clicked his heels and bent forward in a stiff bow. He was thin-faced, a little pallid, unsmiling. His round, dark eyes surveyed her for a second, and then:

"I'm glad to meet you, Miss Leicester," he said, in a high, harsh voice, that had just the trace of a foreign accent.

This struck the girl with as much surprise as the cold kiss he had implanted upon her hand, and, as if he read her thoughts, he went on quickly:

"I have lived so long abroad that England and English manners are strange to me. Won't you dance? And had you not better mask? I must apologise to you for my costume." He shrugged his shoulders. "But there was no gala dress available."

She fixed the red mask, and in another second she was gliding through the crowd and was presently lost to view.

"I don't understand it all, Benton."

Joan was worried and frightened. She had begun to realize that the game she played was something different... her part more sinister than any role she had yet filled. To jolly along the gilded youth to the green tables of Captain Monty Newton was one thing; but never before had she seen the gang working against a woman.

"I don't know," grumbled the brigand, who was not inaptly arrayed. "There's been a hurry call for everybody." He glanced round uneasily as though he feared his words might be overheard. "All the guns are here—Defson, Cuccini, Jewy Stubbs..."

"The guns?" she whispered in horror, paling under her rouge. "You mean...?"

"The guns are out: that's all I know," he said doggedly. "They started drifting in half an hour before you came."

Joan was silent, her heart racing furiously. Then Monty had told her the truth. She knew that somewhere behind Oberzohn, behind Monty Newton, was a force perfectly dovetailed into the machine, only one cog of which she had seen working. These card parties of Monty's were profitable enough, but for a long time she had had a suspicion that they were the merest sideline. The organization maintained a regular corps of gunmen, recruited from every quarter of the globe. Monty Newton talked sometimes in his less sober moments of what he facetiously described as the "Old Guard." How they were employed, on what excuse, for what purpose, she had never troubled to think. They came and went from England in batches. Once Monty had told her that Oberzohn's people had gone to Smyrna, and he talked vaguely of unfair competition that had come to the traders of the O.&S. outfit. Afterwards she read in the paper of a "religious riot" which resulted in the destruction by fire of a great block of business premises. After that Monty spoke no more of competition. The Old Guard returned to England, minus one of its number, who had been shot in the stomach in the course of this "religious riot." What particular faith he possessed in such a degree as to induce him to take up arms for the cause, she never learned. She knew he was dead, because Monty had written to the widow, who lived in the Bronx.

Joan knew a lot about Monty's business, for an excellent reason. She was with him most of the time; and whether she posed as his niece or daughter, his sister, or some closer relationship, she was undoubtedly the nearest to a confidante he possessed.

"Who is that man with the moustache—is he one?" she asked.

"No; he's Oberzohn's man—for God's sake don't tell Monty I told you all this! I got orders tonight to put wise about the girl."

"What about her... what are they doing with her?" she gasped in terror.

"Let us dance," said Benton, and half guided, half carried her into the throng. They had reached the centre of the floor when, with no warning, every light in the hall went out.

9

BEFORE THE LIGHTS WENT OUT

THE band had stopped, a rustle of hand-clapping came from the hot dancers, and almost before the applause had started the second band struck up "Kulloo."

Mirabelle was not especially happy. Her partner was the most correct of dancers, but they lacked just that unity of purpose, the oneness of interest which makes all the difference between the ill-and the well-matched.

"May we sit down?" she begged. "I am rather hot."

"Will the gracious lady come to the little hall?" he asked. "It is cooler there, and the chairs are comfortable."

She looked at him oddly.

"'Gracious lady' is a German expression—why do you use it, Lord Evington? I think it is very pretty," she hastened to assure him.

"I lived for many years in Germany," said Mr Gurther. "I do not like the German people—they are so stupid."

If he had said "German police" he would have been nearer to the truth; and had he added that the dislike was mutual, he might have gained credit for his frankness.

At the end of the room, concealed by the floral decorations of the bandstand, was a door which led to a smaller room, ordinarily separated from the main hall by folding doors which were seldom opened. Tonight the annexe was to be used as a conservatory. Palms and banked flowers were everywhere. Arbours had been artificially created, and the cosy nooks, half-hidden by shrubs, secluded seats and tables, all that ingenuity could design to meet the wishes of sitters-out.

He stood invitingly at the entrance of a little grotto, dimly illuminated by one Chinese lantern.

"I think we will sit in the open," said Mirabelle, and pulled out a chair.

"Excuse me."

Instantly he was by her side, the chair arranged, a cushion found, and she sank down with a sigh of relief. It was early yet for the loungers: looking round, she saw that, but for a solitary waiter fastening his apron with one eye upon possible customers, they were alone.

"You will drink wine... no? An orangeade? Good!" He beckoned the waiter and gave his order. "You must excuse me if I am a little strange. I have been in Germany for many years—except during the war, when I was in France."

Mr Gurther had certainly been in Germany for many years, but he had never been in France. Nor had he heard a shot fired in the war. It is true that an aerial bomb had exploded perilously near the prison at Mainz in which he was serving ten years for murder, but that represented his sole warlike experience.

"You live in the country, of course?"

"In London: I am working with Mr Oberzohn."

"So: he is a good fellow. A gentleman."

She had not been very greatly impressed by the doctor's breeding, but it was satisfying to hear a stranger speak with such heartiness of her new employer. Her mind at the moment was on Heavytree Farm: the cool parlour with its chintzes—a room, at this hour, fragrant with the night scents of flowers which came stealing through the open casement. There was a fox-terrier, Jim by name, who would be wandering disconsolately from room to room, sniffing unhappily at the hall door. A lump came up into her throat. She felt very far from home and very lonely. She wanted to get up and run back to where she had left Joan and tell her that she had changed her mind and must go back to Gloucester that night... she looked impatiently for the waiter. Mr Gurther was fiddling with some straws he had taken from the glass container in the centre of the table. One end of the straws showed above the edge of the table, the others were thrust deep in the wide-necked little bottle he had in the other hand. The hollow straws held half an inch of the red powder that filled the bottle.

"Excuse!"

The waiter put the orangeades on the table and went away to get change. Mirabelle's eyes were wistfully fixed on a little door at the end of the room. It gave to the street, and there were taxicabs which could get her to Paddington in ten minutes.

When she looked round he was stirring the amber contents of her glass with a spoon. Two straws were invitingly protruding from the foaming orangeade. She smiled and lifted the glass as he fitted a cigarette into his black holder.

"I may smoke—yes?"

The first taste she had through the straws was one of extreme bitterness. She made a wry face and put down the glass.

"How horrid!"

"Did it taste badly... ?" he began, but she was pouring out water from a bottle.

"It was most unpleasant—"

"Will you try mine, please?" He offered the glass to her and she drank. "It may have been something in the straw." Here he was telling her the fact.

"It was..."

The room was going round and round, the floor was rising up and down like the deck of a ship in a stormy sea. She rose, swayed, and caught him by the arm.

"Open the little door, waiter, please—the lady is faint."

The waiter turned to the door and threw it open. A man stood there—just outside the door. He wore over his dinner dress a long cloak in the Spanish style. Gurther stood staring, a picture of amused dismay, his cigarette still unlit. He did not move his hands. Gonsalez was waiting there, alert... death grinning at him... and then the room went inky black. Somebody had turned the main switch.

10

WHEN THE LIGHTS WENT OUT

Five, ten minutes passed before the hall-keeper tripped and stumbled and cursed his way to the smaller room and, smashing down the hired flowers, he passed through the wreckage of earthen pots and tumbled mould to the control. Another second and the rooms were brilliantly lit again—the band struck up a two-step and fainting ladies were escorted to the decent obscurity of their retiring rooms.

The manager of the hall came flying into the annexe.

"What happened—the main fuse gone?"

"No," said the hall-keeper sourly, "some fool turned over the switch."

The agitated waiter protested that nobody had been near the switch-box.

"There was a lady and gentleman here, and another gentleman outside." He pointed to the open door.

"Where are they now?"

"I don't know. The lady was faint."

The three had disappeared when the manager went out into a small courtyard that led round the corner of the building to a side street. Then he came back on a tour of inspection.

"Somebody did it from the yard. There's a window open—you can reach the switch easily."

The window was fastened and locked.

"There is no lady or gentleman in the yard," he said. "Are you sure they did not go into the big hall?"

"In the dark—maybe."

The waiter's nervousness was understandable. Mr Gurther had given him a five-pound note and the man had not as yet delivered the change. Never would he return to claim it if all that his keen ears heard was true.

Four men had appeared in the annexe: one shut the door and stood by it. The three others were accompanied by the manager, who called Phillips, the waiter.

"This man served them," he said, troubled. Even the most innocent do not like police visitations. "What was the gentleman like?"

Phillips gave a brief and not inaccurate description.

"That is your man, I think, Herr Fluen?"

The third of the party was bearded and plump; he wore a Derby hat with evening dress.

"That is Gurther," he nodded. "It will be a great pleasure to meet him. For eight months the Embassy has been striving for his extradition. But our people at home... !"

He shrugged his shoulders. All properly constituted officials behave in such a manner when they talk of Governments.

"The lady now"—Inspector Meadows was patently worried—"she was faint, you say. Had she drunk anything?"

"Orangeade—there is the glass. She said there was something nasty in the straws. These."

Phillips handed them to the detective. He wetted his finger from them, touched his tongue and spat out quickly.

"Yes," he said, and went out by the little door.

Gonsalez, of course: but where had he gone, and how, with a drugged girl on his hands and the Child of the Snake? Gurther was immensely quick to strike, and an icy-hearted man: the presence of a woman would not save Leon.

"When the light went out—" began the waiter, and the trouble cleared from Mr Meadows's face.

"Of course—I had forgotten that," he said softly. "The lights went out!"

All the way back to the Yard he was trying to bring something from the back of his mind—something that was there, the smooth tip of it tantalizingly displayed, yet eluding every grasp. It had nothing to do with the lights—nor Gonsalez, nor yet the girl. Gurther? No. Nor Manfred? What was it? A name had been mentioned to him that day—it had a mysterious significance. A golden idol! He picked up the end of the thought... Johnny! Manfred's one mystery. That was the dust which lay on all thought. And now that he remembered he was disappointed. It was so ridiculously unimportant a matter to baffle him.

He left his companions at the corner of Curzon Street and went alone to the house. There was a streak of light showing between the curtains in the upstairs room. The passage was illuminated—Poiccart answered his ring at once.

"Yes, George and Leon were here a little time back—the girl? No, they said nothing about a girl. They looked rather worried, I thought. Miss Leicester, I suppose? Won't you come in?"

"No, I can't wait. There's a light in Manfred's room."

The ghost of a smile lit the heavy face and faded as instantly.

"My room also," he said. "Butlers take vast liberties in the absence of their masters. Shall I give a message to George?"

"Ask him to call me at the Yard."

Poiccart closed the door on him; stopped in the passage to arrange a salver on the table and hung up a hat. All this Meadows saw through the fanlight and walking-stick periscope which is so easily fitted and can be of such value. And seeing, his doubts evaporated.

Poiccart went slowly up the stairs into the little office room, pulled back the curtains and opened the window at the top.

The next second, the watching detective saw the light go out and went away.

"I'm sorry to keep you in the dark," said Poiccart.

The men who were in the room waited until the shutters were fast and the curtains pulled across, and then the light flashed on. White of face, her eyes closed, her breast scarcely moving, Mirabelle Leicester lay on the long settee. Her domino was a heap of shimmering green and scarlet on the floor, and Leon was gently sponging her face, George Manfred watching from the back of the settee, his brows wrinkled.

"Will she die?" he asked bluntly.

"I don't know: they sometimes die of that stuff," replied Leon cold-bloodedly. "She must have had it pretty raw. Gurther is a crude person."

"What was it?" asked George.

Gonsalez spread out his disengaged hand in a gesture of uncertainty.

"If you can imagine morphia with a kick in it, it was that. I don't know. I hope she doesn't die: she is rather young—it would be the worst of bad luck."

Poiccart stirred uneasily. He alone had within his soul what Leon would call "a trace" of sentiment.

"Could we get Elver?" he asked anxiously, and Leon looked up with his boyish smile. "Growing onions in Seville has softened you, Raymondo mio!" He never failed in moments of great strain to taunt the heavy man with his two years of agricultural experiment, and they knew that the gibes were deliberately designed to steady his mind. "Onions are sentimental things—they make you cry: a vegetable muchos simpatico! This woman is alive!"

Her eyelids had fluttered twice. Leon lifted the bare arm, inserted the needle of a tiny hypodermic and pressed home the plunger.

"Tomorrow she will feel exactly as if she had been drunk," he said calmly, "and in her mouth will be the taste of ten rank cigars. Oh, señorinetta, open thy beautiful eyes and look upon thy friends!"

The last sentence was in Spanish. She heard: the lids fluttered and rose.

"You're a long way from Heavytree Farm, Miss Leicester."

She looked up wonderingly into the kindly face of George Manfred.

"Where am I?" she asked faintly, and closed her eyes again with a grimace of pain.

"They always ask that—just as they do in books," said Leon oracularly. "If they don't say 'Where am I?' they ask for their mothers. She's quite out of danger."

One hand was on her wrist, another at the side of her neck.

"Remarkably regular. She has a good head—mathematical probably."

"She is very beautiful," said Poiccart in a hushed voice.

"All people are beautiful—just as all onions are beautiful. What is the difference between a lovely maid and the ugliest of duennas—what but a matter of pigmentation and activity of tissue? Beneath that, an astounding similarity of the circulatory, sustentacular, motorvascular—"

"How long have we got?" Manfred interrupted him, and Leon shook his head.

"I don't know—not long, I should think. Of course, we could have told Meadows and he'd have turned out police reserves, but I should like to keep them out of it."

"The Old Guard was there?"

"Every man jack of them—those tough lads! They will be here just as soon as the Herr Doktor discovers what is going forward. Now, I think you can travel. I want her out of the way."

Stooping, he put his hands under her and lifted her. The strength in his frail body was a never-ending source of wonder to his two friends.

They followed him down the stairs and along the short passage, down another flight to the kitchen. Manfred opened a door and went out into the paved yard. There was a heavier door in the boundary wall. He opened this slowly and peeped out. Here was the inevitable mews. The sound of an engine running came from a garage near by. Evidently somebody was on the look out for them. A long-bodied car drew up noiselessly and a woman got out. Beside the driver at the wheel sat two men.

"I think you'll just miss the real excitement," said Gonsalez, and then to the nurse he gave a few words of instruction and closed the door on her.

"Take the direct road," he said to the driver. "Swindon—Gloucester. Good night."

"Good night, sir."

He watched anxiously as the machine swung into the main road. Still he waited, his head bent. Two minutes went by, and the faint sound of a motor-horn, a long blast and a short, and he sighed.

"They're clear of the danger zone," he said.

Plop!

He saw the flash, heard the smack of the bullet as it struck the door, and his hand stiffened. There was a thudding sound—a scream of pain from a dark corner of the mews and the sound of voices. Leon drew back into the yard and bolted the door.

"He had a new kind of silencer. Oberzohn is rather a clever old bird. But my air pistol against their gun for noiselessness."

"I didn't expect the attack from that end of the mews." Manfred was slipping a Browning back to his pocket.

"If they had come from the other end the car would not have passed—I'd like to get one of those silencers."

They went into the house. Poiccart had already extinguished the passage light.

"You hit your man—does that thing kill?"

"By accident—it is possible. I aimed at his stomach: I fear that I hit him in the head. He would not have squealed for a stomach wound. I fear he is alive."

He felt his way up the stairs and took up the telephone. Immediately a voice said, "Number?"

"Give me 8877 Treasury."

He waited, and then a different voice asked: "Yes—Scotland Yard speaking."

"Can you give me Mr Meadows?"

Manfred was watching him frowningly.

"That you, Meadows?... They have shot Leon Gonsalez—can you send police reserves and an ambulance?"

"At once."

Leon hung up the receiver, hugging himself. "The idea being—?" said Poiccart.

"These people are clever." Leon's voice was charged with admiration. "They haven't cut the wires—they've simply tapped it at one end and thrown it out of order on the exchange side."

"Phew!" Manfred whistled. "You deceived me—you were talking to Oberzohn?"

"Captain Monty and Lew Cuccini. They may or may not be deceived, but if they aren't, we shall know all about it."

He stopped dead. There was a knock on the front door, a single, heavy knock. Leon grinned delightedly.

"One of us is now supposed to open an upper window cautiously and look out, whereupon he is instantly gunned. I'm going to give these fellows a scare."

He ran up the stairs to the top floor, and on the landing, outside an attic door, pulled at a rope. A fire ladder lying flat against the ceiling came down, and at the same time a small skylight opened. Leon went into the room, and his pocket-lamp located what he needed: a small papier-mache cylinder, not unlike a seven-pound shell. With this on his arm, he climbed up the ladder on to the roof, fixed the cylinder on a flat surface, and, striking a match, lit a touch-paper. The paper sizzled and spluttered, there was a sudden flash and "boom!" a dull explosion, and a white ball shot up into the sky, described a graceful curve and burst into a shower of brilliant crimson stars. He waited till the last died out; then, with the hot cylinder under his arm, descended the ladder, released the rope that held it in place, and returned to his two friends.

"They will imagine a secret arrangement of signals with the police," he said; "unless my knowledge of their psychology is at fault, we shall not be bothered again."

Ten minutes later there was another knock at the door, peremptory, almost official in its character.

"This," said Leon, "is a policeman to summon us for discharging fireworks in the public street!"

He ran lightly down into the hall and without hesitation pulled open the door. A tall, helmeted figure stood on the doorstep, notebook in hand.

"Are you the gentleman that let off that rocket—" he began.

Leon walked past him, and looked up and down Curzon Street. As he had expected, the Old Guard had vanished.

11

GURTHER

Monty Newton dragged himself home, a weary angry man, and let himself in with his key. He found the footman lying on the floor of the hall asleep, his greatcoat pulled over him, and stirred him to wakefulness with the toe of his boot.

"Get up," he growled. "Anybody been here?"

Fred rose, a little dazed, rubbing his eyes.

"The old man's in the drawing-room," he said, and his employer passed on without another word.

As he opened the door, he saw that all the lights in the drawing-room were lit. Dr Oberzohn had pulled a small table near the fire, and before this he sat bolt upright, a tiny chessboard before him; immersed in a problem. He looked across to the newcomer for a second and then resumed his study of the board, made a move...

"Ach!" he said in tones of satisfaction. "Leskina was wrong! It is possible to mate in five moves!"

He pushed the chessmen into confusion and turned squarely to face Newton.

"Well, have you concluded these matters satisfactorily?"

"He brought up the reserves," said Monty, unlocking a tantalus on a side table and helping himself liberally to whisky. "They got Cuccini through the jaw. Nothing serious."

Dr Oberzohn laid his bony hands on his knees.

"Gurther must be disciplined," he said. "Obviously he has lost his nerve; and when a man loses his nerve also he loses his sense of time. And his timing—how deplorable! The car had not arrived; my excellent police had not taken position... deplorable!"

"The police are after him: I suppose you know that?" Newton looked over his glass.

Dr Oberzohn nodded.

"The extradition so cleverly avoided is now accomplished. But Gurther is too good a man to be lost. I have arranged a hiding-place for him. He is of many uses."

"Where did he go?"

Dr Oberzohn's eyebrows wrinkled up and down.

"Who knows?" he said. "He has the little machine. Maybe he has gone to the house—the green light in the top window will warn him and he will move carefully."

Newton walked to the window and looked out. Chester Square looked ghostly in the grey light of dawn. And then, out of the shadows, he saw a figure move and walk slowly towards the south side of the square. "They're watching this house," he said, and laughed.

"Where is my young lady?" asked Oberzohn, who was staring glumly into the fire.

"I don't know... there was a car pulled out of the mews as one of our men 'closed' the entrance. She has probably gone back to Heavytree Farm, and you can sell that laboratory of yours. There is only one way now, and that's the rough way. We have time—we can do a lot in six weeks. Villa is coming this morning—I wish we'd taken that idol from the trunk. That may put the police on to the right track."

Dr Oberzohn pursed his lips as though he were going to whistle, but he was guilty of no such frivolity.

"I am glad they found him," he said precisely. "To them it will be a scent. What shall they think, but that the unfortunate

Barberton had come upon an old native treasure-house? No, I do not fear that" He shook his head. "Mostly I fear Mr Johnson Lee and the American, Elijah Washington."

He put his hand into his jacket pocket and took out a thin pad of letters. "Johnson Lee is for me difficult to understand. For what should a gentleman have to do with this boor that he writes so friendly letters to him?"

"How did you get these?"

"Villa took them: it was one of the intelligent actions also to leave the statue."

He passed one of the letters across to Newton. It was addressed "Await arrival, Paste Restante, Mosamedes." The letter was written in a curiously round, boyish hand. Another remarkable fact was that it was perforated across the page at regular intervals, and upon the lines formed by this perforation Mr Johnson Lee wrote:

"Dear B.," the letter ran, "I have instructed my bankers to cable you £500. I hope this will carry you through and leave enough to pay your fare home. You may be sure that I shall not breathe a word, and your letters, of course, nobody in the house can read but me. Your story is amazing and I advise you to come home at once and see Miss Leicester.

Your friend,
JOHNSON LEE."

The note-paper was headed *"Rath Hall, January 13th."*

"They came to me today. If I had seen them before, there would have been no need for the regrettable happening."

He looked thoughtfully at his friend. "They will be difficult: I had that expectation," he said; and Monty knew that he referred to the Three Just Men. "Yet they are mortal also—remember that, my Newton: they are mortal also."

"As we are," said Newton gloomily

"That is a question," said Oberzohn, "so far as I am concerned."

Dr Oberzohn never jested; he spoke with the greatest calm and assurance. The other man could only stare at him.

Although it was light, a green lamp showed clearly in the turret room of the doctor's house as he came within sight of the ugly place. And, seeing that warning, he did not expect to be met in the passage by Gurther. The man had changed from his resplendent kit and was again in the soiled and shabby garments he had discarded the night before.

"You have come, Gurther?"

"Ja, Herr Doktor."

"To my parlour!" barked Dr Oberzohn, and marched ahead.

Gurther followed him and stood with his back to the door, erect, his chin raised, his bright, curious eyes fixed on a point a few inches above his master's head.

"Tell me now." The doctor's ungainly face was working ludicrously.

"I saw the man and struck, Herr Doktor, and then the lights went out and I went to the floor, expecting him to shoot... I think he must have taken the gracious lady. I did not see, for there was a palm between us. I returned at once to the greater hall, and walked through the people on the floor. They were very frightened."

"You saw them?"

"Yes, Herr Doktor," said Gurther. "It is not difficult for me to see in the dark. After that I ran to the other entrance, but they were gone."

"Come here."

The man took two stilted paces towards the doctor and Oberzohn struck him twice in the face with the flat of his hand. Not a muscle of the man's face moved: he stood erect, his lips framed in a half-grin, his curious eyes staring straight ahead.

"That is for bad time, Gurther. Nobody saw you return?"

"No, Herr Doktor, I came on foot."

"You saw the light?"

"Yes, Herr Doktor, and I thought it best to be here."

"You were right," said Oberzohn. "March!"

He went into the forbidden room, turned the key, and passed into the super-heated atmosphere. Gurther stood attentively at the door. Presently the doctor came out, carrying a long case covered with baize under his arm. He handed it to the waiting man, went into the room, and, after a few minutes' absence, returned with a second case, a little larger.

"March!" he said.

Gurther followed him out of the house and across the rank, weed-grown "garden" towards the factory. A white mist had rolled up from the canal, and factory and grounds lay under the veil.

He led the way through an oblong gap in the wall where once a door had stood, and followed a tortuous course through the blackened beams and twisted girders that littered the floor. Only a half-hearted attempt had been made to clear up the wreckage after the fire, and the floor was ankle-deep in charred shreds of burnt cloth. Near the far end of the building, Oberzohn stopped, put down his box and pushed aside the ashes with his foot until he had cleared a space about three feet square. Stooping, he grasped an iron ring and pulled, and a flagstone came up with scarcely an effort, for it was well counter-weighted. He took up the box again and descended the stone stairs, stopping only to turn on a light.

The vaults of the store had been practically untouched by the fire. There were shelves that still carried dusty bales of cotton goods. Oberzohn was in a hurry. He crossed the stone floor in two strides, pulled down the bar of another door, and, walking into the darkness, deposited his box on the floor.

The electric power of the factory had, in the old days, been carried on two distinct circuits, and the connection with the vaults was practically untouched by the explosion.

They were in a smaller room now, fairly comfortably furnished. Gurther knew it well, for it was here that he had spent the greater part of his first six months in England. Ventilation came through three small gratings near the roof. There was a furnace, and, as Gurther knew, an ample supply of fuel in one of the three cellars that opened into the vault.

"Here will you stay until I send for you," said Oberzohn. "Tonight, perhaps, after they have searched. You have a pistol?"

"Ja, Herr Doktor."

"Food, water, bedding—all you need." Oberzohn jerked open another of the cellars and took stock of the larder. "Tonight I may come for you—tomorrow night—who knows? You will light the fire at once." He pointed to the two baize-covered boxes. "Good morning, Gurther."

"Good morning, Herr Doktor."

Oberzohn went up to the factory level, dropped the trap and his foot pushed back the ashes which hid its presence, and with a cautious look round he crossed the field to his house. He was hardly in his study before the first police car came bumping along the lane.

12

LEON THEORIZES

Making inquiries, Detective-Inspector Meadows discovered that, on the previous evening at eight o'clock, two men had called upon Barberton. The first of these was described as tall and rather aristocratic in appearance. He wore dark, horn-rimmed spectacles. The hotel manager thought he might have been an invalid, for he walked with a stick. The second man seemed to have been a servant of some kind, for he spoke respectfully to the visitor.

"No, he gave no name, Mr Meadows," said the manager. "I told him of the terrible thing which had happened to Mr Barberton, and he was so upset that I didn't like to press the question."

Meadows was on his circuitous way to Curzon Street when he heard this, and he arrived in time for breakfast. Manfred's servants regarded it as the one eccentricity of an otherwise normal gentleman that he invariably breakfasted with his butler and chauffeur. This matter had been discussed threadbare in the tiny servants' hall, and it no longer excited comment when Manfred telephoned down to the lower regions and asked for another plate.

The Triangle were in cheerful mood. Leon Gonsalez was especially bright and amusing, as he invariably was after such a night as he had spent.

"We searched Oberzohn's house from cellar to attic," said Meadows when the plate had been laid.

"And of course you found nothing. The elegant Gurther?"

"He wasn't there. That fellow will keep at a distance if he knows that there's a warrant out for him. I suspect some sort of signal. There was a very bright green light burning in one of those ridiculous Gothic turrets." Manfred stifled a yawn.

"Gurther went back soon after midnight," he said, "and was there until Oberzohn's return."

"Are you sure?" asked the astonished detective.

Leon nodded, his eyes twinkling.

"After that, one of those infernal river mists blotted out observation," he said, "but I should imagine Herr Gurther is not far away. Did you see his companion, Pfeiffer?"

Meadows nodded. "Yes, he was cleaning boots when I arrived."

"How picturesque!" said Gonzalez. "I think he will have a valet the next time he goes to prison, unless the system has altered since your days, George?"

George Manfred, who had once occupied the condemned cell in Chelmsford Prison, smiled.

"An interesting man, Gurther," mused Gonsalez. "I have a feeling that he will escape hanging. So you could not find him? I found him last night. But for the lady, who was both an impediment and an interest, we might have put a period to his activities." He caught Meadows' eye. "I should have handed him to you, of course."

"Of course," said the detective dryly.

"A remarkable man, but nervous. You are going to see Mr Johnson Lee?"

"What made you say that?" asked the detective in astonishment, for he had not as yet confided his intention to the three men.

"He will surprise you," said Leon. "Tell me, Mr Meadows: when you and George so thoroughly and carefully searched

Barberton's box, did you find anything that was suggestive of his being a cobbler, let us say—or a bookbinder?"

"I think in his sister's letter there was a reference to the books he had made. I found nothing particular except an awl and a long oblong of wood which was covered with pinpricks. As a matter of fact, when I saw it my first thought was that, living the kind of life he must have done in the wilderness, it was rather handy to be able to repair his own shoes. The idea of bookbinding is a new one."

"I should say he never bound a book in his life, in the ordinary sense of the word," remarked Manfred; "and as Leon says, you will find Johnson Lee a very surprising man."

"Do you know him?"

Manfred nodded gravely.

"I have just been on the telephone to him," he said. "You'll have to be careful of Mr Lee Meadows. Our friend the snake may be biting his way, and will, if he hears a breath of suspicion that he was in Barberton's confidence."

The detective put down his knife and fork.

"I wish you fellows would stop being mysterious," he said, half annoyed, half amused. "What is behind this business? You talk of the snake as though you could lay your hands on him."

"And we could," they said in unison.

"Who is he?" challenged the detective.

"The Herr Doktor," smiled Gonsalez.

"Oberzohn?"

Leon nodded.

"I thought you would have discovered that by connecting the original three murders together—and murders they were. First"—he ticked the names off on his fingers—"we have a stockbroker. This gentleman was a wealthy speculator who occasionally financed highly questionable deals. Six months before his death he drew from the bank a very large sum of money in notes. By an odd coincidence the bank clerk, going

LEON THEORIZES

out to luncheon, saw his client and Oberzohn driving past in a taxicab, and as they came abreast he saw a large blue envelope go into Oberzohn's pocket. The money had been put into a blue envelope when it was drawn. The broker had financed the doctor, and when the scheme failed and the money was lost, he not unnaturally asked for its return. He trusted Oberzohn not at all; carried his receipt about in his pocket, and never went anywhere unless he was armed—that fact did not emerge at the inquest, but you know it is true."

Meadows nodded.

"He threatened Oberzohn with exposure at a meeting they had in Winchester Street, on the day of his death. That night he returns from a theatre or from his club, and is found dead on the doorstep. No receipt is found. What follows?

"A man, a notorious blackmailer, homeless and penniless, was walking along the Bayswater Road, probably looking for easy money, when he saw the broker's car going into Orme Place. He followed on the off-chance of begging a few coppers. The chauffeur saw him. The tramp, on the other hand, must have seen something else. He slept the next night at Rowton House, told a friend, who had been in prison with him, that he had a million pounds as good as in his hand..."

Meadows laughed helplessly.

"Your system of investigation is evidently more thorough than ours!"

"It is complementary to yours," said George quietly. "Go on, Leon."

"Now what happened to our friend the burglar? He evidently saw somebody in Orme Place whom he either recognized or trailed to his home. For the next day or two he was in and out of public telephone booths, though no number has been traced. He goes to Hyde Park, obviously by appointment—and the snake bites!

"There was another danger to the confederacy. The bank clerk, learning of the death of the client, is troubled. I have proof that he called Oberzohn on the 'phone. If you remember, when the broker's affairs were gone into, it was found that he was almost insolvent. A large sum of money had been drawn out of the bank and paid to 'X.' The certainty that he knew who 'X' was worried this decent bank clerk, and he called Oberzohn, probably to ask him why he had not made a statement. On the day he telephoned the snake man, that day he died."

The detective was listening in silent wonder. "It sounds like a page out of a sensational novel," he said, "yet it hangs together."

"It hangs together because it is true." Poiccart's deep voice broke into the conversation. "This has been Oberzohn's method all his life. He is strong for logic, and there is no more logical action in the world than the destruction of those who threaten your safety and life."

Meadows pushed away his plate, his breakfast half eaten. "Proof," he said briefly.

"What proof can you have, my dear fellow?" scoffed Leon.

"The proof is the snake," persisted Meadows. "Show me how he could educate a deadly snake to strike, as he did, when the victim was under close observation, as in the case of Barberton, and I will believe you."

The Three looked at one another and smiled together. "One of these days I will show you," said Leon. "They have certainly tamed their snake! He can move so quickly that the human eye cannot follow him. Always he bites on the most vital part, and at the most favourable time. He struck at me last night, but missed me. The next time he strikes"—he was speaking slowly and looking at the detective through the veriest slits of his half-closed eyelids—"the next time he strikes, not all Scotland Yard on the one side, nor his agreeable company of gunmen on the other, will save him!"

Poiccart rose suddenly. His keen ears had heard the ring of a bell, and he went noiselessly down the stairs.

"The whole thing sounds like a romance to me." Meadows was rubbing his chin irritably. "I am staring at the covers of a book whilst you are reading the pages. I suppose you devils; have the A and Z of the story?" Leon nodded. "Why don't you tell me?"

"Because I value your life," said Leon simply. "Because I wish—we all wish—to keep the snake's attention upon ourselves."

Poiccart came back at that moment and put his head in the door.

"Would you like to see Mr Elijah Washington?" he asked, and they saw by the gleam in his eyes that Mr Elijah Washington was well worth meeting.

He arrived a second or two later, a tall, broad-shouldered man with a reddish face. He wore pince-nez, and behind the rimless glasses his eyes were alive and full of bubbling laughter. From head to foot he was dressed in white; the cravat which flowed over the soft silk shirt was a bright yellow; the belt about his waist as bright as scarlet.

He stood beaming upon the company, his white panama crushed under his arm, both huge hands thrust into his trousers pockets.

"Glad to know you folks," he greeted them in a deep boom of a voice. "I guess Mr Barberton told you all about me. That poor little guy! Listen: he was a he-man all right, but kinder mysterious. They told me I'd find the police chief here— Captain Meadows?"

"Mister," said the inspector, "I'm that man."

Washington put out his huge paw and caught the detective's hand with a grip that would have been notable in a boa constrictor.

"Glad to know you! My name is Elijah Washington—the Natural History Syndicate, Chicago."

"Sit down Mr Washington." Poiccart pushed forward a chair.

"I want to tell you gentleman that this Barberton was murdered. Snake? Listen, I know snakes—brought up with 'um! Snakes are my hobby: I know 'um from egg-eaters to 'tigers'—notechis sentatus, moccasins, copperheads, corals mamba, fer de lance—gosh! Snakes are just common objects like flies. An' I tell you boys right here and now, that there ain't a snake in this or the next world that can climb up a parapet, bite a man and get away with it with a copper looking on."

He beamed from one to the other: he was almost paternal.

"I'd like to have shown you folks a worse-than-mamba," he said regretfully, "but carrying round snakes in your pocket is just hot dog: it's like a millionaire wearin' diamond ear-rings just to show he can afford 'em. I liked that little fellow; I'm mighty sorry he's dead, but if any man tells you that a snake bit him, go right up to him, hit him on the nose, and say 'Liar!'"

"You will have some coffee?" Manfred had rung the bell.

"Sure I will: never have got used to this tea-drinking habit. I'm on the wagon too: got scared up there in the back-lands of Angola—"

"What were you doing there?" asked Leon.

"Snakes," said the other briefly. "I represent an organization that supplies specimens to zoos and museums. I was looking for a flying snake—there ain't such a thing, though the natives say there is. I got a new kinder cobra—viperidae crotalinae—and yet not!"

He scratched his head, bringing his scientific perplexity into the room. Leon's heart went out to him.

He had met Barberton by accident. Without shame he confessed that he had gone to a village in the interior for a real solitary jag, and returning to such degree of civilization as Mossamedes represented, he found a group of Portuguese breeds squatting about a fire at which the man's feet were toasting.

"I don't know what he was—a prospector, I guess. He was one of those what-is-its you meet along that coast. I've met his kind most everywhere—as far south as Port Nottosh. In Angola there are scores: they go native at the end."

"You can tell us nothing about Barberton?"

Mr Elijah Washington shook his head.

"No, sir: I know him same as I might know you. It got me curious when I found out the why of the torturing: he wouldn't tell where it was."

"Where what was?" asked Manfred quickly, and Washington was surprised.

"Why, the writing they wanted to get. I thought maybe he'd told you. He said he was coming right along to spill all that part of it. It was a letter he'd found in a tin box—that was all he'd say."

They looked at one another.

"I know no more about it than that," Mr Washington added, when he saw Gonsalez' lips move. "It was just a letter. Who it was from, why, what it was about, he never told me. My first idea was that he'd been flirting round about here, but divorce laws are mighty generous and they wouldn't trouble to get evidence that way. A man doesn't want any documents to get rid of his wife. I dare say you folks wonder why I've come along." Mr Washington raised his steaming cup of coffee, which must have been nearly boiling, and drank it at one gulp. "That's fine," he said, "the nearest to coffee I've had since I left home."

He wiped his lips with a large and vivid silk handkerchief.

"I've come along, gentleman, because I've got a pretty good idea that I'd be useful to anybody who's snake-hunting in this little dorp."

"It's rather a dangerous occupation, isn't it?" said Manfred quietly.

Washington nodded.

"To you, but not to me," he said. "I am snake-proof."

He pulled up his sleeve: the forearm was scarred and pitted with old wounds.

"Snakes," he said briefly. "That's cobra." He pointed proudly. "When that snake struck, my boys didn't wait for anything, they started dividing my kit. Sort of appointed themselves a board of executors and joint heirs of the family estate."

"But you were very ill?" said Gonsalez.

Mr Washington shook his head.

"No, sir, not more than if a bee bit me, and not so much as if a wasp had got in first punch. Some people can eat arsenic, some people can make a meal of enough morphia to decimate a province. I'm snake-proof—been bitten ever since I was five."

He bent over towards them, and his jolly face went suddenly serious. "I'm the man you want," he said.

"I think you are," said Manfred slowly.

"Because this old snake ain't finished biting. There's a graft in it somewhere, and I want to find it. But first I want to vindicate the snake. Anybody who says a snake's naturally vicious doesn't understand. Snakes are timid, quiet, respectful things, and don't want no trouble with nobody. If a snake sees you coming, he naturally lights out for home. When momma snake's running around with her family, she's naturally touchy for fear you'd tread on any of her boys and girls, but she's a lady, and if you give her time she'll Maggie 'um and get 'um into the parlour where the foot of white man never trod."

Leon was looking at him with a speculative eye.

"It is queer to think," he said, speaking half to himself, "that you may be the only one of us who will be alive this day week!"

Meadows, not easily shocked, felt a cold shiver run down his spine.

13

MIRABELLE GOES HOME

The prediction that Leon Gonsalez had made was not wholly fulfilled, though he himself had helped to prevent the supreme distress he prophesied. When Mirabelle Leicester awoke in the morning, her head was thick and dull, and for a long time she lay between sleeping and waking, trying to bring order to the confusion of her thoughts, her eyes on the ceiling towards a gnarled oak beam which she had seen before somewhere; and when at last she summoned sufficient energy to raise herself on her elbow, she looked upon the very familiar surroundings of her own pretty little room.

Heavytree Farm! What a curious dream she had had! A dream filled with fleeting visions of old men with elongated heads, of dance music and a crowded ball-room, of a slightly over-dressed man who had been very polite to her at dinner. Where did she dine? She sat up in bed, holding her throbbing head.

Again she looked round the room and slowly, out of her dreams, emerged a few tangible facts. She was still in a state of bewilderment when the door opened and Aunt Alma came in, and the unprepossessing face of her relative was accentuated by her look of anxiety.

"Hullo, Alma!" said Mirabelle dully. "I've had such a queer dream."

Alma pressed her lips tightly together as she placed a tray on a table by the side of the bed.

"I think it was about that advertisement I saw." And then, with a gasp: "How did I come here?"

"They brought you," said Alma. "The nurse is downstairs having her breakfast. She's a nice woman and keeps press-cuttings."

"The nurse?" asked Mirabelle in bewilderment.

"You arrived here at three o'clock in the morning in a motor-car. You had a nurse with you." Alma enumerated the circumstances in chronological order. "And two men. First one of the men got out and knocked at the door. I was worried to death. In fact, I'd been worried all the afternoon, ever since I had your wire telling me not to come up to London."

"But I didn't send any such wire," replied the girl.

"After I came down, the man—he was really a gentleman and very pleasantly spoken—told me that you'd been taken ill and a nurse had brought you home. They then carried you, the two men and the nurse, upstairs and laid you on the bed, and nurse and I undressed you. I simply couldn't get you to wake up: all you did was to talk about the orangeade."

"I remember! It was so bitter, and Lord Evington let me drink some of his. And then I... I don't know what happened after that," she said, with a little grimace.

"Mr Gonsalez ordered the car, got the nurse from a nursing home," explained Alma.

"Gonsalez! Not my Gonsalez—the—the Four Just Men Gonsalez?" she asked in amazement.

"I'm sure it was Gonsalez: they made no secret about it. You can see the gentleman who brought you: he's about the house somewhere. I saw him in Heavytree Lane not five minutes ago, strolling up and down and smoking. A pipe.", added Alma.

The girl got out of bed; her knees were curiously weak under her, but she managed to stagger to the window, and, pushing

MIRABELLE GOES HOME

open the casement still farther, looked out across the patchwork quilt of colour. The summer flowers were in bloom; the delicate scents came up on the warm morning air, and she stood for a moment, drinking in great draughts of the exquisite perfume, and then, with a sigh, turned back to the waiting Alma.

"I don't know how it all happened and what it's about, but my word, Alma, I'm glad to be back! That dreadful man... ! We lunched at the Ritz-Carlton... I never want to see another restaurant or a ball-room or Chester Square, or anything but old Heavytree!"

She took the cup of tea from Alma's hand, drank greedily, and put it down with a little gasp.

"That was wonderful! Yes, the tea was too, but I'm thinking about Gonsalez. If it should be he!"

"I don't see why you should get excited over a man who's committed I don't know how many murders."

"Don't be silly, Alma!" scoffed the girl. "The Just Men have never murdered, any more than a judge and jury murder."

The room was still inclined to go round, and it was with the greatest difficulty that she could condense the two Almas who stood before her into one tangible individual.

"There's a gentleman downstairs: he's been waiting since twelve."

And when she asked, she was to learn, to her dismay, that it was half-past one.

"I'll be down in a quarter of an hour," she said recklessly. "Who is it?"

"I've never heard of him before, but he's a gentleman," was the unsatisfactory reply. "They didn't want to let him come in."

"Who didn't?"

"The gentlemen who brought you here in the night."

Mirabelle stared at her.

"You mean... they're guarding the house?"

"That's how it strikes me," said Alma bitterly. "Why they should interfere with us, I don't know. Anyway, they let him in. Mr Johnson Lee."

The girl frowned.

"I don't know the name," she said.

Alma walked to the window.

"There's his car," she said, and pointed.

It was just visible, standing at the side of the road beyond the box hedge, a long-bodied Rolls, white with dust. The chauffeur was talking to a strange man, and from the fact that he was smoking a pipe Mirabelle guessed that this was one of her self-appointed custodians.

She had her bath, and with the assistance of the nurse, dressed and came shakily down the stairs. Alma was waiting in the brick-floored hall.

"He wants to see you alone," she said in a stage whisper. "I don't know whether I ought to allow it, but there's evidently something wrong. These men prowling about the house have got thoroughly on my nerves."

Mirabelle laughed softly as she opened the door and walked in. At the sound of the door closing, the man who was sitting stiffly on a deep settee in a window recess got up. He was tall and bent, and his dark face was lined. His eyes she could not see; they were hidden behind dark green glasses, which were turned in her direction as she came across the room to greet him.

"Miss Mirabelle Leicester?" he asked, in the quiet, modulated voice of an educated man. He took her hand in his.

"Won't you sit down?" she said, for he remained standing after she had seated herself.

"Thank you." He sat down gingerly, holding between his knees the handle of the umbrella he had brought into the drawing-room. "I'm afraid my visit may be inopportune, Miss Leicester," he said. "Have you by any chance heard about Mr Barberton?"

Her brows wrinkled in thought. "Barberton? I seem to have heard the name."

"He was killed yesterday on the Thames Embankment."

Then she recollected. "The man who was bitten by the snake?" she asked in horror.

The visitor nodded.

"It was a great shock to me, because I have been a friend of his for many years, and had arranged to call at his hotel on the night of his death." And then abruptly he turned the conversation in another and a surprising direction. "Your father was a scientist, Miss Leicester?"

She nodded.

"Yes, he was an astronomer, an authority upon meteors."

"Exactly. I thought that was the gentleman. I have only recently had his book read to me. He was in Africa for some years?"

"Yes," she said quietly, "he died there. He was studying meteors for three years in Angola. You probably know that a very large number of shooting stars fall in that country. My father's theory was that it was due to the ironstone mountains which attract them—so he set up a little observatory in the interior." Her lips trembled for a second. "He was killed in a native rising," she said.

"Do you know the part of Angola where be had his observatory?"

She shook her head.

"I'm not sure. I have never been in Africa, but perhaps Aunt Alma may know."

She went out to find Alma waiting in the passage, in conversation with the pipe-smoker. The man withdrew hastily at the sight of her.

"Alma, do you remember what part of Angola father had his observatory?" she asked.

Alma did not know off-hand, but one of her invaluable scrapbooks contained all the information that the girl wanted, and she carried the book to Mr Lee.

"Here are the particulars," she said, and laid the book open before them.

"Would you read it for me?" he requested gently, and she read to him the three short paragraphs which noted that Professor Leicester had taken up his residence in Bishaka.

"That is the place," interrupted the visitor. "Bishaka! You are you sure that Mr Barberton did not communicate with you?"

"With me?" she said in amazement "No—why should he?"

He did not answer, but sat for a long time, turning the matter over in his mind.

"You're perfectly certain that nobody sent you a document, probably in the Portuguese language, concerning"—he hesitated—"Bishaka?"

She shook her head, and then, as though he had not seen the gesture, he asked the question again.

"I'm certain," she said. "We have very little correspondence at the farm, and it isn't possible that I could overlook anything so remarkable."

Again he turned the problem over in his mind.

"Have you any documents in Portuguese or in English... any letters from your father about Angola?"

"None," she said. "The only reference my father ever made to Bishaka was that he was getting a lot of information which he thought would be valuable, and that he was a little troubled because his cameras, which he had fixed in various parts of the country to cover every sector of the skies, were being disturbed by wandering prospectors."

"He said that, did he?" asked Mr Lee eagerly. "Come now, that explains a great deal!"

In spite of herself she laughed. "It doesn't explain much to me, Mr Lee," she said frankly. And then, in a more serious tone: "Did Barberton come from Angola?"

"Yes, Barberton came from that country," he said in a lower voice. "I should like to tell you,"—he hesitated—"but I am rather afraid."

"Afraid to tell me? Why?"

He shook his head.

"So many dreadful things have happened recently to poor Barberton and others, that knowledge seems a most dangerous thing. I wish I could believe that it would not be dangerous to you," he added kindly, "and then I could speak what is in my mind and relieve myself of a great deal of anxiety." He rose slowly. "I think the best thing I can do is to consult my lawyer. I was foolish to keep it from him so long. He is the only man I can trust to search my documents."

She could only look at him in astonishment

"But surely you can search your own documents?" she said good humouredly.

"No, I'm afraid I can't. Because"—he spoke with the simplicity of a child—"I am blind."

"Blind?" gasped Mirabelle, and the man laughed gently.

"I am pretty capable for a blind man, am I not? I can walk across a room and avoid all the furniture. The only thing I cannot do is to read—at least, read the ordinary print. I can read Braille: poor Barberton taught me. He was a school-master," he explained, "at a blind school near Brightlingsea. Not a particularly well-educated man, but a marvellously quick writer of Braille. We have corresponded for years through that medium. He could write a Braille letter almost as quickly as you can with pen and ink."

Her heart was full of pity for the man: he was so cheery, so confident, and withal so proud of his own accomplishments, that pity turned to admiration. He had the ineffable air of obstinacy which is the possession of so many men similarly stricken, and she began to realize that self-pity, that greatest of all afflictions which attends blindness, had been eliminated from his philosophy.

"I should like to tell you more," he said, as he held out his hand. "Probably I will dictate a long letter to you tomorrow, or else my lawyer will do so, putting all the facts before you. For the moment, however, I must be sure of my ground. I have no desire to raise in your heart either fear or—hope. Do you know a Mr Manfred?"

"I don't know him personally," she said quickly. "George Manfred?"

He nodded.

"Have you met him?" she asked eagerly. "And Mr Poiccart, the Frenchman?"

"No, not Mr Poiccart. Manfred was on the telephone to me very early this morning. He seemed to know all about my relationships with my poor friend. He knew also of my blindness. A remarkable man, very gentle and courteous. It was he who gave me your address. Perhaps," he roused, "it would be advisable if I first consulted him."

"I'm sure it would!" she said enthusiastically. "They are wonderful. You have heard of them, of course, Mr Lee—the Four Just Men?"

He smiled.

"That sounds as though you admire them," he said. "Yes, I have heard of them. They are the men who, many years ago, set out to regularize the inconsistencies of the English law, to punish where no punishment is provided by the code. Strange I never associated them..."

He meditated upon the matter in silence for a long while, and then: "I wonder," he said, but did not tell her what he was wondering.

She walked down the garden path with him into the roadway and stood chatting about the country and the flowers that he had never seen, and the weather and such trivialities as people talk about when their minds are occupied with more serious thoughts which they cannot share, until the big limousine pulled up and he stepped into its cool interior. He had the independence which comes to the educated blind and gently refused the offer of her guidance, an offer she did not attempt to repeat, sensing the satisfaction he must have had in making his way without help. She waved her hand to the car as it moved off, and so naturally did his hand go up in salute that for a moment she thought he had seen her.

So he passed cut of her sight, and might well have passed out of her life, for Mr Oberzohn had decreed that the remaining hours of blind Johnson Lee were to be few.

But it happened that the Three Men had reached the same decision in regard to Mr Oberzohn, only there was some indecision as to the manner of his passing. Leon Gonsalez had original views.

14

THE PEDLAR

The man with the pipe was standing within half a dozen paces of her. She was going back through the gate, when she remembered Aunt Alma's views on the guardianship.

"Are you waiting here all day?" she asked.

"Till this evening, miss. We're to be relieved by some men from Gloucester—we came from town, and we're going back with the nurse, if you can do without her?"

"Who placed you here?" she asked.

"Mr Gonsalez. He thought it would be wise to have somebody around."

"But why?"

The big man grinned.

"I've known Mr Gonsalez many years," he said. "I'm a police pensioner, and I can remember the time when I'd have given a lot of money to lay my hands on him—but I've never asked him why, miss. There is generally a good reason for everything he does."

Mirabelle went back into the farmhouse, very thoughtful. Happily, Alma was not inquisitive; she was left alone in the drawing-room to reconstruct her exciting yesterday.

Mirabelle harboured very few illusions. She had read much, guessed much, and in the days of her childhood had been in the habit of linking cause to effect. The advertisement was designed especially for her: that was her first conclusion. It was designed to bring her into the charge of Oberzohn. For now she recognized this significant circumstance: never once, since she had entered the offices of Oberzohn & Smitts, until the episode of the orangeade, had she been free to come and go as she wished. He had taken her to lunch, he had brought her back; Joan Newton had been her companion in the drive from the house, and from the house to the hall; and from then on she did not doubt that Oberzohn's surveillance had continued, until...

Dimly she remembered the man in the cloak who had stood in the rocking doorway. Was that Gonsalez? Somehow she thought it must have been. Gonsalez, watchful, alert—why? She had been in danger—was still in danger. Though why anybody should have picked unimportant her was the greatest of all mysteries.

In some inexplicable way the death of Barberton had been associated with that advertisement and the attention she had received from Dr Oberzohn and his creatures. Who was Lord Evington? She remembered his German accent and his "gracious lady," the curious click of his heels and his stiff bow. That was a clumsy subterfuge which she ought to have seen through from the first. He was another of her watchers. And the drugged orangeade was his work. She shuddered. Suppose Leon Gonsalez, or whoever it was, had not arrived so providentially, where would she be at this moment?

Walking to the window, she looked out, and the sight of the two men just inside the gate gave her a sense of infinite relief and calm; and the knowledge that she, for some reason, was under the care and protection of this strange organization about which she had read, thrilled her.

She walked into the vaulted kitchen, to find the kitchen table covered with fat volumes, and Aunt Alma explaining to the interested nurse her system of filing. Two subjects interested that hard-featured lady: crime and family records. She had two books filled with snippings from country newspapers relating to the family of a distant cousin who had been raised to a peerage during the war. She had another devoted to the social triumphs of a distant woman, Goddard, who had finally made a sensational appearance as petitioner in the most celebrated divorce suit of the age. But crime, generally speaking, was Aunt Alma's chief preoccupation. It was from these voluminous cuttings that Mirabelle had gained her complete knowledge of the Four Just Men and their operations. There were books packed with the story of the Ramon murder, arranged with loving care in order of time, for chronology was almost a vice in Alma Goddard. Only one public sensation was missing from her collection, and she was explaining the reason to the nurse as Mirabelle came into the kitchen.

"No, my dear," she was saying, "there is nothing about The Snake. I won't have anything to do with that: it gives me the creeps. In fact, I haven't read anything that has the slightest reference to it."

"I've got every line," said the nurse enthusiastically. "My brother is a reporter on the *Megaphone*, and he says this is the best story they've had for years—"

Mirabelle interrupted this somewhat gruesome conversation to make inquiries about luncheon. Her head was steady now and she had developed an appetite.

The front door stood open, and as she turned to go into the dining-room to get her writing materials, she heard an altercation at the gate. A third man had appeared: a grimy-looking pedlar who carried a tray before him, packed with all manner of cheap buttons and laces. He was a middle-aged man with a ragged beard, and despite the warmth of the day, was wearing a long overcoat that almost reached to his heels.

"You may or you may not be," the man with the pipe was saying, "but you're not going in here."

"I've served this house for years," snarled the pedlar. "What do you mean by interfering with me? You're not a policeman."

"Whether I'm a policeman or a dustman or a postman," said the patient guard, "you don't pass through this gate—do you understand that?"

At this moment the pedlar caught sight of the girl at the door and raised his battered hat with a grin. He was unknown to the girl; she did not remember having seen him at the house before. Nor did Alma, who came out at that moment.

"He's a stranger here, but we're always getting new people up from Gloucester," she said. "What does he want to sell?"

She stalked out into the garden, and at the sight of her the grin left the pedlar's face.

"I've got some things I'd like to sell to the young lady, ma'am," he said.

"I'm not so old, and I'm a lady," replied Alma sharply. "And how long is it since you started picking and choosing your customers?"

The man grumbled something under his breath, and without waiting even to display his wares, shuffled off along the dusty road, and they watched him until he was out of sight.

Heavytree Farm was rather grandly named for so small a property. The little estate followed the road to Heavytree Lane, which formed the southern boundary of the property. The lane itself ran at an angle to behind the house, where the third boundary was formed by a hedge dividing the farmland from the more pretentious estate of a local magnate. It was down the lane the pedlar turned.

"Excuse me, ma'am," said the companion of the man with the pipe.

He opened the gate, walked in, and, making a circuit of the house, reached the orchard behind. Here a few outhouses were scattered, and, clearing these, he came to the meadow, where Mirabelle's one cow ruminated in the lazy manner of her kind. Half hidden by a thick-boled apple-tree, the watcher waited, and presently, as he expected, he saw a head appear through the boundary hedge. After an observation the pedlar sprang into the meadow and stood, taking stock of his ground. He had left his tray and his bag, and, running with surprising swiftness for a man of his age, he gained a little wooden barn, and, pulling open the door, disappeared into its interior. By this time the guard had been joined by his companion and they had a short consultation, the man with the pipe going back to his post before the house, whilst the other walked slowly across the meadow until he came to the closed door of the barn.

Wise in his generation, he first made a circuit of the building, and discovered there were no exits through the blackened gates. Then, pulling both doors open wide:

"Come out, bo'!" he said.

The barn was empty, except for a heap of hay that lay in one corner and some old and wheel-less farm-wagons propped up on three trestles awaiting the wheelwright's attention.

A ladder led to a loft, and the guard climbed slowly. His head was on a level with the dark opening, when: "Put up your hands!"

He was looking into the adequate muzzle of an automatic pistol.

"Come down, bo'!"

"Put up your hands," hissed the voice in the darkness, "or you're a dead man!"

The watcher obeyed, cursing his folly that he had come alone.

"Now climb up."

With some difficulty the guard brought himself up to the floor level.

"Step this way, and step lively," said the pedlar. "Hold your hands out."

He felt the touch of cold steel on his wrist, heard a click.

"Now the other hand."

The moment he was manacled, the pedlar began a rapid search.

"Carry a gun, do you?" he sneered, as he drew a pistol from the man's hip pocket. "Now sit down."

In a few seconds the discomfited guard was bound and gagged. The pedlar, crawling to the entrance of the loft, looked out between a crevice in the boards. He was watching, not the house, but the hedge through which he had climbed. Two other men had appeared there, and he grunted his satisfaction. Descending into the barn, he pulled away the ladder and let it fall on the floor, before he came out into the open and made a signal.

The second guard had made his way back by the short cut to the front of the house, passing through the garden and in through the kitchen door. He stopped to shoot the bolt, and the girl, coming into the kitchen, saw him.

"Is anything wrong?" she asked anxiously.

"I don't know, miss." He was looking at the kitchen windows: they were heavily barred. "My mate has just seen that pedlar go into the barn."

She followed him to the front door. He had turned to go, but, changing his mind, came back, and she saw him put his hand into his hip pocket and was staggered to see him produce a long-barrelled Browning.

"Can you use a pistol, miss?"

She nodded, too surprised to speak, and watched him as he jerked back the jacket and put up the safety catch.

"I want to be on the safe side, and I'd feel happier if you were armed."

There was a gun hanging on the wall and he took it down.

"Have you any shells for this?" he asked.

She pulled open the drawer of the hall-stand and took out a cardboard carton.

"They may be useful," he said.

"But surely, Mr—"

"Digby." He supplied his name.

"Surely you're exaggerating? I don't mean that you're doing it with any intention of frightening me, but there isn't any danger to us?"

"I don't know. I've got a queer feeling—had it all morning. How far is the nearest house from here?"

"Not half a mile away," she said.

"You're on the phone?"

She nodded.

"I'm scared, maybe. I'll just go out into the road and have a look round. I wish that fellow would come back," he added fretfully.

He walked slowly up the garden path and stood for a moment leaning over the gate. As he did so, he heard the rattle and asthmatic wheezing of an ancient car, and saw a tradesman's trolley come round a corner of Heavytree Lane. Its pace grew slower as it got nearer to the house, and opposite the gate it stopped altogether. The driver, getting down with a curse, lifted up the battered tin bonnet, and, groping under the seat, brought out a long spanner. Then, swift as thought, he half turned and struck at Digby's head. The girl heard the sickening impact, saw the watcher drop limply to the path, and in another second she had slammed the door and thrust home the bolts.

She was calm; the hand that took the revolver from the hall-table did not tremble.

"Alma!" she called, and Alma came running downstairs.

"What on earth—?" she began, and then saw the pistol in Mirabelle's hands.

THE PEDLAR

"They are attacking the house," said the girl quickly. "I don't know who 'they' are, but they've just struck down one of the men who was protecting us. Take the gun, Alma."

Alma's face was contorted, and might have expressed fear or anger or both. Mirabelle afterwards learnt that the dominant emotion was one of satisfaction to find herself in so war-like an environment.

Running into the drawing-room, the girl pushed open the window, which commanded a view of the road. The gate was unfastened and two men, who had evidently been concealed inside the trolley, were lifting the unconscious man, and she watched, with a calm she could not understand in herself, as they threw him into the interior and fastened the tailboard. She counted four in all, including the driver, who was climbing back to his seat. One of the newcomers, evidently the leader, was pointing down the road towards the lane, and she guessed that he was giving directions as to where the car should wait, for it began to go backwards almost immediately and with surprising smoothness, remembering the exhibition it had given of decrepitude a few minutes before.

The man who had given instructions came striding down the path towards the door.

"Stop!"

He looked round with a start into the levelled muzzle of a Browning, and his surprise would, in any other circumstances, have been comical.

"It's all right, miss—" he began.

"Put yourself outside that gate," said Mirabelle coolly.

"I wanted to see you... very important—"

Bang!

Mirabelle fired a shot, aimed above his head, towards the old poplar. The man ducked and ran. Clear of the gate he dropped to the cover of a hedge, where his men already were, and she heard the murmur of their voices distinctly, for the day was still, and the far-off chugging of the trolley's engine sounded close at hand. Presently she saw a head peep round the hedge.

"Can I have five minutes' talk with you?" asked the leader loudly.

He was a thick-set, bronzed man, with a patch of lint plastered to his face, and she noted unconsciously that he wore gold ear-rings.

"There's no trouble coming to you," he said, opening the gate as he spoke. "You oughtn't to have fired, anyway. Nobody's going to hurt you—"

He had advanced a yard into the garden as he spoke.

Bang, bang!

In her haste she had pressed butt and trigger just a fraction too long, and, startled by the knowledge that another shot was coming, her hand jerked round, and the second shot missed his head by the fraction of an inch. He disappeared in a flash, and a second later she saw their hats moving swiftly above the box. They were running towards the waiting car.

"Stay here, Alma!"

Alma Goddard nodded grimly, and the girl flew up the stairs to her room. From this elevation she commanded a better view. She saw them climb into the van, and in another second the limp body of the guard was thrown out into the hedge; then, after a brief space of time, the machine began moving and, gathering speed, disappeared in a cloud of dust on the Highcombe Road.

Mirabelle came down the stairs at a run, pulled back the bolts and flew out and along the road towards the still figure of the detective. He was lying by the side of the ditch, his head a mass of blood, and she saw that he was still breathing. She tried to lift him, but it was too great a task. She ran back to the house. The telephone was in the hall: an old-fashioned instrument with a handle that had to be turned, and she had not made two revolutions before she realized that the wire had been cut.

THE PEDLAR

Alma was still in the parlour, the gun gripped tight in her hand, a look of fiendish resolution on her face.

"You must help me to get Digby into the house," she said. "Where is he?"

Mirabelle pointed, and the two women, returning to the man, half lifted, half dragged him back to the hall. Laying him down on the brick floor, the girl went in search of clean linen. The kitchen, which was also the drying place for Alma's more intimate laundry, supplied all that she needed. Whilst Alma watched unmoved the destruction of her wardrobe, the girl bathed the wound and the frightened nurse (who had disappeared at the first shot) applied a rough dressing. The wound was an ugly one, and the man showed no signs of recovering consciousness.

"We shall have to send Mary into Gloucester for an ambulance," said Mirabelle. "We can't send nurse—she doesn't know the way."

"Mary," said Alma calmly, "is at this moment having hysterics in the larder. I'll harness the dog-cart and go myself. But where is the other man?"

Mirabelle shook her head.

"I don't like to think what has happened to him," she said. "Now, Alma, do you think we can get him into the drawing-room?"

Together they lifted the heavy figure and staggered with it into the pretty little room, laying him at last upon the settee under the window.

"He can rest there till we get the ambulance," began Mirabelle, and a chuckle behind her made her turn with a gasp.

It was the pedlar, and in his hand he held the pistol which she had discarded.

"I only want you"—he nodded to the girl. "You other two women can come out here." He jerked his head to the passage.

Under the stairs was a big cupboard and he pulled the door open invitingly. "Get in here. If you make a noise, you'll be sorry for yourselves."

Alma's eyes wandered longingly to the gun she had left in the corner, but before she could make a move he had placed himself between her and the weapon.

"Inside," said the pedlar, and Mirabelle was not much surprised when Aunt Alma meekly obeyed.

He shut the door on the two women and fastened the latch.

"Now, young lady, put on your hat and be lively!"

He followed her up the stairs into her room and watched her while she found a hat and a cloak. She knew only that it was a waste of time even to temporize with him. He, for his part, was so exultant at his success that he grew almost loquacious.

"I suppose you saw the boys driving away and you didn't remember that I was somewhere around. Was that you doing the shooting?"

She did not answer.

"It couldn't have been Lew, or you'd have been dead," he said. He was examining the muzzle of the pistol. "It was you all right." He chuckled. "Ain't you the game one! Sister, you ought to be—"

He stopped dead, staring through the window. He was paralysed with amazement at the sight of a bare-headed Aunt Alma flying along the Gloucester Road. With an oath he turned to the girl.

"How did she get out? Have you got anybody here? Now speak up."

"The cupboard under the stairs leads to the wine cellar," said Mirabelle coolly, "and there are two ways out of the wine cellar I think Aunt Alma found one of them."

With an oath, he took a step towards her, gripped her by the arm and jerked her towards the door.

"Lively!" he said, and dragged her down the stairs through the hall, into the kitchen.

He shot back the bolts, but the lock of the kitchen door had been turned.

"This way." He swore cold-bloodedly, and, her arm still in his powerful grip, he hurried along the passage and pulled open the door.

It was an unpropitious moment. A man was walking down the path, a half smile on his face, as though he was thinking over a remembered jest. At the sight of him the pedlar dropped the girl's arm and his hand went like lightning to his pocket.

"When will you die?" said Leon Gonsalez softly. "Make a choice, and make it quick!"

And the gun in his hand seemed to quiver with homicidal eagerness.

15

TWO "ACCIDENTS"

The pedlar, his face twitching, put up his shaking hands.

Leon walked to him, took the Browning from his moist grip and dropped it into his pocket.

"Your friends are waiting, of course?" he said pleasantly.

The pedlar did not answer.

"Cuccini too? I thought I had incapacitated him for a long time."

"They've gone," growled the pedlar.

Gonsalez looked round in perplexity.

"I don't want to take you into the house. At the same time, I don't want to leave you here," he said. "I almost wish you'd drawn that gun of yours," he added regretfully. "It would have solved so many immediate problems."

This particular problem was solved by the return of the dishevelled Alma and the restoration to her of her gun.

"I would so much rather you shot him than I," said Leon earnestly. "The police are very suspicious of my shootings, and they never wholly believe that they are done in self-defence."

With a rope he tied the man, and tied him uncomfortably, wrists to ankles. That done, he made a few inquiries and went swiftly out to the barn, returning in a few minutes with the unhappy guard.

"It can't be helped," said Leon, cutting short the man's apologies. "The question is, where are the rest of the brethren?"

Something zipped past him: it had the intensified hum of an angry wasp, and a second later he heard a muffled "Plop!" In a second he was lying flat on the ground, his Browning covering the hedge that hid Heavytree Lane.

"Run to the house," he called urgently. "They won't bother about you." And the guard, nothing loth, sprinted for the cover of walls.

Presently Leon located the enemy, and at a little distance off he saw the flat top of the covered trolley. A man walked invitingly across the gap in the hedge, but Gonsalez held his fire, and presently the manoeuvre was repeated. Obviously they were trying to concentrate his mind upon the gap whilst they were moving elsewhere. His eyes swept the meadow boundary — running parallel, he guessed, was a brook or ditch which would make excellent cover.

Again the man passed leisurely across the gap. Leon steadied his elbow, and glanced along the sight. As he did so, the man reappeared.

Crack!

Gonsalez aimed a foot behind him. The man saw the flash and jumped back, as he had expected. In another second he was writhing on the ground with a bullet through his leg.

Leon showed his teeth in a smile and switched his body round to face the new point of attack. It came from the spot that he had expected: a little rise of ground that commanded his position.

The first bullet struck the turf to his right with an angry buzz, sent a divot flying heavenward, and ricocheted with a smack against a tree. Before the raised head could drop to cover, Gonsalez fired; fired another shot to left and right, then, rising, raced for the shelter of the tree, and reached it in time to see three heads bobbing back to the road. He waited, covering the gap, but the people who drew the wounded man out of sight did not show themselves, and a minute later he saw the trolley moving swiftly down the by-road, and knew that danger was past.

The firing had attracted attention. He had not been back in the house a few minutes before a mounted policeman, his horse in a lather, came galloping up to the gate and dismounted. A neighbouring farm had heard the shots and telephoned to constabulary headquarters. For half an hour the mounted policeman took notes, and by this time half the farmers in the neighbourhood, their guns under their arms, had assembled in Mirabelle's parlour.

She had not seen as much of the redoubtable Leon as she could have wished, and when they had a few moments to themselves she seized the opportunity to tell him of the call which Lee had made that morning. Apparently he knew all about it, for he expressed no surprise, and was only embarrassed when she showed a personal interest in himself and his friends.

It was not a very usual experience for him, and he was rather annoyed with himself at this unexpected glimpse of enthusiasm and hero-worship, sane as it was, and based, as he realized, upon her keen sense of justice.

"I'm not so sure that we've been very admirable really," he said. "But the difficulty is to produce at the moment a judgement which would be given from a distance of years. We have sacrificed everything which to most men would make life worth living, in our desire to see the scales held fairly."

"You are not married, Mr Gonsalez?"

He stared into the frank eyes. "Married! Why, no," he said, and she laughed.

"You talk as though that were a possibility that had never occurred to you."

"It hasn't," he admitted. "By the very nature of our work we are debarred from that experience. And is it an offensive thing to say that I have never felt my singleness to be a deprivation?"

"It is very rude," she said severely, and Leon was laughing to himself all the way back to town as at a great joke that improved upon repetition.

"I think we can safely leave her for a week," he reported, on his return to Curzon Street. "No, nothing happened. I was held up in a police trap near Newbury for exceeding the speed limit. They said I was doing fifty, but I should imagine it was nearer eighty. Meadows will get me out of that. Otherwise, I must send the inevitable letter to the magistrate and pay the inevitable fine. Have you done anything about Johnson Lee?"

Manfred nodded. "Meadows and the enthusiastic Mr Washington have gone round to see him. I have asked Washington to go because"—he hesitated—"the snake is a real danger, so far as he is concerned. Elijah Washington promises to be a very real help. He is afraid of nothing, and has undertaken to stay with Lee and to apply such remedies for snake-bites as he knows."

He was putting on his gloves as he spoke, and Leon Gonsalez looked at him with a critical admiration.

"Are you being presented at Court, or are you taking tea with a duchess?"

"Neither. I'm calling upon friend Oberzohn."

"The devil you are!" said Leon, his eyebrows rising.

"I have taken the precaution of sending him a note, asking him to keep his snakes locked up," said Manfred, "and as I have pointedly forwarded the carbon copy of the letter, to impress the fact that another exists and may be brought in evidence against him, I think I shall leave Oberzohn & Smitts' main office without hurt. If you are not too tired, Leon, I would rather prefer the Buick to the Spanz."

"Give me a quarter of an hour," said Leon, and went up to his room to make himself tidy.

It was fifteen minutes exactly when the Buick stopped at the door, and Manfred got into the saloon. There was no partition between driver and passenger, and conversation was possible.

"It would have been as well if you'd had Brother Newton there," he suggested.

"Brother Newton will be on the spot: I took the precaution of sending him a similar note," said Manfred. "I shouldn't imagine they'll bring out their gunmen."

"I know two, and possibly three, they won't bring out." Gonsalez grinned at the traffic policeman who waved him into Oxford Street. "That Browning of mine throws high, Manfred: I've always had a suspicion it did. Pistols are queer things, but this may wear into my hand." He talked arms and ammunition until the square block of Oberzohn & Smitts came into sight. "Good hunting!" he said, as he got out, opened the saloon door and touched his hat to Manfred as he alighted.

He got back into his seat, swung the little car round in a circle, and sat on the opposite side of the road, his eyes alternately on the entrance and on the mirror which gave him a view of the traffic approaching him from the rear.

Manfred was not kept in the waiting-room for more than two minutes. At the end of that time, a solemn youth in spectacles, with a little bow, led him across the incurious office into the presence of the illustrious doctor.

The old man was at his desk. Behind him, his debonair self, Monty Newton, a large yellow flower in his buttonhole, a smile on his face. Oberzohn got up like a man standing to attention.

"Mr Manfred, this is a great honour," he said, and held at his hand stiffly.

An additional chair had been placed for the visitor: a rich-looking tapestried chair, to which the doctor waved the hand which Manfred did not take.

"Good morning, Manfred." Newton removed his cigar and nodded genially. "Were you at the dance last night?"

"I was there, but I didn't come in," said Manfred, seating himself. "You did not turn up till late, they tell me?"

"It was of all occurrences the most unfortunate," said Dr Oberzohn, and Newton laughed.

"I've lost his laboratory secretary and he hasn't forgiven me," he said almost jovially. "The girl he took on yesterday. Rather a stunner in the way of looks. She didn't wish to go back to the country where she came from, so my sister offered to put her up for the night in Chester Square. I'm blessed if she didn't lose herself at the dance, and we haven't seen her since!"

"It was a terrible thing," said Oberzohn sadly. "I regard her as in my charge. For her safety I am responsible. You, I trust, Mr Newton—"

"I don't think I should have another uneasy moment if I were you, doctor," said Manfred easily. "The young lady is back at Heavytree Farm. I thought that would surprise you. And she is still there: that will surprise you more, if you have not already heard by telephone that your Old Guard failed dismally to—er—bring her back to work. I presume that was their object?"

"My old guard, Mr Manfred?" Oberzohn shook his head in bewilderment. "This is beyond my comprehension."

"Is your sister well?" asked Manfred blandly. Newton shrugged his shoulders.

"She is naturally upset. And who wouldn't be? Joan is a very tender-hearted girl."

"She has been that way for years," said Manfred offensively. "May I smoke?"

"Will you have one of my cigarettes?" Manfred's grave eyes fixed the doctor in a stare that held the older man against his will.

"I have had just one too many of your cigarettes," he said. His words came like a cold wind. "I do not want any more, Herr Doktor, or there will be vacancies in your family circle. Who knows that, long before you compound your wonderful elixir, you may be called to normal immortality?"

The yellow face of Oberzohn had turned to a dull red.

"You seem to know so much about me, Mr Manfred, as myself," he said in a husky whisper.

Manfred nodded.

"More. For whilst you are racing against time to avoid the end of a life which does not seem especially worthy of preservation, and whilst you know not what day or hour that end may come, I can tell you to the minute," The finger of his gloved hand pointed the threat.

All trace of a smile had vanished from Monty Newton's face. His eyes did not leave the caller's.

"Perhaps you shall tell me." Oberzohn found a difficulty in speaking. Rage possessed him, and only his iron will choked down the flames from view.

"The day that injury comes to Mirabelle Leicester, that day you go out—you and those who are with you!"

"Look here, Manfred, there's a law in this country—" began Monty Newton hotly.

"I am the law." The words rang like a knell of fate. "In this matter I am judge, jury, hangman. Old or young, I will not spare," he said evenly.

"Are you immortal too?" sneered Monty.

Only for a second did Manfred's eyes leave the old man's face.

"The law is immortal," he said. "If you dream that, by some cleverly concerted coup, you can sweep me from your path before I grow dangerous, be sure that your sweep is clean."

"You haven't asked me to come here to listen to this stuff, have you?" asked Newton, and though his words were bold, his manner aggressive, there were shadows on his face which were not there when Manfred had come into the room—shadows under his eyes and in his cheeks where plumpness had been.

"I've come here to tell you to let up on Miss Leicester. You're after something that you cannot get, and nobody is in a position to give you. I don't know what it is—I will make you a present of that piece of information. But it's big—bigger than any prize you've ever gone after in your wicked lives. And to get that, you're prepared to sacrifice innocent lives with the recklessness of spendthrifts who think there is no bottom to their purse. The end is near!"

He rose slowly and stood by the table, towering over the stiff-backed doctor.

"I cannot say what action the police will take over this providential snake-bite, Oberzohn, but I'll make you this offer: I and my friends will stand out of the game and leave Meadows to get you in his own way. You think that means you'll go scot-free? But it doesn't. These police are like bull-dogs: once they've got a grip of you, they'll never let go."

"What is the price you ask for this interesting service?" Newton was puffing steadily at his cigar, his hands clasped behind him, his feet apart, a picture of comfort and well-being.

"Leave Miss Leicester alone. Find a new way of getting the money you need so badly."

Newton laughed.

"My dear fellow, that's a stupid thing to say. Neither Oberzohn nor I are exactly poor."

"You're bankrupt, both of you," said Manfred quietly. "You are in the position of gamblers when the cards have run against you for a long time. You have no reserve, and your expenses are enormous. Find another way, Newton—and tell your sister"— he paused by the door, looking down into the white lining of his silk hat—"I'd like to see her at Curzon Street tomorrow morning at ten o'clock."

"Is that an order?" asked Newton sarcastically.

Manfred nodded.

"Then let me tell you," roared the man, white with passion, "that I take no orders for her or for me. Got swollen heads since you've had your pardon, haven't you? You look out for me, Manfred. I'm not exactly harmless."

He felt the pressure of the doctor's foot upon his and curbed his temper.

"All right," he growled, "but don't expect to see Joan."

He added a coarse jest, and Manfred raised his eyes slowly and met his.

"You will be hanged by the State or murdered by Oberzohn—I am not sure which," he said simply, and he spoke with such perfect confidence that the heart of Monty Newton turned to water.

Manfred stood in the sidewalk and signalled, and the little car came swiftly and noiselessly across. Leon's eyes were on the entrance. A tall man standing in the shadow of the hall was watching. He was leaning against the wall in a negligent attitude, and for a second Leon was startled.

"Get in quickly!"

Leon almost shouted the words back, and Manfred jumped into the machine, as the chauffeur sent the car forward, with a jerk that strained every gear.

"What on—?" began Manfred, but the rest of his words were lost in the terrific crash which followed.

The leather hood of the machine was ripped down at the back, a splinter of glass struck Leon's cap and sliced a half-moon neatly. He jammed on the brakes, threw open the door of the saloon and leaped out. Behind the car was a mass of wreckage; a great iron casting lay split into three pieces amidst a tangle of broken packing-case. Leon looked up; immediately above the entrance to Oberzohn & Smitts' was a crane, which had swung out with a heavy load just before Manfred came out. The steel wire hung loosely from the derrick. He heard excited voices speaking from the open doorway three floors above, and two men in large glasses were looking down and gabbling in a language he did not understand.

"A very pretty accident. We might have filled half a column in the evening newspapers if we had not moved."

"And the gentleman in the hall—what was he doing?"

Leon walked back through the entrance: the man had disappeared, but near where he had been standing was a small bell-push which, it was obvious, had recently been fixed, for the wires ran loosely on the surface of the wall and were new.

He came back in time to see a policeman crossing the road.

"I wish to find out how this accident occurred, constable," he said. "My master was nearly killed."

The policeman looked at the ton of debris lying half on the sidewalk, half on the road, then up at the slackened hawser.

"The cable has run off the drum, I should think."

"I should think so," said Leon gravely.

He did not wait for the policeman to finish his investigations, but went home at a steady pace, and made no reference to the "accident" until he had put away his car and had returned to Curzon Street.

"The man in the hall was put there to signal when you were under the load—certain things must not happen," he said. "I am going out to make a few inquiries."

Gonsalez knew one of Oberzohn's staff: a clean young Swede, with that knowledge of English which is normal in Scandinavian countries; and at nine o'clock that night he drifted into a Swedish restaurant in Dean Street and found the young man at the end of his meal. It was an acquaintance—one of many—that Leon had assiduously cultivated. The young man, who knew him as Mr Heinz—Leon spoke German remarkably well—was glad to have a companion with whom he could discuss the inexplicable accident of the afternoon.

"The cable was not fixed to the drum," he said. "It might have been terrible: there was a gentleman in a motor-car outside, and he had only moved away a few inches when the case fell. There is bad luck in that house. I am glad that I am leaving at the end of the week."

Leon had some important questions to put, but he did not hurry, having the gift of patience to a marked degree. It was nearly ten when they parted, and Gonsalez went back to his garage, where he spent a quarter of an hour.

At midnight, Manfred had just finished a long conversation with the Scotland Yard man who was still at Brightlingsea, when Leon came in, looking very pleased with himself. Poiccart had gone to bed, and Manfred had switched out one circuit of lights when his friend arrived.

"Thank you, my dear George," said Gonsalez briskly. "It was very good of you, and I did not like troubling you, but—"

"It was a small thing," said Manfred with a smile, "and involved merely the changing of my shoes. But why? I am not curious, but why did you wish me to telephone the night watchman at Oberzohn's to be waiting at the door at eleven o'clock for a message from the doctor?"

"Because," said Leon cheerfully, rubbing his hands, "the night watchman is an honest man; he has a wife and six children, and I was particularly wishful not to hurt anybody. The building doesn't matter: it stands, or stood, isolated from all others. The only worry in my mind was the night watchman. He was at the door—I saw him."

Manfred asked no further questions. Early the next morning he took up the paper and turned to the middle page, read the account of the "Big Fire in City Road" which completely gutted the premises of Messrs. Oberzohn & Smitts; and, what is more, he expected to read it before he had seen the paper.

"Accidents are accidents," said Leon the philosopher that morning at breakfast. "And that talk I had with the clerk last night told me a lot: Oberzohn has allowed his fire insurance to lapse!"

16

RATH HALL

In one of the forbidden rooms that was filled with the apparatus which Dr Oberzohn had accumulated for his pleasure and benefit, was a small electrical furnace which was the centre of many of his most interesting experiments. There were, in certain known drugs, constituents which it was his desire to eliminate. Dr Oberzohn believed absolutely in many things that the modern chemist would dismiss as fantastical.

He believed in the philosopher's stone, in the transmutation of base metals to rare; he had made diamonds, of no great commercial value, it is true; but his supreme faith was that somewhere in the materia medica was an infallible elixir which would prolong life far beyond the normal span. It was to all other known properties as radium is to pitchblende. It was something that only the metaphysician could discover, only the patient chemist could materialize. Every hour he could spare he devoted himself to his obsession; and he was in the midst of one of his experiments when the telephone bell called him back to his study. He listened, every muscle of his face moving, to the tale of disaster that Monty Newton wailed. "It is burning still? Have you no fire-extinguishing machinery in London?"

"Is the place insured or is it not?" asked Monty for the second time.

Dr Oberzohn considered. "It is not," he said. "But this matter is of such small importance compared with the great thing which is coming, that I shall not give it a thought."

"It was incendiary," said Newton angrily. "The fire brigade people are certain of it. That cursed crowd are getting back on us for what happened this afternoon."

"I know of nothing that happened this afternoon," said Dr Oberzohn coldly. "You know of nothing either. It was an accident which we all deplored. As to this man... we shall see."

He hung up the telephone receiver very carefully, went along the passage, down a steep flight of dark stairs, and into a basement kitchen. Before he opened the door he heard the sound of furious voices, and he stood for a moment surveying the scene with every feeling of satisfaction. Except for two men, the room was empty. The servants used the actual kitchen at the front of the house, and this place was little better than a scullery. On one side of the deal table stood Gurther, white as death, his round eyes red with rage. On the other, the short, stout Russian Pole, with his heavy pasty face and baggy eyes; his little moustache and beard bristling with anger. The cards scattered on the table and the floor told the Herr Doktor that this was a repetition of the quarrel which was so frequent between them.

"Schweinhund!" hissed Gurther. "I saw you palm the King as you dealt. Thief and robber of the blind—"

"You German dog! You—"

They were both speaking in German. Then the doctor saw the hand of Gurther steal down and back.

"Gurther!" he called, and the man spun round. "To my parlour—march!"

Without a word, the man strode past him, and the doctor was left with the panting Russian.

"Herr Doktor, this Gurther is beyond endurance!" His voice trembled with rage. "I would sooner live with a pig than this man, who is never normal unless he is drugged."

"Silence!" shouted Oberzohn, and pointed to the chair. "You shall wait till I come," he said.

When he came back to his room, he found Gurther standing stiffly to attention.

"Now, Gurther," he said—he was almost benevolent as he patted the man on the shoulder—"this matter of Gonsalez must end. Can I have my Gurther hiding like a worm in the ground? No, that cannot be. Tonight I will send you to this man, and you are so clever that you cannot fail. He whipped you, Gurther—tied you up and cruelly beat you—always remember that, my brave fellow—he beat you till you bled. Now you shall see the man again. You will go in a dress for-every-occasion," he said. "The city-clerk manner. You will watch him in your so clever way, and you shall strike—it is permitted."

"Ja, Herr Doktor."

He turned on his heels and disappeared through the door. The doctor waited till he heard him going up the stairs, and then he rang for Pfeiffer. The man came in sullenly. He lacked all the precision of the military Gurther; yet, as Oberzohn knew, of the two he was the more alert, the more cunning.

"Pfeiffer, it has come to me that you are in some danger. The police wish to take you back to Warsaw, where certain unpleasant things happened, as you well know. And I am told"—he lowered his voice—"that a friend of ours would be glad to see you go, hein?"

The man did not raise his sulky eyes from the floor, did not answer, or by any gesture or movement of body suggest that he had heard what the older man had said.

"Gurther goes tomorrow, perhaps on our good work, perhaps to speak secretly to his friends in the police—who knows? He has work to do: let him do it, Pfeiffer. All my men will be there—at a place called Brightlingsea. You also shall go. Gurther would rob a blind man? Good! You shall rob one also. As for Gurther, I do not wish him back. I am tired of him: he is a madman. All men are mad who sniff that white snuff up their foolish noses—eh, Pfeiffer?"

Still the awkward-looking man made no reply.

"Let him do his work: you shall not interfere, until—it is done."

Pfeiffer was looking at him now, a cold sneer on his face.

"If he comes back, I do not," he said. "This man is frightening me. Twice the police have been here—three times... you remember the woman. The man is a danger, Herr Doktor. I told you he was the day you brought him here."

"He can dress in the gentleman-club manner," said the doctor gently.

"Pshaw!" said the other scornfully. "Is he not an actor who has postured and painted his face and thrown about his legs for so many marks a week?"

"If he does not come back I shall be relieved," murmured the doctor. "Though it would be a mistake to leave him so that these cunning men could pry into our affairs."

Pfeiffer said nothing: he understood his instructions; there was nothing to be said. "When does he go?"

"Early tomorrow, before daylight. You will see him, of course."

He said something in a low tone, that only Pfeiffer heard. The shadow who stood in stockinged feet listening at the door only heard two words. Gurther grinned in the darkness; his bright eyes grew luminous. He heard his companion move towards the door and sped up the stairs without a sound.

Rath Hall was a rambling white building of two stories, set in the midst of a little park, so thickly wooded that the house was invisible from the road; and since the main entrance to the estate was a very commonplace gate, without lodge or visible drive beyond, Gonsalez would have missed the place had he not recognized the man who was sitting on the moss-grown and broken wall who jumped down as Leon stopped his car.

RATH HALL

"Mr Meadows is at the house, sir. He said he expected you."

"And where on earth is the house?" asked Leon Gonsalez, as he went into reverse.

For answer the detective opened the gate wide and Leon sent his car winding between the trees, for close at hand he recognized where a gravel drive had once been, and, moreover, he saw the tracks of cars in the soft earth. He arrived just as Mr Johnson Lee was taking his two guests in to dinner; and Meadows was obviously glad to see him. He excused himself, and took Leon aside into the hall, where they could not be overheard.

"I have had your message," he said. "The only thing that happened out of the ordinary is that the servants have an invitation to a big concert at Brightlingsea. You expected that?"

Leon nodded.

"Yes: I hope Lee will let them go. I prefer that they should be out of the way. A crude scheme—but Oberzohn does these things. Has anything else happened?"

"Nothing. There have been one or two queer people around."

"Has he showed you the letters he had from Barberton?"

To his surprise the inspector answered in the affirmative.

"Yes, but they are worse than Greek to me. A series of tiny protuberances on thick brown paper. He keeps them in his safe. He read some of the letters to me: they were not very illuminating."

"But the letter of letters?" asked Leon anxiously. "That which Lee answered—by the way, you know that Mr Lee wrote all his letters between perforated lines?"

"I've seen the paper," nodded the detective. "No, I asked him about that, but apparently he is not anxious to talk until he has seen his lawyer, who is coming down tonight. He should have been here, in fact, in time for dinner."

They passed into the dining-room together. The blind man was waiting patiently at the head of the table, and with an apology Leon took the place that had been reserved for him. He sat with his back to the wall, facing one of the three long windows that looked out upon the park. It was a warm night and the blinds were up, as also was the middle window that faced him. He made a motion to Mr Washington, who sat opposite him, to draw a little aside, and the American realized that he wished an uninterrupted view of the park.

"Would you like the window closed?" asked Mr Lee, leaning forward and addressing the table in general. "I know it is open," he said with a little laugh, "because I opened it! I am a lover of fresh air."

They murmured their agreement and the meal went on without any extraordinary incident. Mr Washington was one of those adaptable people who dovetail into any environment in which they find themselves. He was as much at home at Rath Hall as though he had been born and bred in the neighbourhood. Moreover, he had a special reason for jubilation: he had found a rare adder when walking in the woods that morning, and spent ten minutes explaining in what respect it differed from every other English adder.

"Is it dead?" asked Meadows nervously.

"Kill it?" said the indignant Mr Washington. "Why should I kill it? I saw a whole lot of doves out on the lawn this morning—should I kill 'em? No, sir! I've got none of those mean feelings towards snakes. I guess the Lord sent snakes into this world for some other purpose than to be chased and killed every time they're seen. I sent him up to London today by train to a friend of mine at the Zoological Gardens. He'll keep him until I'm ready to take him back home."

Meadows drew a long sigh.

"As long as he's not in your pocket," he said.

"Do you mind?"

Leon's voice was urgent as he signalled Washington to move yet farther to the left, and when the big man moved his chair,

Leon nodded his thanks. His eyes were on the window and the darkening lawn. Not once did he remove his gaze.

"It's an extraordinary thing about Poole, my lawyer," Mr Lee was saying. "He promised faithfully he'd be at Rath by seven o'clock. What is the time?"

Meadows looked at his watch.

"Half-past eight," he said. He saw the cloud that came over the face of the blind owner of Rath Hall.

"It is extraordinary! I wonder if you would mind—"

His foot touched a bell beneath the table and his butler came in.

"Will you telephone to Mr Poole's house and ask if he has left?"

The butler returned in a short time.

"Yes, sir, Mr Poole left the house by car at half-past six."

Johnson Lee sat back in his chair.

"Half-past six? He should have been here by now."

"How far away does he live?"

"About fifteen miles. I thought he might have come down from London rather late. That is extraordinary."

"He may have had tyre trouble," said Leon, not shifting his fixed stare.

"He could have telephoned."

"Did anyone know he was coming—anybody outside your own household?" asked Gonsalez.

The blind man hesitated.

"Yes, I mentioned the fact to the post office this morning. I went in to get my letters, and found that one I had written to Mr Poole had been returned through a mistake on my part. I told the postmaster that he was coming this evening and that there was no need to forward it."

"You were in the public part of the post office?"

"I believe I was."

"You said nothing else, Mr Lee—nothing that would give any idea of the object of this visit?"

Again his host hesitated. "I don't know. I'm almost afraid that I did," he confessed. "I remember telling the postmaster that I was going to talk to Mr Poole about poor Barberton—Mr Barberton was very well known in this neighbourhood."

"That is extremely unfortunate," said Leon.

He was thinking of two things at the same time: the whereabouts of the missing lawyer, and the wonderful cover that the wall between the window and the floor gave to any man who might creep along out of sight until he got back suddenly to send the snake on its errand of death.

"How many men have you got in the grounds, by the way, Meadows?"

"One, and he's not in the grounds but outside on the road. I pull him in at night, or rather in the evening, to patrol the grounds, and he is armed." He said this with a certain importance. An armed English policeman is a tremendous phenomenon that few have seen.

"Which means that he has a revolver that he hasn't fired except at target practice," said Leon. "Excuse me—I thought I heard a car."

He got up noiselessly from the table, went round the back of Mr Lee, and, darting to the window, looked out. A flower-bed ran close to the wall, and beyond that was a broad gravel drive. Between gravel and flowers was a wide strip of turf. The drive continued some fifty feet to the right before it turned under an arch of rambler roses. To the left it extended for less than a dozen feet, and from this point a path parallel the side of the house ran into the drive.

"Do you hear it?" asked Lee.

"No, sir, I was mistaken."

Leon dipped his hand into his side pocket, took out a handful of something that looked like tiny candles wrapped in coloured paper. Only Meadows saw him scatter them left and right, and he was too discreet to ask why, Leon saw the inquiring lift of his eyebrows as he came back to his seat, but was wilfully dense. Thereafter, he ate his dinner with only an occasional glance towards the window.

"I'm not relying entirely upon my own lawyer's advice," I said Mr Lee. "I have telegraphed to Lisbon to ask Dr Pinto Caillao to come to England, and he may be of greater service even than Poole, though where—" The butler came in at this moment.

"Mrs Poole has just telephoned, sir. Her husband has had a bad accident: his car ran into a tree trunk which was lying across the road near Lawley. It was on the other side of the bend, and he did not see it until too late."

"Is he very badly hurt?"

"No, sir, but he is in the Cottage Hospital. Mrs Poole says he is fit to travel home."

The blind man sat open-mouthed. "What a terrible thing to have happened!" he began. "A very lucky thing for Mr Poole," said Leon cheerfully. "I feared worse than that—"

From somewhere outside the window came a "snap!"—the sound that a Christmas cracker makes when it is exploded. Leon got up from the table, walked swiftly to the side of the window and jumped out. As he struck the earth, he trod on one of the little bon-bons he had scattered and it cracked viciously under his foot.

There was nobody in sight. He ran swiftly along the grass-plot, slowing his pace as came to the end of the wall, and then jerked round, gun extended stiffly. Still nobody. Before him was a close-growing box hedge, in which had been cut an opening. He heard the crack of a signal behind him, guessed that it was Meadows, and presently the detective joined him. Leon put his fingers to his lips, leapt the path to the grass on the other side, and dodged behind a tree until he could see straight through the opening in the box hedge. Beyond was a rose-garden, a mass of pink and red and golden blooms.

Leon put his hand in his pocket and took out a black cylinder, fitting it, without taking his eyes from the hedge opening, to the muzzle of his pistol. Meadows heard the dull thud of the explosion before he saw the pistol go up. There was a scatter of leaves and twigs and the sound of hurrying feet. Leon dashed through the opening in time to see a man plunge into a plantation.

"Plop!"

The bullet struck a tree not a foot from the fugitive.

"That's that!" said Leon, and took off his silencer. "I hope none of the servants heard it, and most of all that Lee, whose hearing is unfortunately most acute, mistook the shot for something else."

He went back to the window, stopping to pick up such of his crackers as had not exploded.

"They are useful things to put on the floor of your room when you're expecting to have your throat cut in the middle of the night," he said pleasantly. "They cost exactly two dollars a hundred, and they've saved my life more often than I can count. Have you ever waited in the dark to have your throat cut?" he asked. "It happened to me three times, and I will admit that it is not an experience that I am anxious to repeat. Once in Bohemia, in the city of Prague; once in New Orleans, and once in Ortona."

"What happened to the assassins?" asked Meadows with a shiver.

"That is a question for the theologian, if you will forgive the well-worn jest," said Leon. "I think they are in hell, but then I'm prejudiced."

Mr Lee had left the dining-table and was standing at the front door, leaning on his stick; and with him an interested Mr Washington.

"What was the trouble?" asked the old man in a worried voice. "It is a great handicap not being able to see things. But I thought I heard a shot fired."

"Two," said Leon promptly. "I hoped you hadn't heard them. I don't know who the man was, Mr Lee, but he certainly had no right in the grounds, and I scared him off."

"You must have used a silencer: I did not hear the shots fully. Did you catch a view of the man's face?"

"No, I saw his back," he said. Leon thought it was unnecessary to add that a man's back was as familiar to him as his face. For when he studied his enemies, his study was a very thorough and complete one. Moreover, Gurther ran with a peculiar swing of his shoulder.

He turned suddenly to the master of Rath Hall. "May I speak with you privately for a few minutes, Mr Lee?" he asked. He had taken a sudden resolution.

"Certainly," said the other courteously, and tapped his way into the hall and into his private study.

For ten minutes Leon was closeted with him. When he came out, Meadows had gone down to his man at the gate, and Washington was standing disconsolately alone. Leon took him by the arm and led him on to the lawn.

"There's going to be real trouble here tonight," he said, and told him the arrangement he had made with Mr Johnson Lee. "I've tried to persuade him to let me see the letter which is in his safe, but he is like rock on that matter, and I'd hate to burgle the safe of a friend. Listen."

Elijah Washington listened and whistled.

"They stopped the lawyer coming," Gonsalez went on, "and now they're mortally scared if, in his absence, the old man tells us what he intended keeping for his lawyer."

"Meadows is going to London, isn't he?"

Leon nodded slowly.

"Yes, he is going to London—by car. Did you know all the servants were going out tonight?"

Mr Washington stared at him.

"The women, you mean?"

"The women and the men," said Leon calmly. "There is an excellent concert at Brightlingsea tonight, and though they will be late for the first half of the performance, they will thoroughly enjoy the latter portion of the programme. The invitation is not mine, but it is one I thoroughly approve."

"But does Meadows want to go away when the fun is starting?"

Apparently Inspector Meadows was not averse from leaving at this critical moment. He was, in fact, quite happy to go. Mr Washington's views on police intelligence underwent a change for the worse.

"But surely he had better stay?" said the American. "If you're expecting an attack... they are certain to marshal the whole of their forces?"

"Absolutely certain," said the calm Gonsalez "Here is the car."

The Rolls came out from the back of the house at that moment and drew up before the door.

"I don't like leaving you," said Meadows, as he swung himself up by the driver's side and put his bag on the seat.

"Tell the driver to avoid Lawley like the plague," said Leon. "There's a tree down, unless the local authorities have removed it—which is very unlikely."

He waited until the tail lights of the machine had disappeared into the gloom, then he went back to the hall.

"Excuse me, sir," said the butler, struggling into his greatcoat as he spoke. "Will you be all right—there is nobody left in the house to look after Mr Lee. I could stay—"

"It was Mr Lee's suggestion you should all go," said Gonsalez briefly. "Just go outside and tell me when the lights of the char-a-banc come into view. I want to speak to Mr Lee before you go."

He went into the library and shut the door behind him. The waiting butler heard the murmur of his voice and had some qualms of conscience. The tickets had come from a local agency; he had never dreamt that, with guests in the house, his employer would allow the staff to go in its entirety.

It was not a char-a-banc but a big closed bus that came lumbering up the apology for a drive, and swept round to the back of the house, to the annoyance of the servants, who were gathered in the hall.

"Don't bother, I will tell him," said Leon. He seemed to have taken full charge of the house, an unpardonable offence in the eyes of well-regulated servants.

He disappeared through a long passage leading into the mysterious domestic regions, and returned to announce that the driver had rectified his error and was coming to the front entrance: an unnecessary explanation, since the big vehicle drew up as he was telling the company.

"There goes the most uneasy bunch of festive souls it has ever been my misfortune to see," he said, as the bus, its brakes squeaking, went down the declivity towards the unimposing gate. "And yet they'll have the time of their lives. I've arranged supper for them at the Beech Hotel, and although they are not aware of it, I am removing them to a place where they'd give a lot of money to be — if they hadn't gone!"

"That leaves you and me alone," said Mr Washington glumly, but brightened up almost at once. "I can't say that I mind a rough house, with or without gun-play," he said. He looked round the dark hall a little apprehensively. "What about fastening the doors behind?" he asked.

"They're all right," said Leon. "It isn't from the back that danger will come. Come out and enjoy the night air... it is a little too soon for the real trouble."

But here, for once, he was mistaken.

Elijah Washington followed him into the park, took two paces, and suddenly Leon saw him stagger. In a second he was by the man's side, bent and peering, his glasses discarded on the grass.

"Get me inside," said Washington's voice. He was leaning heavily upon his companion.

With his arm round his waist, taking half his weight, Leon pushed the man into the hall but did not close the door. Instead, as the American sat down with a thud upon a hall seat, Leon fell to the ground, and peered along the artificial sky-line he had created. There was no movement, no sign of any attacker. Then and only then did he shut the door and drop the bar, and pushing the study door wide, carried the man into the room and switched on the lights.

"I guess something got me then," muttered Washington.

His right cheek was red and swollen, and Leon saw the telltale bite; saw something else. He put his hand to the cheek and examined his finger-tips.

"Get me some whisky, will you?—about a gallon of it."

He was obviously in great pain and sat rocking himself to and fro.

"Gosh! This is awful!" he groaned. "Never had any snake that bit like this!"

"You're alive, my friend, and I didn't believe you when you said you were snake-proof."

Leon poured out a tumbler of neat whisky and held it to the American's lips.

"Down with Prohibition!" murmured Washington, and did not take the glass from his lips until it was empty. "You can give me another dose of that—I shan't get pickled," he said.

He put his hand up to his face and touched the tiny wound gingerly—"It is wet," he said in surprise.

"What did it feel like?"

"Like nothing so much as a snake-bite," confessed the expert.

Already his face was puffed beneath the eyes, and the skin was discoloured black and blue.

Leon crossed to the fire-place and pushed the bell, and Washington watched him in amazement.

"Say, what's the good of ringing? The servants have gone."

There was a patter of feet in the hall, the door was flung open and George Manfred came in, and behind him the startled visitor saw Meadows and a dozen men.

"For the Lord's sake!" he said sleepily.

"They came in the char-a-banc, lying on the floor," explained Leon, "and the only excuse for bringing a char-a-banc here was to send the servants to that concert."

"You got Lee away?" asked Manfred.

Leon nodded.

"He was in the car that took friend Meadows, who transferred to the char-a-banc somewhere out of sight of the house."

Washington had taken a small cardboard box from his pocket and was rubbing a red powder gingerly upon the two white-edged marks, groaning the while.

"This is certainly a snake that's got the cobra skinned to death and a rattlesnake's bite ain't worse than a dog nip," he said. "Mamba nothing! I know the mamba; he is pretty fatal, but not so bad as this."

Manfred looked across to Leon.

"Gurther?" he asked simply, and Gonsalez nodded.

"It was intended for me obviously, but, as I've said before, Gurther is nervous. And it didn't help him any to be shot up."

"Do you fellows mind not talking so loud?" He glanced at the heavy curtains that covered the windows. Behind these the shutters had been fastened, and Dr Oberzohn was an ingenious man.

Leon took a swift survey of the visitor's feet; they wore felt slippers.

"I don't think I can improve upon the tactics of the admirable Miss Leicester," he said, and went up to Mr Lee's bedroom, which was in the centre of the house and had a small balcony, the floor of which was formed by the top of the porch.

The long French windows were open and Leon crawled out into the darkness and took observation through the pillars of the balustrade. They were in the open now, making no attempt to conceal their presence. He counted seven, until he saw the cigarette of another near the end of the drive. What were they waiting for, he wondered. None of them moved; they were not even closing on the house. And this inactivity puzzled him. They were awaiting a signal. What was it to be? Whence would it come?

He saw a man come stealthily across the lawn... one or two? His eyes were playing tricks. If there were two, one was Gurther. There was no mistaking him. For a second he passed out of view behind a pillar of the balcony. Leon moved his head... Gurther had fallen! He saw him stumble to his knees and tumble flat upon the ground. What did that mean?

He was still wondering when he heard a soft scraping, and a deep-drawn breath, and tried to locate the noise. Suddenly, within a few inches of his face, a hand came up out of the darkness and gripped the lower edge of the balcony.

Swiftly, noiselessly, Gonsalez wriggled back to the room, drew erect in the cover of the curtains and waited. His hand touched something: it was a long silken cord by which the curtains were drawn. Leon grinned in the darkness and made a scientific loop.

The intruder drew himself up on to the parapet, stepped quietly across, then tiptoed to the open window. He was not even suspicious, for the French windows had been open all the evening. Without a sound, he stepped into the room and was momentarily silhouetted against the starlight reflected in the window.

"Hatless," thought Leon. That made things easier. As the man took another stealthy step, the noose dropped over his neck, jerked tight and strangled the cry in his throat. In an instant he was lying flat on the ground with a knee in his back. He struggled to rise, but Leon's fist came down with the precision of a piston-rod, and he went suddenly quiet.

Gonsalez loosened the slip-knot, and, flinging the man over his shoulder, carried him out of the room and down the stairs. He could only guess that this would be the only intruder, but left nothing to chance, and after he had handed his prisoner to the men who were waiting in the hall, he ran back to the room, to find, as he had expected, that no other adventurer had followed the lead. They were still standing at irregular intervals where he had seen them last. The signal was to come from the house. What was it to be, he wondered.

He left one of his men on guard in the room and went back to the study, to find that the startled burglar was an old friend. Lew Cuccini was looking from one of his captors to the other, a picture of dumbfounded chagrin. But the most extraordinary discovery that Leon made on his return to the study was that the American snake-charmer was his old cheerful self, and, except for his unsightly appearance, seemed to be none the worse for an ordeal which would have promptly ended the lives of ninety-nine men out of a hundred. "Snake-proof—that's me. Is this the guy that did it?" He pointed to Cuccini.

"Where is Gurther?" asked Manfred,

Cuccini grinned up into his face.

"You'd better find out, boss," he said. "He'll fix you. As soon as I shout—"

"Cuccini—" Leon's voice was gentle. The point of the long-bladed knife that he held to the man's neck was indubitably sharp. Cuccini shrank back. "You will not shout. If you do, I shall cut your throat and spoil all these beautiful carpets—that is a genuine silken Bokhara, George. I haven't seen one in ten years." He nodded to the soft-hued rug on which George Manfred was standing. "What is the signal, Cuccini?" turning his attention again to the prisoner. "And what happens when you give the signal?"

"Listen," said Cuccini, "that throat-cutting stuff don't mean anything to me. There's no third degree in this country, and don't forget it."

"You have never seen my ninety-ninth degree." Leon smiled like a delighted boy. "Put something in his mouth, will you?"

One of the men tied a woollen scarf round Cuccini's head.

"Lay him on the sofa."

He was already bound hand and foot and helpless.

"Have you any wax matches? Yes, here are some." Leon emptied a cut-glass container into the palm of his hand and looked round at the curious company. "Now, gentlemen, if you will leave me alone for exactly five minutes, I will give Mr Cuccini an excellent imitation of the persuasive methods of Gian Visconti, an excellent countryman of his, and the inventor of the system I am about to apply."

Cuccini was shaking his head furiously. A mumble of unintelligible sounds came from behind the scarf.

"Our friend is not unintelligent. Any of you who say that Signer Cuccini is unintelligent will incur my severest displeasure," said Leon.

They sat the man up and he talked brokenly, hesitatingly. "Splendid," said Leon, when he had finished. "Take him into the kitchen and give him a drink—you'll find a tap above the kitchen sink."

"I've often wondered, Leon," said George, when they were alone together, "whether you would ever carry out those horrific threats of yours of torture and malignant savagery?"

"Half the torture of torture is anticipation," said Leon easily, lighting a cigarette with one of the matches he had taken from the table, and carefully guiding the rest back into the glass bowl. "Any man versed in the art of suggestive descriptions can dispense with thumbscrews and branding irons, little maidens and all the ghastly apparatus of criminal justice ever employed by our ancestors. I, too, wonder," he mused, blowing a ring of smoke to the ceiling, "whether I could carry my threats into execution—I must try one day." He nodded pleasantly, as though he were promising himself a great treat.

Manfred looked at his watch.

"What do you intend doing—giving the signal?" Gonsalez nodded. "And then?"

"Letting them come in. We may take refuge in the kitchen. I think it would be wiser."

George Manfred nodded. "You're going to allow them to open the safe?"

"Exactly," said Leon. "I particularly wish that safe to be opened, and since Mr Lee demurs, I think this is the best method. I had that in my mind all the time. Have you seen the safe, George? I have. Nobody but an expert could smash it. I have no tools. I did not provide against such a contingency, and I have scruples. Our friends have tools—and no scruples!"

"And the snake—is there any danger?"

Leon snapped his fingers.

"The snake has struck for the night, and will strike no more! As for Gurther—"

"He owes you something."

Leon sent another ring up and did not speak until it broke on the ceiling.

"Gurther is dead," he said simply. "He has been lying on the lawn in front of the house for the past ten minutes."

17

WRITTEN IN BRAILLE

Leon briefly related the scene he had witnessed from the balcony.

"It was undoubtedly Gurther," he said. "I could not mistake him. He passed out of view for a second behind one of the pillars, and when I looked round he was lying flat on the ground."

He threw his cigarette into the fire-place.

"I think it is nearly time," he said. He waited until Manfred had gone, and, going to the door, moved the bar and pulled it open wide.

Stooping down, he saw that the opening of the door had been observed, for one of the men was moving across the lawn in the direction of the house. From his pocket he took a small electric lamp and sent three flickering beams into the darkness. To his surprise, only two men walked forward to the house. Evidently Cuccini was expected to deal with any resistance before the raid occurred.

The house had been built in the fifteenth century, and the entrance hall was a broad, high barn of a place. Some Georgian architect, in the peculiar manner of his kind, had built a small minstrel gallery over the dining-room entrance and immediately facing the study. Leon had already explored the house and had found the tiny staircase that led to this architectural monstrosity. He had no sooner given the signal than he dived into the dining-room, through the tall door, and was behind the thick curtains at the back of the narrow gallery when the first two men came in. He saw them go straight into the study and push open the door. At the same time a third man appeared under the porch, though he made no attempt to enter the hall.

Presently one of those who had gone into the study came out and called Cuccini by name. When no answer came, he went grumbling back to his task. What that task was, Leon could guess, before the peculiarly acrid smell of hot steel was wafted to his sensitive nostrils.

By crouching down he could see the legs of the men who were working at the safe. They had turned on all the lights, and apparently expected no interruption. The man at the door was joined by another man.

"Where is Lew?"

In the stillness of the house the words, though spoken in a low tone, were audible.

"I don't know—inside somewhere. He had to fix that dago."

Leon grinned. This description of himself never failed to tickle him.

One of the workers in the library came out at this point.

"Have you seen Cuccini?"

"No," said the man at the door.

"Go in and find him. He ought to be here."

Cuccini's absence evidently made him uneasy, for though he returned to the room he was out again in a minute, asking if the messenger had come back. Then, from the back of the passage, came the searcher's voice: "The kitchen's locked."

The safe-cutter uttered an expression of amazement.

"Locked? What's the idea?"

He came to the foot of the stairs and bellowed up: "Cuccini!"

Only the echo answered him.

"That's queer." He poked his head in the door of the study. "Rush that job, Mike. There's some funny business here." And over his shoulder, "Tell the boys to get ready to jump."

The man went out into the night and was absent some minutes, to return with an alarming piece of news.

"They've gone, boss. I can't see one of them."

The "boss" cursed him, and himself went into the grounds on a visit of inspection. He came back in a hurry, ran into the study, and Leon heard his voice: "Stand ready to clear."

"What about Cuccini?"

"Cuccini will have to look after himself... got it, Mike?"

The deep voice said something. There followed the sound of a crack, as though something of iron had broken. It was the psychological moment. Leon parted the curtains and dropped lightly to the floor.

The man at the door turned in a flash at the sound.

"Put 'em up!" he said sharply.

"Don't shoot." Leon's voice was almost conversational in its calmness. "The house is surrounded by police."

With an oath the man darted out of the door, and at that instant came the sound of the first shot, followed by desultory firing from the direction of the road. The second guard had been the first to go. Leon ran to the door, slammed it tight and switched on the lights as the two men came from the study. Under the arm of one was a thick pad of square brown sheets. He dropped his load and put up his hands at the sight of the gun; but his companion was made of harder material, and, with a yell, he leapt at the man who stood between him and freedom. Leon twisted aside, advanced his shoulder to meet the furious drive of the man's fist; then, dropping his pistol, he stooped swiftly and tackled him below the knees. The man swayed, sought to recover his balance and fell with a crash on the stone floor. All the time his companion stood dazed and staring, his hands waving in the air.

There was a knock at the outer door. Without turning his back upon his prisoners, Leon reached for the bar and pulled it up. Manfred came in.

"The gentleman who shouted 'Cuccini' scared them. I think they've got away. There were two cars parked on the road."

His eyes fell upon the brown sheets scattered on the floor and he nodded.

"I think you have all you want, Leon," he said.

The detectives came crowding in at that moment and secured their prisoners whilst Leon Gonsalez and his friend went out on to the lawn to search for Gurther.

The man lay as he had fallen, on his face, and as Leon flashed his lamp upon the figure, he saw that the snake had struck behind the ear.

"Gurther?" frowned Leon.

He turned the figure on its back and gave a little gasp of surprise, for there looked up to the starry skies the heavy face of Pfeiffer.

"Pfeiffer! I could have sworn it was the other! There has been some double-crossing here. Let me think." He stood for fully a minute, his chin on his hand. "I could have understood Gurther; he was becoming a nuisance and a danger to the old man. Pfeiffer, the more reliable of the two, hated him. My first theory was that Gurther had been put out by order of Oberzohn."

"Suppose Gurther heard that order, or came to know of it?" asked Manfred quietly.

Leon snapped his fingers.

"That is it! We had a similar case a few years ago, you will remember, George? The old man gave the 'out' order to Pfeiffer—and Gurther got his blow in first. Shrewd fellow!"

When they returned to the house, the three were seated in a row in Johnson Lee's Library. Cuccini, of course, was an old acquaintance. Of the other two men, Leon recognized one, a notorious gunman whose photograph had embellished the pages of Hue and Cry for months.

The third, and evidently the skilled workman of the party, for he it was whom they had addressed as "Mike" and who had burnt out the lock of Lee's safe, was identified by Meadows as Mike Selwyn, a skilful burglar and bank-smasher, who had, according to his statement, only arrived from the Continent that afternoon in answer to a flattering invitation which promised considerable profit to himself.

"And why I left Milan," he said bitterly, "where the graft is easy and the money's good, I'd like you to tell me!"

The prisoners were removed to the nearest secure lock-up, and by the time Lee's servants returned from their dance, all evidence of an exciting hour had disappeared, except that the blackened and twisted door of the safe testified to the sinister character of the visitation.

Meadows returned as they were gathering together the scattered sheets. There were hundreds of them, all written in Braille characters, and Manfred's sensitive fingers were skimming their surface.

"Oh, yes," he said, in answer to a question that was put to him, "I knew Lee was blind, the day we searched Barberton's effects. That was my mystery." He laughed. "Barberton expected a call from his old friend and had left a message for him on the mantelpiece. Do you remember that strip of paper? It ran: 'Dear Johnny, I will be back in an hour.' These are letters,"— he indicated the papers.

"The folds tell me that," said Meadows. "You may not get a conviction against Cuccini; the two burglars will come up before a judge, but to charge Cuccini means the whole story of the snake coming out, and that means a bigger kick than I'm prepared to laugh away—I am inclined to let Cuccini go for the moment."

Manfred nodded. He sat with the embossed sheets on his knee.

"Written from various places," he went on.

It was curious to see him, his fingers running swiftly along the embossed lines, his eyes fixed on vacancy.

"So far I've learnt nothing, except that in his spare time Barberton amused himself by translating native fairy stories into English and putting them into Braille for use in the blind school. I knew, of course, that he did that, because I'd already interviewed his sister, who is the mistress of the girls' section."

He had gone through half a dozen letters when he rose from the table and walked across to the safe.

"I have a notion that the thing we're seeking is not here," he said. "It is hardly likely that he would allow a communication of that character to be jumbled up with the rest of the correspondence."

The safe door was open and the steel drawer at the back had been pulled out. Evidently it was from this receptacle that the letters had been taken. Now the drawer was empty. Manfred took it out and measured the depth of it with his finger.

"Let me see," said Gonsalez suddenly.

He groped along the floor of the safe, and presently he began to feel carefully along the sides.

"Nothing here," he said. He drew out half a dozen account books and a bundle of documents which at first glance Manfred had put aside as being personal to the owner of Rath Hall. These were lying on the floor amidst the mass of molten metal that had burnt deep holes in the carpet. Leon examined the books one by one, opening them and running his nail along the edge of the pages. The fourth, a weighty ledger, did not open so easily—did not, indeed, open at all. He carried it to the table and tried to pull back the cover. "Now, how does this open?"

The ledger covers were of leather; to all appearance a very ordinary book, and Leon was anxious not to disturb so artistic a camouflage. Examining the edge carefully, he saw a place where the edges had been forced apart. Taking out a knife, he slipped the thin blade into the aperture. There was a click and the cover sprang up like the lid of a box.

"And this, I think, is what we are looking for," said Gonsalez.

The interior of the book had been hollowed out, the edges being left were gummed tight, and the receptacle thus formed was packed close with brown papers; brown, except for one, which was written on a large sheet of foolscap, headed:

"Bureau of the Ministry of Colonies, Lisbon."

Barberton had superimposed upon this long document his Braille writing, and now one of the mysteries was cleared up.

"Lee said he had never received any important documents," said Manfred, "and, of course, he hadn't, so far as he knew. To him this was merely a sheet of paper on which Braille characters were inscribed. Read this, Leon."

Leon scanned the letter. It was dated "July 21st, 1912," and bore, in the lower left-hand corner, the seal of the Portuguese Colonial Office. He read it through rapidly and at the end looked up with a sigh of satisfaction.

"And this settles Oberzohn and Co., and robs them of a fortune, the extent of which I think we shall discover when we read Barberton's letter."

He lit a cigarette and scanned the writing again, whilst Meadows, who did not understand Leon's passion for drama, waited with proving impatience.

"Illustrious Senhor," began Leon, reading. "I have this day had the honour of placing before His Excellency the President, and the Ministers of the Cabinet, your letter dated May 15th, 1912. By a letter dated January 8th, 1911, the lands marked Ex. 275 on the Survey Map of the Biskara district were conceded to you, Illustrious Senhor, in order to further the cause of science—a cause which is very dear to the heart of His Excellency the President. Your further letter, in which you

WRITTEN IN BRAILLE 155

complain, Illustrious Senhor, that the incursion of prospectors upon our land is hampering your scientific work, and your request that an end may be put to these annoyances by the granting to you of an extension of the concession, so as to give you title to all mineral found in the aforesaid area, Ex. 275 on the Survey Map of Biskara, and thus making the intrusion of prospectors illegal, has been considered by the Council, and the extending concession is hereby granted, on the following conditions: The term of the concession shall be for twelve years, as from the 14th day of June, 1912, and shall be renewable by you, your heirs or nominees, every twelfth year, on payment of a nominal sum of 1,000 milreis. In the event of the concessionaire, his heirs or nominees, failing to apply for a renewal on the 14th day of June, 1924, the mineral rights of the said area, Ex. 275 on the Survey Map of Biskara, shall be open to claim in accordance with the laws of Angola—"

Leon sat back.

"Fourteenth of June?" he said, and looked up. "Why, that is next week—five days! We've cut it rather fine, George."

"Barberton said there were six weeks," said Manfred. "Obviously he made the mistake of timing the concession from July 21st—the date of the letter. He must have been the most honest man in the world; there was no other reason why he should have communicated with Miss Leicester. He could have kept quiet and claimed the rights for himself. Go on Leon."

"That is about all," said Leon, glancing at the tail of the letter. "The rest is more or less flowery and complimentary and has reference to the scientific work in which Professor Leicester was engaged. Five days—phew!" he whistled.

"We may now find something in Barberton's long narrative to give us an idea of the value of this property." Manfred turned the numerous pages. "Do any of you gentlemen write shorthand?"

Meadows went out into the hall and brought back an officer. Waiting until he had found pencil and paper, Leon began the extraordinary story of William Barberton—most extraordinary because every word had been patiently and industrially punched in the Braille characters.

18

THE STORY OF MONT D'OR

"Dear Friend Johnny,

"I have such a lot to tell you that I hardly know where to begin. I've struck rich at last, and the dream I've often talked over with you has come true. First of all, let me tell you that I have come upon nearly £50,000 worth of wrought gold. We've been troubled round here with lions, one of which took away a carrier of mine, and at last I decided to go out and settle accounts with this fellow. I found him six miles from the camp and planted a couple of bullets into him without killing him, and decided to follow up his spoor. It was a mad thing to do, trailing a wounded lion in the jungle, and I didn't realize how mad until we got out of the bush into the hills and I found Mrs Lion waiting for me. She nearly got me too. More by accident than anything else, I managed to shoot her dead at the first shot, and got another pot at her husband as he was slinking into a cave which was near our tent.

"As I had gone so far, I thought I might as well go the whole hog, especially as I'd seen two lion cubs playing around the mouth of the cave, and bringing up my boys, who were scared to death, I crawled in, to find, as I expected, that the old lion was nearly gone, and a shot

finished him. I had to kill the cubs: they were too young to be left alone, and too much of a nuisance to bring back to camp. This cave had been used as a lair for years; it was full of bones, human amongst them.

"*But what struck me was the appearance of the roof, which, I was almost certain, had been cut out by hand. It was like a house, and there was a cut door in the rock at the back. I made a torch and went through on a tour of inspection, and you can imagine my surprise when I found myself in a little room with a line of stone niches or shelves. There were three lines on each side. Standing on these at intervals there were little statuettes. They were so covered with dust that I thought they were stone, until I tried to take one down to examine it; then I knew by its weight that it was gold, as they all were.*

"*I didn't want my boys to know about my find, because they are a treacherous lot, so I took the lightest, after weighing them all with a spring balance, and made a note where I'd taken it from. You might think that was enough of a find for one man in a lifetime, but my luck had set in. I sent the boys back and ordered them to break camp and join me on top of the Thaba. I called it the Thaba, because it is rather like a hill I know in Basutoland, and is one of two.*

"*The camp was moved up that night; it was a better pitch than any we had had. There was water, plenty of small game, and no mosquitoes. The worst part of it was the terrific thunderstorms which come up from nowhere, and until you've seen one in this ironstone country you don't know what a thunderstorm is like! The hill opposite was slightly smaller than the one I had taken as a camp, and between was a shallow valley, through which ran a small shallow river—rapids would be a better word.*

"*Early the next morning I was looking round through my glasses, and saw what I thought was a house on the opposite hill. I asked my head-man who lived there, and he told me that it was once the house of the Star Chief; and I remembered that somebody told me, down in Mossamedes, that an astronomer had settled in this neighbourhood and had been murdered by the natives. I thought I would go over and have a look at the place. The day being cloudy and not too hot, I took my gun and a couple of boys and we crossed the river and began climbing the hill. The house was, of course, in ruins; it had only been a wattle hut at the best of times. Part of it was covered with vegetation, but out of curiosity I searched round, hoping to pick up a few things that might be useful to me, more particularly kettles, for my boys had burnt holes in every one I had. I found a kettle, and then, turning over a heap of rubbish which I think must have been his bed, I found a little rusty tin box and broke it open with my stick. There were a few letters which were so faded that I could only read a word here and there, and in a green oilskin, a long letter from the Portuguese Government."*

(It was at this point, either by coincidence or design, that the narrative continued on the actual paper to which he referred.)

"I speak Portuguese and can read it as easily as English, and the only thing that worried me about it was that the concession gave Professor Leicester all rights to my cave. My first idea was to burn it, but then I began to realize what a scoundrelly business that would be, and I took the letters out into the sun and tried to find if he had any relations, hoping that I'd be able to fix it up with them to take at any rate 50 per cent. of my find. There was only one letter that helped me. It was written in a child's hand and was evidently from his daughter. It had no address, but there was the name — 'Mirabelle Leicester.'

"I put it in my pocket with the concession and went on searching, but found nothing more. I was going down the hill towards the valley when it struck me that perhaps this man had found gold, and the excuse for getting the concession was a bit of artfulness. I sent a boy back to the camp for a pick, a hammer and a spade, and when he returned I began to make a cutting in the side of the hill. There was nothing to guide me—no outcrop, such as you usually find near a true reef—but I hadn't been digging for an hour before I struck the richest bed of conglomerate I've ever seen. I was either dreaming, or my good angel had at last led me to the one place in the hill where gold could be found. I had previously sent the boys back to camp and told them to wait for me, because, if I did strike metal, I did not want the fact advertised all over Angola, where they've been looking for gold for years.

"Understand, it was not a reef in the ordinary sense of the word, it was all conglomerate, and the wider I made my cutting, the wider the bed appeared, I took the pick to another part of the hill and dug again, with the same result—conglomerate. It was as though nature had thrown up a huge golden hump in the earth. I covered both cuttings late that night and went back to camp. (I was stalked by a leopard in the low bush, but managed to get him.)

"Early next morning, I started off and tried another spot, and with the same result; first three feet of earth, then about six inches of shale, and then conglomerate. I tried to work through the bed, thinking that it might be just a skin, but I was saved much exertion by coming upon a deep rift in the hill about twenty feet wide at the top and tapering down to about fifty feet below the ground level. This gave me a section to work on, and as near as I can judge, the conglomerate bed is something over fifty feet thick and

I'm not so sure that it doesn't occur again after an interval of twenty feet or more, for I dug more shale and had a showing of conglomerate at the very bottom of the ravine.

"What does this mean, Johnny? It means that we have found a hill of gold; not solid gold, as in the storybooks, but gold that pays ounces and probably pounds to the ton. How the prospectors have missed it all these years I can't understand, unless it is that they've made their cuttings on the north side of the hill, where they have found nothing but slate and sandstone. The little river in the valley must be feet deep in alluvial, for I panned the bed and got eight ounces of pure gold in an hour—and that was by rough-and-ready methods. I had to be careful not to make the boys too curious, and I am breaking camp tomorrow, and I want you to cable or send me £500 to Mossamedes. The statuette I'm bringing home is worth all that. I would bring more, only I can't trust these Angola boys; a lot of them are mission boys and can read Portuguese, and they're too friendly with a half-breed called Villa, who is an agent of Oberzohn & Smitts; the traders and I know these people to be the most unscrupulous scoundrels on the coast.

"I shall be at Mossamedes about three weeks after you get this letter, but I don't want to get back to the coast in a hurry, otherwise people are going to suspect I have made a strike."

Leon put the letter down.

"There is the story in a nutshell, gentlemen," he said. "I don't, for one moment, believe that Mr Barberton showed Villa the letter. It is more likely that one of the educated natives he speaks about saw it and reported it to Oberzohn's agent. Portuguese is the lingua franca of that part of the coast. Barberton was killed to prevent his meeting the girl and telling her of his find—incidentally, of warning her to apply for a renewal of the concession. It wasn't even necessary that they should search his belongings to recover the letter, because once they knew of its existence and the date which Barberton had apparently confounded with the date the letter was written, their work was simply to present an application to the Colonial Office at Lisbon. It was quite different after Barberton was killed, when they learnt or guessed that the letter was in Mr Lee's possession."

Meadows agreed.

"That was the idea behind Oberzohn's engagement of Mirabelle Leicester?"

"Exactly, and it was also behind the attack upon Heavytree Farm. To secure this property they must get her away and keep her hidden either until it is too late for her to apply for a renewal, or until she has been bullied or forced into appointing a nominee."

"Or married," said Leon briskly. "Did that idea occur to you? Our tailor-made friend, Monty Newton, may have had matrimonial intentions. It would have been quite a good stroke of business to secure a wife and a large and auriferous hill at the same time. This, I think, puts a period to the ambitions of Herr Doktor Oberzohn."

He got up from the table and handed the papers to the custody of the detective, and turned with a quizzical smile to his friend.

"George, do you look forward with any pleasure to a two hundred and fifty miles' drive?"

"Are you the chauffeur?" asked George.

"I am the chauffeur," said Leon cheerfully. "I have driven a car for many years and I have not been killed yet. It is unlikely that I shall risk my precious life and yours tonight. Come with me and I promise never to hit her up above sixty except on the real speedways."

Manfred nodded.

"We will stop at Oxley and try to get a 'phone call through to Gloucester," said Leon. "This line is, of course, out of order. They would do nothing so stupid as to neglect the elementary precaution of disconnecting Rath Hall."

At Oxley the big Spanz pulled up before the dark and silent exterior of the inn, and Leon, getting down, brought the half-clad landlord to the door and explained his mission, and also learned that two big cars had passed through half an hour before, going in the direction of London.

"That was the gang. I wonder how they'll explain to their paymaster their second failure?"

His first call was to the house in Curzon Street, but there was no reply. "Ring them again," said Leon. "You left Poiccart there?"

Manfred nodded.

They waited for five minutes; still there was no reply.

"How queer!" said Manfred. "It isn't like Poiccart to leave the house. Get Gloucester."

At this hour of the night the lines are comparatively clear, and in a very short time he heard the Gloucester operator's voice, and a few seconds later the click that told them they were connected with Heavytree Farm. Here there was some delay before the call was answered.

It was not Mirabelle Leicester nor her aunt who spoke. Nor did he recognize the voice of Digby, who had recovered sufficiently to return to duty.

"Who is that?" asked the voice sharply. "Is that you, sergeant?"

"No, it is Mr Meadows," said Leon mendaciously.

"The Scotland Yard gentleman?" It was an eager inquiry.

"I'm Constable Kirk, of the Gloucester Police. My sergeant's been trying to get in touch with you, sir."

"What is the matter?" asked Leon, a cold feeling at his heart.

"I don't know, sir. About half an hour ago, I was riding past here—I'm one of the mounted men—and I saw the door wide open and all the lights on, and when I came in there was nobody up. I woke Miss Goddard and Mr Digby, but the young lady was not in the house."

"Lights everywhere?" asked Leon quickly.

"Yes, sir—in the parlour at any rate."

"No sign of a struggle?"

"No, sir; but a car passed me three miles from the house and it was going at a tremendous rate. I think she may have been in that. Mr Digby and Miss Goddard have just gone into Gloucester."

"All right, officer. I am sending Mr Gonsalez down to see you," said Leon, and hung up the receiver.

"What is it?" asked George Manfred, who knew that something was wrong by his friend's face.

"They've got Mirabelle Leicester after all," said Leon. "I'm afraid I shall have to break my promise to you, George. That machine of mine is going to travel before daybreak!"

19

AT HEAVYTREE FARM

It had been agreed that, having failed in their attack, and their energies for the moment being directed to Rath Hall, an immediate return of the Old Guard to Heavytree Farm was unlikely. This had been Meadows' view, and Leon and his friend were of the same mind. Only Poiccart, that master strategist, working surely with a queer knowledge of his enemies' psychology, had demurred from this reasoning; but as he had not insisted upon his point of view, Heavytree Farm and its occupants had been left to the care of the local police and the shaken Digby.

Aunt Alma offered to give up her room to the wounded man, but he would not hear of this, and took the spare bedroom, an excellent position for a defender, since it separated Mirabelle's apartment from the pretty little room which Aunt Alma used as a study and sleeping-place.

The staff of Heavytree Farm consisted of an ancient cowman, a cook and a maid, the latter of whom had already given notice and left on the afternoon of the attack. She had, as she told Mirabelle in all seriousness, a weak heart.

"And a weak head too!" snapped Alma. "I should not worry about your heart, my girl, if I were you."

"I was top of my class at school," bridled the maid, touched to the raw by this reflection upon her intelligence.

"It must have been a pretty small class," retorted Alma.

A new maid had been found, a girl who had been thrilled by the likelihood that the humdrum of daily labour would be relieved by exciting events out of the ordinary, and before evening the household had settled down to normality. Mirabelle was feeling the reaction and went to bed early that night, waking as the first slant of sunlight poured through her window. She got up, feeling, she told herself, as well as she had felt in her life. Pulling back the chintz curtains, she looked out upon a still world with a sense of happiness and relief beyond measure. There was nobody in sight. Pools of mist lay in the hollows, and from one white farmstead, far away on the slope of the hill, she saw the blue smoke was rising. It was a morning to remember, and, to catch its spirit the better, she dressed hastily and went down into the garden. As she walked along the path she heard a window pulled open and the bandaged head of Mr Digby appeared.

"Oh, it's you, is it, miss?" he said with relief, and she laughed.

"There is nothing more terrible in sight than a big spider," she said, and pointed to a big flat fellow, who was already spinning his web between the tall hollyhocks. And the first of the bees was abroad.

"If anybody had come last night I shouldn't have heard them," he confessed. "I slept like a dead man." He touched his head gingerly. "It smarts, but the ache is gone," he said, not loth to discuss his infirmities. "The doctor said I had a narrow escape; he thought there was a fracture. Would you like me to make some tea, miss, or shall I call the servant?"

She shook her head, but he had already disappeared, and came seeking her in the garden ten minutes later, with a cup of tea in his hand. He told her for the second time that he was a police pensioner and had been in the employ of Gonsalez for three years. The Three paid well, and had, she learned to her surprise, considerable private resources.

"Does it pay them—this private detective business?"

"Lord bless your heart, no, miss!" He scoffed at the idea. "They are very rich men. I thought everybody knew that. They say Mr Gonsalez was worth a million even before the war."

This was astonishing news.

"But why do they do this"—she hesitated—"this sort of thing?"

"It is a hobby, miss," said the man vaguely. "Some people run race-horses, some own yachts—these gentlemen get a lot of pleasure out of their work and they pay well," he added.

Men in the regular employ of the Three Just Men not only received a good wage, but frequently a bonus which could only be described as colossal. Once, after they had rounded up and destroyed a gang of Spanish bank robbers, they had distributed £1,000 to every man who was actively employed. He hinted rather than stated that this money had formed part of the loot which the Three had recovered, and did not seem to think that there was anything improper in this distribution of illicit gains.

"After all, miss," he said philosophically, "when you collect money like that, it's impossible to give it back to the people it came from. This Diego had been holding up banks for years, and banks are not like people—they don't feel the loss of money."

"That's a thoroughly immoral view," said Mirabelle, intent upon her flower-picking.

"It may be, miss," agreed Digby, who had evidently been one of the recipients of bounty, and took a complacent and a tolerant view. "But a thousand pounds is a lot of money."

The day passed without event. From the early evening papers that came from Gloucester she learned of the fire at Oberzohn's, and did not connect the disaster with anything but an accident. She was not sorry. The fire had licked out one ugly from the past. Incidentally it had destroyed a crude painting which was to Dr Oberzohn more precious than any that Leonardo had painted or Raphael conceived, but this she did not know.

It was just before the dinner hour that there came the first unusual incident of the day. Mirabelle was standing by the garden gate, intent upon the glories of the evening sky, which was piled high with red and slate-coloured cumuli. The light was falling and a wet night was promised. But the loveliness of that lavish colouring held her. And then she became dimly aware that a man was coming towards the house from the direction of Gloucester. He walked in the middle of the road slowly, as though he, too, were admiring the view and there was no need to hurry. His hands were behind him, his soft felt hat at the back of his head. A stocky-looking man, but his face was curiously familiar. He turned his unsmiling eyes in her direction, and, looking again at his strong features, at the tiny grey-black moustache under his aquiline nose, she was certain she had seen him before. Perhaps she had passed him in the street, and had retained a subconscious mental picture of him.

He slowed his step until, when he came abreast of her, he stopped.

"This is Heavytree Lane?" he asked, in a deep musical voice.

"No—the lane is the first break in the hedge," she smiled. "I'm afraid it isn't much of a road—generally it is ankle-deep in mud."

He looked past her to the house; his eyes ranged the windows, dropped for a moment upon a climbing clematis, and came back to her.

"I don't know Gloucestershire very well," he said, and added: "You have a very nice house."

"Yes," she said in surprise.

"And a garden." And then, innocently: "Do you grow onions?"

She stared at him and laughed.

"I think we do—I am not sure. My aunt looks after the kitchen garden."

His sad eyes wandered over the house again.

"It is a very nice place," he said, and, lifting his hat, went on.

Digby was out: he had gone for a gentle walk, and, looking up the road after the stranger, she saw the guard appear round a bend in the road, and saw him stop and speak to the stranger. Apparently they knew one another, for they shook hands at meeting, and after a while Digby pointed down the road to where she was standing, and she saw the man nod. Soon after the stranger went out of view. Who could he be? Was it an additional guard that the three men had put to protect her? When Digby came up to her, she asked him. "That gentleman, miss? He is Mr Poiccart."

"Poiccart?" she said, delighted. "Oh, I wish I had known!"

"I was surprised to see him," said the guard. "As a matter of fact, he's the one of the three gentlemen I've met the most. He's generally in Curzon Street, even when the others are away."

Digby had nothing to say about Poiccart except that he was a very quiet gentleman and took no active part in the operations of the Three Just Men.

"I wonder why he wanted to know about onions?" asked the girl thoughtfully. "That sounded awfully mysterious."

It would not have been so mysterious to Leon.

The house retired to bed soon after ten, Alma going the rounds, and examining the new bolts and locks which had been attached that morning to every door which gave ingress to the house.

Mirabelle was unaccountably tired, and was asleep almost as soon as her head touched the pillow.

She heard in her dreams the swish of the rain beating against her window, lay for a long time trying to energise herself to rise and shut the one open window where the curtains were blowing in. Then came the heavier patter against a closed pane, and something rattled on the floor of her room. She sat up. It could not be hail, although there was a rumble of thunder in the distance.

She got out of bed, pulled on her dressing-gown, went to the window, and had all her work to stifle a scream. Somebody was standing on the path below... a woman! She leaned out.

"Who is it?" she asked.

"It is me—I—Joan!" There was a sob in the voice of the girl. Even in that light Mirabelle could see that the girl was drenched. "Don't wake anybody. Come down—I want you."

"What is wrong?" asked Mirabelle in a low voice.

"Everything... everything!"

She was on the verge of hysteria. Mirabelle lit a candle and crossed the room, went downstairs softly, so that Alma should not be disturbed. Putting the candle on the table, she unbarred and unbolted the door, opened it, and as she did so, a man slipped through the half-opened door, his big hands smothering the scream that rose to her lips.

Another man followed and, lifting the struggling girl, carried her into the drawing-room. One of the men took a small iron bottle from his pocket, to which ran a flexible rubber tube ending in a large red cap. Her captor removed his hands just as long as it took to fix the cap over her face. A tiny faucet was turned. Mirabelle felt a puff on her face, a strangely sweet taste, and then her heart began to beat thunderously. She thought she was dying, and writhed desperately to free herself.

* * * * *

"She's all right," said Monty Newton, lifting an eyelid for a second. "Get a blanket." He turned fiercely to the whimpering girl behind him. "Shut up, you!" he said savagely. "Do you want to rouse the whole house?"

A woebegone Joan was whimpering softly, tears running down her face, her hands clasping and unclasping in the agony of her mind.

AT HEAVYTREE FARM

"You told me you weren't going to hurt her!" she sobbed.

"Get out," he hissed, and pointed to the door. She went meekly.

A heavy blanket was wrapped round the unconscious girl, and, lifting her between them, the two men went out into the rain, where the old trolley was waiting, and slid her along the straw-covered floor. In another second the trolley moved off, gathering speed.

By this time the effect of the gas had worn off and Mirabelle had regained consciousness. She put out a hand and touched a woman's knee. "Who is that—Alma?"

"No," said a miserable voice, "it's Joan."

"Joan? Oh, yes, of course... why did you do it?—How wicked!"

"Shut up!" Monty snarled. "Wait until you get to—where you're going before you start these 'whys' and 'wherefores.'"

Mirabelle was deathly sick and bemused, and for the next hour she was too ill to feel even alarmed. Her head was going round and round, and ached terribly, and the jolting of the truck did not improve matters in this respect.

Monty, who was sitting with his back to the truck's side, was smoking. He cursed now and then, as some unusually heavy jolt flung him forward. They passed through the heart of the storm: the flicker of lightning was almost incessant and the thunder was deafening. Rain was streaming down the hood of the trolley, rendering it like a drum.

Mirabelle fell into a sleep and woke feeling better. It was still dark, and she would not have known the direction they were taking, only the driver took the wrong turning coming through a country town, and by the help of the lightning she saw what was indubitably the stand of a race-track, and a little later saw the word "Newbury." They were going towards London, she realized.

At this hour of the morning there was little or no traffic, and when they turned on to the new Great West Road a big car went whizzing past at seventy miles an hour and the roar of it woke the girl. Now she could feel the trolley wheels skidding on tramlines. Lights appeared with greater frequency. She saw a store window brilliantly illuminated, the night watchman having evidently forgotten to turn off the lights at the appointed hour.

Soon they were crossing the Thames. She saw the red and green lights of a tug, and black upon near black a string of barges in mid-stream. She dozed again and was jerked wide awake when the trolley swayed and skidded over a surface more uneven than any. Once its wheels went into a pothole and she was flung violently against the side. Another time it skidded and was brought up with a crash against some obstacle. The bumping grew more gentle, and then the machine stopped, and Monty jumped down and called to her sharply.

Her head was clear now, despite its throbbing. She saw a queer-shaped house, all gables and turrets, extraordinarily narrow for its height. It seemed to stand in the middle of a field. And yet it was in London: she could see the glow of furnace fires and hear the deep boom of a ship's siren as it made its way down the river on the tide.

She had not time to take observations, for Monty fastened to her arm and she squelched through the mud up a flight of stone steps into a dimly lit hall. She had a confused idea that she had seen little dogs standing on the side of the steps, and a big bird with a long bill, but these probably belonged to the smoke dreams which the gas had left.

Monty opened a door and pushed her in before him, and she stared into the face of Dr Oberzohn.

He wore a black velvet dressing-gown that had once been a regal garment but was now greasy and stained. On his egg-shaped head he had an embroidered smoking-cap. His feet were encased in warm velvet slippers. He put down the book he had been reading, rubbed his glasses on one velvet sleeve, and then:

"So!" he said.

He pointed to the remains of a fire.

"Sit down, Mirabelle Leicester, and warm yourself. You have come quickly, my friend."—he addressed Monty.

"I'm black and blue all over," growled Newton. "Why couldn't we have a car?"

"Because the cars were engaged, as I told you."

"Did you—" began Newton quickly, but the old man glanced significantly at the girl, shivering before the fire and warming her hands mechanically.

"I will answer, but you need not ask, in good time. This is not of all moments the most propitious. Where is your woman?"

He had forgotten Joan, and went out to find her shivering in the passage.

"Do you want her?" he asked, poking his head in the door.

"She shall go with this girl. You will explain."

"Where are you going to put her?"

Oberzohn pointed to the floor.

"Here? But—"

"No, no. My friend, you are too quick to see what is not meant. The gracious lady shall live in a palace—I have a certain friend who will no longer need it."

His face twitched in the nearest he ever approached to a smile. Groping under the table, he produced a pair of muddy Wellingtons, kicked off his slippers and pulled on the boots with many gasps and jerks.

"All that they need is there: I have seen to it. March!"

He led the way out of the room, pulling the girl to her feet, and Newton followed, Joan bringing up the rear. Inside the factory, Oberzohn produced a small hand torch from his pocket and guided them through the debris till he came to that part of the floor where the trap was. With his foot he moved the covering of rubbish, pulled up the trap and went down.

"I can't go down there, Monty, I can't!" said Joan's agitated voice. "What are you going to do with us? My God! If I'd known—"

"Don't be a fool," said Newton roughly. "What have you got to be afraid of? There's nothing here. We want you to look after her for a day or two. You don't want her to go down by herself: she'd be frightened to death."

Her teeth chattering, Joan stumbled down the steps behind him. Certainly the first view of her new quarters was reassuring. Two little trestle beds had been made; the underground room had been swept clean, and a new carpet laid on the floor. Moreover, the apartment was brilliantly lit, and a furnace gave almost an uncomfortable warmth which was nevertheless very welcome, for the temperature had dropped 20° since noon.

"In this box there are clothes of all varieties, and expensive to purchase," said Oberzohn, pointing to a brand-new trunk at the foot of one of the beds. "Food you will have in plenty—bread and milk newly every day. By night you shall keep the curtain over the ventilator." On the wall was a small black curtain about ten inches square.

Monty took her into the next apartment and showed her the wash-place. There was even a bath, a compulsory fixture under the English Factory Act in a store of this description, where, in the old days, men had to handle certain insanitary products of the Coast.

"But how do we get out, Monty? Where do we get exercise?"

"You'll come out tomorrow night: I'll see to that," he said, dropping his voice. "Now listen, Joan: you've got to be a sensible girl and help me. There's money in this—bigger money than you've ever dreamed of. And when we've got this unpleasant business over, I'm taking you away for a trip round the world."

It was the old promise, given before, never fulfilled, always hoped for. But this time it did not wholly remove her uneasiness.

"But what are you going to do with the girl?" she asked.

AT HEAVYTREE FARM

"Nothing; she will be kept here for a week. I'll swear to you that nothing will happen to her. At the end of a week she's to be released without a hair of her head being harmed."

She looked at him searchingly. As far as she was able to judge, he was speaking the truth. And yet—

"I can't understand it"—she shook her head, and for once Monty Newton was patient with her.

"She's the owner of a big property in Africa, and that we shall get, if things work out right," he said. "The point is that she must claim within a few days. If she doesn't, the property is ours."

Her face cleared.

"Is that all?" She believed him, knew him well enough to detect his rare sincerity. "That's taken a load off my mind, Monty. Of course I'll stay and look after her for you—it makes it easier to know that nothing will happen. What are those baize things behind the furnace—they look like boxes?"

He turned on her quickly.

"I was going to tell you about those," he said. "You're not to touch them under any circumstances. They belong to the old man and he's very stuffy about such things. Leave them just as they are. Let him touch them and nobody else. Do you understand?"

She nodded, and, to his surprise, pecked his cheek with her cold lips.

"I'll help you, boy," she said tremulously. "Maybe that trip will come off after all, if—"

"If what?"

"Those men—the men you were talking about—the Four Just Men, don't they call themselves? They scare me sick, Monty! They were the people who took her away before, and they'll kill us—even Oberzohn says that. They're after him. Has he"—she hesitated—"has he killed anybody? That snake stuff... you're not in it, are you, Monty?"

She looked more like a child than a sophisticated woman, clinging to his arm, her blue eyes looking pleadingly into his.

"Stuff! What do I know about snakes?" He disengaged himself and came back to where Oberzohn was waiting, a figure of patience.

The girl was lying on the bed, her face in the crook of her arm, and he was gazing at her, his expression inscrutable.

"That is all, then. Good night, gracious ladies."

He turned and marched back towards the step and waved his hand. Monty followed. The girl heard the thud of the trap fall, the scrape of the old man's boots, and then a rumbling sound, which she did not immediately understand. Later, when in a panic she tried the trap, she found that a heavy barrel had been put on top, and that it was immovable.

20

GURTHER REPORTS

Dr Oberzohn had not been to bed for thirty-five years. It was his practice to sleep in a chair, and alternate his dozes with copious draughts from his favourite authors. Mostly the books were about the soul, and free will, and predestination, with an occasional dip into Nietzsche by way of light recreation. In ordinary circumstances he would have had need for all the philosophy he could master; for ruin had come. The destruction of his store, which, to all intents and purposes, was uninsured, would have been the crowning stroke of fate but for the golden vision ahead.

Villa, that handsome half-breed, had arrived in England and had been with the doctor all the evening. At that moment he was on his way to Liverpool to catch the Coast boat, and he had left with his master a record of the claims that had already been pegged out on Monto Doro, as he so picturesquely renamed the new mountain. There were millions there; uncountable wealth. And between the Herr Doktor and the achievement of this colossal fortune was a life which he had no immediate desire to take. The doctor was a bachelor; women bored him. Yet he was prepared to take the extreme step if by so doing he could doubly ensure his fortune. Mirabelle dead gave him one chance; Mirabelle alive and persuaded, multiplied that chance by a hundred.

He opened the book he was reading at the last page and took out the folded paper. It was a special licence to marry, and had been duly registered at the Greenwich Registrar's Office since the day before the girl had entered his employment. This was his second and most powerful weapon. He could have been legally married on this nearly a week ago. It was effective for two months at least, and only five days separated him from the necessity of a decision. If the time expired, Mirabelle could live. It was quite a different matter, killing in cold blood a woman for whom the police would be searching, and with whose disappearance his name would be connected, from that other form of slaying he favoured: the striking down of strange men in crowded thoroughfares. She was not for the snake — as yet.

He folded the paper carefully, put it back in the book and turned the page, when there was a gentle tap at the door and he sat up.

"Come in, Pfeiffer. March!"

The door opened slowly and a man sidled into the room, and at the sight of him Dr Oberzohn gasped.

"Gurther!" he stammered, for once thrown out of his stride.

Gurther smiled and nodded, his round eyes fixed on the tassel of the Herr Doktor's smoking-cap.

"You have returned — and failed?"

"The American, I think, is dead, Herr Doktor," said the man in staccato tone. "The so excellent Pfeiffer is also — dead!"

The doctor blinked twice.

"Dead?" he said gratingly. "Who told you this?"

"I saw him. Something happened... to the snake. Pfeiffer was bitten."

The old man's hard eyes fixed him.

"So!" he said softly.

"He died very quickly — in the usual manner," jerked Gurther, still with that stupid smile.

"So!" said the doctor again. "All then was failure, and out of it comes an American, who is nothing, and Pfeiffer, who is much—dead!"

"God have him in His keeping!" said Gurther, not lowering or raising his eyes. "And all the way back I thought this, Herr Doktor—how much better that it should be Pfeiffer and not me. Though my nerves are so bad."

"So!" said the doctor for the fourth time, and held out his hand.

Gurther slipped his fingers into his waistcoat pocket and took out a gold cigarette-case. The doctor opened it and looked at the five cigarettes that reposed, at the two halves of the long holder neatly lying in their proper place, closed the case with a snap and laid it on the table.

"What shall I do with you, Gurther? Tomorrow the police will come and search this house."

"There is the cellar, Herr Doktor: it is very comfortable there. I would prefer it."

Dr Oberzohn made a gesture like a boy wiping something from a slate.

"That is not possible: it is in occupation," he said. "I must find a new place for you." He stared and mused. "There is the boat," he said.

Gurther's smile did not fade.

The boat was a small barge, which had been drawn up into the private dock of the O.&S. factory, and had been rotting there for years, the playing-ground of rats, the doss-house of the homeless. The doctor saw what was in the man's mind.

"It may be comfortable. I will give you some gas to kill the rats, and it will only be for five-six days."

"Ja, Herr Doktor."

"For tonight you may sleep in the kitchen. One does not expect—"

There was a thunderous knock on the outer door. The two men looked at one another, but still Gurther grinned.

"I think it is the police," said the doctor calmly.

He got to his feet, lifted the seat of a long hard-looking sofa, disclosing a deep cavity, and Gurther slipped in, and the seat was replaced. This done, the doctor waddled to the door and turned the key.

"Good morning, Inspector Meadows,"

"May I come in?" said Meadows.

Behind him were two police officers, one in uniform.

"Do you wish to see me? Certainly." He held the door cautiously open and only Meadows came in, and preceded the doctor into his study.

"I want Mirabelle Leicester," said Meadows curtly. "She was abducted from her home in the early hours of this morning, and I have information that the car which took her away came to this house. There are tracks of wheels in the mud outside."

"If there are car tracks, they are mine," said the doctor calmly. He enumerated the makes of machines he possessed. "There is another matter: as to cars having come here in the night, I have a sense of hearing, Mr Inspector Meadows, and I have heard many cars in Hangman's Lane—but not in my ground. Also, I'm sure you have not come to tell me of abducted girls, but to disclose to me the miscreant who burnt my store. That is what I expected of you."

"What you expect of me and what you will get will be entirely different propositions," said Meadows unpleasantly. "Now come across, Oberzohn! We know why you want this girl—the whole plot has been blown. You think you'll prevent her from making a claim on the Portuguese Government for the renewal of a concession granted in June, 1912, to her father."

If Dr Oberzohn was shocked to learn that his secret was out, he did not show it by his face. Not a muscle moved.

"Of such matters I know nothing. It is a fantasy, a story of fairies. Yet it must be true, Mr Inspector Meadows, if you say it. No: I think you are deceived by the criminals of Curzon

Street, W. Men of blood and murder, with records that are infamous. You desire to search my house? It is your privilege." He waved his hand. "I do not ask you for the ticket of search. From basement to attic the house is yours."

He was not surprised when Meadows took him at his word, and, going out into the hall, summoned his assistants. They visited each room separately, the old cook and the half-witted Danish girl accepting this visitation as a normal occurrence: they had every excuse to do so, for this was the second time in a fortnight that the house had been visited by the police.

"Now I'll take a look at your room, if you don't mind," said Meadows.

His quick eyes caught sight of the box ottoman against the wall, and the fact that the doctor was sitting thereon added to his suspicions.

"I will look in here, if you please," he said.

Oberzohn rose and the detective lifted the lid. It was empty. The ottoman had been placed against the wall, at the bottom of which was a deep recess. Gurther had long since rolled through the false back.

"You see—nothing," said Oberzohn. "Now perhaps you would like to search my factory? Perhaps amongst the rafters and the burnt girders I may conceal a something. Or the barge in my slipway? Who knows what I may place amongst the rats?"

"You're almost clever," said Meadows, "and I don't profess to be a match for you. But there are three men in this town who are! I'll be frank with you, Oberzohn. I want to put you where I can give you a fair trial, in accordance with the law of this country, and I shall resist, to the best of my ability, any man taking the law into his own hands. But whether you're innocent or guilty, I wouldn't stand in your shoes for all the money in Angola!"

"So?" said the doctor politely.

"Give up this girl, and I rather fancy that half your danger will be at an end. I tell you, you're too clever for me. It's a stupid thing for a police officer to say, but I can't get at the bottom of your snake. They have."

The old man's brows worked up and down.

"Indeed?" he said blandly. "And of which snake do you speak?"

Meadows said nothing more. He had given his warning: if Oberzohn did not profit thereby, he would be the loser.

Nobody doubted, least of all he, that, in defiance of all laws that man had made, independent of all the machinery of justice that human ingenuity had devised, inevitable punishment awaited Oberzohn and was near at hand.

21

THE ACCOUNT BOOK

It was five o'clock in the morning when the mud-spattered Spanz dropped down through the mist and driving rain of the Chiltern Hills and struck the main Gloucester Road, pulling up with a jerk before Heavytree Farm. Manfred sprang out, but before he could reach the door, Aunt Alma had opened it, and by the look of her face he saw that she had not slept that night.

"Where is Digby?" he asked.

"He's gone to interview the Chief Constable," said Alma. "Come in, Mr Gonsalez."

Leon was wet from head to foot: there was not a dry square centimetre upon him. But he was his old cheerful self as he stamped into the hall, shaking himself free of his heavy mackintosh.

"Digby, of course, heard nothing, George."

"I'm the lightest sleeper in the world," said Aunt Alma, "but I heard not a sound. The first thing I knew was when a policeman came up and knocked at my door and told me that he'd found the front door open."

"No clue was left at all?"

"Yes," said Aunt Alma. They went into the drawing-room and she took up from the table a small black bottle with a tube and cap attached. "I found this behind the sofa. She'd been lying on the sofa; the cushions were thrown on the floor and she tore the tapestry in her struggle."

Leon turned the faucet, and, as the gas hissed out, sniffed.

"The new dental gas," he said. "But how did they get in? No window was open or forced?"

"They came in at the door: I'm sure of that. And they had a woman with them," said Aunt Alma proudly.

"How do you know?"

"There must have been a woman," said Aunt Alma. "Mirabelle would not have opened the door except to a woman, without waking either myself or Mr Digby."

Leon nodded, his eyes gleaming.

"Obviously," he said.

"And I found the marks of a woman's foot in the passage. It is dried now, but you can still see it."

"I have already seen it," said Leon. "It is to the left of the door: a small pointed shoe and a rubber heel. Miss Leicester opened the door to the woman, the men came in, and the rest was easy. You can't blame Digby," he said appealingly to George.

He was the friend at court of every agent, but this time Manfred did not argue with him.

"I blame myself," he said. "Poiccart told me—"

"He was here," said Aunt Alma.

"Who—Poiccart? asked Manfred, surprised, and Gonsalez slapped his knee.

"That's it, of course! What fools we are! We ought to have known why this wily old fox had left his post. What time was he here?"

Alma told him all the circumstances of the visit.

"He must have left the house immediately after us," said Leon, with a wide grin of amusement, "caught the five o'clock train for Gloucester, taxied across."

"And after that?" suggested Manfred.

Leon scratched his chin.

"I wonder if he's back?" He took up the telephone and put a trunk call through to London. "Somehow I don't think he is. Here's Digby, looking as if he expected to be summarily executed."

The police pensioner was indeed in a mournful and pathetic mood.

"I don't know what you'll think of me, Mr Manfred—" he began.

"I've already expressed a view on that subject." George smiled faintly. "I'm not blaming you, Digby. To leave a man who has been knocked about as you have been without an opposite number was the height of folly. I didn't expect them back so soon. As a matter of fact, I intended putting four men on from today. You've been making inquiries?"

"Yes, sir. The car went through Gloucester very early in the morning and took the Swindon road. It was seen by a cyclist policeman; he said there was a fat roll of tarpaulin lying on the tent of the trolley."

"No sign of anybody chasing it in a car, or on a motor-bicycle?" asked Manfred anxiously.

Poiccart had recently taken to motor-cycling.

"No, sir."

"You saw Mr Poiccart?"

"Yes, he was just going back to London. He said he wanted to see the place with his own eyes."

George was disappointed. If it had been a visit of curiosity, Poiccart's absence from town was understandable. He would not have returned at the hour he was rung up.

Aunt Alma was cooking a hasty breakfast, and they had accepted her offering gratefully, for both men were famished; and they were in the midst of the meal when the London call came through.

"Is that you, Poiccart?"

"That is I," said Poiccart's voice. "Where are you speaking from?"

"Heavytree Farm. Did you see anything of Miss Leicester?"

There was a pause.

"Has she gone?"

"You didn't know?"

Another pause.

"Oh, yes, I knew; in fact, I accompanied her part of the way to London, and was bumped off when the trolley struck a refuge on the Great West Road. Meadows is here: he has just come from Oberzohn's. He says he has found nothing."

Manfred thought for a while.

"We will be back soon after nine," he said.

"Leon driving you?" was the dry response.

"Yes—in spite of which we shall be back at nine."

"That man has got a grudge against my driving," said Leon, when Manfred reported the conversation. "I knew it was he when Digby described the car and said there was a fat roll of mackintosh on the top. 'Fat roll' is not a bad description. Do you know whether Poiccart spoke to Miss Leicester?"

"Yes, he asked her if she grew onions."—a reply which sent Leon into fits of silent laughter.

Breakfast was over and they were making their preparations for departure, when Leon asked unexpectedly: "Has Miss Leicester a writing-table of her own?"

"Yes, in her room," said Alma, and took him up to show him the old bureau.

He opened the drawers without apology, took out some old letters, turned them over, reading them shamelessly. Then he opened the blotter. There were several sheets of blank paper headed "Heavytree Farm," and two which bore her signature at the bottom. Alma explained that the bank account of the establishment was in Mirabelle's name, and, when it was necessary to draw cash, it was a rule of the bank that it should be accompanied by a covering letter—a practice which still exists in some of the old West-country banking establishments. She unlocked a drawer that he had not been able to open and showed him a cheque-book with three blank cheques signed with her name.

"That banker has known me since I was so high," said Alma scornfully. "You wouldn't think there'd be so much red-tape."

Leon nodded.

"Do you keep any account books?"

"Yes, I do," said Alma in surprise. "The household accounts, you mean?"

"Could I see one?"

She went out and returned with a thin ledger, and he made a brief examination of its contents. Wholly inadequate, thought Alma, considering the trouble she had taken and the interest he had shown.

"That's that," he said. "Now, George, en voiture!"

"Why did you want to see the account book?" asked Manfred as they bowled up the road.

"I am naturally commercial-minded," was the unsatisfactory reply. "And, George, we're short of juice. Pray like a knight in armour that we sight a filling station in the next ten minutes."

If George had prayed, the prayer would have been answered: just as the cylinders started to miss they pulled up the car before a garage, and took in a supply which was more than sufficient to carry them to their destination. It was nine o'clock exactly when the car stopped before the house. Poiccart, watching the arrival from George's room, smiled grimly at the impertinent gesture of the chauffeur.

Behind locked doors the three sat in conference.

"This has upset all my plans," said Leon at last. "If the girl was safe, I should settle with Oberzohn tonight."

George Manfred stroked his chin thoughtfully. He had once worn a trim little beard, and had never got out of that beard-stroking habit of his.

"We think exactly alike. I intended suggesting that course," he said gravely.

"The trouble is Meadows. I should like the case to have been settled one way or the other, and for Meadows to be out of it altogether. One doesn't wish to embarrass him. But the urgency is very obvious. It would have been very easy," said Leon, a note of regret in his gentle voice. "Now of course it is impossible until the girl is safe. But for that"—he shrugged his shoulders—"tomorrow friend Oberzohn would have experienced a sense of lassitude. No pain... just a little tiredness. Sleep, coma—death on the third day. He is an old man, and one has no desire to hurt the aged. There is no hurt like fear. As for Gurther, we will try a more violent method, unless Oberzohn gets him first. I sincerely hope he does."

"This is news to me. What is this about Gurther?" asked Poiccart.

Manfred told him.

"Leon is right now," Poiccart nodded. He rose from the table and unlocked the door. "If any of you men wish to sleep, your rooms are ready; the curtains are drawn, and I will wake you at such and such an hour."

But neither was inclined for sleep. George had to see a client that morning: a man with a curious story to tell. Leon wanted a carburettor adjusted. They would both sleep in the afternoon, they said.

The client arrived soon after. Poiccart admitted him and put him in the dining-room to wait before he reported his presence.

"I think this is your harem man," he said, and went downstairs to show up the caller.

He was a commonplace-looking man with a straggling, fair moustache and a weak chin.

"Debilitated or degenerate," he suggested.

"Probably a little of both," assented Manfred, when the butler had announced him.

He came nervously into the room and sat down opposite to Manfred.

"I tried to get you on the 'phone last night," he complained, "but I got no answer."

"My office hours are from ten till two!" said George good-humouredly. "Now will you tell me again this story of your sister?"

The man leaned back in the chair and clasped his knees, and began in a sing-song voice, as though he were reciting something that he had learned by heart.

"We used to live in Turkey. My father was a merchant of Constantinople, and my sister, who went to school in England, got extraordinary ideas, and came back a most violent pro-Turk. She is a very pretty girl and she came to know some of the best Turkish families, although my father and I were dead against her going about with these people. One day she went to call on Hymer Pasha, and that night she didn't come back. We went to the Pasha's house and asked for her, but he told us she had left at four o'clock. We then consulted the police, and they told us, after they had made investigations, that she had been seen going on board a ship which left for Odessa the same night. I hadn't seen her for ten years, until I went down to the Gringo Club, which is a little place in the East End—not high class, you understand, but very well conducted. There was a cabaret show after midnight, and whilst I was sitting there, thinking about going home—very bored, you understand, because that sort of thing doesn't appeal to me—I saw a girl come out from behind a curtain dressed like a Turkish woman, and begin a dance. She was in the middle of the dance when her veil slipped off. It was Marie! She recognized me at once, and darted through the curtains. I tried to follow her, but they held me back."

"Did you go to the police?" asked Manfred.

The man shook his head.

"No, what is the use of the police?" he went on in a monotonous tone. "I had enough of them in Constantinople, and I made up my mind that I would get outside help. And then somebody told me of you, and I came along. Mr Manfred, is it impossible for you to rescue my sister? I'm perfectly sure that she is being detained forcibly and against her will."

"At the Gringo Club?" asked Manfred.

"Yes," he nodded.

"I'll see what I can do," said George. "Perhaps my friends and I will come down and take a look round some evening. In the meantime will you go back to your friend Dr Oberzohn and tell him that you have done your part and I will do mine? Your little story will go into my collection of Unplausible Inventions!"

He touched a bell and Poiccart came in.

"Show Mr Liggins out, please. Don't hurt him—he may have a wife and children, though it is extremely unlikely."

The visitor slunk from the room as though he had been whipped.

The door had scarcely closed upon him when Poiccart called Leon down from his room.

"Son," he said, "George wants that man trailed."

Leon peeped out after the retiring victim of Turkish tyranny.

"Not a hard job," he said. "He has flat feet!"

Poiccart returned to the consulting-room. "Who is he?" he asked.

"I don't know. He's been sent here either by Oberzohn or by friend Newton, the general idea being to bring us all together at the Gringo Club—which is fairly well known to me—on some agreeable evening. A bad actor! He has no tone. I shouldn't be surprised if Leon finds something very interesting about him."

"He's been before, hasn't he?" Manfred nodded.

"Yes, he was here the day after Barberton came. At least, I had his letter the next morning and saw him for a few moments in the day. Queer devil, Oberzohn! And an industrious devil," he added. "He sets everybody moving at once, and of course he's right. A good general doesn't attack with a platoon, but with an army, with all his strength, knowing that if he fails to pierce the line at one point he may succeed at another. It's an interesting thought, Raymond, that at this moment there are probably some twenty separate and independent agencies working for our undoing. Most of them ignorant that their efforts are being duplicated. That is Oberzohn's way—always has been his way. It's the way he has started revolutions, the way he has organized religious riots."

After he had had his bath and changed, he announced his intention of calling at Chester Square.

"I'm rather keen on meeting Joan Newton again, even if she has returned to her normal state of Jane Smith."

Miss Newton was not at home, the maid told him when he called. Would he see Mr Montague Newton, who was not only at home, but anxious for him to call, if the truth be told, for he had seen his enemy approaching.

"I shall be pleased," murmured Manfred, and was ushered into the splendour of Mr Newton's drawing-room.

"Too bad about Joan," said Mr Newton easily. "She left for the Continent this morning."

"Without a passport?" smiled Manfred.

A little slip on the part of Monty, but how was Manfred to know that the authorities had, only a week before, refused the renewal of her passport pending an inquiry into certain irregularities? The suggestion had been that other people than she had travelled to and from the Continent armed with this individual document.

"You don't need a passport for Belgium," he lied readily. "Anyway, this passport stuff's a bit overdone. We're not at war now."

"All the time we're at war," said Manfred. "May I sit down?"

"Do. Have a cigarette?"

"Let me see the brand before I accept," said Manfred cautiously, and the man guffawed as at a great joke.

The visitor declined the offer of the cigarette-case and took one from a box on the table.

"And is Jane making the grand tour?" he asked blandly.

"Jane's run down and wants a rest."

"What's the matter with Aylesbury?"

He saw the man flinch at the mention of the women's convict establishment, but he recovered instantly. "It is not far enough out, and I'm told that there are all sorts of queer people living round there. No, she's going to Brussels and then on to Aix-la-Chapelle, then probably to Spa—I don't suppose I shall see her again for a month or two."

"She was at Heavytree Farm in the early hours of this morning," said Manfred, "and so were you. You were seen and recognized by a friend of mine—Mr Raymond Poiccart. You travelled from Heavytree Farm to Oberzohn's house in a Ford trolley."

Not by a flicker of an eyelid did Monty Newton betray his dismay.

"That is bluff," he said. "I didn't leave this house last night. What happened at Heavytree Farm?"

"Miss Leicester was abducted. You are surprised, almost agitated, I notice."

"Do you think I had anything to do with it?" asked Monty steadily.

"Yes, and the police share my view. A provisional warrant was issued for your arrest this morning. I thought you ought to know."

Now the man drew back, his face went from red to white, and then to a deeper red again. Manfred laughed softly.

"You've got a guilty conscience, Newton," he said, "and that's half-way to being arrested. Where is Jane?"

"Gone abroad, I tell you."

He was thrown off his balance by this all too successful bluff and had lost some of his self-possession.

"She is with Mirabelle Leicester: of that I'm sure," said Manfred. "I've warned you twice, and it is not necessary to warn you a third time. I don't know how far deep you're in these snake murders: a jury will decide that sooner or later. But you're dead within six hours of my learning that Miss Leicester has been badly treated. You know that is true, don't you?"

Manfred was speaking very earnestly.

"You're more scared of us than you are of the law, and you're right, because we do not put our men to the hazard of a jury's intelligence. You get the same trial from us as you get from a judge who knows all the facts. You can't beat an English judge, Newton."

The smile returned and he left the room. Fred, near at hand, waiting in the passage but at a respectful distance from the door, let him out with some alacrity.

Monty Newton turned his head sideways, caught a fleeting glimpse of the man he hated—hated worse than he hated Leon Gonsalez—and then called harshly for his servant.

"Come here," he said, and Fred obeyed. "They'll be sending round to make inquiries, and I want you to know what to tell them," he said. "Miss Joan went away this morning to the Continent by the eight-fifteen. She's either in Brussels or Aix-la-Chapelle. You're not sure of the hotel, but you'll find out. Is that clear to you?"

"Yes, sir."

Fred was looking aimlessly about the room.

"What's the matter with you?"

"I was wondering where the clock is."

"Clock?" Now Monty Newton heard it himself. The tick-tick-tick of a cheap clock, and he went livid. "Find it," he said hoarsely, and even as he spoke his eyes fell upon the little black box that had been pushed beneath the desk, and he groped for the door with a scream of terror.

Passers-by in Chester Square saw the door flung open and two men rush headlong into the street. And the little American clock, which Manfred had purchased a few days before, went on ticking out the time, and was still ticking merrily when the police experts went in and opened the box. It was Manfred's oldest jest, and never failed.

22

IN THE STORE CELLAR

It was impossible that Mirabelle Leicester could fail to realize the serious danger in which she stood. Why she had incurred the enmity of Oberzohn, for what purpose this man was anxious to keep her under his eye, she could not even guess. It was a relief to wake up in the early morning, as she did, and find Joan sleeping in the same room; for though she had many reasons for mistrusting her, there was something about this doll-faced girl that made an appeal to her.

Joan was lying on the bed fully dressed, and at the sound of the creaking bed she turned and got up, fastening her skirt.

"Well, how do you like your new home?" she asked, with an attempt at joviality, which she was far from feeling, in spite of Monty's assurances.

"I've seen better," said Mirabelle coolly.

"I'll bet you have!" Joan stretched and yawned; then, opening one of the cupboards, took a shovelful of coal and threw it into the furnace, clanging the iron door. "That's my job," she said humorously, "to keep you warm."

"How long am I going to be kept here?"

"Five days," was the surprising answer.

"Why five?" asked Mirabelle curiously.

"I don't know. Maybe they'll tell you," said Joan.

She fixed a plug in the wall and turned on the small electric fire. Disappearing, she came back with a kettle which she placed on top of the ring.

"The view's not grand, but the food's good," she said, with a gaiety that Mirabelle was now sure was forced.

"You're with these people, of course—Dr Oberzohn and Newton?"

"Mister Newton," corrected Joan. "Yes, I'm his fiancee. We're going to be married when things get a little better," she said vaguely, "and there's no use in your getting sore with me because I helped to bring you here. Monty's told me all about it. They're going to do you no harm at all."

"Then why—" began Mirabelle.

"He'll tell you," interrupted Joan, "sooner or later. The old man, or—or—well, Monty isn't in this: he's only obliging Oberzohn."

With one thing Mirabelle agreed: it was a waste of time to indulge in recriminations or to reproach the girl for her supreme treachery. After all, Joan owed nothing to her, and had been from the first a tool employed for her detention. It would have been as logical for a convict to reproach the prison guard.

"How do you come to be doing this sort of thing?" she asked, watching the girl making tea.

"Where do you get 'this sort of thing' from?" demanded Joan. "If you suppose that I spend my life chaperoning females, you've got another guess coming. Scared, aren't you?"

She looked across at Mirabelle and the girl shook her head.

"Not really."

"I should be," confessed Joan. "Do you mind condensed milk? There's no other. Yes, I should be writhing under the table, knowing something about Oberzohn."

"If I were Oberzohn," said Mirabelle with spirit, "I should be hiding in a deep hole where the Four Just Men would not find me."

IN THE STORE CELLAR

"Four Just Men!" sneered the girl, and then her face changed. "Were they the people who whipped Gurther?"

Mirabelle had not heard of this exploit, but she gave them credit with a nod.

"Is that so? Does Gurther know they're friends of yours?" she asked significantly.

"I don't know Gurther."

"He's the man who danced with you the other night—Lord—I forget what name we gave him. Because, if he does know, my dear," she said slowly, "you've got two people to be extremely careful with. Gurther's half mad. Monty has always said so. He dopes too, and there are times when he's not a man at all but a low-down wolf. I'm scared of him—I'll admit it. There aren't Four Just Men, anyway," she went off at a tangent. "There haven't been more than three for years. One of them was killed in Bordeaux. That's a town I'd hate to be killed in," said Joan irreverently.

An interval of silence followed whilst she opened an airtight tin and took out a small cake, and, putting it on the table, cut it into slices.

"What are they like?" she asked. Evidently the interval had been filled with thoughts of the men from Curzon Street. "Monty says they're just bluff, but I'm not so sure that Monty tells me all he thinks. He's so scared that he told me to call and see them, just because they gave him an order—which isn't like Monty. They've killed people, haven't they?"

Mirabelle nodded.

"And got away with it? They must be clever." Joan's admiration was dragged from her. "Where do they get their money?"

That was always an interesting matter to Joan.

When the girl explained, she was really impressed. That they could kill and get away with it was wonderful; that they were men of millions placed them in a category apart.

"They'll never find you here," said Joan. "There's nobody living knows about this vault. There used to be eight men working here, sorting monkey hides, and every one of them's dead. Monty told me. He said this place is below the canal level, and Oberzohn can flood it in five minutes. Monty thinks the old man had an idea of running a slush factory here."

"What is a slush factory?" asked Mirabelle, open-mouthed.

"Phoney—snide—counterfeit. Not English, but Continental work. He was going to do that if things had gone really bad, but of course you make all the difference."

Mirabelle put down her cup.

"Does he expect to make money out of me?" she said, trying hard not to laugh.

The girl nodded solemnly.

"Does he think I have a great deal of money?"

"He's sure."

Joan was sure too. Her tone said that plainly enough.

Mirabelle sat down on the bed, for the moment too astonished to speak. Her own financial position was no mystery. She had been left sufficient to bring her in a small sum yearly, and with the produce of the farm had managed to make both ends meet. It was the failure of the farm as a source of profit which had brought her to her new job in London. Alma had also a small annuity; the farm was the girl's property, but beyond these revenues she had nothing. There was not even a possibility that she was an heiress. Her father had been a comparatively poor man, and had been supported in his numerous excursions to various parts of the world in search of knowledge by the scientific societies to which he was attached; his literary earnings were negligible; his books enjoyed only a very limited sale. She could trace her ancestry back for seven generations; knew of her uncles and aunts, and they did not include a single man or woman who, in the best traditions of the story-books, had gone to America and made an immense fortune.

"It is absurd," she said. "I have no money. If Mr Oberzohn puts me up to ransom, it will have to be something under a hundred!"

"Put you up to ransom?" said Joan. "I don't get you there. But you're rich all right—I can tell you that. Monty says so, and Monty wouldn't lie to me."

Mirabelle was bewildered. It seemed almost impossible that a man of Oberzohn's intelligence and sources of information could make such a mistake. And yet Joan was earnest.

"They must have mistaken me for somebody else," she said, but Joan did not answer. She was sitting up in a listening attitude, and her eyes were directed towards the iron door which separated their sleeping apartment from the larger vault. She had heard the creak of the trap turning and the sound of feet coming down the stairs.

Mirabelle rose as Oberzohn came in. He wore his black dressing-gown, his smoking-cap was at the back of his head, and the muddy Wellington boots which he had pulled over his feet looked incongruous, and would at any other time have provoked her to laughter. He favoured her with a stiff nod.

"You have slept well, gracious lady?" he said, and to her amazement took her cold hand in his and kissed it.

She felt the same feeling of revulsion and unreality as had overcome her that night at the dance when Gurther had similarly saluted her.

"It is a nice place, for young people and for old." He looked round the apartment with satisfaction. "Here I should be content to spend my life reading my books, and giving my mind to thought, but"—he spread his hands and shrugged—"what would you? I am a business man, with immense interests in every part of the world. I am rich, too, beyond your dreams! I have stores in every part of the world, and thousands of men and women on my pay-roll."

Why was he telling her all this, she wondered, reciting the facts in a monotonous voice. Surely he had not come down to emphasize the soundness of his financial position?

"I am not very much interested in your business, Mr Oberzohn," she said; "but I want to know why I am being detained here. Surely, if you're so rich, you do not want to hold me to ransom?"

"To ransom?" His forehead went up and down. "That is foolish talk. Did she tell you?" He pointed at the girl, and his face went as black as thunder.

"No, I guessed," said Mirabelle quickly, not wishing to get her companion into bad odour.

"I do not hold you to ransom. I hold you, lovely lady, because you are good for my eyes. Did not Heine say, 'The beauty of women is a sedative to the soul'? You should read Heine: he is frivolous, but in his stupidity there are many clever thoughts. Now tell me, lovely lady, have you all you desire?"

"I want to go out," she said. "I can't stay in this underground room without danger to my health."

"Soon you shall go." He bowed stiffly again, and shuffled across the floor to the furnace. Behind this were the two baize covered boxes, and one he lifted tenderly. "Here are secrets such as you should not pry into," he said in his awkward English. "The most potent of chemicals, colossal in power. The ignorant would touch them and they would explode—you understand?"

He addressed Mirabelle, who did not understand but made no answer.

"They must be kept warm for that reason. One I take, the other I leave. You shall not touch it—that is understood? My good friend has told you?" He brought his eyes to Joan.

"I understand all right," she said. "Listen, Oberzohn: when am I going out for a walk? This place is getting on my nerves already."

"Tonight you shall exercise with the lovely lady. I myself will accompany you."

"Why am I here, Mr Oberzohn?" Mirabelle asked again.

"You are here because you are in danger," said Oberzohn, holding the green box under his arm. "You are in very great danger." He nodded with every word. "There are certain men, of all the most infamous, who have a design upon your life. They are criminal, cunning and wise—but not so cunning or wise as Dr Oberzohn. Because I will not let you fall into their hands I keep you here, young miss. Good morning."

Again he bowed stiffly and went out, the iron door clanging behind him. They heard him climbing the stairs, the thud of the trap as it fell, and the rumble which Joan, at any rate, knew was made by the cement barrel being rolled to the top of the trap.

"Pleasant little fellow, isn't he?" said Joan bitterly. "Him and his chemicals!" She glared down at the remaining box. "If I were sure it wouldn't explode, I should smash it to smithereens!" she said.

Later she told the prisoner of Oberzohn's obsession; of how he spent time and money in his search for the vital elixir.

"Monty thinks he'll find it," she said seriously. "Do you know, that old man has had an ox stewed down to a pint? There used to be a king in Europe—I forget his name—who had the same stuff, but not so strong. Monty says that Oberzohn hardly ever takes a meal—just a teaspoonful of this dope and he's right for the day. And Monty says..."

For the rest of that dreary morning the girl listened without hearing to the wise sayings and clever acts of Monty; and every now and again her eyes strayed to the baize-covered box which contained "the most potent chemicals," and she wondered whether, in the direst extremity, she would be justified in employing these dread forces for her soul's salvation.

23

THE COURIER

Elijah Washington came up to London for a consultation. With the exception of a blue contusion beneath his right eye, he was none the worse for his alarming experience.

Leon Gonsalez had driven him to town, and on the way up the big man had expressed views about snake-bite which were immensely interesting to the man at the wheel. "I've figured it out this way: there is no snake at all. What happens is that these guys have extracted snake venom—and that's easy, by making a poison-snake bite on something soft—and have poisoned a dart or a burr with the venom. I've seen that done in Africa, particularly up in the Ituri country, and it's pretty common in South America. The fellow just throws or shoots it, and just where the dart hits, he gets snake-poisoning right away."

"That is an excellent theory," said Leon, "only—no dart or burr has ever been found. It was the first thing the police looked for in the case of the stockbroker. They had the ground searched for days. And it was just the same in the case of the tramp and the bank clerk, just the same in the case of Barberton. A dart would stick some time and would be found in the man's clothing or near the spot where he was struck down. How do you account for that?"

Mr Washington very frankly admitted that he couldn't account for it at all, and Leon chuckled.

"I can," he said. "In fact, I know just how it's done."

"Great snakes!" gasped Washington in amazement. "Then why don't you tell the police?"

"The police know — now," said Leon. "It isn't snake-bite — it is nicotine poisoning."

"How's that?" asked the startled man, but Leon had his joke to himself.

After a consultation which had lasted most of the night they had brought Washington from Rath Hall, and on the way Leon hinted gently that the Three had a mission for him and hoped he would accept.

"You're much too good a fellow to be put into an unnecessarily dangerous position," he said; "and even if you weren't, we wouldn't lightly risk your blessed life; but the job we should ask you to do isn't exactly a picnic."

"Listen!" said Mr Washington with sudden energy. "I don't want any more snakes — not that kind of snake! I've felt pain in my time, but nothing like this! I know it must have been snake venom, but I'd like to meet the little wriggler who brews the brand that was handed to me, and maybe I'd change my mind about collecting him — alive!"

Leon agreed silently, and for the next few moments was avoiding a street car on one side, a baker's cart on another, and a blah woman who was walking aimlessly in the road, apparently with no other intention than of courting an early death, this being the way of blah women.

"Phew!" said Mr Washington, as the car skidded on the greasy road. "I don't know whether you're a good driver or just naturally under the protection of Providence."

"Both," said Leon, when he had straightened the machine. "All good drivers are that."

Presently he continued:

"It is snake venom all right, Mr Washington; only snake venom that has been most carefully treated by a man who knows the art of concentration of its bad and the extraction of its harmless constituents. My theory is that certain alkaloids are added, and it is possible that there has been a blending of two different kinds of poison. But you're right when you say that no one animal carries in his poison sac that particular variety of death-juice. If it is any value to you, we are prepared to give you a snake-proof certificate!"

"I don't want another experience of that kind," Elijah Washington warned him; but Leon turned the conversation to the state of the road and the problems of traffic control.

There had been nothing seen or heard of Mirabelle, and Meadows' activities had for the moment been directed to the forthcoming inquest on Barberton. Nowadays, whenever he reached Scotland Yard, he moved in a crowd of reporters, all anxious for news of further developments. The Barberton death was still the livest topic in the newspapers: the old scare of the snake had been revived and in some degree intensified. There was not a journal which did not carry columns of letters to the editor denouncing the inactivity of the police. Were they, asked one sarcastic correspondent, under the hypnotic influence of the snake's eyes? Could they not, demanded another, give up trapping speeders on the Lingfield road and bring their mighty brains to the elucidation of a mystery that was to cause every household in London the gravest concern? The Barberton murder was the peg on which every letter-writing faddist had a novel view to hang, and Mr Meadows was not at that time the happiest officer in the force.

"Where is Lee?" asked Washington as they came into Curzon Street.

"He's in town for the moment, but we are moving him to the North of England, though I don't think there is any danger to him, now that Barberton's letters are in our possession. They would have killed him yesterday to prevent our handling the correspondence. Today I should imagine he has no special importance in the eyes of Oberzohn and Company. And here we are!"

Mr Washington got out stiffly and was immediately admitted by the butler. The three men went upstairs to where George Manfred was wrestling with a phase of the problem. He was not alone; Digby, his head swathed in bandages, sat, an unhappy man, on the edge of a chair and answered Leon's cheery greeting with a mournful smile.

"I'm sending Digby to keep observation on Oberzohn's house; and especially do I wish him to search that old boat of his."

He was referring to an ancient barge which lay on the mud at the bottom of Mr Oberzohn's private dock. From the canal there was a narrow waterway into the little factory grounds. It was so long since the small cantilever bridge which covered the entrance had been raised, that locals regarded the bridge floor as part of the normal bank of the canal. But behind the green water-gates was a concrete dock large enough to hold one barge, and here for years a decrepit vessel had wallowed, the hunting-ground of rats and the sleeping-place of the desperately homeless.

"The barge is practically immovable: I've already reported on that," said Leon.

"It certainly has that appearance, and yet I would like a search," replied Manfred. "You understand that this is night duty, and I have asked Meadows to notify the local inspector that you will be on duty—I don't want to be pulled out of my bed to identify you at the Peckham police station. It isn't a cheerful job, but you might be able to make it interesting by finding your way into his grounds. I don't think the factory will yield much, but the house will certainly be a profitable study to an observer of human nature."

"I hope I do better this time, Mr Manfred," said Digby, turning to go. "And, if you don't mind, I'll go by day and take a look at the place. I don't want to fall down this time!"

George smiled as he rose and shook the man's hand at parting. "Even Mr Gonsalez makes mistakes," he said maliciously, and Leon looked hurt.

Manfred tidied some papers on his desk and put them into a drawer, waiting for Poiccart's return. When he had come: "Now, Mr Washington, we will tell you what we wish you to do. We wish you to take a letter to Lisbon. Leon has probably hinted something to that effect, and it is now my duty to tell you that the errand is pretty certain to be an exceedingly dangerous one, but you are the only man I know to whom I could entrust this important document. I feel I cannot allow you to undertake this mission without telling you that the chances are heavily against your reaching Portugal."

"Bless you for those cheerful words," said Washington blankly. "The only thing I want to be certain about is, am I likely to meet Mr Snake?"

Manfred nodded, and the American's face lengthened.

"I don't know that even that scares me," he said at last, "especially now that I know that the dope they use isn't honest snake-spit at all but a synthesized poison. It was having my confidence shaken in snakes that rattled me. When do you want me to go?"

"Tonight."

Mr Washington for the moment was perplexed, and Manfred continued: "Not by the Dover-Calais route. We would prefer that you travelled by Newhaven-Dieppe. Our friends are less liable to be on the alert, though I can't even guarantee that. Oberzohn spends a lot of money in espionage. This house has been under observation for days. I will show you."

He walked to the window and drew aside the curtain.

"Do you see a spy?" he asked, with a twinkle in his eye.

THE COURIER

Mr Washington looked up and down the street.

"Sure!" he said. "That man at the corner smoking a cigar—"

"Is a detective officer from Scotland Yard," said Manfred. "Do you see anybody else?"

"Yes," said Washington after a while, "there's a man cleaning windows on the opposite side of the road: he keeps looking across here."

"A perfectly innocent citizen," said Manfred.

"Well, he can't be in any of those taxis, because they're empty." Mr Washington nodded to a line of taxis drawn up on the rank in the centre of the road.

"On the contrary, he is in the first taxi on the rank—he is the driver! If you went out and called a cab, he would come to you. If anybody else called him, he would be engaged. His name is Clarke, he lives at 43, Portlington Mews; he is an ex-convict living apart from his wife, and he receives seven pounds a week for his services, ten pounds every time he drives Oberzohn's car, and all the money he makes out of his cab."

He smiled at the other's astonishment.

"So the chances are that your movements will be known; even though you do not call the cab, he will follow you. You must be prepared for that. I'm putting all my cards on the table, Mr Washington, and asking you to do something which, if you cannot bring yourself to agree, must be done by either myself, Poiccart or Gonsalez. Frankly, none of us can be spared."

"I'll go," said the American. "Snake or no snake, I'm for Lisbon. What is my route?"

Poiccart took a folded paper from his pocket.

"Newhaven, Dieppe, Paris. You have a reserved compartment on the Sud Express; you reach Valladolid late tomorrow night, and change to the Portuguese mail. Unless I can fix an aeroplane to meet you at Irun. We are trying now. Otherwise, you should be in Lisbon at two o'clock on the following afternoon. He had better take the letter now, George."

Manfred unlocked the wall safe and took out a long envelope. It was addressed to "Senhor Alvaz Manuel y Cintra, Minister of Colonies," and was heavily sealed.

"I want you to place this in Senhor Cintra's hands. You'll have no difficulty there because you will be expected," he said. "Will you travel in that suit?"

The American thought.

"Yes, that's as good as any," he said.

"Will you take off your jacket?"

Mr Washington obeyed, and with a small pair of scissors Manfred cut a slit in the lining and slipped the letter in. Then, to the American's astonishment, Leon produced a rolled housewife, threaded a needle with extraordinary dexterity, and for the next five minutes the snake-hunter watched the deft fingers stitching through paper and lining. So skilfully was the slit sewed that Elijah Washington had to look twice to make sure where the lining had been cut.

"Well, that beats the band!" he said. "Mr Gonsalez, I'll send you my shirts for repair!"

"And here is something for you to carry." It was a black leather portfolio, well worn. To one end was attached a steel chain terminating in a leather belt. "I want you to put this round your waist, and from now on to carry this wallet. It contains nothing more important than a few envelopes imposingly sealed, and if you lose it no great harm will come."

"You think they'll go for the wallet?" Manfred nodded.

"One cannot tell, of course, what Oberzohn will do, and he's as wily as one of his snakes. But my experience has been," he said, "that the cleverer the criminal, the bigger the fool and the more outrageous his mistakes. You will want money."

"Well, I'm not short of that," said the other with a smile. "Snakes are a mighty profitable proposition. Still, I'm a business man…"

For the next five minutes they discussed financial details, and he was more than surprised to discover the recklessness with which money was disbursed.

He went out, with a glance from the corner of his eye at the taximan, whose hand was raised inquiringly, but, ignoring the driver, he turned and walked towards Regent Street, and presently found a wandering taxi of an innocuous character, and ordered the man to drive to the Ritz-Carlton, where rooms had been taken for him.

He was in Regent Street before he looked round through the peep-hole, and, as Manfred had promised him, the taxi was following, its flag down to prevent chance hiring. Mr Washington went up to his room, opened the window and looked out: the taxi had joined a near-by rank. The driver had left his box.

"He's on the 'phone," muttered Mr Washington, and would have given a lot of money to have known the nature of the message.

24

ON THE NIGHT MAIL

A man of habit, Mr Oberzohn missed his daily journey to the City Road. In ordinary circumstances the loss would have been a paralysing one, but of late he had grown more and more wedded to his deep arm-chair and his ponderous volumes; and though the City Road had been a very useful establishment in many ways, and was ill replaced by the temporary building which his manager had secured, he felt he could almost dispense with that branch of his business altogether.

Oberzohn & Smitts was an institution which had grown out of nothing. The energy of the partners, and especially the knowledge of African trading conditions which the departed Smitts possessed, had produced a nourishing business which ten years before could have been floated for half a million pounds.

Orders still came in. There were up-country stores to be restocked; new, if unimportant, contracts to be fulfilled; there was even a tentative offer under consideration from one of the South American States for the armaments of a political faction. But Mr Oberzohn was content to mark time, in the faith that the next week would see him superior to these minor considerations and in a position, if he so wished, to liquidate his business and sell his stores and his trade. There were purchasers ready, but the half million pounds had dwindled to a tenth of that sum, which outstanding bills would more than absorb. As Manfred had said, his running expenses were enormous. He had agents in every central Government office in Europe, and though they did not earn their salt, they certainly drew more than condiment for their services.

He had spent a busy morning in his little workshop-laboratory, and had settled himself down in his chair, when a telegraph messenger came trundling his bicycle across the rough ground, stopped to admire for a second the iron dogs which littered the untidy strip of lawn, and woke the echoes of this gaunt house with a thunderous knock. Mr Oberzohn hurried to the door. A telegram to this address must necessarily be important. He took the telegram, slammed the door in the messenger's face and hurried back to his room, tearing open the envelope as he went.

There were three sheets of misspelt writing, for the wire was in Portuguese and telegraph operators are bad guessers. He read it through carefully, his lips moving silently, until he came to the end, then he started reading all over again, and, for a better understanding of its purport, he took a pencil and paper and translated the message into Swedish. He laid the telegram face downwards on the table and took up his book, but he was not reading. His busy mind slipped from Lisbon to London, from Curzon Street to the factory, and at last he shut his book with a bang, got up, and opening the door, barked Gurther's name. That strange man came downstairs in his stockinged feet, his hair hanging over his eyes, an unpleasant sight. Dr Oberzohn pointed to the room and the man entered.

For an hour they talked behind locked doors, and then Gurther came out, still showing his teeth in a mechanical smile, and went up the stairs two at a time. The half-witted Danish maid, passing the door of the doctor's room, heard his gruff voice booming into the telephone, but since he spoke a language which, whilst it had some relation to her own, was subtly different, she could not have heard the instructions, admonitions, orders and suggestions which he fired in half a dozen different directions, even if she had heard him clearly.

This done, Dr Oberzohn returned to his book and a midday refreshment, spooning his lunch from a small cup at his side containing a few fluid ounces of dark red liquid. One half of his mind was pursuing his well-read philosophers; the other worked at feverish speed, conjecturing and guessing, forestalling and baffling the minds that were working against him. He played a game of mental chess, all the time seeking for a check, and when at last he had discovered one that was adequate, he put down his book and went out into his garden, strolling up and down inside the wire fence, stopping now and again to pick a flower from a weed, or pausing to examine a rain-filled pothole as though it were the star object in a prize landscape.

He loved this ugly house, knew every brick of it, as a feudal lord might have known the castle he had built, the turret, the flat roof with its high parapet, that commanded a view of the canal bank on the one side and the railway arches left and right. They were railway arches which had a value to him. Most of them were blocked up, having been converted into lock-up garages and sheds, and through only a few could ingress be had. One, under which ran the muddy lane—why it was called Hangman's Lane nobody knew; another that gave to some allotments on the edge of his property; and a third through which he also could see daylight, but which spanned no road at all.

An express train roared past in a cloud of steam, and he scanned the viaduct with benignant interest. And then he performed his daily tour of inspection. Turning back into the house, he climbed the stairs to the third floor, opened a little door that revealed an extra flight of steps, and emerged on to the roof. At each corner was a square black shed, about the height of a man's chest. The doors were heavily padlocked, and near by each was a stout black box, equally weatherproof. There were other things here: great, clumsy wall-plugs at regular intervals. Seeing them, it might be thought that Mr Oberzohn contemplated a night when, in the exultation of achievement, he would illuminate his ungainly premises. But up till now that night had not arrived, and in truth the only light usable was one which at the moment was dismantled in the larger of the four sheds.

From here he could look down upon the water cutting into the factory grounds; and the black bulk of the barge, which filled the entire width of the wharf, seemed so near that he could have thrown a stone upon it. His idle interest was in the sluggish black water that oozed through the gates. A slight mist lay upon the canal; a barge was passing down towards Deptford, and he contemplated the straining horse that tugged the barge rope with a mind set upon the time when he, too, might use the waterway in a swifter craft.

London lay around him, its spires and chimneys looming through the thin haze of smoke. Far away the sun caught the golden ball of St. Paul's and added a new star to the firmament. Mr Oberzohn hated London — only this little patch of his had beauty in his eyes. Not the broad green parks and the flowering rhododendrons; not the majestic aisles of pleasure which the rich lounger rode or walked, nor the streets of stone-fronted stores, nor the pleasant green of suburban roads — he loved only these God-forgotten acres, this slimy wilderness in which he had set up his habitation.

He went downstairs, locking the roof door behind him, and, passing Gurther's room, knocked and was asked to enter. The man sat in his singlet; he had shaved once, but now the keen razor was going across his skin for the second time. He turned his face, shining with cream, and grinned round at the intruder, and with a grunt the doctor shut the door and went downstairs, knowing that the man was for the moment happy; for nothing pleased Gurther quite so much as "dressing up."

The doctor stood at the entrance of his own room, hesitating between books and laboratory, decided upon the latter, and was busy for the next two hours. Only once he came out, and that was to bring from the warm room the green baize box which contained "the most potent of chemicals, colossal in power."

The Newhaven-Dieppe route is spasmodically popular. There are nights when the trains to Paris are crowded; other nights when it is possible to obtain a carriage to yourself; and it happened that this evening, when Elijah Washington booked his seat, he might, if it had been physically possible, have sat in one compartment and put his feet on the seat in another.

Between the two great branches of the Anglo-Saxon race there is one notable difference. The Englishman prefers to travel in solitude and silence. His ideal journey is one from London to Constantinople in a compartment that is not invaded except by the ticket collector; and if it is humanly possible that he can reach his destination without having given utterance to anything more sensational than an agreement with some other passenger's comment on the weather, he is indeed a happy man. The American loves company; he has the acquisitiveness of the Latin, combined with the rhetorical virtues of the Teuton. Solitude makes him miserable; silence irritates him. He wants to talk about large and important things, such as the future of the country, the prospects of agriculture and the fluctuations of trade, about which the average Englishman knows nothing, and is less interested. The American has a town pride, can talk almost emotionally about a new drainage system and grow eloquent upon a municipal balance sheet. The Englishman does not cultivate his town pride until he reaches middle age, and then only in sufficient quantities to feel disappointed with the place of his birth after he has renewed its acquaintance.

Mr Washington found himself in an empty compartment, and, grunting his dissatisfaction, walked along the corridor, peeping into one cell after another in the hope of discovering a fellow-countryman in a similar unhappy plight. His search was fruitless and he returned to the carriage in which his bag and overcoat were deposited, and settled down to the study of an English humorous newspaper and a vain search for something at which any intelligent man could laugh.

The doors of the coach were at either end, and most passengers entering had to pass the open entrance of Mr Washington's compartment. At every click of the door he looked up, hoping to find a congenial soul. But disappointment awaited him, until a lady hesitated by the door. It was a smoking carriage, but Washington, who was a man of gallant character, would gladly have sacrificed his cigar for the pleasure of her society. Young, he guessed, and a widow. She was in black, an attractive face showed through a heavy veil.

"Is this compartment engaged?" she asked in a low voice that was almost a whisper.

"No, madam." Washington rose, hat in hand.

"Would you mind?" she asked in a soft voice.

"Why, surely! Sit down, ma'am," said the gallant American. "Would you like the corner seat by the window?"

She shook her head, and sat down near the door, turning her face from him.

"Do you mind my smoking?" asked Washington, after a while.

"Please smoke," she said, and again turned her face away.

"English," thought Mr Washington in disgust, and hunched himself for an hour and a half of unrelieved silence.

A whistle blew, the train moved slowly from the platform, and Elijah Washington's adventurous journey had begun.

They were passing through Croydon when the girl rose, and, leaning out, closed the little glass-panelled door.

"You should let me do that," said Elijah reproachfully, and she murmured something about not wishing to trouble him, and he relapsed into his seat.

One or two of the men who passed looked in, and evidently this annoyed her, for she reached and pulled down the spring blind which partially hid her from outside observation, and after the ticket collector had been and punched the slips, she lowered the second of the three blinds.

"Do you mind?" she asked.

"Sure not, ma'am," said Elijah, without any great heartiness. He had no desire to travel alone with a lady in a carriage so discreetly curtained. He had heard of cases... and by nature he was an extremely cautious man.

The speed of the train increased; the wandering passengers had settled down. The second of the ticket inspections came as they were rushing through Redhill, and Mr Washington thought uncomfortably that there was a significant look in the inspector's face as he glanced first at the drawn blinds, then from the lady to himself.

She affected a perfume of a peculiarly pleasing kind. The carriage was filled with this subtle fragrance. Mr Washington smelt it above the scent of his cigar. Her face was still averted; he wondered if she had gone to sleep, and, growing weary of his search for humour, he put down the paper, folded his hands and closed his eyes, and found himself gently drifting to that medley of the real and unreal which is the overture of dreams.

The lady moved; he looked at her out of the corner of his half-closed eyes. She had moved round so as to half face him. Her veil was still down, her white gloves were reflectively clasped on her knees. He shut his eyes again, until another movement brought him awake. She was feeling in her bag.

Mr Washington was awake now—as wide awake as he had ever been in his life. In stretching out her hand, the lady had pulled short her sleeve, and there was a gap of flesh between the glove and the wrist of her blouse, and on her wrist was hair!

He shifted his position slightly, grunted as in his sleep, and dropped his hand to his pocket, and all the time those cold eyes were watching him through the veil.

Lifting the bottom of the veil, she put the ebony holder between her teeth and searched the bag for a match. Then she turned appealingly to him as though she had sensed his wakefulness. As she rose, Washington rose too, and suddenly he sprang at her and flung her back against the door. For a moment the veiled lady was taken by surprise, and then there was a flash of steel.

From nowhere a knife had come into her hand and Washington gripped the wrist and levered it over, pushing the palm of his hand under the chin. Even through the veil he could feel the bristles, and knew now, if he had not known before, that he had to deal with a man. A live, active man, rendered doubly strong by the knowledge of his danger. Gurther butted forward with his head, but Washington saw the attack coming, shortened his arm and jabbed full at the face behind the veil. The blow stopped the man only for an instant, and again he came on, and this time the point of the knife caught the American's shoulder, and ripped the coat to the elbow. It needed this to bring forth Elijah Washington's mental and physical reserves. With a roar he gripped the throat of his assailant and threw him with such violence against the door that it gave, and the "widow in mourning" crashed against the panel of the outer corridor. Before he could reach the attacker, Gurther had turned and sped along the corridor to the door of the coach. In a second he had flung it open and had dropped to the footboard. The train was slowing to take Horsham Junction, and the cat eyes waited until he saw a good fall, and let go. Staring back into the darkness, Washington saw nothing, and then the train inspector came along.

"It was a man in woman's clothes," he said, a little breathlessly, and they went back to search the compartment, but Mr Gurther had taken bag and everything with him, and the only souvenir of his presence was the heel of a shoe that had been torn off in the struggle.

25

GURTHER RETURNS

The train was going at thirty miles an hour when Gurther dropped on to a ridge of sand by the side of the track, and in the next second he was sliding forward on his face. Fortunately for him the veil, though torn, kept his eyes free. Stumbling to his feet, he looked round. The level-crossing gates should be somewhere here. He had intended jumping the train at this point, and Oberzohn had made arrangements accordingly. A signalman, perched high above the track, saw the figure and challenged.

"I've lost my way," said Gurther. "Where is the level-crossing?"

"A hundred yards farther on. Keep clear of those metals— the Eastbourne express is coming behind."

If Gurther had had his way, he would have stopped long enough to remove a rail for the sheer joy of watching a few hundred of the hated people plunged to destruction. But he guessed that the car was waiting, went sideways through the safety gates into a road which was fairly populous. There were people about who turned their heads and looked in amazement at the bedraggled woman in black, but he had got beyond worrying about his appearance.

He saw the car with the little green light which Oberzohn invariably used to mark his machines from others, and, climbing into the cab (as it was), sat down to recover his breath. The driver he knew as one of the three men employed by Oberzohn, one of whom Mr Washington had seen that morning.

The journey back to town was a long one, though the machine, for a public vehicle, was faster than most. Gurther welcomed the ride. Once more he had failed, and he reasoned that this last failure was the most serious of all. The question of Oberzohn's displeasure did not really arise. He had travelled far beyond the point when the Swede's disapproval meant very much to him. But there might be a consequence more serious than any. He knew well with what instructions Pfeiffer had been primed on the night of the attack at Rath House — only Gurther had been quicker, and his snake had bitten first. Dr Oberzohn had no illusions as to what happened, and if he had tactfully refrained from making reference to the matter, he had his purpose and reasons. And this night journey with Elijah Washington was one of them.

There was no excuse; he had none to offer. His hand wandered beneath the dress to the long knife that was strapped to his side, and the touch of the worn handle was very reassuring. For the time being he was safe; until another man was found to take Pfeiffer's place Oberzohn was working single-handed and could not afford to dispense with the services of this, the last of his assassins.

It was past eleven when he dismissed the taxi at the end of the long lane, and, following the only safe path, came to the unpainted door that gave admission to Oberzohn's property. And the first words of his master told him that there was no necessity for explanation.

"So you did not get him, Gurther?"

"No, Herr Doktor.'

"I should not have sent you." Oberzohn's voice was extraordinarily mild in all the circumstances. "That man you cannot kill — with the snake. I have learned since you went that he was bitten at the blind man's house, yet lives! That is extraordinary. I would give a lot of money to test his blood. You tried the knife?"

"Ja, Herr Doktor." He lifted his veil, stripped off hat and wig in one motion. The rouged and powdered face was bruised; from under the brown wig was a trickle of dried blood.

"Good! You have done as well as you could. Go to your room, Gurther—march!"

Gurther went upstairs, and for a quarter of an hour was staring at his grinning face in the glass, as with cream and soiled towel he removed his make-up.

Oberzohn's very gentleness was a menace. What did it portend? Until that evening neither Gurther nor his dead companion had been taken into the confidence of the two men who directed their activities. He knew there were certain papers to be recovered; he knew there were men to be killed; but what value were the papers, or why death should be directed to this unfortunate or that, he neither knew nor cared. His duty had been to obey, and he had served a liberal paymaster well and loyally. That girl in the underground room? Gurther had many natural explanations for her imprisonment. And yet none of them fitted the conditions. His cogitations were wasted time. That night, for the first time, the doctor took him into his confidence.

He had finished dressing and was on his way to his kitchen when the doctor stood at the doorway and called him in.

"Sit down, Gurther." He was almost kind. "You will have a cigar? These are excellent."

He threw a long, thin, black cheroot, and Gurther caught it between his teeth and seemed absurdly pleased with his trick.

"The time has come when you must know something, Gurther," said the doctor. He took a fellow to the weed the man was smoking, and puffed huge clouds of rank smoke into the room. "I have for a friend—who? Herr Newton?" He shrugged his shoulders. "He is a very charming man, but he has no brains. He is the kind of man, Gurther, who would live in comfort, take all we gave him by our cleverness and industry, and never say thank you! And in trouble what will he do, Gurther? He will go to the police—yes, my dear friend, he will go to the police!"

He nodded. Gurther had heard the same story that night when he had crept soft-footed to the door and had heard the doctor discuss certain matters with the late Mr Pfeiffer.

"He would, without a wink of his eyelash, without a snap of his hand, send you and me to death, and would read about our execution with a smile, and then go forth and eat his plum-pudding and roast beef! That is our friend Herr Newton! You have seen this with your own eyes?"

"Ja, Herr Doktor!" exclaimed the obedient Gurther.

"He is a danger for many reasons," Oberzohn proceeded deliberately. "Because of these three men who have so infamously set themselves out to ruin me, who burnt down my house, and who whipped you, Gurther—they tied you up to a post and whipped you with a whip of nine tails. You have not forgotten, Gurther?"

"Nein, Herr Doktor!" Indeed, Gurther had not forgotten, though the vacant smirk on his face might suggest that he had a pleasant memory of the happening.

"A fool in an organization," continued the doctor oracularly, "is like a bad plate on a ship, or a weak link in a chain. Let it snap, and what happens? You and I die, my dear Gurther. We go up before a stupid man in a white wig and a red cloak, and he hands us to another man who puts a rope around our necks, drops us through a hole in the ground—all because we have a stupid man like Herr Montague Newton to deal with."

"Ja, Herr Doktor," said Gurther as his master stopped. He felt that this comment was required of him.

"Now, I will tell you the whole truth." The doctor carefully knocked off the ash of his cigar into the saucer of his cup.

"There is a fortune for you and for me, and this girl that we have in the quiet place can give it to us. I can marry her, or I can wipe her out, so! If I marry her, it would be better, I think, and this I have arranged."

And then, in his own way, he told the story of the hill of gold, concealing nothing, reserving nothing—all that he knew, all that Villa had told him.

"For three-four days now she must be here. At the end of that time nothing matters. The letter to Lisbon—of what value is it? I was foolish when I tried to stop it. She has made no nominee, she has no heirs, she has known nothing of her fortune, and therefore is in no position to claim the renewal of the concession."

"Herr Doktor, will you graciously permit me to speak?" The doctor nodded. "Does the Newton know this?"

"The Newton knows all this," said the doctor.

"Will you graciously permit me to speak again, Herr Doktor? What was this letter I was to have taken, had I not been overcome by misfortune?"

Oberzohn examined the ceiling.

"I have thought this matter from every angle," he said, "and I have decided thus. It was a letter written by Gonsalez to the Secretary or the Minister of the Colonies, asking that the renewal of the concession should be postponed. The telegram from my friend at the Colonial Office in Lisbon was to this effect." He fixed his glasses, fumbled in his waistcoat and took out the three-page telegram. "I will read it to you in your own language—

"'Application has been received from Leon Gonsalez, asking His Excellency to receive a very special letter which arrives in two days. The telegram does not state the contents of the letter, but the Minister has given orders for the messenger to be received. The present Minister is not favourable to concessions granted to England or Englishmen.'"

He folded the paper.

"Which means that there will be no postponement, my dear Gurther, and this enormous fortune will be ours."

Gurther considered this point and for a moment forgot to smile, and looked what he was in consequence: a hungry, discontented wolf of a man.

"Herr Doktor, graciously permit me to ask you a question?"

"Ask," said Oberzohn magnanimously.

"What share does Herr Newton get? And if you so graciously honoured me with a portion of your so justly deserved gains, to what extent would be that share?"

The other considered this, puffing away until the room was a mist of smoke.

"Ten thousand English pounds," he said at last.

"Gracious and learned doctor, that is a very small proportion of many millions," said Gurther gently.

"Newton will receive one half," said the doctor, his face working nervously, "if he is alive. If misfortune came to him, that share would be yours, Gurther, my brave fellow! And with so much money a man would not be hunted. The rich and the noble would fawn upon him; he would have his lovely yacht and steam about the summer seas everlastingly, huh?"

Gurther rose and clicked his heels.

"Do you desire me again this evening?"

"No, no, Gurther." The old man shook his head. "And pray remember that there is another day tomorrow, and yet another day after. We shall wait and hear what our friend has to say. Good night, Gurther."

"Good night, Herr Doktor."

The doctor looked at the door for a long time after his man had gone and took up his book. He was deep in the chapter which was headed, in the German tongue: "The Subconscious Activity of the Human Intellect in Relation to the Esoteric Emotions." To Dr Oberzohn this was more thrilling than the most exciting novel.

26

IN CAPTIVITY

The second day of captivity dawned unseen, in a world that lay outside the brick roof and glazed white walls of Mirabelle Leicester's prison-house. She had grown in strength and courage, but not so her companion, Joan, who had started her weary vigil with an almost cheerful gaiety, had sunk deeper and deeper into depression as the hours progressed, and Mirabelle woke to the sound of a woman's sobs, to find the girl sitting on the side of her bed, her head in her wet hands.

"I hate this place!" she sobbed. "Why does he keep me here? God! If I thought the hound was double-crossing me... ! I'll go mad if they keep me here any longer. I will, Leicester!" she screamed.

"I'll make some tea," said Mirabelle, getting out of bed and finding her slippers.

The girl sat throughout the operation huddled in a miserable heap, and by and by her whimpering got on Mirabelle's nerves.

"I don't know why you should be wretched," she said. "They're not after your money!"

"You can laugh—and how you can, I don't know," sobbed the girl, as she took the cup in her shaking hands. "I know I'm a fool, but I've never been locked up—like this before. I didn't dream he'd break his word. He swore he'd come yesterday. What time is it?"

"Six o'clock," said Mirabelle.

It might as well have been eight or midday, for all she knew to the contrary.

"This is a filthy place," said the hysterical girl. "I think they're going to drown us all... or that thing will explode"—she pointed to the green baize box—"I know it! I feel it in my blood. That beast Gurther is here somewhere, ugh? He's like a slimy snake. Have you ever seen him?"

"Gurther? You mean the man who danced with me?"

"That's he. I keep telling you who he is," said Joan impatiently. "I wish we could get out of here."

She jumped up suddenly.

"Come and see if you can help me lift the trap."

Mirabelle knew it was useless before she set forth on the quest for freedom. Their united efforts failed to move the stone, and Joan was on the point of collapse when they came back to their sleeping-room.

"I hope Gurther doesn't know that those men are friends of yours," she said, when she became calmer.

"You told me that yesterday. Would that make any difference?"

"A whole lot," said Joan vehemently. "He's got the blood of a fish, that man! There's nothing he wouldn't do. Monty ought to be flogged for leaving us here at his mercy. I'm not scared of Oberzohn—he's old. But the other fellow dopes, and goes stark, staring mad at times. Monty told me one night that he was"—she choked—"a killer. He said that these German criminals who kill people are never satisfied with one murder, they go on and on until they've got twenty or thirty! He says that the German prisons are filled with men who have the murder habit."

"He was probably trying to frighten you."

"Why should he?" said the girl, with unreasonable anger. "And leave him alone! Monty is the best in the world. I adore the ground he walks on!"

Very wisely, Mirabelle did not attempt to traverse this view.

It was only when her companion had these hysterical fits that fear was communicated to her. Her faith was completely and whole-heartedly centred on the three men—upon Gonsalez. She wondered how old he was. Sometimes he looked quite young, at others an elderly man. It was difficult to remember his face; he owed so much to his expression, the smile in his eyes, to the strange, boyish eagerness of gesture and action which accompanied his speech. She could not quite understand herself; why was she always thinking of Gonsalez, as a maid might think of a lover? She went red at the thought. He seemed so apart, so aloof from the ordinary influences of women. Suppose she had committed some great crime and had escaped the vigilance of the law, would he hunt her down in the same remorseless, eager way, planning to cut off every avenue of her escape until he shepherded her into a prison cell? It was a horrible thought, and she screwed up her eyes tight to blot out the mental picture she had made.

It would have given her no ordinary satisfaction to have known how often Gonsalez's thoughts strayed to the girl who had so strangely come into his life. He spent a portion of his time that morning in his bedroom, fixing to the wall a large railway map which took in the south of England and the greater part of the Continent. A red-ink line marked the route from London to Lisbon, and he was fixing a little green flag on the line just south of Paris when Manfred strolled into the room and surveyed his work.

"The Sud Express is about there," he said, pointing to the last of the green flags, "and I think our friend will have a fairly pleasant and uneventful journey as far as Valladolid—where I have arranged for Miguel Garcia, an old friend of mine, to pick him up and shadow him on the westward journey—unless we get the 'plane. I'm expecting a wire any minute. By the way, the Dieppe police have arrested the gentleman who tried to bump him overboard in mid-Channel, but the man who snatched at his portfolio at the Gare St. Lazare is still at liberty."

"He must be getting quite used to it now," said Manfred coolly, and laughed to himself.

Leon turned. "He's a good fellow," he said with quick earnestness. "We couldn't have chosen a better man. The woman on the train, of course, was Gurther. He is the only criminal I've ever known who is really efficient at disguising himself."

Manfred lit his pipe; he had lately taken to this form of smoking. "The case grows more and more difficult every day. Do you realize that?"

Leon nodded. "And more dangerous," he said. "By the laws of average, Gurther should get one of us the next time he makes an attempt. Have you seen the papers?"

Manfred smiled.

"They're crying for Meadows' blood, poor fellow! Which shows the extraordinary inconsistency of the public. Meadows has only been in one snake case. They credit him with having fallen down on the lot."

"They seem to be in remarkable agreement that the snake deaths come into the category of wilful murder," said Gonsalez as they went down the stairs together.

Meadows had been talking to the reporters. Indeed, that was his chief offence from the viewpoint of the official mind. For the first article in the code of every well-constituted policeman is, "Thou shalt not communicate to the Press."

Leon strolled aimlessly about the room. He was wearing his chauffeur's uniform, and his hands were thrust into the breeches pockets. Manfred, recognizing the symptoms, rang the bell for Poiccart, and that quiet man came from the lower regions.

"Leon is going to be mysterious," said Manfred dryly.

"I'm not really," protested Leon, but he went red. It was one of his most charming peculiarities that he had never forgotten how to blush. "I was merely going to suggest that there's a play running in London that we ought to see. I didn't know that 'The Ringer' was a play until this morning, when I saw one of Oberzohn's more genteel clerks go into the theatre, and, being naturally of an inquisitive turn of mind, followed him. A play that interests Oberzohn will interest me, and should interest you, George," he said severely, "and certainly should interest Meadows—it is full of thrilling situations! It is about a criminal who escapes from Dartmoor and comes back to murder his betrayer. There is one scene which is played in the dark, that ought to thrill you—I've been looking up the reviews of the dramatic critics, and as they are unanimous that it is not an artistic success, and is, moreover, wildly improbable, it ought to be worth seeing. I always choose an artistic success when I am suffering from insomnia," he added cruelly.

"Oberzohn is entitled to his amusements, however vulgar they may be."

"But this play isn't vulgar," protested Leon, "except in so far as it is popular. I found it most difficult to buy a seat. Even actors go to see the audience act."

"What seat did he buy?"

"Box A," said Leon promptly, "and paid for it with real money. It is the end box on the prompt side—and before you ask me whence I gained my amazing knowledge of theatrical technique, I will answer that even a child in arms knows that the prompt side is the left-hand side facing the audience."

"For tonight?"

Leon nodded.

"I have three stalls," he said and produced them from his pocket. "If you cannot go, will you give them to the cook? She looks like a woman who would enjoy a good cry over the sufferings of the tortured heroine. The seats are in the front row, which means that you can get in and out between the acts without walking on other people's knees."

"Must I go?" asked Poiccart plaintively. "I do not like detective plays, and I hate mystery plays. I know who the real murderer is before the curtain has been up ten minutes, and that naturally spoils my evening."

"Could you not take a girl?" asked Leon outrageously. "Do you know any who would go?"

"Why not take Aunt Alma?" suggested Manfred, and Leon accepted the name joyously.

Aunt Alma had come to town at the suggestion of the Three, and had opened up the Doughty Court flat.

"And really she is a remarkable woman, and shows a steadiness and a courage in face of the terrible position of our poor little friend, which is altogether praiseworthy. I don't think Mirabelle Leicester is in any immediate danger. I think I've said that before. Oberzohn merely wishes to keep her until the period of renewal has expired. How he will escape the consequences of imprisoning her, I cannot guess. He may not attempt to escape them, may accept the term of imprisonment which will certainly be handed out to him, as part of the payment he must pay for his millions."

"Suppose he kills her?" asked Poiccart.

For a second Leon's face twitched.

"He won't kill her," he said quietly. "Why should he? We know that he has got her—the police know. She is a different proposition from Barberton, an unknown man killed nobody knew how, in a public place. No, I don't think we need cross that bridge, only..." He rubbed his hands together irritably. "However, we shall see. And in the meantime I'm placing a lot of faith in Digby, a shrewd man with a sense of his previous shortcomings. You were wise there, George."

He was looking at the street through the curtains.

"Tittlemouse is at his post, the faithful hound!" he said, nodding towards the solitary taxicab that stood on the rank. "I wonder whether he expects—"

Manfred saw a light creep into his eyes.

"Will you want me for the next two hours?" Leon asked quickly, and was out of the room in a flash.

Ten minutes later, Poiccart and George were talking together when they heard the street door close, and saw Leon stroll to the edge of the pavement and wave his umbrella. The taxi-driver was suddenly a thing of quivering excitement. He leaned down, cranked his engine, climbed back into his seat and brought the car up quicker than any taxicab driver had ever moved before.

"New Scotland Yard," said Leon, and got into the machine.

The cab passed through the forbidding gates of the Yard and dropped him at the staff entrance.

"Wait here," said Leon, and the man shifted uncomfortably.

"I've got to be back at my garage—" he began.

"I shall not be five minutes," said Leon.

Meadows was in his room, fortunately.

"I want you to pull in this man and give him a dose of the third degree you keep in this country," said Leon. "He carries a gun; I saw that when he had to get down to crank up his cab in Piccadilly Circus. The engine stopped."

"What do you want to know?"

"All that there is to be known about Oberzohn. I may have missed one or two things. I've seen him outside the house. Oberzohn employs him for odd jobs and occasionally he acts as the old man's chauffeur. In fact, he drove the machine the day Miss Leicester lunched with Oberzohn at the Ritz-Carlton.

He may not have a cabman's licence, and that will make it all the easier for you."

A few minutes later, a very surprised and wrathful man was marched into Cannon Row and scientifically searched. Leon had been right about the revolver; it was produced and found to be loaded, and his excuse that he carried the weapon as a protection following upon a recent murder of a cab-driver had not the backing of the necessary permit. In addition—and this was a more serious offence—he held no permit from Scotland Yard to ply for hire on the streets, and his badge was the property of another man.

"Put him inside," said Meadows, and went back to report to the waiting Leon. "You've hit the bull's-eye first time. I don't know whether he will be of any use to us, but I don't despise even the smallest fish."

Whilst he was waiting, Leon had been engaged in some quick thinking.

"The man has been at Greenwich lately. One of my men saw him there twice, and I needn't say that he was driving Oberzohn."

"I'll talk to him later and telephone you," said Meadows, and Leon Gonsalez went back to Curzon Street, one large smile.

"You have merely exchanged a spy you know for a spy you don't know," said George Manfred, "though I never question these freakish acts of yours, Leon. So often they have a trick of turning up trumps. By the way, the police are raiding the Gringo Club in the Victoria Dock Road tonight, and they may be able to pick up a few of Mr Oberzohn's young gentlemen who are certain to be regular users of the place."

The telephone bell rang shrilly, and Leon took up the receiver, and recognized Meadows' voice.

"I've got a queer story for you," said the inspector immediately.

"Did he talk?" asked the interested Leon.

"After a while. We took a finger-print impression, and found that he was on the register. More than that, he is a ticket-of-leave man. As an ex-convict we can send him back to finish his unexpired time. I promised to say a few words for him, and he spilt everything. The most interesting item is that Oberzohn is planning to be married."

"To be married? Who is this?" asked Manfred, in surprise. "Oberzohn?"

Leon nodded.

"Who is the unfortunate lady?" asked Leon.

There was a pause, and then:

"Miss Leicester."

Manfred saw the face of his friend change colour, and guessed.

"Does he know when?" asked Leon in a different voice.

"No. The licence was issued over a week ago, which means that Oberzohn can marry any morning he likes to bring along his bride. What's the idea, do you think?"

"Drop in this evening and either I or George will tell you," said Leon.

He put the telephone on the hook very carefully.

"That is a danger I had not foreseen, although it was obviously the only course Oberzohn could take. If he marries her, she cannot be called in evidence against him. May I see the book, George?"

Manfred unlocked the wall safe and brought back a small ledger. Leo Gonsalez turned the pages thoughtfully.

"Dennis—he has done good work for us, hasn't he?" he asked.

"Yes, he's a very reliable man. He owes us, amongst other things, his life. Do you remember, his wife was—"

"I remember." Leon scribbled the address of a man who had proved to be one of the most trustworthy of his agents.

"What are you going to do?" asked Manfred.

"I've put Dennis on the doorstep of the Greenwich registrar's office from nine o'clock in the morning until half-past three in the afternoon, and he will have instructions from me that, the moment he sees Oberzohn walk out of a cab with a lady, he must push him firmly but gently under the wheels of the cab and ask the driver politely to move up a yard."

Leon in his more extravagantly humorous moods was very often in deadly earnest.

27

MR NEWTON'S DILEMMA

The most carefully guided streaks of luck may, in spite of all precautions, overflow into the wrong channel, and this had happened to Mr Montague Newton, producing an evening that was financially disastrous and a night from which sleep was almost banished. He had had one of his little card parties; but whether it was the absence of Joan, and the inadequacy of her fluffy-haired substitute, or whether the wine had disagreed with one of the most promising victims, the result was the same. They had played chemin de fer, and the gilded pigeon, whose feathers seemed already to be ornamenting the headdress of Monty Newton, had been successful, and when he should have been signing cheques for large amounts, he was cashing his counters with a reluctant host.

The night started wrong with Joan's substitute, whose name was Lisa. She had guided to the establishment, via an excellent dinner at Mero's, the son of an African millionaire. Joan, of course, would have brought him alone, but Lisa, less experienced, had allowed a young-looking friend of the victim to attach himself to the party, and she had even expected praise for her perspicacity and enterprise in producing two birds for the stone which Mr Newton so effectively wielded, instead of one.

Monty did not resent the presence of the newcomer, and rather took the girl's view, until he learnt that Lisa's "find" was not, as she had believed, an officer of the Guards, but a sporting young lawyer with a large criminal practice, and one who had already, as a junior, conducted several prosecutions for the Crown. The moment his name was mentioned, Monty groaned in spirit. He was, moreover, painfully sober. His friend was not so favourably situated.

That was the first of the awkward things to happen. The second was the bad temper of the player, who, when the bank was considerably over £3,000, had first of all insisted upon the cards being reshuffled, and then he had gone banquo—the game being baccarat. Even this contretemps might have been overcome, but after he had expressed his willingness to "give it," the card which Monty had so industriously palmed slipped from his hand to the table, and though the fact was unnoticed by the players, the lawyer's attention being diverted at the moment, it was impossible to recover that very valuable piece of pasteboard. And Monty had done a silly thing. Instead of staging an artistic exhibition of annoyance at remarks which the millionaire's son had made, he decided to take a chance on the natural run of the cards. And he had lost. On top of that, the slightly inebriated player had decided that when a man had won a coup of £3,000 it was time to stop playing. So Monty experienced the mortification of paying out money, and accompanying his visitor to the door with a smile that was so genial and so full of good-fellowship that the young gentleman was compelled to apologize for his boorishness.

"Come along some other night and give me my revenge," said Monty.

"You bet I will! I'm going to South Africa tomorrow, but I shall be back early next year, and I'll look you up."

Monty watched him going down the steps and hoped he would break his neck.

He was worried about Joan—more worried than he thought it was possible for him to be about so light a girl. She was necessary to him in many ways. Lisa was a bungling fool, he decided, though he sent her home without hurting her feelings. She was a useful girl in many ways, and nothing spoils a tout quicker than constant nagging.

He felt very lonely in the house, and wandered from room to room, irritated with himself that the absence of this featherbrained girl, who had neither the education nor the breed of his own class, should make such a big difference. And it did; he had to admit as much to himself. He hated the thought of that underground room. He knew something of her temperament, and how soon her experience would get on her nerves. In many respects he wished he did not feel that way about her, because she had a big shock coming, and it was probably because he foresaw this hurt that he was anxious to make the present as happy as he could for her.

After he had done what he was to do, there was no reason in the world why they should be bad friends, and he would give her a big present. Girls of that class soon forget their miseries if the present is large enough. Thus he argued, tossing from side to side in his bed, and all the time his thoughts playing about that infernal cellar. What she must be feeling! He did not worry at all about Mirabelle, because—well, she was a principal in the case. To him, Joan was the real victim.

Sleep did not come until daybreak, and he woke in his most irritable frame of mind. He had promised the girl he would call and see her, though he had privately arranged with Oberzohn not to go to the house until the expiry of the five days.

By lunch-time he could stand the worry no longer, and, ordering his car, drove to a point between New Cross and Bermondsey, walking on foot the remainder of the distance. Mr Oberzohn expected the visit. He had a shrewd knowledge of his confederate's mental outfit, and when he saw this well-dressed man picking a dainty way across the littered ground, he strolled out on the steps to meet him.

"It is curious you should have come," he said.

"Why didn't you telephone?" growled Newton. This was his excuse for the visit.

"Because there are human machines at the end of every wire," said Oberzohn. "If they were automatic and none could listen, but you and I, we would talk and talk and then talk! All day long would I speak with you and find it a pleasure. But not with Miss This and Miss That saying, 'One moment, if you please,' and saying to the Scotland Yard man, 'Now you cut in'!"

"Is Gurther back?"

"Gurther is back," said the doctor soberly.

"Nothing happened to that bird? At least, I saw nothing in the evening papers."

"He has gone to Lisbon," replied the doctor indifferently. "Perhaps he will get there, perhaps he will not—what does it matter? I should like to see the letter, because it is data, and data has an irresistible charm for a poor old scientist. You will have a drink?"

Monty hesitated, as he always did when Oberzohn offered him refreshment. You could never be sure with Oberzohn.

"I'll have a whisky," he said at last, "a full bottle—one that hasn't been opened. I'll open it myself."

The doctor chuckled unevenly.

"You do not trust?" he said. "I think you are wise. For who is there in this world of whom a man can say, 'He is my friend. To the very end of my life I will have confidence in him'?"

Monty did not feel that the question called for an answer.

He took the whisky bottle to the light, examined the cork and drove in the corkscrew.

"The soda water—that also might be poisoned," said Dr Oberzohn pleasantly.

MR NEWTON'S DILEMMA

At any other time he would not have made that observation. That he said it at all betrayed a subtle but ominous change in their relationship. If Monty noticed this, he did not say a word, but filled his glass and sat down on the sofa to drink. And all the time the doctor was watching him interestedly.

"Yes, Gurther is back. He failed, but you must excuse failure in a good man. The perfect agent has yet to be found, and the perfect principal also. The American, Washington, had left Paris when I last heard of him. He is to be congratulated. If I myself lived in Paris I should always be leaving. It is a frivolous city."

Monty lit a cigar, and decided to arrive at the object of his visit by stages. For he had come to perform two important duties. He accounted as a duty a call upon Joan. No less was it a duty, and something of a relief also, to make his plan known to his partner.

"How are the girls?" he asked.

"They are very happy," said Dr Oberzohn, who had not resumed his seat, but stood in an attitude somewhat reminiscent of Gurther, erect, staring, motionless. "Always my guests are happy."

"In that dog-hole?" said the other contemptuously. "I don't want Joan to be here."

The Herr Doktor shrugged.

"Then take her away, my friend," he said. "Why should she stay, if you are unhappy because this woman is not with you? She serves no purpose. Possibly she is fretting. By all means—I will bring her to you." He moved to the door.

"Wait a moment," said Monty. "I'll see her later and take her out perhaps, but I don't want her to be away permanently. Somebody ought to stay with that girl."

"Why? Am I not here?" asked Oberzohn blandly.

"You're here, and Gurther's here." Monty was looking out of the window and did not meet the doctor's eyes. "Especially

Gurther. That's why I think that Mirabelle Leicester should have somebody to look after her. Has it ever struck you that the best way out of this little trouble is—marriage?"

"I have thought that," said the doctor. "You also have thought it? This is wonderful! You are beginning to think."

The change of tone was noticeable enough now. Monty snapped round at the man who had hitherto stood in apparent awe of him and his judgments.

"You can cut that sarcasm right out, Oberzohn," he said, and, without preamble: "I'm going to marry that girl." Oberzohn said nothing to this. "She's not engaged; she's got no love affairs at all. Joan told me, and Joan is a pretty shrewd girl. I don't know how I'm going to fix it, but I guess the best thing I can do is to pretend that I am a real friend and get her out of your cellar. She'll be so grateful that maybe she will agree to almost anything. Besides, I think I made an impression the first time I saw her. And I've got a position to offer her, Oberzohn: a house in the best part of London—"

"My house," interrupted Oberzohn's metallic voice.

"Your house? Well, our house, let us say. We're not going to quarrel about terms,"

"I also have a position to offer her, and I do not offer her any other man's."

Oberzohn was looking at him wide-eyed, a comical figure; his elongated face seemed to stand out in the gloom like a pantomime mask.

"You?" Monty could hardly believe his ears.

"I, Baron Eruc Oberzohn."

"A baron, are you?" The room shook with Monty's laughter. "Why, you damned old fool, you don't imagine she'd marry you, do you?"

Oberzohn nodded.

"She would do anythings what I felt her." In his agitation his English was getting a little ragged. "A girl may not like a mans, but she might hate something worse—you understand? A woman says death is nothing, but a woman is afeard of death, isn't it?"

"You're crazy," said Monty scornfully.

"I am crazy, am I? And a damned old fool also—yes? Yet I shall marry her."

There was a dead silence, and then Oberzohn continued the conversation, but on a much calmer note.

"Perhaps I am what you call me, but it is not a thing worthy for two friends to quarrel. Tomorrow you shall come here, and we will discuss this matter like a business proposition, hein?"

Monty examined him as though he were a strange insect that had wandered into his ken.

"You're not a Swede, you're German," he said. "That baron stuff gave you away."

"I am from the Baltic, but I have lived many years in Sweden," said Oberzohn shortly. "I am not German: I do not like them."

More than this he would not say. Possibly he shared Gurther's repugnance towards his sometime neighbours.

"We shall not quarrel, anyway," he continued. "I am a fool, you are a fool, we are all fools. You wish to see your woman?"

"I wish to see Joan," said Monty gruffly. "I don't like that 'your woman' line of yours."

"I will go get her. You wait."

Again the long boots came from under the table, were dragged on to the doctor's awkward feet, and Monty watched him from the window as he crossed to the factory and disappeared.

He was gone five minutes before he came out again, alone. Monty frowned. What was the reason for this?

"My friend," panted Oberzohn, to whom these exertions were becoming more and more irksome, "it is not wise."

"I want to see her—" began Monty.

"Gently, gently; you shall see her. But on the canal bank Gurther has also seen a stranger, who has been walking up and down, pretending to fish. Who can fish in a canal, I ask you?"

"What is he to do with it?"

"Would it be wise to bring her in daylight, I ask you again? Do not the men think that your—that this girl is in Brussels?"

This had not occurred to Monty.

"I have an idea for you. It is a good idea. The brain of old fool Oberzohn sometimes works remarkably. This morning a friend sent to me a ticket for a theatre. Now you shall take her tonight. There is always a little fog when the sun is setting and you can leave the house in a car. Presently I will send a man to attract this watcher's attention, and then I will bring her to the house and you can call for her."

"I will wait for her." Monty was dogged on this point.

And wait he did, until an hour later a half-crazy girl came flying into the room and into his arms.

Dr Oberzohn witnessed the reunion unmoved.

"That is a pretty scene for me," he said, "for one to be so soon married," and he left them alone.

* * * * *

"Monty, I can't possibly go back to that beastly place tonight. She'll have to stay by herself. And she's not a bad kid Monty, but she doesn't know she's worth a lot of money."

"Have you been talking to her?" he asked angrily. "I told you—"

"No, I've only just asked her a few questions. You can't be in a poky hole like that, thrown together day and night, without talking, can you? Monty, you're absolutely sure nothing can happen to her?"

Monty cleared his throat.

"The worst thing that can happen to her," he said, "is to get married."

She opened her eyes at this.

"Does somebody want to marry her?"

"Oberzohn," he said.

"That old thing!" she scoffed.

Again he found a difficulty in speaking.

"I have been thinking it over, honey," he said. "Marriage doesn't mean a whole lot to anybody."

"It'll mean a lot to me," she said quietly.

"Suppose I married her?" he blurted.

"You!" She stepped back from him in horror.

"Only just a... well, this is the truth, Joan. It may be the only way to get her money. Now you're in on this graft, and you know what you are to me. A marriage—a formal marriage—for a year or two, and then a divorce, and we could go away together, man and wife."

"Is that what he meant?" She jerked her head to the door. "About 'married so soon'?"

"He wants to marry her himself."

"Let him," she said viciously. "Do you think I care about money? Isn't there any other way of getting it?"

He was silent. There were too many other ways of getting it for him to advance a direct negative.

"Oh, Monty, you're not going to do that?"

"I don't know what I'm going to do yet," he said.

"But not that?" she insisted, clinging to him by his coat.

"We'll talk about it tonight. The old man's got us tickets for the theatre. We'll have a bit of dinner up West and go on, and it really doesn't matter if anybody sees us, because they know very well you're not in Brussels. What is that queer scent you've got?"

Joan laughed, forgetting for the moment the serious problem which faced her.

"Joss-sticks," she said. "The place got so close and stuffy, and I found them in the pantry with the provisions. As a matter of fact, it was a silly thing to do, because we had the place full of smoke. It's gone now, though. Monty, you do these crazy things when you're locked up," she said seriously. "I don't think I can go back again."

"Go back tomorrow," he almost pleaded. "It's only for two or three days, and it means a lot to me. Especially now that Oberzohn has ideas."

"You're not going to think any more about—about marrying her, are you?"

"We'll talk of it tonight at dinner. I thought you'd like the idea of the graft," he added untruthfully.

Joan had to return to her prison to collect some of her belongings. She found the girl lying on the bed, reading, and Mirabelle greeted her with a smile.

"Well, is your term of imprisonment ended?"

Joan hesitated.

"Not exactly. Do you mind if I'm not here tonight?"

Mirabelle shook her head. If the truth be told, she was glad to be alone. All that day she had been forced to listen to the plaints and weepings of this transfigured girl, and she felt that she could not well stand another twenty-four hours.

"You're sure you won't mind being alone?"

"No, of course not. I shall miss you," added Mirabelle, more in truth than in compliment. "When will you return?"

The girl made a little grimace.

"Tomorrow."

"You don't want to come back, naturally? Have you succeeded in persuading your—your friend to let me out too?"

Joan shook her head.

"He'll never do that, my dear, not till..." She looked at the girl. "You're not engaged, are you?"

"I? No. Is that another story they've heard?" Mirabelle got up from the bed, laughing. "An heiress, and engaged?"

"No, they don't say you were engaged." Joan hastened to correct the wrong impression. There was genuine admiration in her voice when she said: "You're wonderful, kid! If I were in your shoes I'd be quaking. You're just as cheerful as though you were going to the funeral of a rich aunt!"

She did not know how near to a breakdown her companion had been that day, and Mirabelle, who felt stronger and saner now, had no desire to tell her.

"You're rather splendid," Joan nodded. "I wish I had your pluck."

And then, impulsively, she came forward and kissed the girl.

"Don't feel too sore at me," she said, and was gone before Mirabelle could make a reply.

The doctor was waiting for her in the factory.

"The spy has walked up to the canal bridge. We can go forward," he said. "Besides"—he had satisfaction out of this—"he cannot see over high walls."

"What is this story about marrying Mirabelle Leicester?"

"So he has told you? Also did he tell you that—that he is going to marry her?"

"Yes, and I'll tell you something, doctor. I'd rather he married her than you."

"So!" said the doctor.

"I'd rather anybody else married her, except that snake of yours."

Oberzohn looked round sharply. She had used the word quite innocently, without any thought of its application, and uttered an "Oh!" of dismay when she realized her mistake.

"I meant Gurther," she said.

"Well, I know you meant Gurther, young miss," he said stiffly.

To get back to the house they had to make a half-circle of the factory and pass between the canal wall and the building itself. The direct route would have taken them into a deep hollow into which the debris of years had been thrown, and which now Nature, in her kindness, had hidden under a green mantle of wild convolvulus. It was typical of the place that the only beautiful picture in the grounds was out of sight.

They were just turning the corner of the factory when the doctor stopped and looked up at the high wall, which was protected by a cheval de frise of broken glass. All except in one spot, about two feet wide, where not only the glass but the mortar which held it in place had been chipped off. There were fragments of the glass, and, on the inside of the wall, marks of some implement on the hard surface of the mortar.

"So!" said the doctor.

He was examining the scratches on the wall.

"Wait," he ordered, and hurried back into the factory, to return, carrying in each hand two large rusty contraptions which he put on the ground.

One by one he forced open the jagged rusty teeth until they were wide apart and held by a spring catch. She had seen things like that in a museum. They were man-traps—relics of the barbarous days when trespass was not only a sin but a crime.

He fixed the second of the traps on the path between the factory and the wall.

"Now we shall see," he said. "Forward!"

Monty was waiting for her impatiently. The Rolls had been turned out in her honour, and the sulky-looking driver was already in his place at the wheel.

"What is the matter with that chauffeur?" she asked, as they bumped up the lane towards easier going. "He looks so happy that I shouldn't be surprised to hear that his mother was hanged this morning."

"He's sore with the old man," explained Monty. "Oberzohn has two drivers. They do a little looking round in the morning. The other fellow was supposed to come back to take over duty at three o'clock, and he hasn't turned up. He was the better driver of the two."

The chauffeur was apparently seeking every pothole in the ground, and in the next five minutes she was alternately clutching the support of the arm-strap and Monty. They were relieved when at last the car found a metal road and began its noiseless way towards the lights. And then her hand sought his, and for a moment this beautiful flower which had grown in such foul soil, bloomed in the radiance of a love common to every woman, high and low, good and bad.

28

AT PRATER'S

Manfred suggested an early dinner at the Lasky, where the soup was to his fastidious taste. Leon, who had eaten many crumpets for tea—he had a weakness for this indigestible article of diet—was prepared to dispense with the dinner, and Poiccart had views, being a man of steady habits. They dined at the Lasky, and Leon ordered a baked onion, and expatiated upon the two wasted years of Poiccart's life, employing a wealth of imagery and a beauty of diction worthy of a better subject.

Manfred looked at his watch.

"Where are they dining?" he asked.

"I don't know yet," said Leon. "Our friend will be here in a few minutes: when we go out he will tell us. You don't want to see her?"

Manfred shook his head.

"No," he said.

"I'm going to be bored," complained Poiccart.

"Then you should have let me bring Alma," said Leon promptly.

"Exactly." Raymond nodded his sober head. "I have the feeling that I am saving a lady from an unutterably dreary evening."

There was a man waiting for them when they came out of the restaurant—a very uninteresting-looking man who had three sentences to say sotto voce as they stood near him, but apparently in ignorance of his presence.

"I did not wish to go to Mero's," said Manfred, "but as we have the time, I think it would be advisable to stroll in that direction. I am curious to discover whether this is really Oberzohn's little treat, or whether the idea emanated from the unadmirable Mr Newton."

"And how will you know, George?" asked Gonsalez.

"By the car. If Oberzohn is master of the ceremonies, we shall find his machine parked somewhere in the neighbourhood. If it is Newton's idea, then Oberzohn's limousine, which brought them from South London, will have returned, and Newton's car will be in its place."

Mero's was one of the most fashionable of dining clubs, patronized not only by the elite of society, but having on its books the cream of the theatrical world. It was situated in one of those quiet, old-world squares which are to be found in the very heart of London, enjoying, for some mysterious reason, immunity from the hands of the speculative property owner. The square retained the appearance it had in the days of the Georges; and though some of the fine mansions had been given over to commerce and the professions, and the lawyer and the manufacturer's agent occupied the drawing-rooms and bedrooms sacred to the bucks and beauties of other days, quite a large number of the houses remained in private occupation.

There was nothing in the fascia of Mero's to advertise its character. The club premises consisted of three of these fine old dwellings. The uninitiated might not even suspect that there was communication between the three houses, for the old doorways and doorsteps remained untouched, though only one was used.

They strolled along two sides of the square before, amidst the phalanx of cars that stood wheel to wheel, their backs to the railings of the centre gardens, they saw Oberzohn's car. The driver sat with his arms folded on the wheel, in earnest conversation with a pale-faced man, slightly and neatly bearded, and dressed in faultless evening dress. He was evidently a cripple: one shoulder was higher than the other; and when he moved, he walked painfully with the aid of a stick.

Manfred saw the driver point up the line of cars, and the lame gentleman limped in the direction the chauffeur had indicated and stopped to speak to another man in livery. As they came abreast of him, they saw that one of his boots had a thick sole, and the limp was explained.

"The gentleman has lost his car," said Manfred, for now he was peering short-sightedly at the number-plates.

The theft of cars was a daily occurrence. Leon had something to say on the potentialities of that branch of crime. He owned to an encyclopaedic knowledge of the current fashions in wrongdoing, and in a few brief sentences indicated the extent of these thefts.

"Fifty a week are shipped to India and the Colonies, after their numbers are erased and another substituted. In some cases the 'knockers off,' as they call the thieves, drive them straightway into the packing-cases which are prepared for every make of car; the ends are nailed up, and they are waiting shipment at the docks before the owner is certain of his loss. There are almost as many stolen cars in India, South Africa and Australia as there are honest ones!"

They walked slowly past the decorous portals of Mero's, and caught a glimpse, through the curtained windows, of soft table lamps burning, of bare-armed women and white-shirted men, and heard faintly the strains of an orchestra playing a Viennese waltz.

"I should like to see our Jane," said Gonsalez. "She never came to you, did she?"

"She came, but I didn't see her," said Manfred. "From the moment she leaves the theatre she must not be left."

Leon nodded.

"I have already made that arrangement," he said. "Digby—"

"Digby takes up his duty at midnight," said Manfred. "He has been down to Oberzohn's place to get the lie of the land: he thought it advisable that he should study the topography in daylight, and I agreed. He might get himself into an awkward tangle if he started exploring the canal bank in the dark hours. Summer or winter, there is usually a mist on the water."

They reached Prater's theatre so early that the queues at the pit door were still unadmitted, and Leon suggested that they make a circuit of this rambling house of entertainment. It stood in Shaftesbury Avenue and occupied an island site. On either side two narrow streets flanked the building, whilst the rear formed the third side of a small square, one of which was taken up by a County Council dwelling, mainly occupied by artisans. From the square a long passageway led to Cranbourn Street; whilst, in addition to the alley which opened just at the back of the theatre, a street ran parallel to Shaftesbury Avenue from Charing Cross Road to Rupert Street.

The theatre itself was one of the best in London, and although it had had a succession of failures, its luck had turned, and the new mystery play was drawing all London.

"That is the stage door," said Leon—they had reached the square—"and those are emergency exits"—he pointed back the way they had come—"which are utilized at the end of a performance to empty the theatre."

"Why are you taking such an interest in the theatre itself?" asked Poiccart.

"Because," said Gonsalez slowly, "I am in agreement with George. We should have found Newton's car parked in

Fitzreeve Gardens—not Oberzohn's. And the circumstances are a little suspicious."

The doors of the pit and gallery were open now; the queues were moving slowly to the entrances; and they watched the great building swallow up the devotees of the drama, before they returned to the front of the house.

Cars were beginning to arrive, at first at intervals, but, as the hour of the play's beginning approached, in a ceaseless line that made a congestion and rendered the traffic police articulate and occasionally unkind. It was short of the half-hour after eight when Manfred saw Oberzohn's glistening car in the block, and presently it pulled up before the entrance of the theatre. First Joan and then Monty Newton alighted and passed out of view.

Gonsalez thought he had never seen the girl looking quite as radiantly pretty. She had the colouring and the shape of youth, and though the more fastidious might object to her daring toilette, the most cantankerous could not cavil at the pleasing effect.

"It is a great pity"—Leon spoke in Spanish—"a thousand pities! I have the same feeling when I see a perfect block of marble placed in the hands of a tombstone-maker to be mangled into ugliness!"

Manfred put out his hand and drew him back into the shadow. A cab was dropping the lame man. He got out with the aid of a linkman, paid the driver, and limped into the vestibule. It was not a remarkable coincidence: the gentleman had evidently come from Mero's, and as all London was flocking to the drama, there was little that was odd in finding him here. They saw that he went up into the dress circle, and later, when they took their places in the stalls, Leon, glancing up, saw the pale, bearded face and noted that he occupied the end seat of the front row.

"I've met that man somewhere," he said, irritated. "Nothing annoys me worse than to forget, not a face, but where I have seen it!"

Did Gurther but know, he had achieved the height of his ambition: he had twice passed under the keen scrutiny of the cleverest detectives in the world, and had remained unrecognized.

29

WORK FOR GURTHER

Gurther was sleeping when he was called for duty, but presented himself before his director as bright and alert as though he had not spent a sleepless night, nor yet had endured the strain of a midnight train jump.

"Once more, my Gurther, I send you forth." Dr Oberzohn was almost gay. "This time to save us all from the Judas treachery of one we thought was our friend. Tonight the snake must bite, and bite hard, Gurther. And out into the dark goes the so-called Trusted! And after that, my brave boy, there shall be nothing to fear."

He paused for approval, and got it in a snapped agreement.

"Tonight we desire from you a chef d'oeuvre, the supreme employment of your great art, Gurther; the highest expression of genius! The gentleman-club manner will not do. They may look for you and find you. Better it should be, this time, that you—"

"Herr Doktor, will you graciously permit me to offer a humble suggestion?" said Gurther eagerly.

The doctor nodded his head slowly.

"You may speak, Gurther," he said. "You are a man of intelligence; I would not presume to dictate to an artist."

"Let me go for an hour, perhaps two hours, and I will return to you with a manner that is unique. Is it graciously permitted, Herr Doktor?"

"March!" said the doctor graciously, waving his hand to the door.

Nearly an hour and a half passed before the door opened and a gentleman came in who for a moment even the doctor thought was a stranger. The face had an unearthly ivory pallor; the black brows, the faint shadows beneath the eyes that suggested a recent illness, the close-cropped black beard in which grey showed—these might not have deceived him. But the man was obviously the victim of some appalling accident of the past. One shoulder was hunched, the hand that held the stick was distorted out of shape, and as he moved, the clump of his club foot advertised his lameness.

"Sir, you desire to see me—?" began the doctor, and then stared open-mouthed. "It is not... !"

Gurther smiled.

"Herr Doktor, are you condescendingly pleased?"

"Colossal!" murmured Oberzohn, gazing in amazement. "Of all accomplishments this is supreme! Gurther, you are an artist. Some day we shall buy a theatre for you in Unter den Linden, and you shall thrill large audiences."

"Herr Doktor, this is my own idea; this I have planned for many months. The boots I made myself; even the coat I altered"—he patted his deformed shoulder proudly.

"An eyeglass?"

"I have it," said Gurther promptly.

"The cravat—is it not too proper?"

Gurther fingered his tie.

"For the grand habit I respectfully claim that the proper tie is desirable, if you will graciously permit."

The Herr Doktor nodded.

"You shall go with God, Gurther," he said piously, took a golden cigarette-case from his pocket and handed it to the man. "Sit down, my dear friend."

He rose and pointed to the chair he had vacated.

"In my own chair, Gurther. Nothing is too good for you. Now here is the arrangement..."

Step by step he unfolded the time-table, for chronology was almost as great a passion with this strange and wicked man as it was with Aunt Alma.

So confident was Gurther of his disguise that he had gone in the open to speak to Oberzohn's chauffeur, and out of the tail of his eye he had seen Manfred and Gonsalez approaching. It was the supreme test and was passed with credit to himself.

He did not dine at Mero's; Gurther never ate or drank when he was wearing a disguise, knowing just how fatal that occupation could be. Instead, he had called a taxi, and had killed time by being driven slowly round and round the Outer Circle of Regent's Park.

Gurther was doing a great deal of thinking in these days, and at the cost of much physical discomfort had curtailed his pernicious practices, that his head might be clear all the time. For if he were to live, that clear head of his was necessary.

The prisoner in the cellar occupied his thoughts. She had an importance for two reasons: she was a friend of the men whom he hated with a cold and deadly malignity beyond description; she represented wealth untold, and the Herr Doktor had even gone to the length of planning a marriage with her. She was not to be killed, not to be hurt; she was so important that the old man would take the risks attendant upon a marriage. There must be an excellent reason for that, because Dr Oberzohn had not a very delicate mind.

He seemed to remember that, by the English law, a wife could not give evidence against her husband. He was not sure, but he had a dim notion that Pfeiffer had told him this: Pfeiffer was an educated man and had taken high honours at the gymnasium.

Gurther was not well read. His education had been of a scrappy character, and once upon a time he had been refused a leading part because of his provincial accent. That fault he had corrected in prison, under the tuition of a professor who was serving a life sentence for killing two women; but by the time Gurther had been released, he was a marked man, and the stage was a career lost to him for ever.

Oberzohn possessed advantages which were not his. He was the master; Gurther was the servant. Oberzohn could determine events by reason of his vast authority, and the strings which he pulled in every part of the world. Even Gurther had accepted this position of blind, obedient servant, but now his angle had shifted, even as Oberzohn's had moved in relation to Montague Newton. Perhaps because of this. The doctor, in curtailing one confidence, was enlarging another, and in the enlargement his prestige suffered.

Gurther was now the confidant, therefore the equal, and logically, the equal can always become the superior. He had dreamed dreams of a life of ease, a gratification of his sense of luxury without the sobering thought that somewhere round the corner was waiting a man ready to tap him on the shoulder... a white palace in a flowery land, with blue swimming pools, and supple girls who called him Master. Gurther began to see the light.

Until he had taken his seat in the theatre, he had not so much as glimpsed the man and the woman in the end box.

Joan was happy—happier than she remembered having been. Perhaps it was the reaction from her voluntary imprisonment. Certainly it was Monty's reluctant agreement to a change of plans which so exalted her. Monty had dropped the thin pretence of an accommodation marriage; and once he was persuaded to this, the last hindrance to enjoyment was dissipated. Let Oberzohn take the girl if he wanted her; take, too, such heavy responsibility as followed. Monty Newton would get all that he wanted without the risk. Having arrived at this decision, he had ordered another bottle of champagne to seal the bargain, and they left Mero's club a much happier couple than they had been when they entered.

"As soon as we've carved up this money, we'll get away out of England," he told her as they were driving to the theatre. "What about Buenos Ayres for the winter, old girl?"

She did not know where Buenos Ayres was, but she gurgled her delight at the suggestion, and Monty expatiated upon the joys of the South American summer, the beauties of B.A., its gaieties and amusements.

"I don't suppose there'll be any kick coming," he said, "but it wouldn't be a bad scheme if we took a trip round the world, and came back in about eighteen months' time to settle down in London. My hectic past would have been forgotten by then—why, I might even get into Parliament."

"How wonderful!" she breathed, and then: "What is this play about, Monty?"

"It's a bit of a thrill, the very play for you—a detective story that will make your hair stand on end."

She had all the gamin's morbid interest in murder and crime, and she settled down in the box with a pleasant feeling of anticipation, and watched the development of the first act.

The scene was laid in a club, a low-down resort where the least desirable members of society met, and she drank in every word, because she knew the life, had seen that type of expensively dressed woman who swaggered on to the stage and was addressed familiarly by the club proprietor. She knew that steady-eyed detective when he made his embarrassing appearance. The woman was herself. She even knew the cadaverous wanderer who approached stealthily at the door: a human wolf that fled at the sight of the police officer.

The three who sat in the front row of the stalls—how Leon Gonsalez secured these tickets was one of the minor mysteries of the day—saw her, and one at least felt his heart ache.

Monty beamed his geniality. He had taken sufficient wine to give him a rosy view of the world, and he was even mildly interested in the play, though his chief pleasure was in the girl's enchantment. He ordered ices for her after the first interval.

"You're getting quite a theatre fan, kiddie," he said. "I must take you to some other shows. I had no idea you liked this sort of thing."

She drew a long breath and smiled at him.

"I like anything when I'm with you," she said, and they held hands foolishly, till the house lights dimmed and the curtain rose upon a lawyer's office.

The lawyer was of the underworld: a man everlastingly on the verge of being struck off the rolls. He had betrayed a client with whom he had had dealings, and the man had gone to prison for a long term, but had escaped. Now the news had come that he had left Australia and was in London, waiting his opportunity to destroy the man whose treachery was responsible for his capture.

Here was a note to which the heart of the girl responded. Even Monty found himself leaning forward, as the old familiar cant terms of his trade came across the footlights.

"It is quite all right," he said, at the second interval, "only"—he hesitated—"isn't it a bit too near the real thing? After all, one doesn't come to the theatre to see..."

He stopped, realizing that conditions and situations familiar to him were novel enough to a fashionable audience which was learning for the first time that a "busy" was a detective, and that a police informer went by the title of "nose."

The lights up, he glanced round the house, and suddenly he started and caught her arm.

"Don't look for a moment," he said, averting his eyes, "then take a glance at the front row. Do you see anybody you know?"

Presently she looked.

"Yes, that is the fellow you hate so much, isn't it—Gonsalez?"

"They're all there—the three of them," said Monty. "I wonder"—he was troubled at the thought— "I wonder if they're looking for you?"

"For me? They've nothing on me, Monty."

He was silent.

"I'm glad you're not going back to that place tonight. They'll trail you sure—sure!"

He thought later that it was probably a coincidence that they were there at all. They seemed to show no interest in the box, but were chattering and talking and laughing to one another. Not once did their eyes come up to his level, and after a while he gained in confidence, though he was glad enough when the play was resumed.

There were two scenes in the act: the first was a police station, the second the lawyer's room. The man was drunk, and the detective had come to warn him that The Ringer was after him. And then suddenly the lights on the stage were extinguished and the whole house was in the dark. It was part of the plot. In this darkness, and in the very presence of the police, the threatened man was to be murdered. They listened in tense silence, the girl craning her head forward, trying to pierce the dark, listening to the lines of intense dialogue that were coming from the blackness of the stage. Somebody was in the room—a woman, and they had found her. She slipped from the stage detective's grasp and vanished, and when the lights went up she was gone.

"What has happened, Monty?" she whispered.

He did not answer.

"Do you think—?"

She looked round at him. His head was resting on the plush-covered ledge of the box. His face, turned towards her, was grey; the eyes were closed, and his teeth showed in a hideous grin.

She screamed.

"Monty! Monty!"

She shook him. Again her scream rang through the house. At first the audience thought that it was a woman driven hysterical by the tenseness of the stage situation, and then one or two people rose from their stalls and looked up.

"Monty! Speak to me! He's dead, he's dead!"

Three seats in the front row had emptied. The screams of the hysterical girl made it impossible for the scene to proceed, and the curtain came down quickly.

The house was seething with excitement. Every face was turned towards the box where she knelt by the side of the dead man, clasping him in her arms, and the shrill agony in her voice was unnerving.

The door of the box swung open, and Manfred dashed in. One glance he gave at Monty Newton, and he needed no other.

"Get the girl out," he said curtly.

Leon tried to draw her from the box, but she was a shrieking fury.

"You did it, you did it!... Let me go to him!"

Leon lifted her from her feet, and, clawing wildly at his face, she was carried from the box.

The manager was running along the passage, and Leon sent him on with a jerk of his head. And then a woman in evening dress came from somewhere.

"May I take her?" she said, and the exhausted girl collapsed into her arms.

Gonsalez flew back to the box. The man was lying on the floor, and the manager, standing at the edge of the box, was addressing the audience.

"The gentleman has fainted, and I'm afraid his friend has become a little hysterical. I must apologize to you, ladies and gentlemen, for this interruption. If you will allow us a minute to clear the box, the play will be resumed. If there is a doctor in the house, I should be glad if he would come."

There were two doctors within reach, and in the passage, which was now guarded by a commissionaire, a hasty examination was made. They examined the punctured wound at the back of the neck and then looked at one another.

"This is The Snake," said one.

"The house musn't know," said Manfred. "He's dead, of course?"

The doctor nodded.

Out in the passage was a big emergency exit door, and this the manager pushed open, and, running out into the street, found a cab, into which all that was mortal of Monty Newton was lifted.

Whilst this was being done, Poiccart returned.

"His car has just driven off," he said. "I saw the number-plate as it turned into Lisle Street."

"How long ago?" asked Gonsalez quickly.

"At this very moment."

Leon pinched his lip thoughtfully.

"Why didn't he wait, I wonder?"

He went back through the emergency door, which was being closed, and passed up the passage towards the entrance. The box was on the dress-circle level, and the end of a short passage brought him into the circle itself.

And then the thought of the lame man occurred to him, and his eyes sought the first seat in the front row, which was also the seat nearest to the boxes. The man had gone.

As he made this discovery, George emerged from the passage.

"Gurther!" said Leon. "What a fool I am! But how clever!"

"Gurther?" said Manfred in amazement. "Do you mean the man with the club foot?"

Leon nodded.

"He was not alone, of course," said Gonsalez. "There must have been two or three of the gang here, men and women— Oberzohn works these schemes out with the care and thoroughness of a general. I wonder where the management have taken the girl?"

He found the manager discussing the tragedy with two other men, one of whom was obviously associated with the production, and he signalled him aside.

"The lady? I suppose she's gone home. She's left the theatre."

"Which way did she go?" asked Gonsalez, in a sudden panic.

The manager called a linkman, who had seen a middle-aged woman come out of the theatre with a weeping girl, and they had gone down the side-street towards the little square at the back of the playhouse.

"She may have taken her home to Chester Square," said Manfred. His voice belied the assumption of confidence.

Leon had not brought his own machine, and they drove to Chester Square in a taxi. Fred, the footman, had neither heard nor seen the girl, and nearly fainted when he learned of the tragic ending to his master's career.

"Oh, my God!" he groaned. "And he only left here this afternoon... dead, you say?"

Gonsalez nodded.

"Not—not The Snake?" faltered the man.

"What do you know about the snake?" demanded Manfred sternly.

"Nothing, except—well, the snake made him nervous, I know. He told me today that he hoped he'd get through the week without a snake-bite."

He was questioned closely, but although it was clear that he knew something of his master's illicit transactions, and that he was connected in business with Oberzohn, the footman had no connection with the doctor's gang. He drew a large wage and a percentage of profits from the gaming side of the business, and confessed that it was part of his duties to prepare stacks of cards and pass them to his master under cover of bringing in the drinks. But of anything more sinister he knew nothing.

"The woman, of course, was a confederate, who had been planted to take charge of the girl the moment the snake struck. I was in such a state of mind," confessed Leon, "that I do not even remember what she looked like. I am a fool—a double-distilled idiot! I think I must be getting old. There's only one thing for us to do, and that is to get back to Curzon Street—something may have turned up."

"Did you leave anybody in the house?"

Leon nodded. "Yes, I left one of our men, to take any 'phone messages that came through."

They paid off the taxi before the house, and Leon sprinted to the garage to get the car. The man who opened the door to them was he who had been tied up by the pedlar at Heavy-tree Farm, and his first words came as a shock to Manfred: "Digby's here, sir."

"Digby?" said the other in surprise. "I thought he was on duty?"

"He's been here since just after you left, sir. If I'd known where you had gone, I'd have sent him to you."

Digby came out of the waiting-room at that moment, ready to apologize.

"I had to see you, sir, and I'm sorry I'm away from my post."

"You may not be missing much," said Manfred unsmilingly. "Come upstairs and tell me all about it."

Digby's story was a strange one. He had gone down that afternoon to the canal bank to make a reconnaissance of ground which was new to him.

"I'm glad I did too, because the walls have got broken glass on top. I went up into the Old Kent Road and bought a garden hoe, and prised the mortar loose, so that if I wanted, I could get over. And then I climbed round the water-gate and had a look at that barge of his. There was nobody about, though I think they spotted me afterwards. It is a fairly big barge, and, of course, in a terrible state, but the hold is full of cargo—you know that, sir?"

"You mean there is something in the barge?"

Digby nodded.

"Yes, it has a load of some kind. The after part, where the bargee's sleeping quarters are, is full of rats and water, but the fore part of the vessel is water-tight, and it holds something heavy too. That is why the barge is down by its head in the mud. I was in the Thames police and I know a lot about river craft."

"Is that what you came to tell me?"

"No, sir, it was something queerer than that. After I'd given the barge a look over and tried to pull up some of the boards—which I didn't manage to do—I went along and had a look at the factory. It's not so easy to get in, because the entrance faces the house, but to get to it you have to go half round the building, and that gives you a certain amount of cover. There was nothing I could see in the factory itself. It was in a terrible mess, full of old iron and burnt-out boxes. I was coming round the back of the building," he went on impressively, "when I smelt a peculiar scent."

"A perfume?"

"Yes, sir, it was perfume, but stronger—more like incense. I thought at first it might be an old bale of stuff that had been thrown out, or else I was deceiving myself. I began poking about in the rubbish heaps—but they didn't smell of scent! Then I went back into the building again, but there was no smell at all. It was very strong when I returned to the back of the factory, and then I saw a little waft of smoke come out of a ventilator close to the ground. My first idea was that the place was on fire, but when I knelt down, it was this scent."

"Joss-sticks?" said Poiccart quickly.

"That's what it was!" said the detective. "Like incense, yet not like it. I knelt down and listened at the grating, and I'll swear that I heard voices. They were very faint."

"Men's?"

"No, women's."

"Could you see anything?"

"No, sir, it was a blind ventilator there was probably a shaft there—in fact, I'm sure there was, because I pushed a stone through one of the holes and heard it drop some distance down."

"There may be an underground room there," said Poiccart, "and somebody's burnt joss-sticks to sweeten the atmosphere."

"Under the factory? It's not in the plans of the building. I've had them from the surveyor's office and examined them," said George, "although surveyors' plans aren't infallible. A man like Oberzohn would not hesitate to break so unimportant a thing as a building law!"

Leon came in at that moment, heard the story and was in complete agreement with Poiccart's theory.

"I wondered at the time we saw the plans whether we ought to accept that as conclusive," he said. "The store was built at the end of 1914, when architects and builders took great liberties and pleaded the exigencies of the war."

Digby went on with his story.

"I was going back to the barge to get past the water-gate, but I saw the old man coming down the steps of the house, so I climbed the wall, and very glad I was that I'd shifted that broken glass, or I should never have got over."

Manfred pulled his watch from his pocket with a frown. They had lost nearly an hour of precious time with their inquiries in Chester Square.

"I hope we're not too late," he said ominously. "Now Leon... "

But Leon had gone down the stairs in three strides.

30

JOAN A PRISONER

Dazed with grief, not knowing, not seeing, not caring, not daring to think, Joan suffered herself to be led quickly into the obscurity of the side-street, and did not even realize that Oberzohn's big limousine had drawn up by the sidewalk.

"Get in," said the woman harshly.

Joan was pushed through the door and guided to a seat by somebody who was already in the machine.

She collapsed in a corner moaning as the door slammed and the car began to move.

"Where are we going? Let me get back to him!"

"The gracious lady will please restrain her grief," said a hateful voice, and she swung round and stared unseeingly to the place whence the voice had come.

The curtains of the car had been drawn; the interior was as black as pitch.

"You—you beast!" she gasped. "It's you, is it?... Gurther! You murdering beast!"

She struck at him feebly, but he caught her wrist.

"The gracious lady will most kindly restrain her grief," he said suavely. "The Herr Newton is not dead. It was a little trick in order to baffle certain interferers."

"You're lying, you're lying!" she screamed, struggling to escape from those hands of steel. "He's dead! You know he's dead, and you killed him! You snake-man!"

"The gracious lady must believe me," said Gurther earnestly. They were passing through a public part of the town and at any moment a policeman might hear her shrieks. "If Herr Newton had not pretended to be hurt, he would have been arrested... he follows in the next car."

"You're trying to quieten me," she said, "but I won't be quiet."

And then a hand came over her mouth and pressed her head back against the cushions. She struggled desperately, but two fingers slid up her face and compressed her nostrils. She was being suffocated. She struggled to free herself from the tentacle hold of him, and then slipped into unconsciousness.

Gurther felt the straining figure go limp and removed his hands. She did not feel the prick of the needle on her wrist, though the drugging was clumsily performed in the darkness and in a car that was swaying from side to side. He felt her pulse, his long fingers pressed her throat and felt the throb of the carotid artery; propping her so that she could not fall, Herr Gurther sank back luxuriously into a corner of the limousine and lit a cigar.

The journey was soon over. In a very short time they were bumping down Hangman's Lane and turned so abruptly into the factory grounds that one of the mudguards buckled to the impact of the gate-post.

It must have been two hours after the departure of her companion, when Mirabelle, lying on her bed, half dozing, was wakened by her book slipping to the floor, and sat up quickly to meet the apprising stare of the man whom, of all men in the world, she disliked most cordially. Dr Oberzohn had come noiselessly into the room and under his arm was a pile of books.

"I have brought these for you," he said, in his booming voice, and stacked them neatly on the table.

She did not answer.

"Novels of a frivolous kind, such as you will enjoy," he said, unconscious of offence. "I desired the seller of the books to pick them for me. Fiction stories of adventure and of amorous exchanges. These will occupy your mind, though to me they would be the merest rubbish and nonsense."

She stood silently, her hands clasped behind her, watching him. He was neater than usual, had resumed the frock-coat he wore the day she had first met him—how long ago that seemed!—his collar was stiffly white, and if his cravat was more gorgeous than is usually seen in a man correctly arrayed, it had the complementary value of being new.

He held in his hands a small bouquet of flowers tightly packed, their stems enclosed in silver foil, a white paper frill supplying an additional expression of gentility.

"These are for you." He jerked out his hand towards her.

Mirabelle looked at the flowers, but did not take them. He seemed in no way disconcerted, either by her silence, or by the antagonism which her attitude implied, but, laying the flowers on top of the books, he clasped his hands before him and addressed her. He was nervous, for some reason; the skin of his forehead was furrowing and smoothing with grotesque rapidity. She watched the contortions, fascinated.

"To every man," he began, "there comes a moment of domestic allurement. Even to the scientific mind, absorbed in its colossal problems, there is this desire for family life and for the haven of rest which is called marriage."

He paused, as though he expected her to offer some comment upon his platitude.

"Man alone," he went on, when she did not speak, "has established an artificial and unnatural convention that, at a certain age, a man should marry a woman of that same age.

Yet it has been proved by history that happy marriages are often between a man who is in the eyes of the world old, and a lady who is youthful."

She was gazing at him in dismay. Was he proposing to her? The idea was incredible, almost revolting. He must have read in her face the thoughts that were uppermost in her mind, the loathing, the sense of repulsion which filled her, yet he went on, unabashed: "I am a man of great riches. You are a girl of considerable poverty. But because I saw you one day in your poor house, looking, gracious lady, like a lily growing amidst foul weeds, my heart went out to you, and for this reason I brought you to London, spending many thousands of pounds in order to give myself the pleasure of your company."

"I don't think you need go any farther, Dr Oberzohn," she said quietly, "if you're proposing marriage, as I think you are."

He nodded emphatically.

"Such is my honourable intention," he said.

"I would never marry you in any circumstances," she said. "Not even if I had met you under the happiest conditions. The question of your age"—she nearly added "and of your appearance," but her natural kindness prevented that cruel thrust, though it would not have hurt him in the slightest degree— "has nothing whatever to do with my decision. I do not even like you, and have never liked you, Mr Oberzohn."

"Doctor," he corrected, and in spite of her woeful plight she could have laughed at this insistence upon the ceremonial title.

"Young miss, I cannot woo you in the way of my dear and sainted brother, who was all for ladies and had a beautiful manner."

She was amazed to hear that he had a brother at all—and it was almost a relief to know that he was dead.

"Martyred, at the hands of wicked and cunning murderers, slain in his prime by the assassin's pistol..." His voice trembled and broke. "For that sainted life I will some day take vengeance."

It was not wholly curiosity that impelled her to ask who killed him.

"Leon Gonsalez." The words in his lips became the grating of a file. "Killed... murdered! And even his beautiful picture destroyed in that terrible fire. Had he saved that, my heart would have been soft towards him." He checked himself, evidently realizing that he was getting away from the object of his call. "Think over this matter, young lady. Read the romantic books and the amorous books, and then perhaps you will not think it so terrible a fate to drift at moonlight through the canals of Venice, with the moon above and the gondoliers."

He wagged his head sentimentally.

"There is no book which will change my view, doctor," she said. "I cannot understand why you propose such an extraordinary course, but I would rather die than marry you."

His cold eyes filled her with a quick terror.

"There are worse things than death, which is but sleep—many worse things, young miss. Tomorrow I shall come for you, and we will go into the country, where you will say 'yes' and 'no' according to my desire. I have many—what is the word?—certificates for marriage, for I am too clever a man to leave myself without alternatives."

(This was true; he had residential qualifications in at least four counties, and at each he had given legal notice of his intended marriage.)

"Not tomorrow or any other day. Nothing would induce me."

His eyebrows went almost to the top of his head.

"So!" he said, with such significance that her blood ran cold. "There are worse men than the Herr Doktor"—he raised a long finger warningly—"terrible, men with terrible minds. You have met Gurther?"

She did not answer this.

"Yes, yes, you danced with him. A nice man, is he not, to ladies? Yet this same Gurther... I will tell you something."

He seated himself on a corner of the table and began talking, until she covered her ears with her hands and hid her white face from him.

"They would have killed him for that," he said, when her hands came down, "but Gurther was too clever, and the poor German peasants too stupid. You shall remember that, shall you not?"

He did not wait for her answer. With a stiff bow he strutted out of the room and up the stairs. There came the thud of the trap falling and the inevitable rumble of the concrete barrel.

He had some work to do, heavy work for a man who found himself panting when he climbed stairs. And though four of his best and most desperate men were waiting in his parlour drinking his whisky and filling the little room with their rank cigar smoke, he preferred to tackle this task which he had already begun as soon as night fell, without their assistance or knowledge.

On the edge of the deep hole in his grounds, where the wild convolvulus grew amidst the rusty corners of discarded tins and oil barrels, was a patch of earth that yielded easily to the spade. When the factory had been built, the depression had been bigger, but the builders had filled in half the hole with the light soil that they had dug out of the factory's foundations.

He took his spade, which he had left in the factory, and, skirting the saucer-shaped depression, he reached a spot where a long trench had already been dug. Taking off his fine coat and waistcoat, unfastening cravat and collar and carefully depositing them upon the folded coat, he continued his work, stopping now and again to wipe his streaming brow.

He had to labour in the dark, but this was no disadvantage; he could feel the edges of the pit. In an hour the top of the trench was level with his chin, and, stooping to clear the bottom of loose soil, he climbed up with greater difficulty than he had anticipated, and it was only after the third attempt that he managed to reach the top, out of breath and short of temper.

He dressed again, and with his electric torch surveyed the pit he had made and grunted his satisfaction.

He was keenly sensitive to certain atmospheres, and needed no information about the change which had come over his subordinates. In their last consultation Gurther had been less obsequious, had even smoked in his presence without permission—absent-mindedly, perhaps, but the offence was there. And Dr Oberzohn, on the point of smacking his face for his insolence, heard a warning voice within himself which had made his hand drop back at his side. Or was it the look he saw on Gurther's face? The man was beyond the point where he could discipline him in the old Junker way. For although Dr Oberzohn condemned all things Teutonic, he had a sneaking reverence for the military caste of that nation.

He left the spade sticking in a heap of turned earth. He would need that again, and shortly. Unless Gurther failed. Somehow he did not anticipate a failure in this instance. Mr Monty Newton had not yet grown suspicious, would not be on his guard. His easy acceptance of the theatre tickets showed his mind in this respect.

The four men in his room rose respectfully as he came in. The air was blue with smoke, and Lew Cuccini offered a rough apology. He had been released that morning from detention, for Meadows had found it difficult to frame a charge which did not expose the full activities of the police, and the part they were playing in relation to Mirabelle Leicester. Evidently Cuccini had been reproaching, in his own peculiar way and in his own unprincipled language, the cowardice of his three companions, for the atmosphere seemed tense when the doctor returned. Yet, as was subsequently proved, the appearance of discord was deceptive; might indeed have been staged for their host's benefit.

"I've just been telling these birds—" began Cuccini.

"Oh, shut up, Lew!" growled one of his friends. "If that crazy man hadn't been shouting your name, we should not have gone back! He'd have wakened the dead. And our orders were to retire at the first serious sign of an alarm. That's right, doctor, isn't it?"

"Sure it's right," said the doctor blandly. "Never be caught— that is a good motto. Cuccini was caught."

"And I'd give a year of my life to meet that Dago again," said Cuccini, between his teeth.

He was delightfully inconsistent, for he came into the category, having been born in Milan, and had had his early education in the Italian quarter of Hartford, Connecticut.

"He'd have tortured me too… he was going to put lighted wax matches between my fingers—"

"And then you spilled it!" accused one of the three hotly. "You talk about us bolting!"

"Silence!" roared the doctor. "This is unseemly! I have forgiven everything. That shall be enough for you all. I will hear no other word."

"Where is Gurther?" Cuccini asked the question.

"He has gone away. Tonight he leaves for America. He may return—who knows? But that is the intention."

"Snaking?" asked somebody, and there was a little titter of laughter.

"Say, doctor, how do you work that stunt?" Cuccini leaned forward, his cigar between his fingers, greatly intrigued. "I saw no snakes down at Rath Hall, and yet he was bitten, just as that Yankee was bitten—Washington."

"He will die," said the doctor complacently. He was absurdly jealous for the efficacy of his method.

"He was alive yesterday, anyway. We shadowed him to the station."

"Then he was not bitten—no, that is impossible. When the snake bites"—Oberzohn raised his palms and gazed piously at the ceiling—"after that there is nothing. No, no, my friend, you are mistaken."

"I tell you I'm not making any mistake," said the other doggedly. "I was in the room, I tell you, soon after they brought him in, and I heard one of the busies say that his face was all wet."

"So!" said Oberzohn dully. "That is very bad."

"But how do you do it, doctor? Do you shoot or sump'n?"

"Let us talk about eventual wealth and happiness," said the doctor. "Tonight is a night of great joy for me. I will sing you a song."

Then, to the amazement of the men and to their great unhappiness, he sang, in a thin reedy old voice, the story of a young peasant who had been thwarted in love and had thrown himself from a cliff into a seething waterfall. It was a lengthy song, intensely sentimental, and his voice held few of the qualities of music. The gang had never been set a more difficult job than to keep straight faces until he had finished.

"Gee! You're some artist, doctor!" said the sycophantic Cuccini, and managed to get a simulation of envy into his voice.

"In my student days I was a great singer," said the doctor modestly.

Over the mantelpiece was a big, old clock, with a face so faded that only a portion of the letters remained. Its noisy ticking had usually a sedative effect on the doctor. But its main purpose and value was its accuracy. Every day it was corrected by a message from Greenwich, and as Oberzohn's success as an organizer depended upon exact timing, it was one of his most valuable assets.

He glanced up at the clock now, and that gave Cuccini his excuse.

"We'll be getting along, doctor," he said. "You don't want anything tonight? I'd like to get a cut at that Gonsalez man. You won't leave me out if there's anything doing?"

Oberzohn rose and went out of the room without another word, for he knew that the rising of Cuccini was a signal that not only was the business of the day finished, but also that the gang needed its pay.

Every gang-leader attended upon Mr Oberzohn once a week with his pay-roll, and it was usually the custom for the Herr Doktor to bring his cash-box into the room and extract sufficient to liquidate his indebtedness to the leader. It was a big box, and on pay-day, as this was, filled to the top with banknotes and Treasury bills. He brought it back now, put it on the table, consulted the little slip that Cuccini offered to him, and, taking out a pad of notes, fastened about by a rubber band, he wetted his finger and thumb.

"You needn't count them," said Cuccini. "We'll take the lot."

The doctor turned to see that Cuccini was carelessly holding a gun in his hand.

"The fact is, doctor," said Cuccini coolly, "we've seen the red light, and if we don't skip now, while the skipping's good, there's going to be no place we can stay comfortable in this little island, and I guess we'll follow Gurther."

One glance the doctor gave at the pistol and then he resumed his counting, as though nothing had happened.

"Twenty, thirty, forty, fifty... "

"Now quit that," said Cuccini roughly. "I tell you, you needn't count."

"My friend, I prefer to know what I am going to lose. It is a pardonable piece of curiosity."

He raised his hand to the wall, where a length of cord hung, and pulled it gently, without taking his eyes from the banknotes.

"What are you doing? Put up your hands!" hissed Cuccini.

"Shoot, I beg." Oberzohn threw a pad of notes on the table. "There is your pay." He slammed down the lid of the box. "Now you shall go, if you can go! Do you hear them?" He raised his hand, and to the strained ears of the men came a gentle rustling sound from the passage outside as though somebody were dragging a piece of parchment along the floor. "Do you hear? You shall go if you can," said the doctor again, with amazing calmness.

"The snakes!" breathed Cuccini, going white, and the hand that held the pistol shook.

"Shoot them, my friend," sneered Oberzohn. "If you see them, shoot them. But you will not see them, my brave man. They will be—where? No eyes shall see them come or go. They may lie behind a picture, they may wait until the door is opened, and then... !"

Cuccini's mouth was dry.

"Call 'em off, doctor," he said tremulously.

"Your gun—on the table."

Still the rustling was audible. Cuccini hesitated for a second, then obeyed, and took up the notes.

The other three men were huddled together by the fireplace, the picture of fear.

"Don't open the door, doc," said Cuccini, but Oberzohn had already gripped the handle and turned it.

They heard another door open and the click of the passage light as it had come on. Then he returned.

"If you go now, I shall not wish to see you again. Am I not a man to whom all secrets are known? You are well aware!"

Cuccini looked from the doctor to the door.

"Want us to go?" he asked, troubled.

Oberzohn shrugged.

"As you wish! It was my desire that you should stay with me tonight—there is big work and big money for all of you."

The men were looking at one another uneasily.

"How long do you want us to stay?" asked Cuccini.

"Tonight only; if you would not prefer..."

Tonight would come the crisis. Oberzohn had realized this since the day dawned for him.

"We'll stay—where do we sleep?"

For answer Oberzohn beckoned them from the room and they followed him into the laboratory. In the wall that faced them was a heavy iron door that opened into a concrete storehouse, where he kept various odds and ends of equipment, oil and spirit for his cars, and the little gas engine that worked a small dynamo in the laboratory and gave him, if necessary a lighting plant independent of outside current.

There were three long windows heavily barred and placed just under the ceiling.

"Looks like the condemned cell to me," grumbled Cuccini suspiciously.

"Are the bolts on the inside of a condemned cell?" asked Oberzohn. "Does the good warden give you the key as I give you?"—

Cuccini took the key.

"All right," he said ungraciously, "there are plenty of blankets here, boys—I guess you want us where the police won't look, eh?"

"That is my intention," replied the doctor.

Dr Oberzohn closed the door on them and re-entered his study, his big mouth twitching with amusement. He pulled the cord again and closed the ventilator he had opened. It was only a few days before that he had discovered that there were dried leaves in the ventilator shaft, and that the opening of the inlet made them rustle, disturbingly for a man who was engaged in a profound study of the lesser known, and therefore the more highly cultured, philosophers.

31

THE THINGS IN THE BOX

He heard the soft purr of engines, and, looking through the hall window, saw the dim lights of the car approaching the house, and turned out the hall lamp. There he waited in the darkness, till the door of the limousine opened and Gurther jumped out. "I respectfully report that it is done, Herr Doktor," he said.

Oberzohn nodded.

"The woman of Newton—where is she?"

"She is inside. Is it your wish that I should bring her? She was very troublesome, Herr Doktor, and I had to use the needle."

"Bring her in—you!" He barked to the chauffeur. "Help our friend."

Together they lifted the unconscious girl, but carried her no farther than the steps. At this point Oberzohn decided that she must return to the prison. First they sent the chauffeur away; the car was garaged at New Cross (it was one of Oberzohn's three London depots), where the man also lived. After he had gone, they carried Joan between them to the factory, taking what, to Gurther, seemed an unnecessarily circuitous route. If it was necessary, it was at least expedient, for the nearest way to the factory led past the yawning hole that the doctor had dug with such labour.

There was no mistaking Oberzohn's arrival this time. The trap went up with a thud, and Mirabelle listened, with a quickly beating heart, to the sound of feet coming down the stone stairs. There were two people, and they were walking heavily. Somehow she knew before she saw their burden that it was Joan. She was in evening dress, her face as white as chalk and her eyes closed; the girl thought she was dead when she saw them lay her on the bed.

"You have given her too much, Gurther," said Oberzohn.

Gurther? She had not recognized him. It was almost impossible to believe that this was the dapper young man who had danced with her at the Arts Ball.

"I had to guess in the dark, Herr Doktor," said Gurther.

They were talking in German, and Mirabelle's acquaintance with that language was very slight. She saw Gurther produce a small flat case from his pocket, take out a little phial, and shake into the palm of his hand a small brown capsule. This he dissolved in a tiny tube which, with the water he used, was also extracted from the case. Half filling a minute syringe, he sent the needle into Joan's arm. A pause, and then: "Soon she will wake, with your kind permission, Herr Doktor," said Gurther.

Mirabelle was not looking at him, but she knew that his hot eyes were fixed on her, that all the time except the second he was operating, he was looking at her; and now she knew that this was the man to be feared. A cold hand seemed to grip at her heart.

"That will do, Gurther." Oberzohn's voice was sharp. He, too, had interpreted the stare. "You need not wait."

Gurther obediently stalked from the room, and the doctor followed. Almost before the trap had fastened down she was by the girl's side, with a basin of water and a wet towel. The second the water touched her face, Joan opened her eyes and gazed wildly up at the vaulted ceiling, then rolling over from the bed to her knees, she struggled to her feet, swayed and would have fallen, had not Mirabelle steadied her.

"They've got him! They've got my boy... killed him like a dog!"

"What — Mr — Mr Newton?" gasped Mirabelle, horrified.

"Killed him — Monty — Monty!"

And then she began to scream and run up and down the room like a thing demented. Mirabelle, sick at heart, almost physically sick at the sight, caught her and tried to calm her, but she was distracted, half mad. The drug and its antidote seemed to have combined to take away the last vestige of restraint. It was not until she fell, exhausted, that Mirabelle was able to drag her again to the bed and lay her upon it.

Montague Newton was dead! Who had killed him? Who were the "they"? Then she thought of Gurther in his strange attire; white dress-front crumpled, even his beard disarranged in the struggle he had had with the overwrought woman.

In sheer desperation she ran up the steps and tried the trap, but it was fast. She must get away from here — must get away at once. Joan was moaning pitiably, and the girl sat by her side, striving to calm her. She seemed to have passed into a state of semi-consciousness; except for her sobs, she made no sound and uttered no intelligible word. Half an hour passed — the longest and most dreadful half-hour in Mirabelle Leicester's life. And then she heard a sound. It had penetrated even to the brain of this half-mad girl, for she opened her eyes wide, and, gripping Mirabelle, drew herself up.

"He's coming," she said, white to the lips, "coming... the Killer is coming!"

"For God's sake don't talk like that!" said Mirabelle, beside herself with fear.

There it was, in the outer room; a stealthy shuffle of feet. She stared at the closed door, and the strain of the suspense almost made her faint. And then she saw the steel door move slowly, and first a hand came through, the edge of a face... Gurther was leering at her. His beard was gone, and his wig; he was collarless, and had over his white shirt the stained jacket that was his everyday wear.

"I want you." He was talking to Mirabelle. Her tongue clave to the roof of her mouth, but she did not speak.

"My pretty little lady—" he began, and then, with a shriek, Joan leapt at him.

"Murderer, murderer... ! Beast!" she cried, striking wildly at his face. With a curse, he tried to throw her off, but she was clinging to him; a bestial lunatic thing, hardly human.

He flung her aside at last, and then he put up his hand to guard his face as she leapt at him again. This time she went under his arm and was through the door in a flash. He heard the swift patter of her feet on the stairs, and turned in pursuit. The trap was open. He stumbled and tripped in the dark across the floor of the gaunt factory. Just as she reached the open, he grabbed at her and missed. Like a deer she sped, but he was fleeter-footed behind her; and suddenly his hand closed about her throat.

"You had better go out, my friend," he said, and tightened his grip.

As she twisted to avoid him, he put out his foot. There was a grating snap, something gripped his legs, and the excruciating pain of it was agonizing. He loosened his hold of her throat, but held her arm tightly. With all his strength he threw her against the wall and she fell in a heap. Then, leaning down, he forced apart the cruel jagged teeth of the mantrap on to which he had put his foot, and drew his leg clear. He was bleeding; his trouser leg was torn to ribbons. He stopped only long enough to drag the girl to her feet, and, throwing her across his shoulder as though she were a sack, he went back into the factory, down the stairs, and threw her on to the bed with such violence that the spring supports broke. It had a strange effect upon the dazed woman, but this he did not see, for he had turned to Mirabelle.

"My little lady, I want you!" he breathed.

Blood was trickling down from his wounded calf, but he did not feel the pain any more; felt nothing, save the desire to hurt those who hunted him; wanted nothing but the materialization of crude and horrid dreams.

She stood, frozen, paralysed, incapable of movement. And then his hand came under her chin and he lifted her face; and she saw the bright, hungry eyes devouring her, saw the thin lips come closer and closer, could not move; had lost all sentient impressions, and could only stare into the eyes of this man-snake, hypnotized by the horror of the moment.

And then a raging fury descended upon him. Narrow fingers tore at his face, almost blinding him. He turned with a howl of rage, but the white-faced Joan had flown to the furnace and taken up a short iron bar that had been used to rake the burning coals together. She struck at him and missed. He dodged past her and she flung the bar at him, and again missed him. The iron struck the green box, behind the furnace, there was a sound of smashing glass. He did not notice this, intent only upon the girl, and Mirabelle closed her eyes and heard only the blow as he struck her.

When she looked again, Joan was lying on the bed and he was tying one of her hands to the bed-rail with a strap which he had taken from his waist. Then Mirabelle saw a sight that released her pent speech. He heard her scream and grinned round at her... saw where she was looking and looked too.

Something was coming from the broken green box! A black, spade-shaped head, with bright, hard eyes that seemed to survey the scene in a malignant stare. And then, inch by inch, a thick shining thing, like a rubber rope, wriggled slowly to the floor, coiled about upon itself, and raised its flat head. "Oh, God, look!"

He turned about at the sight, that immovable grin of his upon his face, and said something in a guttural tongue. The snake was motionless, its baleful gaze first upon the sinking girl, then upon the man.

Gurther's surprise was tragic; it was as though he had been confronted with some apparition from another world. And then his hand went to his hip pocket; there was a flash of light and a deafening explosion that stunned her. The pistol dropped from his hand and fell with a clatter to the floor, and she saw his arm was stiffly extended, and protruding from the cuff of his coat a black tail that wound round and round his wrist. It had struck up his sleeve. The cloth about his biceps was bumping up and down erratically.

He stood straightly erect, grinning, the arm still outflung, his astonished eyes upon the coil about his wrist. And then, slowly his other hand came round, gripped the tail and pulled it savagely forth. The snake turned with an angry hiss and tried to bite back at him; but raising his hand, he brought the head crashing down against the furnace. There was a convulsive wriggle as the reptile fell among the ashes.

"Gott in himmel!" whispered Gurther, and his free hand went up to his arm and felt gingerly. "He is dead, gracious lady. Perhaps there is another?"

He went, swaying as he walked, to the green box, and put in his hand without hesitation. There was another—a bigger snake, roused from its sleep and angry. He bit twice at the man's wrist, but Gurther laughed, a gurgling laugh of pure enjoyment. For already he was a dead man; that he knew. And it had come to him, at the moment and second of his dissolution, when the dread gates of judgment were already ajar, that he should go to his Maker with this clean space in the smudge of his life.

"Go, little one," he said, grinning into the spade-face. "You have no more poison; that is finished!"

He put the writhing head under his heel, and Mirabelle shut her eyes and put her hands to her ears. When she looked again, the man was standing by the door, clinging to the post and slipping with every frantic effort to keep himself erect. He grinned at her again; this man of murder, who had made his last kill.

"Pardon, gracious lady," he said thickly, and went down on his knees, his head against the door, his body swaying slowly from side to side, and finally tumbled over.

She heard Oberzohn's harsh voice from the floor above. He was calling Gurther, and presently he appeared in the doorway, and there was a pistol in his hand.

"So!" he said, looking down at the dying man.

And then he saw the snake, and his face wrinkled. He looked from Mirabelle to the girl on the bed, went over and examined her, but did not attempt to release the strap. It was Mirabelle who did that; Mirabelle who sponged the bruised face and loosened the dress.

So doing, she felt a hand on her shoulder.

"Come," said Oberzohn.

"I'm staying here with Joan, until—"

"You come at once, or I will give you to my pretty little friends." He pointed to the two snakes on the floor who still moved spasmodically.

She had to step past Gurther, but that seemed easier than passing those wriggling, shining black ropes; and, her hand in his, she stumbled up the dark steps and eventually into the clean, sweet air of the night.

He was dressed for a journey; she had noticed that when he appeared. A heavy cloth cap was on his curious-shaped head, and he looked less repulsive with so much of his forehead hidden. Though the night was warm, he wore an overcoat.

They were passing between the wall and the factory when he stopped and put his hand before her mouth. He had heard voices, low voices on the other side of the wall, and presently the scrape of something. Without removing his hand from her face, he half dragged, half pushed her until they were clear of the factory.

She thought they were going back to the house, which was in darkness, but instead, he led her straight along the wall, and presently she saw the bulk of the barge.

"Stay, and do not speak," he said, and began to turn a rusty wheel. With a squeak and a groan the water-gates opened inwards. What did he intend doing? There was no sign of a boat, only this old dilapidated barge. She was presently to know.

"Come," he said again. She was on the deck of the barge, moving forward to its bow, which pointed towards the open gate and the canal beyond.

She heard him puff and groan as he strained at a rope he had found, and then, looking down, she saw the front of the barge open, like the two water-gates of a lock. Displaying remarkable agility, he lowered himself over the edge; he seemed to be standing on something solid, for again he ordered her to join him.

"I will not go," she said breathlessly, and turning, would have fled, but his hand caught her dress and dragged at her.

"I will drown you here, woman," he, said, and she knew that the threat would have a sequel.

Tremblingly she lowered herself over the edge until her foot touched something hard and yet yielding. He was pushing at the barge with all his might, and the platform beneath her grew in space. First the sharp nose and then the covered half-deck of the fastest motor-boat that Mr Oberzohn's money could buy, or the ingenuity of builders could devise. The old barge was a boat-house, and this means of escape had always been to his hand. It was for this reason that he lived in a seemingly inaccessible spot.

The men who had been on the canal bank were gone. The propellers revolving slowly, the boat stole down the dark waters,

THE THINGS IN THE BOX

after a short time slipped under a bridge over which street-cars were passing, and headed for Deptford and the river.

Dr Oberzohn took off his overcoat and laid it tenderly inside the shelter of the open cabin, tenderly because every pocket was packed tight with money.

To Mirabelle Leicester, crouching in the darkness of that sheltered space, the time that passed had no dimension. Once an authoritative voice hailed them from the bank. It was a policeman; she saw him after the boat had passed. A gas-lamp showed the glitter of his metal buttons. But soon he was far behind.

Deptford was near when they reached a barrier which neither ingenuity nor money could pass; a ragged night-bird peered down curiously at the motor-boat. "You can't get through here, guv'nor," he said simply. "The lock doesn't open until high tide."

"When is this high tide?" asked Oberzohn breathlessly.

"Six o'clock tomorrow morning," said the voice.

For a long time he was stricken to inactivity by the news, and then he sent his engines into reverse and began circling round.

"There is one refuge for us, young miss," he said. "Soon we shall see it. Now I will tell you something. I desire so much to live. Do you also?"

She did not answer.

"If you cry out, if you will make noises, I will kill you—that is all," he said; and the very simplicity of his words, the lack of all emphasis behind the deadly earnestness, told her that he would keep his word.

32

THE SEARCH

"'Ware man-traps," said Gonsalez.

The white beam of his lamp had detected the ugly thing. He struck at it with his stick, and with a vicious snap it closed.

"Here's one that's been sprung," he said, and examined the teeth. "And, what's more, it has made a catch! There's blood here."

Manfred and Digby were searching the ground cautiously. Then Manfred heard the quick intake of his breath, and he stooped again, picked up a strip of braided cloth.

"A man's," he said, and his relief betrayed his fear. "Somebody in evening dress, and quite recent." He looked at his finger. "The blood is still wet."

Digby showed him the ventilator grating through which he had smelt the incense, and when Leon stooped, the faint aroma still remained.

"We will try the factory first. If that draws blank, we'll ask Dr Oberzohn's guidance, and if it is not willingly given I shall persuade him." And in the reflected light of the lamp George Manfred saw the hard Leon he knew of old. "This time I shall not promise: my threat will be infinitely milder than my performance."

They came to the dark entry of the factory, and Manfred splashed his light inside.

"You'll have to walk warily here," he said,

Progress was slow, for they did not know that a definite path existed between the jagged ends of broken iron and debris. Once or twice Leon stopped to stamp on the floor; it gave back a hollow sound.

The search was long and painfully slow: a quarter of an hour passed before Leon's lamp focussed on the upturned flagstone and the yawning entrance of the vault. He was the first to descend, and, as he reached the floor, he saw silhouetted in the light that flowed from the inner room, a man, as he thought, crouching in the doorway, and covered him.

"Put up your hands!" he said.

The figure made no response, and Manfred ran to the shape. The face was in the shadow, but he brought his own lamp down and recognized the set grin of the dead man.

Gurther!

So thus he had died, in a last effort to climb out for help.

"The Snake," said Manfred briefly. "There are no marks on his face, so far as I can see."

"Do you notice his wrist, George?"

Then, looking past the figure, Gonsalez saw the girl lying on the bed, and recognized Joan before he saw her face. Halfway across the room he slipped on something. Instinctively he knew it was a snake and leapt around, his pistol balanced.

"Merciful heaven! Look at this!"

He stared from the one reptile to the other.

"Dead!" he said. "That explains Gurther."

Quickly he unstrapped Joan's wrists and lifted up her head, listening, his ear pressed to the faintly fluttering heart. The basin and the sponge told its own story. Where was Mirabelle?

There was another room, and a row of big cupboards, but the girl was in no place that he searched.

"She's gone, of course," said Manfred quietly. "Otherwise, the trap would not have been open. We'd better get this poor girl out of the way and search the grounds. Digby, go to—"

He stopped.

If Oberzohn were in the house, they must not take the risk of alarming him.

But the girl's needs were urgent. Manfred picked her up and carried her out into the open, and, with Leon guiding them, they came, after a trek which almost ended in a broken neck for Leon, to within a few yards of the house.

"I presume," said Gonsalez, "that the hole into which I nearly dived was dug for a purpose, and I shouldn't be surprised to learn it was intended that the late Mr Gurther should find a permanent home there. Shall I take her?"

"No, no," said Manfred, "go on into the lane. Poiccart should be there with the car by now."

"Poiccart knows more about growing onions than driving motor-cars." The gibe was mechanical; the man's heart and mind were on Mirabelle Leicester.

They had to make a circuit of the stiff copper-wire fence which surrounded the house, and eventually reached Hangman's Lane just as the headlamps of the Spanz came into view.

"I will take her to the hospital and get in touch with the police," said Manfred. "I suppose there isn't a near-by telephone?"

"I shall probably telephone from the house," said Leon gravely.

From where he stood he could not tell whether the door was open or closed. There was no transom above the door, so that it was impossible to tell whether there were lights in the passage or not. The house was in complete darkness.

He was so depressed that he did not even give instructions to Poiccart, who was frankly embarrassed by the duty which had been imposed upon him, and gladly surrendered the wheel to George.

THE SEARCH

They lifted the girl into the tonneau, and, backing into the gate, went cautiously up the lane—Leon did not wait to see their departure, but returned to the front of the house.

The place was in darkness. He opened the wire gate and went silently up the steps. He had not reached the top before he saw that the door was wide open. Was it a trap? His lamp showed him the switch: he turned on the light and closed the door behind him, and, bending his head, listened.

The first door on the right was Oberzohn's room. The door was ajar, but the lamps were burning inside. He pushed it open with the toe of his boot, but the room was empty.

The next two doors he tried on that floor were locked. He went carefully down to the kitchens and searched them both. They were tenantless. He knew there was a servant or two on the premises, but one thing he did not know, and this he discovered in the course of his tour, was that Oberzohn had no bedroom. One of the two rooms above had evidently been occupied by the servants. The door was open, the room was empty and in some confusion; a coarse night-dress had been hastily discarded and left on the tumbled bedclothes. Oberzohn had sent his servants away in a hurry—why?

There was a half-smoked cigarette on the edge of a deal wash-stand. The ash lay on the floor. In a bureau every drawer was open and empty, except one, a half-drawer filled with odd scraps of cloth. Probably the cook or the maid smoked. He found a packet of cigarettes under one pillow to confirm this view, and guessed they had gone to bed leisurely with no idea that they would be turned into the night.

He learned later that Oberzohn had bundled off his servants at ten minutes' notice, paying them six months' salary as some salve for the indignity.

Pfeiffer's room was locked; but now, satisfied that the house was empty, he broke the flimsy catch, made a search but found nothing. Gurther's apartment was in indescribable disorder.

He had evidently changed in a hurry. His powder puffs and beards, crepe hair and spirit bottles, littered the dressing-table. He remembered, with a pang of contrition, that he had promised to telephone the police, but when he tried to get the exchange he found the line was dead: a strange circumstance, till he discovered that late that evening Meadows had decided to cut the house from all telephonic communication, and had given orders accordingly.

It was a queerly built house: he had never realized its remarkable character until he had examined it at these close quarters. The walls were of immense thickness: that fact was brought home to him when he had opened the window of the maid's room to see if Digby was in sight. The stairs were of concrete, the shutters which covered the windows of Oberzohn's study were steel-faced. He decided, pending the arrival of the police, to make an examination of the two locked rooms. The first of these he had no difficulty in opening. It was a large room on the actual ground level, and was reached by going down six steps. A rough bench ran round three sides of this bare apartment, except where its continuity broke to allow entrance to a further room. The door was of steel and was fastened.

The room was dusty but not untidy. Everything was in order. The various apparatus was separated by a clear space. In one corner he saw a gas engine and dynamo covered with dust. There was nothing to be gained here. The machine which interested him most was one he knew all about, only he had not guessed the graphite moulds. The contents of a small blue bottle, tightly corked, and seemingly filled with discoloured swabs of cotton-wool, however, revived his interest. With a glance round the laboratory, he went out and tried the second of the locked doors.

This room, however, was well protected, both in the matter of stoutness of door and complication of locks. Leon tried all his keys, and then used his final argument. This he carried in a small leather pouch in his hip pocket; three steel pieces that screwed together and ended in a bright claw. Hammering the end of the jemmy with his fist, he forced the claw between door and lintel, and in less than a minute the lock had broken, and he was in the presence of the strangest company that had ever been housed.

Four electric radiators were burning. The room was hot and heavy, and the taint of it caught his throat, as it had caught the throat of the Danish servant. He put on all the lights—and they were many—and then began his tour.

There were two lines of shelves, wide apart, and each supporting a number of boxes, some of which were wrapped in baize, some of which, however, were open to view. All had glass fronts, all had steel tops with tiny air-holes, and in each there coiled, in its bed of wool or straw, according to its requirements, one or two snakes. There were cobras, puff-adders, two rattlesnakes, seemingly dead, but, as he guessed, asleep; there was a South American fer-de-lance, that most unpleasant representative of his species; there were little coral snakes, and, in one long box, a whole nest of queer little things that looked like tiny yellow lobsters, but which he knew as scorpions.

He was lifting a baize cover when:

"Don't move, my friend! I think I can promise you more intimate knowledge of our little family."

Leon turned slowly, his hands extended. Death was behind him, remorseless, unhesitating. To drop his hand to his pocket would have been the end for him—he had that peculiar instinct which senses sincerity, and when Dr Oberzohn gave him his instructions he had no doubt whatever that his threat was backed by the will to execute.

Oberzohn stood there, and a little behind him, white-faced, open-eyed with fear, Mirabelle Leicester.

Digby—where was he? He had left him in the grounds.

The doctor was examining the broken door and grunted his annoyance.

"I fear my plan will not be good," he said, "which was to lock you in this room and break all those glasses, so that you might become better acquainted with the Quiet People. That is not to be. Instead, march!"

What did he intend? Leon strolled out nonchalantly, but Oberzohn kept his distance, his eyes glued upon those sensitive hands that could move so quickly and jerk and fire a gun in one motion.

"Stop!"

Leon halted, facing the open front door and the steps.

"You will remember my sainted brother, Señor Gonsalez, and of the great loss which the world suffered when he was so vilely murdered?"

Leon stood without a quiver. Presently the man would shoot. At any second a bullet might come crashing on its fatal errand. This was a queer way to finish so full a life. He knew it was coming, had only one regret; that this shaken girl should be called upon to witness such a brutal thing. He wanted to say good-bye to her, but was afraid of frightening her.

"You remember that so sainted brother?" Oberzohn's voice was raucous with fury. Ahead of him the light fell upon a face.

"Digby! Stay where you are!" shouted Leon.

The sound of the explosion made him jump. He saw the brickwork above the doorway splinter, heard a little scuffle, and turned, gun in hand. Oberzohn had pulled the girl in front of him so that she afforded a complete cover: under her arm he held his pistol.

"Run!" she screamed.

He hesitated a second. Again the pistol exploded and a bullet ricochetted from the door. Leon could not fire. Oberzohn so crouched that nothing but a trick shot could miss the girl and hit him. And then, as the doctor shook free the hand that gripped his wrist, he leapt down the steps and into the darkness. Another second and the door slammed. He heard the thrust of the bolts and a clang as the great iron bar fell into its place. Somehow he had a feeling as of a citadel door being closed against him.

Dr Oberzohn had returned unobserved, though the night was clear. Passing through the open water-gate he had tied up to the little quay and landed his unwilling passenger. Digby, according to instructions, had been making a careful circuit of the property, and at the moment was as far away from the barge as it was humanly possible to be. Unchallenged, the doctor had worked his way back to the house. The light in the hall warned him that somebody was there. How many? He could not guess.

"Take off your shoes," he growled in Mirabelle's ear, and she obeyed.

Whatever happened, he must not lose touch of her, or give her an opportunity to escape. Still grasping her arm with one hand and his long Mauser pistol in the other, he went softly up the steps, got into the hall and listened, locating the intruder instantly.

It all happened so quickly that Mirabelle could remember nothing except the desperate lunge she made to knock up the pistol that had covered the spine of Leon Gonsalez. She stood dumbly by, watching this horrible old man fasten the heavy door, and obediently preceded him from room to room. She saw the long cases in the hot room and shrank back. And then began a complete tour of the house. There were still shutters to be fastened, peep-holes to be opened up. He screwed up the shutters of the servants' room, and then, with a hammer, broke the thumb-piece short.

"You will stay here," he said. "I do not know what they will do. Perhaps they will shoot. I also am a shooter!"

Not satisfied with the lock that fastened her door, he went into his workshop, found a staple, hook and padlock, and spent the greater part of an hour fixing this additional security. At last he had finished, and could put the situation in front of four very interested men.

He unlocked the door of the concrete annexe and called the crestfallen gunmen forth, and in a very few words explained the situation and their danger.

"For every one of you the English police hold warrants," he said. "I do not bluff, I know. This afternoon I was visited by the police. I tell you I do not bluff you—me they cannot touch, because they know nothing, can prove nothing. At most I shall go to prison for a few years, but with you it is different."

"Are they waiting outside?" asked one suspiciously. "Because, if they are, we'd better move quick."

"You do not move, quick or slow," said Oberzohn. "To go out from here means certain imprisonment for you all. To stay, if you follow my plan, means that every one of you may go free and with money."

"What's the idea?" asked Cuccini. "Are you going to fight them?"

"Sure I am going to fight them," nodded Oberzohn. "That is my scheme. I have the young miss upstairs; they will not wish to do her any harm. I intend to defend this house."

"Do you mean you're going to hold it?" asked one of the staggered men.

"I will hold it until they are tired, and make terms."

Cuccini was biting his nails nervously.

"Might as well be hung for a sheep as a lamb, boss," he growled. "I've got an idea you've roped us into this."

"You may rope yourself out of it!" snapped Oberzohn. "There is the door—go if you wish. There are police there; make terms with them. A few days ago you were in trouble, my friend. Who saved you? The doctor Oberzohn. There is life imprisonment for every one of you, and I can hold this house myself. Stay with me, and I will give you a fortune greater than any you have dreamt about. And, more than this, at the end you shall be free."

"Where's Gurther?"

"He has been killed—by accident." Oberzohn's face was working furiously. "By accident he died," he said, and told the truth unconvincingly. "There is nothing now to do but to make a decision."

Cuccini and his friends consulted in a whisper.

"What do we get for our share?" he asked, and Oberzohn mentioned a sum which staggered them.

"I speak the truth," he said. "In two days I shall have a goldmine worth millions."

The habit of frankness was on him, and he told them the story of the golden hill without reservations. His agents at Lisbon had already obtained from the Ministry an option upon the land and its mineral rights. As the clock struck twelve on June 14, the goldfield of Biskara automatically passed into his possession.

"On one side you have certain imprisonment, on the other you have great moneys and happiness."

"How long will we have to stay here?" asked Cuccini.

"I have food for a month, even milk. They will not cut the water because of the girl. For the same reason they will not blow in the door."

Again they had a hasty consultation and made their decision.

"All right, boss, we'll stay. But we want that share-out put into writing."

"To my study," said Oberzohn promptly, "march!"

He was half-way through writing the document when there came a thunderous knock on the door and he got up, signalling for silence. Tiptoeing along the passage, he came to the door.

"Yes—who is that?" he asked.

"Open, in the name of the law!" said a voice, and he recognized Meadows. "I have a warrant for your arrest, and if necessary the door will be broken in."

"So!" said Oberzohn, dropped the muzzle of his pistol until it rested on the edge of the little letter-slit and fired twice.

33

THE SIEGE

But Meadows had already been warned to keep clear of the letter-box, and the bullets eventually reached one of the railway viaducts, to the embarrassment of a road ganger who happened to be almost in the line of fire.

Meadows slipped down the steps to cover. Inside the wire fence a dozen policemen were waiting. "Sergeant, go back to the station in the police car and bring arms," he said. "This is going to be a long job."

Gonsalez had made a very careful reconnaissance of the ground, and from the first had recognized the difficulties which lay ahead of the attacking party. The wall rose sheer without any break; such windows as were within reach were heavily shuttered; and even the higher windows, he guessed, had been covered. The important problem in his mind was to locate the room in which the girl was imprisoned, and making a mental review of the house, he decided that she was either in the servants' apartment or in that which had held Gurther. By the light of the lantern he made a rapid sketch plan of the floors he had visited.

Meadows had gone away to telephone to police headquarters. He had decided to re-establish telephone connection with the doctor, and when this was done, he called the house and Oberzohn's voice answered him.

The colloquy was short and unsatisfactory. The terms which the doctor offered were such as no self-respecting Government could accept. Immunity for himself and his companions (he insisted so strongly upon this latter offer that Meadows guessed, accurately, that the gang were standing around the instrument).

"I don't want your men at all. So far as I am concerned, they can go free," said Meadows. "Ask one of them to speak on the 'phone."

"Oh, indeed, no," said Oberzohn. "It is ridiculous to ask me that."

He hung up at this point and explained to the listening men that the police had offered him freedom if he would surrender the gang.

"As I already told you," he said in conclusion, "that is not the way of Dr Oberzohn. I will gain nothing at the expense of my friends."

A little later, when Cuccini crept into the room to call police head-quarters and confirm this story of the doctor, he found that not only had the wire been cut, but a yard of the flex had been removed. Dr Oberzohn was taking no risks.

The night passed without any further incident. Police reserves were pouring into the neighbourhood; the grounds had been isolated, and even the traffic of barges up and down the canal prohibited. The late editions of the morning newspapers had a heavily head-lined paragraph about the siege of a house in the New Cross area, and when the first reporters arrived a fringe of sightseers had already gathered at every police barrier. Later, special editions, with fuller details, begun to roll out of Fleet Street; the crowd grew in density, and a high official from Scotland Yard, arriving soon after nine, ordered a further area to be cleared, and with some difficulty the solid wedge of humanity at the end of Hangman's Lane was slowly pushed back until the house was invisible to them. Even here, a passageway was kept for police cars and only holders of passes were allowed to come within the prohibited area.

The three men, with the police chief, had taken up their head-quarters in the factory, from which the body of Gurther had been removed in the night. The Deputy Commissioner, who came on the spot at nine and examined the dead snakes, was something of a herpetologist, and pronounced them to be veritable *fers-de-lance*, a view from which Poiccart differed.

"They are a species of African tree snakes that the natives call mamba. There are two, a black and a green. Both of these are the black type."

"The Zoo mamba?" said the official, remembering the sensational disappearance of a deadly snake which had preceded the first of the snake mysteries.

"You will probably find the bones of the Zoo mamba in some mole run in Regent's Park—he must have been frozen to death the night of his escape," said Poiccart. "It was absolutely impossible that at that temperature he could live. I have made a very careful inspection of the land, and adjacent to the Zoological Gardens is a big stretch of earth which is honeycombed by moles. No, this was imported, and the rest of his menagerie was imported."

The police chief shook his head.

"Still, I'm not convinced that a snake could have been responsible for these deaths," he said, and went over the ground so often covered.

The three listened in polite silence, and offered no suggestion.

The morning brought news of Washington's arrival in Lisbon. He had left the train at Irun, Leon's agent in Madrid having secured a relay of aeroplanes, and the journey from Irun to Lisbon had been completed in a few hours. He was now on his way back.

"If he makes the connections he will be here tonight," he told Manfred. "I rather think he will be a very useful recruit to our forces."

"You're thinking of the snakes in the house?"

Leon nodded.

"I know Oberzohn," he said simply, and George Manfred thought of the girl, and knew the unspoken fears of his friend were justified.

The night had not been an idle one for Oberzohn and his companions. With the first light of dawn they had mounted to the roof, and, under his direction, the gunmen had dismantled the four sheds which stood at each corner of the parapet. Unused to the handling of such heavy metal, the remnants of the Old Guard gazed in awe upon the tarnished jackets of the Maxim guns that were revealed.

Oberzohn understood the mechanism of the machines so thoroughly that in half an hour he had taught his crew the method of handling and sighting. In the larger shed was a collapsible tripod, which was put together, and on this he mounted a small but powerful searchlight and connected it up with one of the plugs in the roof.

He pointed to them the three approaches to the house: the open railway arches and the long lane, at the end of which the crowd at that moment was beginning to gather.

"From only these places can the ground be approached," he said, "and my little quick-firers cover them!"

Just before eleven there came down Hangman's Lane, drawn by a motor tractor, a long tree-trunk, suspended about the middle by chains, and Oberzohn, examining it carefully through his field-glasses, realized that no door in the world could stand against the attack of that battering-ram. He took up one of the dozen rifles that lay on the floor, sighted it carefully, resting his elbow on the parapet, and fired.

He saw the helmet of a policeman shoot away from the head of the astonished man, and fired again. This time he was more successful, for a policeman who was directing the course of the tractor crumpled up and fell in a heap.

A shrill whistle blew; the policemen ran to cover, leaving the machine unattended. Again he fired, this time at the driver of the tractor. He saw the man scramble down from his seat and run for the shelter of the fence.

A quarter of an hour passed without any sign of activity on the part of his enemies, and then eight men, armed with rifles, came racing across the ground towards the wire barrier. Oberzohn dropped his rifle, and, taking a grip of the first machine-gun in his hand, sighted it quickly. The staccato patter of the Maxim awakened the echoes. One man dropped; the line wavered. Again the shrill whistle, and they broke for cover, dragging their wounded companion with them.

"I was afraid of that," said Leon, biting his knuckles—sure evidence of his perturbation.

He had put a ladder against the wall of the factory, and now he climbed up on to the shaky roof and focussed his glasses.

"There's another Maxim on this side," he shouted down. And then, as he saw a man's head moving above the parapet, he jerked up his pistol and fired. He saw the stone splinters fly up and knew that it was not bad practice at four hundred yards. The shot had a double effect; it made the defenders cautious and aroused in them the necessary quantity of resentment.

He was hardly down before there was a splutter from the roof, and the whine and snap of machine-gun bullets; one slate tile shivered and its splinters leapt high in the air and dropped beside his hand.

The presence of the girl was the only complication. Without her, the end of Oberzohn and his companions was inevitable.

Nobody realized this better than the doctor, eating a huge ham sandwich in the shelter of the parapet—an unusual luxury, for he ate few solids.

"This will be very shocking for our friends of Curzon Street," he said. "At this moment they bite their hands in despair." (He was nearly right here.)

He peeped over the parapet. There was no policeman in sight. Even the trains that had roared at regular intervals along the viaduct had ceased to run, traffic being diverted to another route.

At half-past twelve, looking through a peep-hole, he saw a long yellow line of men coming down Hangman's Lane, keeping to the shelter of the fence.

"Soldiers," he said, and for a second his voice quavered.

Soldiers they were. Presently they began to trickle into the grounds, one by one, each man finding his own cover. Simultaneously there came a flash and a crack from the nearest viaduct. A bullet smacked against the parapet and the sound of the ricochet was like the hum of a bee.

Another menace had appeared simultaneously; a great, lumbering, awkward vehicle, that kept to the middle of the lane and turned its ungainly nose into the field. It was a tank, and Oberzohn knew that only the girl's safety stood between him and the dangling noose.

He went down to see her, unlocked the door, and found her, to his amazement, fast asleep. She got up at the sound of the key in the lock, and accepted the bread and meat and water he brought her without a word.

"What time is it?"

Oberzohn stared at her.

"That you should ask the time at such a moment!" he said.

The room was in darkness but for the light he had switched on.

"It is noon, and our friends have brought soldiers. Ach! How important a woman you are, that the whole army should come out for you!"

Sarcasm was wasted on Mirabelle.

"What is going to happen—now?"

"I do not know." He shrugged his shoulders. "They have brought a diabolical instrument into the grounds. They may use it, to give them cover, so that the door may be blown in. At that moment I place you in the snake-room. This I shall tell our friends very quickly."

She gazed at him in horror.

"You wouldn't do anything so wicked, Mr Oberzohn!"

Up and down went the skin of his forehead.

"That I shall tell them and that I shall do," he said, and locked her in with this comfortless assurance.

He went into his study and, fastening the door, took two strands of wire from his pocket and repaired the broken telephone connections.

"I wish to speak to Meadows," he said to the man who answered him—a police officer who had been stationed at the exchange to answer any call from this connection.

"I will put you through to him," was the reply.

For a moment the doctor was surprised that Meadows was not at the exchange. He did not know then that a field telephone line had been organized, and that the factory headquarters of the directing staff was in communication with the world.

It was not Meadows, but another man who answered him, and by his tone of authority Oberzohn guessed that some higher police official than Meadows was on the spot.

"I am the doctor Oberzohn," he barked. "You have brought a tank machine to attack me. If this approaches beyond the wire fence, I shall place the woman Leicester in the home of the snakes, and there I will bind her and release my little friends to avenge me."

"Look here—" began the officer, but Oberzohn hung up on him.

He went out and locked the door, putting the key in his pocket. His one doubt was of the loyalty of his companions. But here, strangely enough, he underrated their faith in him. The very mildness of the attack, the seeming reluctance of the soldiers to fire, had raised their hopes and spirits; and when, a quarter of an hour later, they saw the tank turn and go out into Hangman's Lane, they were almost jubilant.

"You're sure that he will carry out his threat?" asked the police chief.

"Certain," said Leon emphatically. "There is nothing on earth that will stop Oberzohn. You will force the house to find a man who has died by his own hand, and—" He shuddered at the thought. "The only thing to be done is to wait for the night. If Washington arrives on time, I think we can save Miss Leicester."

From the roof Dr Oberzohn saw that the soldiers were digging a line of trenches, and sent a spatter of machine-gun bullets in their direction. They stopped their work for a moment to look round, and then went on digging, as though nothing had happened.

The supply of ammunition was not inexhaustible, and he determined to reserve any further fire until the attack grew more active. Looking over the top of the parapet to examine the ground immediately below, something hot and vicious snicked his ear. He saw the brickwork of the chimney behind him crumble and scatter, and, putting up his hand, felt blood.

"You'd better keep down, Oberzohn," said Cuccini, crouching in the shelter of the parapet. "They nearly got you then. They're firing from that railway embankment. Have you had a talk with the boss of these birds?"

"They are weakening," said Oberzohn promptly. "Always they are asking me if I will surrender the men; always I reply, 'Never will I do anything so dishonourable.'"

Cuccini grunted, having his own views of the doctor's altruism.

Late in the afternoon, a flight of aeroplanes appeared in, the west: five machines flying in V formation. None of the men on the roof recognized the danger, standing rather in the attitude and spirit of sightseers. The machines were flying low; with the naked eye Cuccini could read their numbers long before they came within a hundred yards of the house. Suddenly the roof began to spout little fountains of asphalt. Oberzohn screamed a warning and darted to the stairway, and three men followed him out. Cuccini lay spread-eagled where he fell, two machine-gun bullets through his head.

The fighting machines mounted, turned and came back. Standing on the floor below, Oberzohn heard the roar of their engines as they passed, and went incautiously to the roof, to discover that the guns of flying machines fire equally well from the tail. He was nearer to death then than he had ever been. One bullet hit the tip of his finger and sliced it off neatly. With a scream of pain he half fell, half staggered to safety, spluttering strange oaths in German.

The aeroplanes did not return. He waited until their noise had died away before he again ventured to the roof, to find the sky clear. Cuccini was dead, and it was characteristic of his three friends that they should make a thorough search of his pockets before they heaved the body over the parapet.

Oberzohn left the three on the roof, with strict instructions that they were to dive to cover at the first glint of white wings, and went down into his study. The death of Cuccini was in some ways a blessing. The man was full of suspicion; his heart was not in the fight, and the aeroplane gunner had merely anticipated the doctor's own plan.

Cuccini was a Latin, who spoke English well and wrote it badly. He had a characteristic hand, which it amused Oberzohn to copy, for the doctor was skilful with his pen. All through the next three hours he wrote, breaking off his labours at intervals to visit the guard on the roof. At last he had finished, and Cuccini's sprawling signature was affixed to the bottom of the third page. Oberzohn called down one of the men.

"This is the statement of Cuccini which he left. Will you put your name to his signature?"

"What is it?" asked the man surlily.

"It is a letter which the good Cuccini made—what generosity! In this he says that he alone was to blame for bringing you here, and nobody else. Also that he kept you by threats."

"And you?" asked the man.

"Also me," said Oberzohn, unabashed. "What does it matter? Cuccini is dead. May he not in his death save us all? Come, come, my good friend, you are a fool if you do not sign. After that, send down our friends that they may also sign."

A reluctant signature was fixed, and the other men came one by one, and one by one signed their names, content to stand by the graft which the doctor indicated, exculpating themselves from all responsibility in the defence.

Dusk fell and night came blackly, with clouds sweeping up from the west and a chill rain falling. Gonsalez, moodily apart from his companions, watched the dark bulk of the house fade into the background with an ever-increasing misery. What these men did after did not matter—to them. A policeman had been killed, and they stood equally guilty of murder in the eyes of the law. They could now pile horror upon horror, for the worst had happened. His only hope was that they did not know the inevitability of their punishment.

No orders for attack had been given. The soldiers were standing by, and even the attack by the aeroplanes had been due to a misapprehension of orders. He had seen Cuccini's body fall, and as soon as night came he determined to approach the house to discover if there was any other way in than the entrance by the front door.

The aeroplanes had done something more than sweep the roof with their guns. Late in the evening there arrived by special messenger telescopic photographs of the building, which the military commander and the police chief examined with interest.

Leon was watching the house when he saw a white beam of light shoot out and begin a circular sweep of the grounds. He expected this; the meaning of the connections in the wall was clear. He knew, too, how long that experiment would last. A quarter of an hour after the searchlight began its erratic survey of the ground, the lamp went out, the police having disconnected the current. But it was only for a little while, and in less than an hour the light was showing again.

"He has power in the house—a dynamo and a gas engine," explained Gonsalez.

Poiccart had been to town and had returned with a long and heavy steel cylinder, which Leon and Manfred carried between them into the open and left. They were sniped vigorously from the roof, and although the firing was rather wild, the officer in charge of the operations forbade any further movement in daylight.

At midnight came the blessed Washington. They had been waiting for him with eagerness, for he, of all men, knew something that they did not know. Briefly, Leon described the snake-room and its contents. He was not absolutely certain of some of the species, but his description was near enough to give the snake expert an idea of the species.

"Yes, sir, they're all deadly," said Washington, shaking his head. "I guess there isn't a thing there, bar the scorps, who wouldn't put a grown man to sleep in five minutes—ten minutes at the most."

They showed him the remains of the dead snake and he instantly recognized the kind, as the zoological expert had done in the afternoon.

"That's mamba. He's nearly the deadliest of all. You didn't see a fellow with a long bill-shaped head? You did? Well that's fer-de-lance, and he's almost as bad. The little red fellows were corals..."

Leon questioned him more closely.

"No, sir, they don't leap—that's not their way. A tree snake will hang on to something overhead and get you as you pass, and they'll swing from the floor, but their head's got to touch the floor first. The poor little fellow that killed Gurther was scared, and when they're scared they'll lash up at you—I've known a man to be bitten in the throat by a snake that whipped up from the ground. But usually they're satisfied to get your leg."

Leon told him his plan.

"I'll come along with you," said Washington without hesitation.

But this offer neither of the three would accept. Leon had only wanted the expert's opinion. There were scores of scientists in London, curators of museums and keepers of snakes, who could have told him everything there was to be known about the habits of the reptile in captivity. He needed somebody who had met the snake in his native environment.

An hour before daylight showed in the sky, there was a council of war, Leon put his scheme before the authorities, and the plan was approved. He did not wait for the necessary orders to be given, but, with Poiccart and Manfred, went to the place where they had left the cylinder, and, lifting it, made their slow way towards the house. In addition, Leon carried a light ladder and a small bag full of tools.

The rays of the searchlight were moving erratically, and for a long time did not come in their direction. Suddenly they found themselves in a circle of dazzling light and fell flat on their faces. The machine-gun spat viciously, the earth was churned up under the torrent of bullets, but none of the men was hit; and, more important, the cylinder was not touched.

Then suddenly, from every part of the ground, firing started. The target was the searchlight, and the shooting had not gone on for more than a minute before the light went out, so jerkily that it was obvious that one bullet at least had got home.

"Now," said Manfred, and, lifting up the cylinder, they ran. Poiccart put his hand on the fence wire and was hurled back. The top wire was alive, but evidently the doctor's dynamo was not capable of generating a current that would be fatal. Leon produced an insulated wire cutter and snipped off a six-foot length, earthing the broken ends of the wire. They were now under the shadow of the wall of the house, and out of danger so far as bullets were concerned.

Leon planted his ladder against the window under which they stopped, and in a second had broken the glass, turned the catch and sent up the sash. From his bag he produced a small diamond drill and began to work through the thick steel plate. It was a terribly arduous job, and after ten minutes' labour he handed over the work to Manfred, who mounted in his place.

Whatever damage had been done to the searchlight had now been repaired, and its beam had concentrated on the spot where they had been last seen. This time no fusillade greeted its appearance, and Oberzohn was surprised and troubled by the inaction.

The light came into the sky, the walls grew grey and all objects sharply visible, when he saw the tank move out of the lane where it had been standing all the previous day, turn into the field, and slowly move towards the house. He set his teeth in a grin and, darting down the stairs, flung himself against the door of the girl's room, and his agitation was such that for a time he could not find the keyhole of the two locks that held the door secure.

It opened with a crash, and he almost fell into the room in his eagerness. Mirabelle Leicester was standing by the bed, her face white as death. Yet her voice was steady, almost unconcerned, when she asked:

"What do you want?"

"You!" he hissed. "You, my fine little lady—you are for the snakes!"

He flung himself upon her, though she offered no resistance, threw her back on the bed and snapped a pair of rusty handcuffs on her wrists. Pulling her to her feet, he dragged her from the room and down the stairs. He had some difficulty in opening the door of the snake-room, for he had wedged it close. The door was pushed open at last: the radiators were no longer burning. He could not afford the power. But the room was stiflingly hot, and when he turned on the lights, and she saw the long line of boxes, her knees gave way under her, and she would have fallen had he not put his arm about her waist. Dragging a heavy chair to the centre of the room, he pushed her down into it.

"Here you wait, my friend!" he yelled. "You shall wait... but not long!"

On the wall there were three long straps which were used for fastening the boxes when it was necessary to travel with them. In a second one thong was about her and buckled tight to the back of the chair. The second he put under the seat and fastened across her knee.

"Good-bye, gracious lady!"

The rumble of the tank came to him in that room. But he had work to do. There was no time to open the boxes. The glass fronts might easily be broken. He ran along the line, hitting the glass with the barrel of his Mauser. The girl, staring in horror, saw a green head come into view through one opening; saw a sinuous shape slide gently to the floor. And then he turned out the lights, the door was slammed, and she was left alone in the room of terror.

Oberzohn was no sooner in the passage than the first bomb exploded at the door. Splinters of wood flew past him, as he turned and raced up the stairs, feeling in his pocket as he went for the precious document which might yet clear him.

Boom!

He had not locked the door of the snake-room; Leon had broken the hasp. Let them go in, if they wished. The front door was not down yet. From the landing above he listened over the balustrade. And then a greater explosion than ever shook the house, and after an interval of silence he heard somebody running along the passage and shake at the snake-room door.

Too late now! He grinned his joy, went up the last flight to the roof, to find his three men in a state of mutiny, the quelling of which was not left to him. The glitter of a bayonet came through the door opening, a khaki figure slipped on to the roof, finger on trigger.

"Hands up, you!" he said, in a raucous Cockney voice.

Four pairs of hands went upward.

Manfred followed the second soldier and caught the doctor by the arm.

"I want you, my friend," he said, and Oberzohn went obediently down the stairs.

They had to pass Gurther's room: the door was open, and Manfred pushed his prisoner inside, as Poiccart and Leon ran up the stairs.

"The girl's all right. The gas killed the snakes the moment they touched the floor, and Brother Washington is dealing with the live ones," said Leon rapidly.

He shut the door quickly. The doctor was alone for the first time in his life with the three men he hated and feared.

"Oberzohn, this is the end," said Manfred.

That queer grimace that passed for a smile flitted across the puckered face of the doctor.

"I think not, my friends," he said. "Here is a statement by Cuccini. I am but the innocent victim, as you will see. Cuccini has confessed to all and has implicated his friends. I would not resist—why should I? I am an honest, respectable man, and a citizen of a great and friendly country. Behold!"

He showed the paper. Manfred took it from his hand but did not read it.

"Also, whatever happens, your lady loses her beautiful hill of gold." He found joy in this reflection. "For tomorrow is the last day—"

"Stand over there, Oberzohn," said Manfred, and pushed him against the wall. "You are judged. Though your confession may cheat the law, you will not cheat us."

And then the doctor saw something and he screamed his fear. Leon Gonsalez was fixing a cigarette to the long black holder he had found in Gurther's room.

"You hold it thus," said Leon, "do you not?" He dipped the cigarette down and pressed the small spring that was concealed in the black ebonite. "The holder is an insulated chamber that holds two small icy splinters—I found the mould in your laboratory, Herr Doktor. They drop into the cigarette, which is a metal one, and then..."

He lifted it to his lips and blew. None saw the two tiny icicles fly. Only Oberzohn put his hand to his cheek with a strangled scream, glared for a second, and then went down like a heap of rags.

Leon met Inspector Meadows on his way up.

"I'm afraid our friend has gone," he said. "He has cheated the hangman of ten pounds."

"Dead?" said Meadows. "Suicide?"

"It looks like a snake-bite to me," said Leon carelessly, as he went down to find Mirabelle Leicester, half laughing, half crying, whilst an earnest Elijah Washington was explaining to her the admirable domestic qualities of snakes.

"There's five thousand dollars' worth dead," he said, in despair, "but there's enough left to start a circus!"

34

THE DEATH TUBE

Later Manfred explained to an interested police chief.

"Oberzohn secured the poison by taking a snake and extracting his venom—a simple process: you have but to make him angry, and he will bite on anything. The doctor discovered a way of blending these venoms to bring out the most deadly qualities of them all—it sounds fantastic, and, from the scientists' point of view, unlikely. But it is nevertheless the fact. The venom was slightly diluted with water and enough to kill a dozen people was poured into a tiny mould and frozen."

"Frozen?" said the chief, in astonishment.

Manfred nodded.

"There is no doubt about it," he said. "Snake venom does not lose its potency by being frozen, and this method of moulding their darts was a very sane one, from their point of view. It was only necessary for a microscopic portion of the splinter to pierce the flesh. Sufficient instantly melted to cause death, and if the victim rubbed the place where he had been struck, it was more certain that he would rub some of the venom, which had melted on his cheek, into the wound. Usually they died instantly. The cigarette holders that were carried by Gurther and the other assassin, Pfeiffer, were blowpipes, the cigarette a hollow metal fake. By the time they blew their little ice darts, it was in a half-molten condition and carried sufficient liquid poison to kill, even if the skin was only punctured. And, of course, all that did not enter the skin melted before there could be any examination by the police. That is why you never found darts such as the bushmen use, slithers of bamboo, thorns from trees. Oberzohn had the simplest method of dealing with all opposition: he sent out his snake-men to intercept them, and only once did they fail—when they aimed at Leon and caught that snake-proof man, Elijah Washington!"

"What about Miss Leicester's claim to the goldfields of Biskara?"

Manfred smiled.

"The renewal has already been applied for and granted. Leon found at Heavytree Farm some blank sheets of notepaper signed with the girl's name. He stole one during the aunt's absence and filled up the blank with a formal request for renewal. I have just had a wire to say that the lease is extended."

He and Poiccart had to walk the best part of the way to New Cross before they could find a taxicab. Leon had gone on with the girl. Poiccart was worried about something, and did not speak his mind until the providential cab appeared on the scene and they were trundling along the New Cross Road.

"My dear George, I am a little troubled about Leon," he said at last. "It seems almost impossible to believe, but—"

"But what?" asked Manfred good-humouredly, and knowing what was coming.

"You don't believe," said Poiccart in a hushed voice, as though he were discussing the advent of some world cataclysm—"you don't believe that Leon is in love, do you?"

Manfred considered for a moment.

"Such things happen, even to Just Men," he said, and Poiccart shook his head sadly.

"I have never contemplated such an unhappy contingency," he said, and Manfred was laughing to himself all the way back to town.

AGAIN THE THREE
OR, THE LAW OF THE THREE

CONTENTS

1. The Rebus — 323
2. The Happy Travellers — 334
3. The Abductor — 345
4. The Third Coincidence — 357
5. The Slane Mystery — 367
6. The Marked Cheque — 376
7. Mr Levingrou's Daughter — 386
8. The Share Pusher — 397
9. The Man Who Sang in Church — 408
10. The Lady from Brazil — 424
11. The Typist Who Saw Things — 439
12. The Mystery of Mr Drake — 454
13. "The Englishman Konnor" — 467

1

THE REBUS
(Published as "The Four Just Men" in
Detective Story Magazine, July 2, 1927)

As *the Megaphone* once said, in its most pessimistic and wondering mood, recording rather than condemning the strangeness of the time:

> "Even The Four Just Men have become a respectable institution. Not more than fifteen years ago we spoke of them as 'a criminal organization'; rewards were offered for their arrest... today you may turn into Curzon Street and find a silver triangle affixed to the sedate door which marks their professional headquarters... The hunted and reviled have become a most exclusive detective agency... We can only hope that their somewhat drastic methods of other times have been considerably modified."

It is sometimes a dangerous thing to watch a possible watcher.

'What is Mr Lewis Lethersohn afraid of?' asked Manfred, as he cracked an egg at breakfast. His handsome, clean-shaven face was tanned a teak-brown, for he was newly back from the sun and snows of Switzerland.

Leon Gonsalez sat opposite, absorbed in The Times; at the end of the table was Raymond Poiccart, heavy-featured and saturnine. Other pens than mine have described his qualities and his passion for growing vegetables.

He raised his eyes to Gonsalez.

'Is he the gentleman who has had this house watched for the past month?' he asked.

A smile quivered on Leon's lips as he folded the newspaper neatly.

'He is the gentleman—I'm interviewing him this morning,' he said. 'In the meantime, the sleuth hounds have been withdrawn—they were employed by the Ottis Detective Agency.'

'If he is watching us, he has a bad conscience,' said Poiccart, nodding slowly. 'I shall be interested to hear all about this.'

Mr Lewis Lethersohn lived in Lower Berkeley Street—a very large and expensive house. The footman who opened the door to Leon was arrayed in a uniform common enough in historical films but rather out of the picture in Lower Berkeley Street. Mulberry and gold and knee breeches... Leon gazed at him with awe.

'Mr Lethersohn will see you in the library,' said the man—he seemed; thought Leon, rather conscious of his own magnificence.

A gorgeous house this, with costly furnishings and lavish decorations. As he mounted the wide stairs he had a glimpse of a beautiful woman passing across the landing. One disdainful glance she threw in his direction and passed, leaving behind her the faint fragrance of some exotic perfume.

The room into which he was shown might have been mistaken for a bedroom, with its bric-a-brac and its beauty of appointments.

Mr Lethersohn rose from behind the Empire writing table and offered a white hand. He was thin, rather bald, and there was a suggestion of the scholar in his lined face.

'Mr Gonsalez?' His voice was thin and not particularly pleasant. 'Won't you sit down? I had your inquiry—there seems to be some mistake.'

He had resumed his own seat. Though he might endeavour, to cover up his uneasiness by this cold attitude of his, he could not quite hide his perturbation.

'I know you, of course—but it is ridiculous that I should set men to watch your house. Why?'

Gonsalez was watching him intently.

'That is what I have come to learn,' he said, 'and I think it would be fairest to tell you that there is no doubt that you are watching us. We know the agency you employed—we know the fees you have paid and the instructions you have given. The only question is, why?'

Mr Lethersohn moved uncomfortably and smiled. 'Really... I suppose there is no wisdom in denying that I did employ detectives. The truth is, the Four Just Men is rather a formidable organization—and—er—Well, I am a rich man...'

He was at a loss how to go on.

The interview ended lamely with polite assurances on either side. Leon Gonsalez went back to Curzon Street a very thoughtful man.

'He's afraid of somebody consulting us, and the detective people have been employed to head off that somebody. Now who?'

The next evening brought the answer.

It was a grey April night, chill and moist. The woman who walked slowly down Curzon Street, examining the numbers on the doors, was an object of suspicion to the policeman standing on Claridge's corner. She was in the region of thirty, rather slim, under the worn and soddened coat. Her face was faded and a little pinched. 'Pretty once,' mused Leon Gonsalez, observing her from behind the net curtain that covered the window. 'A working woman without a thought beyond keeping her body and soul together.'

He had time enough to observe her, since she stood for a long time by the kerb, looking up and down the street hopelessly.

'Notice the absence of any kind of luring finery—and this is the hour when even the poorest find a scarf or a pair of gloves.'

Manfred rose from the table where he had been taking his frugal meal and joined the keen-faced observer.

'Provincial, I think,' said Leon thoughtfully. 'Obviously a stranger to the West End—she's coming here!'

As he was speaking, the woman had turned, made a brief scrutiny of the front door... They heard the bell ring.

'I was mistaken—she hadn't lost her way; she was plucking up courage to ring—and if she isn't Lethersohn's bete noire I'm a Dutchman!'

He heard Poiccart's heavy tread in the passage—Poiccart played butler quite naturally. Presently he came in and closed the door behind him.

'You will be surprised,' he said in his grave way. That was peculiarly Poiccart—to say mysterious things gravely.

'About the lady? I refuse to be surprised.' Leon was vehement. 'She has lost something—a husband, a watch, something. She has the "lost" look—an atmosphere of vague helplessness surrounds her. The symptoms are unmistakable!'

'Ask her to come in,' said Manfred, and Poiccart retired.

A second later Alma Stamford was ushered into the room.

That was her name. She came from Edgware and she was a widow... Long before she came to the end of preliminaries Poiccart's promised surprise had been sprung, for this woman, wearing clothes that a charwoman would have despised, had a voice which was soft and educated. Her vocabulary was extensive and she spoke of conditions which could only be familiar to one who had lived in surroundings of wealth.

She was the widow of a man who—they gathered—had not been in his lifetime the best of husbands. Rich beyond the ordinary meaning of the term, with estates in Yorkshire and Somerset, a fearless rider to hounds, he had met his death in the hunting field.

'My husband had a peculiar upbringing,' she said. 'His parents died at an early age and he was brought up by his uncle. He was a terrible old man who drank heavily, was coarse to the last degree, and was jealous of outside interference. Mark saw practically nobody until, in the last year of the old man's life, he brought in a Mr Lethersohn, a young man a little older than Mark, to act as tutor—for Mark's education was terribly backward. My husband was twenty-one when his uncle died, but he retained a gentleman to act for him as companion and secretary.'

'Mr Lewis Lethersohn,' said Leon promptly, and she gasped.

'I can't guess how you know, but that is the name. Although we weren't particularly happy,' she went on, 'my husband's death was a terrible shock. But almost as great a shock was his will. In this he left one half of his fortune to Lethersohn, the other half to me at the expiration of five years from his death, provided that I carried out the conditions of the will. I was not to marry during that period, I was to live at a house in Harlow and never to leave the Harlow district. Mr Lethersohn was given absolute power as sole executor to dispose of property for my benefit. I have lived in Harlow until this morning.'

'Mr Lethersohn is of course married?' said Leon, his bright eyes fixed on the lady.

'Yes—you know him?'

Leon shook his head.

'I only know that he is married and very much in love with his wife.'

She was astounded at this.

'You must know him. Yes, he married just before Mark was killed. A very beautiful Hungarian girl—he is half Hungarian and I believe he adores her. I heard that she was very extravagant—I only saw her once.'

'What has happened at Harlow?' It was the silent, watchful Poiccart who asked the question.

He saw the woman's lips tremble.

'It has been a nightmare,' she said with a break in her voice. 'The house was a beautiful little place—miles from Harlow really, and off the main road. There I have been for two years practically a prisoner. My letters have been opened, I have been locked in my room every night by one of the two women Mr Lethersohn sent to look after me, and men have been patrolling the grounds day and night.'

'The suggestion is that you are not quite right in your head?' asked Manfred.

She looked startled at this.

'You don't think so?' she asked quickly, and, when he shook his head: 'Thank God for that! Yes, that was the story they told. I wasn't supposed to see newspapers, though I had all the books I wanted. One day I found a scrap of paper with the account of a bank fraud which you gentlemen had detected, and there was a brief account of your past. I treasured that because it had your address in the paragraph. To escape seemed impossible—I had no money, it was impossible to leave the grounds. But they had a woman who came to do the rough work twice a week. I think she came from the village. I managed to enlist her sympathy, and yesterday she brought me these clothes. Early this morning I changed, dropped out of my bedroom window and passed the guard. Now I come to my real mystery.'

She put her hand into the pocket of her wet coat and took out a small package. This she unwrapped.

'My husband was taken to the cottage hospital after his accident; he died early the next morning. He must have recovered consciousness unknown to the nurses, for the top of the sheet was covered with little drawings. He had made them with an indelible pencil attached to his temperature chart and hanging above his head—he must have reached up for it and broken it off.'

She spread out the square of soiled linen on the table.

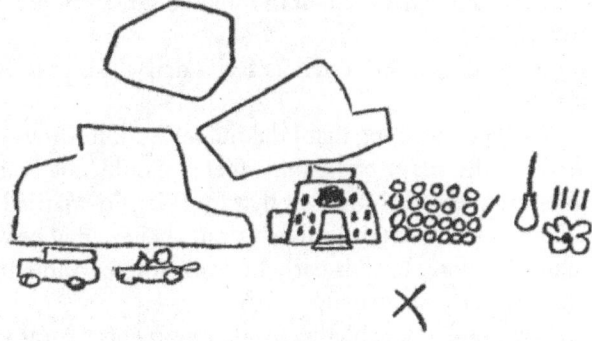

'Poor Mark was very fond of drawing the figures that children and idle people who have no real knowledge of art love to scribble.'

'How did you get this?' asked Leon.

'The matron cut it off for me.'

Manfred frowned. 'The sort of things a man might draw in his delirium,' he said.

'On the contrary,' said Leon coolly, 'it is as clear as daylight to me. Where were you married?'

'At the Westminster Registry Office.'

Leon nodded.

'Take your mind back: was there anything remarkable about the marriage—did your husband have a private interview with the registrar?'

She opened her big blue eyes at this.

'Yes—Mr Lethersohn and my husband interviewed him in his private office.'

Leon chuckled, but was serious again instantly.

'One more question. Who drew up the will? A lawyer?'

She shook her head.

'My husband—it was written in his own hand from start to finish. He wrote rather a nice hand, very easily distinguishable from any other.'

'Were there any other conditions imposed upon you in your husband's will?'

She hesitated, and the watchers saw a dark flush pass over her face.

'Yes... it was so insulting that I did not tell you. It was this—and this was the main condition—that I should not at any time attempt to establish the fact that I was legally married to Mark. That was to me inexplicable—I can't believe that he was ever married before, but his early life was so remarkable that anything may have happened.'

Leon was smiling delightedly. In such moments he was as a child who had received a new and entrancing toy.

'I can relieve your mind,' he said, to her amazement. 'Your husband was never married before!'

Poiccart was studying the drawings.

'Can you get the plans of your husband's estates?' he asked, and Leon chuckled again.

'That man knows everything, George!' he exclaimed. 'Poiccart, mon vieux, you are superb!' He turned quickly to Mrs Stamford. 'Madam, you need rest, a change of clothing, and—protection. The first and the last are in this house, if you dare be our guest. The second I will procure for you in an hour—together with a temporary maid.'

She looked at him, a little bewildered... Five minutes later, an embarrassed Poiccart was showing her to her room, and a nurse of Leon's acquaintance was hurrying to Curzon Street with a bulging suitcase—Leon had a weakness for nurses, and knew at least a hundred by name.

Late as was the hour, he made several calls—one as far as Strawberry Hill, where a certain assistant registrar of marriages lived.

It was eleven o'clock that night when he rang the bell at the handsome house in Upper Berkeley Street. Another footman admitted him.

'Are you Mr Gonsalez? Mr Lethersohn has not returned from the theatre, but he telephoned asking you to wait in the library.'

'Thank you,' said Leon gratefully, though there was no need for gratitude, for he it was who had telephoned.

He was bowed into the ornate sanctum and left alone.

The footman had hardly left the room before Leon was at the Empire desk, turning over the papers rapidly. But he found what he sought on the blotting-pad, face downwards.

A letter addressed to a firm of wine merchants complaining of some deficiency in a consignment of champagne. He read this through rapidly—it was only half finished—folded the paper and put it into his pocket.

Carefully and rapidly he examined the drawers of the table: two were locked—the middle drawer was, however, without fastening. What he found interested him and gave him some little occupation. He had hardly finished before he heard a car stop before the house and, looking through the curtains, saw a man and woman alight.

Dark as it was, he recognized his unconscious host, and he was sitting demurely on the edge of a chair when Lethersohn burst into the room, his face white with fury.

'What the hell is the meaning of this?' he demanded as he slammed the door behind him. 'By God, I'll have you arrested for impersonating me—'

'You guessed that I had telephoned—that was almost intelligent,' smiled Leon Gonsalez.

The man swallowed.

'Why are you here—I suppose it concerns the poor woman who escaped from a mental hospital today—I only just heard before I went out...'

'So we gathered from the fact that your watchers have been on duty again tonight,' said Leon, 'but they were a little too late.'

The man's face went a shade paler.

'You've seen her?' he asked jerkily. 'And I suppose she told you a cock and bull story about me?'

Leon took from his pocket a piece of discoloured linen and held it up.

'You've not seen this?' he asked. 'When Mark Stamford died, this drawing was found on his sheet. He could draw these strange little things, you know that?'

Lewis Lethersohn did not answer.

'Shall I tell you what this is—it is his last will.

'That's a lie!' croaked the other.

'His last will,' nodded Leon sternly. 'Those three queer rhomboids are rough plans of his three estates. That house is a pretty fair picture of the Southern Bank premises and the little circles are money.'

Lethersohn was staring at the drawing.

'No court would accept that foolery,' he managed to say.

Leon showed his teeth in a mirthless grin..

'Nor the "awl" which means "all," nor the four strokes which stand as "for," nor the "Margaret," nor the final "Mark"? be asked.

With an effort Lethersohn recovered his composure. 'My dear man, the idea is fantastical—he wrote a will with his own hand—'

Leon stood with his head thrust forward. So far Lethersohn got, when:

'He couldn't write!' he said softly, and Lethersohn turned pale. 'He could draw these pictures but he couldn't write his own name. If Mrs Stamford had seen the registrar's certificate she would have seen that it was signed with a cross—that is why you put in the little bit about her not attempting to prove her marriage—why you kept her prisoner at Harlow in case she made independent inquiries.'

Suddenly Lethersohn flew to his desk and jerked open a drawer. In a second an automatic appeared in his hand. Running back to the door, he flung it open.

'Help... murder!' he shouted.

He swung round on the motionless Gonsalez and, levelling his gun, pulled the trigger. A click—and no more.

'I emptied the magazine,' said Leon coolly, 'so the little tragedy you so carefully staged has become a farce. Shall I telephone to the police or will you?'

Scotland Yard men arrested Lewis Lethersohn as he was stepping on to the boat at Dover.

'There may be some difficulty in proving the will,' said Manfred, reading the account in the evening newspapers; 'but the jury will not take long to put friend Lewis in his proper place...'

Later, when they questioned Leon—Poiccart was all for pinning down his psychology—he condescended to explain.

'The rebus told me he could not write—the fact that the will did not instruct Mrs Stamford to marry Lewis showed me that he was married and loved his wife. The rest was ridiculously easy.'

2

THE HAPPY TRAVELLERS
(Reprinted in *The Saint Magazine*,
UK edition, April 1959)

Of the three men who had their headquarters in Curzon Street, George Manfred was by far the best looking. His were the features and poise of an aristocrat. In a crowd he stood out by himself, not alone because of his height, but the imponderable something which distinguishes breeding.

'George looks like a racehorse in a herd of Shetland ponies!' said the enthusiastic Leon Gonsalez on one occasion. Which was very nearly true.

Yet it was Leon who attracted the average woman, and even women above the average. It was fatal to send him to deal with a case in which women were concerned, not because he himself was given to philandering, but because it was as certain as anything could be that he would come back leaving at least one sighing maiden to bombard him with letters ten pages long.

Which really made him rather unhappy.

'I'm old enough to be their father,' he wailed on one occasion, 'and as I live I said no more than "Good morning" to the wench. Had I held her hand or chanted a canto or two into her pink ear, I would stand condemned. But, George, I swear—'

But George was helpless with laughter.

Yet Leon could act the perfect lover. Once in Cordova he paid court to a certain senorita—three knife scars on his right breast testify to the success of his wooing. As to the two men who attacked him, they are dead, for by his courting he lured into the open the man for whom the police of Spain and France were searching.

And he was especially effusive one spring morning to a slim and beautiful dark-eyed lady whom he met in Hyde Park. He was on foot, when he saw her walking past slowly and unattended. A graceful woman of thirty with a faultless skin and grey eyes that were almost black.

It was by no accident that they met, for Leon had been studying her movements for weeks.

'This is an answer to prayer, beautiful lady,' he said, and his extravagance was the more facile since he spoke in Italian.

She laughed softly, gave him one swift, quizzical glance from under the long lashes, and signalled him to replace the hat that was now in his hand.

'Good morning, Signor Carrelli,' she smiled, and gave him a small gloved hand. She was simply but expensively dressed. The only jewels she wore were the string of pearls about her white throat.

'I see you everywhere,' she said. 'You were dining at the Carlton on Monday night, and before that I saw you in a box at a theatre, and yesterday afternoon I met you!'

Leon showed his white teeth in a delighted smile.

'That is true, illustrious lady,' he said, 'but you make no reference to my searching London to find somebody who would introduce me. Nor do you pity my despair as I followed you, feasting my eyes upon your beauty, or my sleepless nights—'

All this he said with the fervour of a love-sick youth, and she listened without giving evidence of disapproval.

'You shall walk with me,' she said, in the manner of a queen conveying an immense privilege.

They strolled away from the crowd towards the open spaces of the park, and they talked of Rome and the hunting season, of runs on Campagna and the parties of Princess Leipnitz-Savalo—Leon read the society columns of the Roman press with great assiduity and remembered all that he read.

They came at last to a place of trees and comfortable garden chairs. Leon paid the watchful attendant, and, after he had strolled away:

'How beautiful it is to sit alone with divinity!' he began ecstatically. 'For I tell you this, signorita...'

'Tell me something else, Mr Leon Gonsalez,' said the lady, and this time she spoke in English and her voice had the qualities of steel and ice. 'Why are you shadowing me?'

If she expected to confound him it was because she did not know her Leon.

'Because you are an extremely dangerous lady, Madame Koskina,' he said coolly, 'and all the more dangerous because the Lord has given you kissable lips and a graceful body. How many impressionable young attachés of embassies have discovered these charms in you!'

She laughed at this and was seemingly well pleased.

'You have been reading,' she said. 'No, my dear Mr Gonsalez, I am out of politics—they bore me. Poor Ivan is in Russia struggling with the work of the Economic Commission and living in dread because of his well-known Liberal views, and I am in London, which is delightfully capitalistic and comfortable! Believe me, Leningrad is no place for a lady!'

Isola Koskina had been Isola Caprevetti before she married a dashing young Russian attache. She had been a revolutionary from birth; and now she had developed a zeal for revolution that amounted to fanaticism.

Leon smiled.

'There are worse places for a lady even than Leningrad. I should be grieved indeed, my dear Isola, to see you making coarse shirts in Aylesbury convict establishment.'

She looked at him steadily, insolently.

'That is a threat, and threats bore me. In Italy I have been threatened with... all sorts of dreadful things if I ever showed myself on the wrong side of the Simplon Pass. And really I am the most inoffensive person in the world, Monsieur Gonsalez. You are, or course, employed by the Government—how eminently respectable! Which Government?'

Leon grinned, but was serious again in a second.

'The Italian frontiers are practically closed since the last attempt,' he said. 'You and your friends are causing everybody an immense amount of trouble. Naturally the Government are concerned. They do not wish to wake up one morning and find that they are implicated, and that some successful assassin made a jump from—England, shall we say?'

The lady shrugged her pretty shoulders. 'How very dramatic! And therefore poor Isola Koskina must be watched by detectives and reformed murderers—I suppose you and your precious comrades are reformed?'

The smile on the thin face of Leon Gonsalez widened. 'If we were not, signorita, what would happen? Should I be sitting here talking pretty-pretty talk with you? Would you not be picked out of the Thames at Limehouse all cold and clammy some morning, and lie on the slab till a coroner's jury returned a verdict of "Found drowned"?'

He saw the colour leave her face: fear came to her eyes. 'You had better threaten Ivan—' she began.

'I will cable him: he is not in Leningrad but living in Berlin under the name of Petersohn—Martin Lutherstrasse 904. How easy it would be if we were not reformed! A dead man in a gutter and a policeman searching his pockets for a card of identity—'

She rose hurriedly; her very lips were bloodless.

'You do not amuse me,' she said and, turning from him, walked quickly away.

Leon made no attempt to follow her. It was two days after this encounter that the letter came. Many people wrote to the Just Men, a few abusively, quite a number fatuously. But now and again there could be extracted from the morning correspondence quite a pretty little problem. And the dingy letter with its finger-marks and creases was quite worth the amount that the postman charged them—for it came unstamped. The address was:

Four Just Men, Curzon Street, May Fair,
West End, London.

The writing was that of an illiterate, and the letter went:

DEAR SIR,
You are surposed to go in for misteries well hear is a mistery. I was a boiler makers mate in Hollingses but now out of work and one Sunday I was photoed by a foren lady she come in front of me with a camra and took me. There was a lot of chaps in the park but she only took me. Then she ast me my name and address and ast me if I knew a clergyman. And when I said yes she wrote down the name of the Rev J. Crewe, and then she said shed send me a picture dear sir she didn't send me a pictur but ast me to joyne the Happy Travlers to go to Swizzleland Rome, etc. and nothing to pay all expences payed also loss of time (Ten £) and soots of close everything done in stile. Well dear sir I got ready and she did everything close ten £ &c. also she got tickets &c. But now the lady says I got to go to Devonshire not that I mind. Now dear sir thats a mistery because I just met a gentleman from Leeds and has had his photo took and joyned the Happy Travlers and hes

*going to Cornwall and this lady who took the picture of
him ast him if he knew a clergyman and wrote it down.
Now what is the mistery is it something to do with religion?
Yours Sincerely,*
T. BARGER.

George Manfred read the ill-spelt scrawl and threw the letter across the breakfast table to Leon Gonsalez.

'Read me that riddle, Leon,' he said.

Leon read and frowned.

'"Happy Travellers," eh? That's odd.'

The letter went to Raymond, who studied it with an expressionless face.

'Eh, Raymond?' Leon asked, his eyes alight.

'I think so,' said Raymond, nodding slowly.

'Will you let me into your "mistery"?' asked Manfred.

Leon chuckled.

'No mystery at all, my dear George. I will see this T. Barger, whose name is surely "Thomas" and will learn certain particulars as, for example, the colour of his eyes and the testimonial he has received from the Foreign Secretary.'

'Mistery on mistery,' murmured George Manfred as he sipped his coffee—though in truth the matter was no longer a mystery to him. The reference to the Foreign Secretary was very illuminating.

'As to the lady—' said Leon, and shook his head.

His big Bentley created a mild sensation in the street where T. Barger lived. It was situated near the East India Dock, and T. Barger—whose front name was surprisingly Theophilus—proved to be a tall, dark man of thirty with a small black moustache and rather heavy black eyebrows. He was obviously wearing his new 'soot' and had expended at least a portion of his 'ten £' on alcoholic refreshment, for he was in a loud and confident mood.

'I'm leavin' tomorrow,' he said thickly, 'for Torquay—everything paid. Travellin' like a swell... first class. You one of them Justers!'

Leon induced him to go into the house.

'It's a myst'ry to me,' said Mr Barger, 'why she done it. Happy Trav'ler—that's what I am. She might have took me abroad—I'd like to have seen them mountains, but she says if I don't speak the Swiss language I'd be out of it. Anyway, what's the matter with Torquay?'

'The other man is going to Cornwall?'

Mr Barger nodded solemnly. 'An' his mate's goin' to Somerset—funny meetin' him at all...' He explained the coincidence, which had to do with a public-house where Mr Barger had called for a drink.

'What was his name?'

'Rigson—Harry Rigson. I told him mine, he told me his. The other man? Harry's pal? I call him Harry—we're like pals—now let me think, mister...'

Leon let him think.

'Tunny name... Coke... no, Soke... Lokely! That's it—Joe Lokely.'

Leon asked a few more questions which were seemingly irrelevant but were not.

'Of course I had to be passed by the committee,' said the communicative Theophilus. 'Accordin' to Harry, this lady photoed a friend of his but he didn't pass.'

'I see,' said Leon. 'What time do you leave for Devonshire?'

'Tomorrow mornin'—seven o'clock. Bit early, ain't it? But this lady says that Happy Travellers must be early risers. Harry's goin' by the same train but in another coach...'

Leon went back to Curzon Street well satisfied. The question he had to decide was: was Isola an early riser too?

'I hardly think so,' said Raymond Poiccart. 'She would not take the risk—especially if she knows that she is watched.'

THE HAPPY TRAVELLERS

That night Scotland Yard was a very hive of industry, and Leon Gonsalez did without sleep. Fortunately Isola had been under police observation, and the Yard knew every district in England she had visited for the past month. By midnight two thousand ministers of religion had been awakened from their sleep by local police and asked to furnish certain particulars.

Isola went to a dinner and dance that night and her partner was a very nice young man, tall and dark of face. She chose the L'Orient, which is the most exclusive and plutocratic of night clubs. Men and women turned to admire or criticize her beauty as she entered, a radiant figure in a scarlet dress with a dull gold stole. The colours set off the glories of her lovely face, and there was sinuous grace in every movement.

They had reached the dessert when suddenly she laid two fingers on the table-cloth.

'Who is it?' asked her companion carelessly as he saw the danger signal.

'The man I told you about—he is at the table immediately opposite.'

Presently the dark young man looked.

'So that is the famous Gonsalez! A wisp of a man that I could break—'

'A wisp of a man who has broken giants, Emilo,' she interrupted. 'Have you heard of Saccoriva—was he not a giant? That man killed him—shot him down in his own headquarters when there was a guard of revolutionary brethren within call—and escaped!'

'He is anti-revolutionary?' Emilo was impressed.

She shook her head. 'Comrade Saccoriva was very foolish—with women. It was over some girl he had taken—and left. He is looking this way: I will call him over.'

Leon rose lazily at the signal and came across the crowded dance floor.

'Signorita, you will never forgive me!' he said in despair. 'Here am I watching you again! And yet I only came here because I was bored.'

'Bore me also,' she said with her sweetest smile, and then, remembering her companion: 'This is Herr Halz from Leipzig.'

Leon's eyes twinkled.

'Your friends change their nationalities as often as they change their names,' he said. 'I remember Herr Halz of Leipzig when he was Emilo Cassini of Turin!'

Emilo shifted uncomfortably, but Isola was amused.

'This man is omniscient! Dance with me, Senor Gonsalez, and promise that you will not murder me!'

They went twice round the dance floor before Leon spoke. 'If I had your face and figure and youth, I should have a good time and not bother with politics,' he said.

'And if I had your wisdom and cunning I should remove tyrants from their high positions,' she retorted, her voice quivering.

That was all that was said. Going out into the vestibule, Leon discovered the girl and her escort waiting. It was raining heavily and Isola's car could not be found.

'May I drop you, gracious lady?' Leon's smile was most entrancing. 'I have a poor car but it is at your disposition.'

Isola hesitated.

'Thank you,' she said.

Leon, ever the soul of politeness, insisted on taking one of the seats that put his back to the driver. It was not his own car. Usually he was very nervous about other drivers, but tonight he did not mind.

They crossed Trafalgar Square.

'The man is taking the wrong turning,' said Isola with quick vehemence.

'This is the right road to Scotland Yard,' said Leon. 'We call this the Way of the Happy Traveller—keep your hand away from your pocket, Emilo. I have killed men on less provocation, and I have been covering you ever since we left the club!'

In the early hours of the morning telegrams were despatched to police headquarters at Folkestone and Dover:

'Arrest and detain Theophilus Barger, Joseph Lokely, Harry Rigson'—here followed five other names—'travelling to the Continent by boat either today or tomorrow.'

There was no need to give instructions about Isola. For a perfect lady, her behaviour was indefensible.

'She blotted her copybook,' said Leon sadly. 'I've never seen a Happy Traveller less happy when we got her to Scotland Yard.'

Considering the matter at the morning conference which was part of the daily routine in Curzon Street, Manfred was inclined to regard the plot as elementary.

'If you speak disparagingly of my genius and power of deduction I shall burst into tears,' said Leon. 'Raymond thinks I was clever—I will not have that verdict challenged. George, you're getting old and grouchy.'

'The detection was clever,' Manfred hastened to placate his smiling friend.

'And the scheme was clever,' insisted Leon, 'and terribly like Isola. One of these days she'll do something awfully original and be shot. Obviously, what she set out to do was to collect seven men who bore some resemblance to the members of her murder gang. When she had found them, she made them get passports—that of course is why she asked if they knew a clergyman, for a padre's signature on the photograph and application form is as good as a lawyer's. Seven poor innocent men with passports which she handed over to her friends while the happy travellers were sent into out-of-the-way places. She was heading the gang into Italy—all the passports were visaed for that country.'

'Tell me,' said Manfred, 'did they arrest the spurious T. Barger at Dover?'

Leon shook his head.

'The man who was to have travelled with T. Barger's passport was one Emilo Casbini—I spotted the likeness immediately. Isola was very abusive—but I quietened her by suggesting that her husband might like to know something about her friendship with Emilo... I have been watching Isola for a long time and I have seen things.'

3

THE ABDUCTOR
(No record of prior magazine publication found)

It was a year since Lord Geydrew invoked the aid of the Just Men who lived at the sign of the Triangle in Curzon Street. He was a narrow-headed man; the first time they met with him, Poiccart hazarded the opinion that he was constitutionally mean. The last time they met it was not so much an opinion as stark knowledge, for his lordship had most boldly repudiated the bill of expenses that Poiccart had rendered—even though Manfred and Gonsalez had risked their lives to recover the lost Geydrew diamond.

The Three did not take him to court. Not one of them had need of money. Manfred was satisfied with the experience; Poiccart was cock-a-hoop because a theory of his had worked home; Gonsalez found his consolation in the shape of the client's head.

'The most interesting recession of the parietal and malformation of the occiput I have ever seen,' he said enthusiastically.

The Just Men shared one extraordinary gift—a prodigious memory for faces and an extraordinary facility for attaching those faces to disreputable names. There was, however, no credit due for remembering the head of his lordship.

Manfred was sitting in his small room overlooking Curzon Street one night in spring, and he was in his most thoughtful mood when Poiccart—who invariably undertook the job of butler—came hobbling in to announce Lord Geydrew.

'Not the Geydrew of Gallat Towers?' Manfred could be massively ironical. 'Has he come to pay his bill?'

'God knows,' said Poiccart piously. 'Do peers of the realm pay their bills? For the moment I am less concerned about the peerage than I am about my ankle—really, Leon is a careless devil. I had to take a taxi... .'

Manfred chuckled. 'He will be penitent and interesting,' he said, 'as for his lordship. Show him up.'

Lord Geydrew came in a little nervously, blinking at the bright light that burnt on Manfred's table. Evidently he was unusually agitated. The weak mouth was tremulous, he opened and closed his eyes with a rapidity for which the bright light was not wholly responsible. His long, lined face was twitching spasmodically; from time to time he thrust his fingers through the scanty, reddish-grey hair.

'I hope, Mr Manfred, there is no—um—er—'

He fumbled in his pocket, produced an oblong slip of paper and pushed it across the desk. Manfred looked and wondered. Poiccart, forgetful of his role as butler, watched interestedly. Besides, there was no need to pretend that he was anything but what he was.

Lord Geydrew looked from one to the other.

'I was hoping your friend—um—'

'Mr Gonsalez is out: he will be back later in the evening,' said Manfred, wondering what was coming.

Then his lordship collapsed with a groan, and let his head fall upon the arms that lay on the desk.

'Oh, my God!' he wailed... 'The most terrible thing... It doesn't bear thinking about.'

THE ABDUCTOR

Manfred waited patiently. Presently the older man looked up.

'I must tell you the story from the beginning, Mr Manfred,' he said. 'My daughter Angela—you may have met her?'

Manfred shook his head.

'She was married this morning. To Mr Guntheimer, a very wealthy Australian banker and an immensely nice fellow.' He shook his head and dabbed his eyes with a handkerchief.

Light was beginning to dawn on Manfred.

'Mr Guntheimer is considerably older than my daughter,' his lordship went on, 'and I will not conceal from you the fact that Angela has certain objections to the match. In fact, she had very stupidly arrived at some sort of understanding with young Sidworth—good family and all that, but not a penny in the world... It would have been madness.'

Manfred now understood quite clearly.

'We had to hurry the marriage, since Guntheimer is leaving for Australia much earlier than he expected. Happily my daughter gave way to my legitimate wishes and they were married this morning at a registrar's office and were due to leave for the Isle of Wight by the three o'clock train.

'We did not go to see her off, and the only account I have of the occurrence was from the mouth of my son-in-law. He said that he was walking up to his reserved compartment, when suddenly he missed my daughter from his side. He looked round, retraced his steps, but could see nothing of her. Thinking that she might have gone ahead, he returned to the compartment, but it was empty. He then went back beyond the barrier: she was not in sight, but a porter whom he had engaged to carry his luggage and who followed him, said that he had seen her in earnest conversation with an elderly man and that they walked into the booking hall together and disappeared. Another porter on duty in the courtyard of the station saw them get into a car and drive off.'

Manfred was jotting down his notes on his blotting-pad. Poiccart never lifted his eyes from the visitor.

'The story the porter tells—the outside porter, I mean,' went on his lordship, 'is that my daughter seemed reluctant to go, and that she was almost thrust into the car, which had to pass him. As the car came abreast, the man was pulling down the blinds, and the porter says that he has no doubt that my daughter was struggling with him.'

'With the elderly man?' said Manfred.

Lord Geydrew nodded.

'Mr Manfred'—his voice was a wail—'I am not a rich man, and perhaps I would be wise to leave this matter in the hands of the police. But I have such extraordinary faith in your intelligence and acumen—I think you will find that cheque right—and in spite of your exorbitant charges I wish to engage you. She is my only daughter...' His voice broke.

'Did the porter take the number of the car?'

Lord Geydrew shook his head. 'No,' he said. 'Naturally I wish to keep this out of the press—'

'I'm afraid you've failed,' said Manfred, and took a paper from a basket that was at his side, pointing out a paragraph in the stop press.

"REPORTED ABDUCTION OF BRIDE

"It is reported that a bride, just before leaving Waterloo on her honeymoon trip, was forcibly abducted by an elderly man. Scotland Yard have been notified."

'Porters will talk,' said Manfred, leaning back in his chair. 'Have the police a theory?'

'None,' snapped his lordship.

'Has Mr Sidworth been interviewed?'

Lord Geydrew shook his head vigorously.

'Naturally that was the first thought I had. Sidworth, I thought, has persuaded this unfortunate girl—'

'Is he an elderly man?' asked Manfred, with a twinkle in his eye which only Poiccart understood.

'Of course he isn't,' snapped his lordship. 'I told you he was young. At the present moment he's staying with some very dear friends of mine at Newbury—I think he took the marriage rather badly. At any rate, my friend says that he has not left Kingshott Manor all day, and that he has not once used the telephone.'

Manfred rubbed his shapely nose thoughtfully.

'And Mr Guntheimer—?'

'Naturally he's distracted. I have never known a man so upset. He's almost mad with grief. Can you gentlemen give me any hope?'

He looked from one to the other, and his lean face brightened at Manfred's nod.

'Where is Mr Guntheimer staying?' asked Poiccart, breaking his silence.

'At the Gayborough Hotel,' said Lord Geydrew.

'Another point—what was his present to the bride?' asked Manfred.

His visitor looked surprised, and then: 'A hundred thousand pounds,' he said impressively. 'Mr Guntheimer doesn't believe in our old method of settlement. I may say that his cheque for that amount is in my pocket now.'

'And your present to the bride?' asked Manfred.

Lord Geydrew showed some signs of impatience.

'My dear fellow, you're on the wrong track. Angela was not spirited away for purposes of property. The jewel case containing her diamonds was carried by Guntheimer. She had nothing of value in her possession except for a few odd pounds in her handbag.'

Manfred rose.

'I think that is all I want to ask you, Lord Geydrew. Unless I'm greatly mistaken, your daughter will come back to you in twenty-four hours.'

Poiccart showed the comforted man to his car, and returned to find Manfred reading the sporting column in an evening newspaper.

'Well?' asked Poiccart.

'A curious case and one in which my soul revels.' He put down the paper and stretched himself. 'If Leon comes in, will you ask him to wait my return unless there is something urgent takes him elsewhere?' He lifted his head. 'I think that is him,' he said, at the sound of squealing brakes.

Poiccart shook his head.

'Leon is more noiseless,' he said, and went down to admit an agitated young man.

Mr Harry Sidworth was that type of youth for which Manfred had a very soft spot. Lank of body, healthy of face, he had all the incoherence of his age.

'I say, are you Mr Manfred?' he began, almost before he got into the room. 'I've been to that old devil's house and his secretary told me to come here, though for the Lord's sake don't tell anybody he said so!'

'You're Mr Sidworth, of course?'

The young man nodded vigorously. His face was anxious, his air wild; he was too young to hide his evident distress.

'Isn't it too terrible for words—' he began.

'Mr Sidworth'—Manfred fixed him with a kindly eye— 'you've come to ask me about your Angela, and I'm telling you, as I told Lord Geydrew, that I'm perfectly certain that she will come back to you unharmed. There's one thing I might ask— how long has she known her husband?'

The young man made a wry face.

'That's a hateful word to me,' he groaned. 'Guntheimer? About three months. He isn't a bad fellow. I've nothing against him, except that he got Angela. Old Geydrew thought I'd taken her away. He rang up the people I was staying with, and that was the first news I had that she'd disappeared. It's the most ghastly thing that's ever happened to me.'

'Have you heard from her lately?' asked Manfred.

Sidworth nodded.

'Yes, this morning,' he said dolefully. 'Just a little note thanking me for my wedding present. I gave her a jewel case—'

'A what?' asked Manfred sharply, and the young man, surprised at his vehemence, stared at him.

'A jewel case—my sister bought one about a month ago, and Angela was so taken with it that I had an exact copy made.'

Manfred was looking at him absently.

'Your sister?' he said slowly. 'Where does your sister live?'

'Why, she's at Maidenhead,' said the young man, surprised.

Manfred looked at his watch.

'Eight o'clock,' he said. 'This is going to be rather an amusing evening.'

The clocks were striking the half-hour after ten when the telephone in Mr Guntheimer's private suite buzzed softly. Guntheimer ceased his restless pacing and went to the instrument.

'I can't see anybody,' he said. 'Who?' He frowned. 'All right, I'll see him.'

It had been raining heavily and Manfred apologized for his wet raincoat and waited for an invitation to remove it. But apparently Mr Guntheimer was too preoccupied with his unhappy thoughts to be greatly concerned about his duties as host.

He was a tall, good-looking man, rather haggard of face now, and the hand that stroked the iron-grey moustache trembled a little.

'Geydrew told me he was going to see you—what is your explanation of this extraordinary happening, Mr Manfred?'

Manfred smiled.

'The solution is a very simple one, Mr Guntheimer,' he said. 'It is to be found in the pink diamond.'

'In the what?' asked the other, startled.

'Your wife has a rather nice diamond brooch,' said Manfred. 'Unless I am misinformed, the third from the end of the bar is of a distinctly pinkish hue. It is, or was, the property of the Rajah of Komitar, and on its topmost facet you will find an Arabic word, meaning "Happiness."'

Guntheimer was gazing at him open-mouthed.

'What has that to do with it?'

Again Manfred smiled.

'If there is a pink diamond and it is inscribed as I say, I can find your wife, not in twenty-four but in six hours.'

Guntheimer fingered his chin thoughtfully.

'That matter's easily settled,' he said. 'My wife's jewels are in the hotel safe. Just wait.'

He was gone five minutes and returned carrying a small scarlet box. He put this on the table and opened it with a key which he took from his pocket. Lifting the lid, he took out a pad of wash-leather and revealed a trayful of glittering jewels.

'There's no brooch there,' he said after a search; he pulled out the tray and examined the padded bottom of the box.

There were brooches and bars of all kinds. Manfred pointed to one, and this was inspected—but there was no pink diamond; nor was there in any other brooch.

'Is that the best you can do in the way of detective work?' demanded Mr Guntheimer as he closed and locked the box. 'I thought that tale was a little fantastic... '

Crash! A stone came hurtling through the window, smashing the glass, and fell on the carpet. With an oath Guntheimer spun round.

'What was that?'

He grabbed the jewel box that was on the table and ran to the window. Outside the window was a small balcony which ran the length of the building.

'Somebody standing on the balcony must have thrown that,' said Guntheimer.

The sound of smashing glass had been heard in the Corridor, and two hotel servants came in and examined the damage without, however, offering a solution to the mystery.

Manfred waited until the distracted bridegroom had locked away the jewel box in a strong trunk, and by this time Guntheimer was in a better humour.

'I've heard about you fellows,' he said, 'and I know you're pretty clever; otherwise, I should have thought that story of the pink diamond was all bunkum. Perhaps you will tell me what the Rajah of Who-was-it has to do with Angela's disappearance?'

Manfred was biting his lip thoughtfully.

'I don't wish to alarm you,' he said slowly. 'But has it occurred to you, Mr Guntheimer, that you may share her fate?'

Again that quick turn and look of apprehension.

'I don't quite understand you.'

'I wondered if you would,' said Manfred and, holding out his hand, he left his astonished host staring after him.

When he got to Curzon Street he found Gonsalez, his head in one deep armchair, his feet on another. Apparently Poiccart, who had reached home first, had told him of the callers, for he was holding forth on women.

'They are wilful, they are unreasonable,' he said bitterly. 'You remember, George, that woman at Cordova, how we saved her life from her lover and how we barely saved our own at her infuriated hands—there should be a law prohibiting women from possessing firearms. Here is a case in point. Tomorrow the newspapers will tell you the harrowing story of a bride torn from the arms of her handsome bridegroom. The old ladies of Bayswater will shed tears over the tragedy, knowing nothing of the aching heart of Mr Harry Sidworth or the great inconvenience to which this strange and tragic happening has put George Manfred, Raymond Poiccart, and Leon Gonsalez.'

Manfred opened the safe in a corner of the room and put into it something he had taken from his pocket. Characteristically, Gonsalez asked no questions, and it was remarkable and significant that nobody discussed the pink diamond.

The following morning passed uneventfully, save that Leon had much to say about the hardness of the drawing-room sofa, where he had spent the night, and the three men had finished lunch and were sitting smoking over their coffee, when a ring of the bell took Poiccart into the hall.

'Geydrew, full of bad tidings,' said George Manfred, as the sound of a voice came to them.

Lord Geydrew it was, shrill with his tremendous information.

'Have you heard the news?... Guntheimer has disappeared! The waiter went to his room this morning, could get no answer, opened the door with his key and walked in. The bed had not been slept in... all his luggage was there, and on the floor—'

'Let me guess,' said Manfred, and held his forehead. 'The jewel case was smashed to smithereens, without a single jewel in it! Or was it—'

But Lord Geydrew's face told him that his first guess was accurate.

'How did you know?' he gasped. 'It wasn't in the papers—my God, this is awful!'

In his agitation, he did not notice that Leon Gonsalez had slipped from the room, and only missed him when he turned to find the one man in whom, for some extraordinary reason, he had faith.

('Geydrew never did trust you or me,' said George afterwards.)

'I'm ashamed to confess it,' smiled Manfred. 'That was sheer guesswork. The jewel case had the appearance of being jumped on—I don't wonder!'

'But—but—' stammered the nobleman, and at that minute the door opened and he stood amazed.

A smiling girl was there, and in another instant was in his arms.

'Here's your Angela,' said Leon, with great coolness, 'and with all due respect to everybody, I shan't be sorry to sleep in my own bed tonight. George, that sofa must be sent back to the brigands who supplied it.'

But George was at the safe, lifting out a red leather jewel case.

It was a long time before Geydrew was calm enough to hear the story.

'My friend Leon Gonsalez,' said Manfred, 'has a wonderful memory for faces—so have we all, for the matter of that. But Leon is specially gifted. He was waiting at Waterloo to drive friend Poiccart home. Raymond had been to Winchester to see a surgeon friend of ours over a matter of a sprained leg. Whilst Leon was waiting he saw Guntheimer and your daughter and instantly recognized Guntheimer whose other name is Lanstry, or Smith, or Malikin. Guntheimer's graft is bigamy, and Leon happens to know him rather well. A few inquiries made of the porter, and he discovered, not the identity of your daughter, but that this man had married that day. He approached Angela with a cock and bull story that some mysterious body was waiting to see her outside the station. I will not say that she imagined that mysterious body was Harry Sidworth, but at any rate she went very willingly. She showed some little fight when friend Leon pushed her into the car and drove away with her—'

'Anybody who has tried to drive a car and control an infuriated and terrified lady will sympathize with me,' broke in Leon.

'By the time Miss Angela Geydrew reached Curzon Street she was in full possession of the facts as Leon knew them,' Manfred went on. 'Leon's one object was to postpone the honeymoon until he could get somebody to identify Guntheimer. The young lady told us nothing about her jewel case, but we all guessed the hundred-thousand-pound cheque, presented too late to be banked; before it could be cleared, Guntheimer would be well out of the country with any loot he was able to gather—in this case the family diamonds—and of course it would have been pretty easy to arrest him last night. When your lordship called yesterday Leon was out finishing his investigations. Before he returned, I learnt where I could get a duplicate jewel box, and with Poiccart made a call on friend bigamist. Poiccart was on the balcony, listening, and at an agreed word signal he smashed the window, which gave me just the opportunity I wanted to change the jewel boxes. Later, I presume, Mr Guntheimer opened the box, found it was empty, realized the game was up and fled.'

'But how did you induce him to show you the jewel box?' asked Lord Geydrew.

Manfred smiled cryptically. The tale of the pink diamond was too crude to be repeated.

4

THE THIRD COINCIDENCE
No record of prior magazine
publication found

Leon Gonsalez, like the famous scientist, had an unholy knack of collecting coincidences. He had, too, strange faiths, and believed that if a man saw a pink cow with one horn in the morning, he must, by the common workings of a certain esoteric law, meet another pink cow with one horn later in the day.

'Coincidences, my dear George,' he said, 'are inevitabilities—not accidents.'

Manfred murmured something in reply—he was studying the dossier of one William Yape, of whom something may be told at a later period.

'Now here is a coincidence.' Leon was in no sense abashed, for it was after dinner, the hour of the day when he was most confident. 'This morning I took the car for a run to Windsor—she was a trifle sticky yesterday—and at Langley what did I find? A gentleman sitting before an inn, very drunk. He was, I imagined, an agricultural labourer in his best Sunday suit, and it was remarkable that he wore a diamond ring worth five hundred pounds. He had, he told me, been to Canada, and had stayed at the Chateau Fronteuse—which is an expensive hotel.'

Poiccart was interested.

'And the coincidence?'

'If George will listen.' Manfred looked up with a groan. 'Thank you. Hardly had I begun questioning this inebriated son of the soil when a Rolls drove up, and there stepped down a rather nice-looking gentleman who also wore a diamond ring on his little finger.'

'Sensation,' said George Manfred, and went back to his dossier.

'I shall be offended if you do not listen. Imagine the agriculturist suddenly jumping to his feet as if he had seen a ghost. "Ambrose!" he gasped. I tell you his face was the colour of milk. Ambrose—if he will pardon the liberty—could not have heard him, and passed into the inn. The labourer went stumbling away—it is remarkable that one's head sobers so much more quickly than one's legs—as though the devil was after him.

'I went into the inn and found Ambrose drinking tea—a man who drinks tea at eleven o'clock in the morning has lived either in South Africa or Australia. It proved to be South Africa. An alluvial diamond digger, an ex-soldier and a most gentlemanly person, though not very communicative. After he had gone I went in search of the labourer—overtook him as he entered a most flamboyant villa.'

'Which, with your peculiar disregard for the sacredness of the Englishman's home, you entered.'

Leon nodded.

'Truth is in you,' he said. 'Imagine, my dear George, a suburban villa so filled with useless furniture that you could hardly find a place to sit. Satin-covered settees, pseudo-Chinese cabinets, whatnots and wherefores crowding space. Ridiculous oil paintings, painted by the yard, in heavy gold frames, simpering enlargements of photographs covering hideous wallpaper—and two ladies, expensively dressed, bediamonded but without an "h" between them; common as the dirt on my shoes, shrill, ugly, coarse.

'As I entered the hall on the trail of the labourer I heard him say: "He wasn't killed—he's back," and a woman say:

"Oh, my God!" And then the second woman said: "He must be killed—it was in the list on New Year's Day!"—after which I was so busy explaining my presence that further enlightenment was out of the question.'

George Manfred had tied his dossier neatly with a strip of red tape, and now he leaned back in his chair.

'You took the number of the Ambrose car, of course?'

Leon nodded.

'And he wore a diamond ring?'

'A lady's—it was on his little finger. A not very magnificent affair. It was the sort of dress ring that a girl would wear.'

Poiccart chuckled.

'Now we sit down and wait for the third coincidence,' he said. 'It is inevitable.'

A few minutes later Leon was on his way to Fleet Street, for he was a man whose curiosity was insatiable. For two hours, in the office of a friendly newspaper, he pored over the casualty lists that were published on four New Year's Days, looking for a soldier whose first name was 'Ambrose'.

'The Three Just Men,' said the Assistant Commissioner cheerfully, 'are now so eminently respectable that we give them police protection.'

You must allow for the fact that this was after dinner, when even an Assistant Commissioner grows a little expansive, especially when he is host in his nice house in Belgravia. You must also allow for the more interesting fact that one of the famous organization had been seen outside Colonel Yenford's house that very night.

'They are strange devils—why they should be watching this place beats me; if I'd known I should have asked the fellow in!'

Lady Irene Belvinne looked at one of the portraits on the wall: she seemed scarcely interested in the Three Just Men. Yet every word Colonel Yenford spoke was eagerly stored in her memory.

A beautiful woman of thirty-five, the widow of a man who had held Cabinet rank, she might claim to be especially favoured. She had been the wife of a many-times millionaire who had left her his entire fortune; she had the lineless face and serene poise of one who had never known care...

'I don't exactly know what they do?' Her voice was a soft drawl. 'Are they detectives? Of course, I know what they were.'

Who did not know what that ruthless trio were in the days when every hand was against them? When swift death followed their threat, when a whole world of secret lawbreakers trembled at their names.

'They're tame enough now,' said somebody. 'They wouldn't have played their monkey tricks today, eh, Yenford?'

Colonel Yenford was not so confident.

'It's strange,' mused Irene. 'I didn't think of them.'

She was so wholly absorbed in her thoughts that she did not realize she was speaking aloud.

'Why on earth should you think about them?' demanded Yenford, a little astonished.

She started at this and changed the subject.

It was past midnight when she reached her beautiful flat in Piccadilly, and all the staff except her maid had gone to bed. At the sound of a key turning in the lock the maid came flying into the hall, and with a sinking of heart Irene Belvinne knew that something was wrong.

'She's been waiting since nine, m'lady,' said the girl in a low voice.

Irene nodded.

'Where is she?' she asked.

'I put her in the study, madam.'

Handing her coat to the maid, the woman walked up the broad passage, opened a door and entered the library. The woman who had been sitting on the hide-covered settee rose awkwardly at the sight of the radiant woman who entered. The visitor was poorly dressed, had a long, not too clean face, and a mouth that drooped pathetically. She looked up slyly from under her lowered lids, and though her tone was humble it also held a suggestion of menace.

'He's terribly bad again tonight, m'lady,' she said. 'We had all our work cut out to keep him in bed. He wanted to come here, he said, him being delirious. The doctor says that we ought to get him away to—' her eyes rose quickly and fell again '— South Africa.'

'It was Canada last time,' said Irene steadily. 'That was rather an expensive trip, Mrs Dennis.'

The woman mumbled something, rubbing her hands still more nervously.

'I'm sure I'm worried to death about the whole business, me being his aunt, and I'm sure I can't afford no five thousand pounds to take him to South Africa—'

Five thousand pounds! Irene was aghast at the demand. The Canadian trip had cost three thousand, but the original request was for one.

'I should like to see him myself,' she said with sudden determination.

Again that swift, sly look.

'I wouldn't let you come and see him, me lady, unless you brought a gentleman. I'd say your 'usband, but I know he's no more. I wouldn't take the responsibility, I wouldn't indeed. That's why I never tell you where we're living, in case you was tempted, me lady. He'd think no more of cutting your throat than he would of looking at you!'

A smile of contempt hardened the beautiful face.

'I am not so sure that really terrifies me,' said Irene quietly. 'You want five thousand pounds—when do you sail?'

'Next Saturday, me lady,' said the woman eagerly. 'And Jim say you was to pay the money in notes.'

Irene nodded.

'Very well,' she said. 'But you mustn't come here again unless I send for you.'

'Where shall I get the money, me lady?'

'Here at twelve o'clock tomorrow. And won't you please make yourself a little more presentable when you call?'

The woman grinned.

'I ain't got your looks or your clothes, me lady,' she sneered. 'Every penny piece I earn goes on poor Jim, a-trying to save his life, when if he had his rights he'd have millions.'

Irene walked to the door and opened it, waited in the passage until the maid had shut out the unprepossessing visitor.

'Open the windows and air the room,' said Irene.

She went upstairs and sat down before her dressing table, eyeing her reflection thoughtfully.

Then, of a sudden, she got up and crossed the room to the telephone. She lifted the receiver and then realized that she did not know the number. A search of the book gave her the information she wanted. The Triangle Detective Agency had their headquarters in Curzon Street. But they would be in bed by now, she thought; and even if the members of this extraordinary confederation were not, would they be likely to interest themselves at this late hour?

She had hardly given the number before she was through. She heard the rattle of the receiver as it was raised, and the distinctive tinkle of a guitar; then an eager voice asked her who she was.

'Lady Irene Belvinne,' she said. 'You don't know me, but—'

'I know you very well. Lady Irene.' She could almost detect the unknown smiling as he answered. 'You dined at Colonel

Yenford's tonight and left the house at twelve minutes to twelve. You told your chauffeur to go back by way of Hyde Park...'

The guitar had ceased. She heard a distant voice say: 'Listen to Leon: he's being all Sherlock Holmes.' And then a laugh. She smiled in sympathy.

'Do you want to see me?' This was Leon Gonsalez speaking, then.

'When can I?' she asked.

'Now. I'll come right away, if you're in any serious trouble—I have an idea that you are.'

She hesitated. An immediate decision was called for and she set her teeth.

'Very well. Will you come? I'll wait up for you.'

In her nervousness she dropped the receiver down while he was answering her.

Five minutes later the maid admitted a slim, good-looking man. He wore a dark suit, and was strangely like a Chancery barrister she knew. On her part the greeting was awkward, for the interval had been too short for her to make up her mind what she should tell him, and how she should begin.

It was in the library tainted, to her sensitive nostrils, with her late frowsy visitor, that she made her confession, and he listened with an expressionless face.

'... I was very young—that is my only excuse; and he was a very handsome, very attractive young man... and a chauffeur isn't a servant... I mean, one can be quite good friends with him, as one couldn't be with—well, with other servants.'

He nodded.

'It was an act of lunacy, and nasty, and everything you can say. When my father sent him away I thought my heart would break.'

'Your father knew?' asked Gonsalez gravely.

She shook her head.

'No. Father was rather quick-tempered, and he bullied Jim for some fault that was not his—that was the end of it. I had one letter and then I heard no more until two or three years after I was married, when I got a letter from this woman, saying that her nephew was consumptive and she knew what—good friends we'd been.'

To her surprise her visitor was smiling, and at first she was hurt.

'You have told me only what I've guessed,' he said to her amazement.

'You guessed... but you didn't know—'

He interrupted her brusquely.

'Was your second marriage happy, Lady Irene? I am not being impertinent.'

She hesitated.

'It was quite happy. My husband was nearly thirty years older than I—why do you ask?'

Leon smiled again.

'I am a sentimentalist—which is a shocking confession for one who boasts of his scientific mind. I am a devourer of love stories, both in fiction and in life. This Jim was not unpleasant?'

She shook her head.

'No,' she said, and then added simply: 'I loved him—I love him still. That is the ghastly part of it. It is dreadful to think of him lying ill with this dreadful aunt looking after him—'

'Landlady,' broke in Leon calmly. 'He had no relations.'

She was on her feet now, staring at him.

'What do you know?'

He had a gesture which was almost mesmeric in its calming effect.

'I went to Colonel Yenford's house tonight—I happened to learn that you were his guest and I wanted to see your mouth. I'm sorry if I am being mysterious, but I judge women by their mouths—the test is infallible. That is why I knew the hour you left.'

Irene Belvinne was frowning at him.

'I don't understand, Mr Gonsalez,' she began. 'What has my mouth to do with the matter?'

He nodded slowly.

'If you had a certain type of mouth I should not have been interested — as it is...'

She waited, and presently he spoke.

'You will find James Ambrose Clynes in his suite at the Piccadilly Hotel. The dress ring you gave him is on his little finger, and your photograph is the only one in his room.'

He put out his hand and steadied her as, white and shaking, she sank into a chair.

'He's a very rich man and a very nice man... and a very stupid man, or he would have come to see you.'

A car drew up before an ornate villa in the village of Langley and a poorly-dressed woman got down. The door was opened by a thickset man and the two passed into the over-furnished parlour. On the face of Mrs Dennis was a smile of satisfaction.

'It's all right — she'll part,' she said, throwing off her old coat.

The coarse-looking man with the diamond ring turned to his other sister.

'As soon as we get the money it's Canada for us,' he said ominously. 'I won't have another fright like I had on Tuesday — why were you so late, Maria?'

'A tyre burst on the Great West Road,' she said, rubbing her hands at the fire. 'What are you worrying about, Saul? We've done nothing. It ain't as though we ever threatened her. That'd be crime. Just askin' her to help a poor feller who's ill, that ain't crime.'

They discussed the pros and cons of this for nearly an hour. Then came the knock at the door.

It was the man who went out to interview the visitor...

'If I don't come in,' said Leon Gonsalez pleasantly, 'the police will. There will be a warrant issued tomorrow morning and you will be held on a charge of conspiring to defraud.'

A few seconds later he was questioning a trembling audience...

Poiccart and George Manfred were waiting up for him when he returned in the early hours of the morning.

'Rather a unique case,' said Leon, glancing through his notes. 'Our Ambrose, a well-educated man, had a love affair with the Earl of Carslake's daughter. He loses his job—because he loves the girl he decides not to communicate with her. He goes into the Army and, before he is sent overseas, he writes to his landlady, asks her to take out a sealed envelope, full of letters from Irene and burn them. By the time she gets these instructions, Ambrose is reported killed. The landlady, Mrs Dennis, with the inquisitiveness of her class, opens the envelope and learns enough to be able to blackmail this unfortunate girl. But Ambrose isn't dead—he is discharged from the army on account of wounds and, accepting the invitation of a South African soldier, goes to the Cape, where he makes good.

'In the meantime the Dennises wax rich. They pretend that "Jim", as they called him, is desperately ill, trusting that Irene has not heard of his death. By this means, and on the threat of telling her husband, they extract nearly twenty thousand pounds.'

'What shall we do to them?' asked Poiccart.

Leon took something from his pocket—a glittering diamond ring. 'I took this as payment for my advice,' he said.

George smiled.

'And your advice, Leon?'

'Was to get out of the country before Ambrose found them,' said Leon.

5

THE SLANE MYSTERY
(Reprinted in *The Saint Magazine*,
UK edition, July 1962)

The killing of Bernard Slane was one of those mysteries which delight the Press and worry the police. Mr Slane was a rich stockbroker, a bachelor and a good fellow. He had dined at a Pall Mall club and, his car being in the garage for repairs, he took a taxi and ordered the driver to take him to his flat in Albert Palace Mansions. The porter of the mansions had taken the elevator to the fifth floor at the time Mr Slane arrived.

The first intimation that there was anything wrong was when the porter came down to find the taxi-driver standing in the hall, and asked him what he wanted.

'I've just brought a gentleman here — Mr Slane, who lives at Number Seven,' said the driver. 'He hadn't got any change so he's gone in to get it.'

This was quite likely, because Slane lived on the first floor and invariably used the stairs. They chatted together, the porter and the driver, for some five minutes, and then the porter undertook to go up and collect the money for the fare.

Albert Palace Mansions differed from every other apartment-house of its kind in that, on the first and the most expensive floor, there was one small flat consisting of four rooms, which was occupied by Slane.

A light showed through the transom, but then it had been burning all the evening. The porter rang the bell and waited, rang it again, knocked—without, however, getting an answer. He returned to the driver.

'He must have gone to sleep—how was he?' he asked.

By his question he meant to inquire whether the stockbroker was quite sober. It is a fact that Slane drank rather heavily, and had come home more than once in a condition which necessitated the help of the night porter to get him to bed.

The driver, whose name was Reynolds, admitted his passenger had had as much as, and probably more than, was good for him. Again the porter attempted to get a reply from the flat and, when this failed, he paid the driver out of his own pocket, four shillings and sixpence.

The porter was on duty all night, and made several journeys up and down his shaft. Through the open grille on the first floor he commanded a view of No 7. His statement was that he saw nothing of Mr Slane that night, that it was impossible for the stockbroker to have left the building without his seeing him.

At half past five the next morning a policeman patrolling Green Park saw a man sitting huddled up on a garden chair. He wore a dinner jacket and, his attitude was so suspicious that the policeman stepped over the rails and crossed the stretch of grass which intervened between the pathway and the chair which was placed near a clump of rhododendrons. He came up to the man, to find his fears justified. The man was dead; he had been terribly battered with some blunt instrument, and a search of the pockets revealed his identity as Bernard Slane.

Near the spot was an iron gateway set in the rails leading to the Mall, and the lock of this was discovered to be smashed. Detectives from Scotland Yard were at once on the spot; the porter of Albert Palace Mansions was questioned; and a call was sent round, asking the driver Reynolds to call at the Yard. He was there by twelve o'clock, but could throw no light on the mystery.

Reynolds was a respectable man without any record against him, and was a widower who lived over a garage near Dorset Square, Baker Street.

'A most amusing crime,' said Leon Gonsalez, his elbows on the breakfast table, his head between his hands.

'Why amusing?' asked George.

Leon read on, his lips moving, a trick of his, as he devoured every printed line. After a while he leaned back in his chair and rubbed his eyes.

'It is amusing,' he said, 'because of the hotel bill that was found in the dead man's pocket.'

He put his finger on a paragraph and Manfred drew the paper towards him and read:

'The police discovered in the right hand pocket of the murdered man's overcoat a bloodstained paper which proved to be an hotel bill, issued by the Plage Hotel, Ostend, five years ago. The bill was made out in the name of Mr and Mrs Wilbraham and was for 7,500 francs.'

Manfred pushed the paper back.

'Isn't the mystery why this half-drunken man left his flat and went back to Green Park, some considerable distance from Albert Palace Mansions?' he asked.

Leon, who was staring blankly at the farther wall, shook his head slowly; and then, in his characteristic way, went off at a tangent:

'There's a lot to be said for the law which prohibited the publication of certain details in divorce cases,' he said, 'but I believe that the circumstances which surrounded the visit of Mr and Mrs Wilbraham to the Plage would have been given the fullest publicity if the case had come into court.'

'Do you suspect a murder of revenge?' Leon shrugged his shoulders and changed the subject. George Manfred used to say that Leon had the most amazing pigeon-hole of a mind that it had been his fortune to meet with. Very seldom indeed did he have to consult the voluminous notes and data he had collected during his life, and which made one room in that little house uninhabitable.

There was a man at Scotland Yard, Inspector Meadows, who was on the friendliest terms with the Three. It was his practice to smoke a pipe, indeed many pipes, of evenings in the little Curzon Street house. He came that night, rather full of the Slane mystery.

'Slane was a pretty rapid sort,' he said. 'From the evidence that was found in his house, it is clear that he was the one man in London who ought not to be a bachelor if about two dozen women had their rights! By the way, we've traced Mr and Mrs Wilbraham. Wilbraham was of course Slane. The lady isn't so easy to find; one of his pick-ups, I suppose—'

'And yet the only girl he was willing to marry,' said Gonsalez.

'How did you know that?' asked the startled detective.

Leon chuckled.

'The bill was obviously sent to give the husband evidence. The husband, either because he was willing to give his wife another chance or because he was a Roman Catholic, did not divorce her. Now tell me'—he leaned forward over the table and beamed on the detective—'when the taxi drew up before the door of Albert Palace Mansions, did Slane immediately alight?—I can tell you he didn't.'

'You've been making inquiries,' said the other suspiciously.

'No, he waited there. The driver, being a tactful individual, thought it best to keep him inside until the people who were in the hall had gone up in the lift—which is visible from the door.'

THE SLANE MYSTERY

'Exactly. Was it the driver's idea or Slane's?'

'The driver's,' said Meadows. 'Slane was half asleep when the man pulled him out.'

'One more question: when the elevator man took this party to the fifth floor, did he come down immediately?'

The Inspector shook his head.

'No, he stayed up there talking to the tenants. He heard Slane's door slam, and that was the first intimation he had that somebody had come in.'

Leon jerked back into his chair, a delighted smile on his face.

'What do you think, Raymond?' He addressed the saturnine Poiccart.

'What do you think?' said the other.

Meadows looked from Poiccart to Gonsalez.

'Have you any theory as to why Slane went out again?'

'He didn't go out again,' said the two men in unison.

Meadows caught George Manfred's smiling eyes.

'They're trying to mystify you, Meadows, but what they say is true. Obviously he didn't go out again.'

He rose and stretched himself.

'I'm going to bed; and I'd like to bet you fifty pounds that Leon finds the murderer tomorrow, though I won't swear that he will hand him over to Scotland Yard.'

At eight o'clock next morning, when, with a cigarette in his mouth, Reynolds, the taxi-driver, was making a final inspection of his cab before taking it out for the day, Leon Gonsalez walked into the mews.

Reynolds was a man of forty, a quiet, good-looking fellow. He had a soft voice and was courteous in a particularly pleasing way.

'You're not another detective, are you?' he asked, smiling ruefully. 'I've answered as many foolish questions as I care to answer.'

'Is this your own cab?' Leon nodded to the shining vehicle.

'Yes, that's mine,' said the driver. 'Cab-owning is not the gold mine some people think it is. And if you happen to get mixed up in a case like this, your takings fall fifty per cent.'

Very briefly Leon explained his position.

'The Triangle Agency—oh, yes, I remember: you're the Four Just Men, aren't you? Good Lord! Scotland Yard haven't put you on the job?'

'I'm on the job for my own amusement,' said Leon, giving smile for smile. 'There are one or two matters which weren't quite clear to me, and I wondered if you would mind telling me something that the police don't seem to know.'

The man hesitated, and then: 'Come up to my room,' he said, and led the way up the narrow stairs.

The room was surprisingly well furnished. There were one or two old pieces, Leon noticed, which must have been worth a lot of money. On a gate-legged table in the centre of the room was a suitcase and near the table a trunk. The driver must have noticed his eyes rest on these, for he said quickly: 'They belong to a customer of mine. I'm taking them to the station.'

From where he stood, Leon could see they were addressed to the Tetley cloak room to be called for; he made no comment on this, but his observation evidently disconcerted his host for his manner changed.

'Now, Mr Gonsalez, I'm a working man, so I'm afraid I can't give you very much time. What is it you want to know?'

'I particularly wish to know,' said Leon, 'whether the day you brought Slane to his house had been a very busy one for you?'

'It was fairly profitable,' said the other. 'I've already given the police an account of my fares, including the hospital case—but I suppose you know that.'

'Which hospital case was this?'

The man hesitated.

'I don't want you to think I'm boasting about doing a thing like that—it was just humanity. A woman was knocked down by a bus in Baker Street: I picked her up and took her to the hospital.'

'Was she badly hurt?'

'She died.' His voice was curt.

Leon looked at him thoughtfully. Again his eyes roved to the trunk.

'Thank you,' he said. 'Will you come to Curzon Street tonight at nine o'clock? Here's my address.' He took a card from his pocket.

'Why?' There was a note of defiance in the voice.

'Because I want to ask you something that I think you'll be glad to answer,' said Leon.

His big car was waiting at the end of the mews, and he set it flying in the direction of the Walmer Street hospital. He learnt there no more than he expected, and returned to Curzon Street, a very silent and uninformative man.

At nine o'clock that night came Reynolds, and for an hour he and Leon Gonsalez were closeted together in the little room downstairs. Happily, Meadows did not consider it necessary to call. It was not until a week afterwards that he came with a piece of information that surprised only himself.

'It was rather a rum thing—that driver who took Slane back to his flat has disappeared—sold his taxi and cleared out. There's nothing to associate him with the murder or I should get a warrant for him. He has been straightforward from the very first.'

Manfred politely agreed. Poiccart was staringly vacant. Leon Gonsalez yawned and was frankly bored with all mysteries.

'It's very curious,' said Gonsalez, when he condescended to tell the full story, 'that the police never troubled to investigate Slane's life at Tetley. He had a big house there for some years. If they had, they couldn't have failed to hear the story of young Doctor Grain and his beautiful wife, who ran away from him. She and Slane disappeared together; and of course he was passionately fond of her and was ready to marry her. But then, Slane was the type who was passionately fond of people for about three months, and unless the marriage could be arranged instantly the unfortunate girl had very little chance of becoming his wife.

'The doctor offered to take his wife back, but she refused, and disappeared out of his life. He gave up the practice of medicine, came to London, invested his savings in a small garage, went broke, as all garage proprietors do unless they're backed with good capital, and having to decide whether he'd go back to the practice of medicine and pick up all that he'd lost in the years he'd been trying to forget his wife, he chose what to him was the less strenuous profession of cab-driver. I know another man who did exactly the same thing: I will tell you about him one of these days.

'He never saw his wife again, though he frequently saw Slane. Reynolds, or Grain, as I will call him, had shaved off his moustache and generally altered his appearance, and Slane never recognized him. It became an obsession of Grain's to follow his enemy about, to learn of his movements, his habits. The one habit he did discover, and which proved to be Slane's undoing, was his practice of dining at the Real Club in Pall Mall every Wednesday evening and of leaving the club at eleven-thirty on those occasions.

'He put his discovery to no use, nor did he expect he would, until the night of the murder. He was driving somewhere in the north-west district when he saw a woman knocked down by a bus and he himself nearly ran over the prostrate figure. Stopping his cab, he jumped down and, to his horror, as he picked her up, he found himself gazing into the emaciated face of his wife. He lifted her into the cab, drove full pelt to the nearest hospital. It was while they were in the waiting-room, before the house surgeon's arrival, that the dying woman told him, in a few broken, half-delirious words, the story of her downward progress... She was dead before they got her on to the operating table—mercifully, as it proved.

'I knew all this before I went to the hospital and found that some unknown person had decided that she should be buried at Tetley and had made the most lavish arrangements for her removal. I guessed it before I saw Grain's suitcase packed ready for that tragedy. He left the hospital, a man mad with hate. It was raining heavily. He crawled down Pall Mall, and luck was with him, for just as the porter came out to find an empty taxi, Grain pulled up before the door.

'On the pretext of a tyre burst he stopped in the Mall, forced open one of the gates that led to the park, and waited until no pedestrian was in sight before he dragged the half-drunken man into the gardens... He was sober enough before Grain finished his story. Grain swears that he gave him the chance of his life, but Slane pulled a gun on him, and he had to kill him in self-defence. That may or may not be true.

'He never lost his nerve. Reaching his cab without observation, he drove to Albert Palace Mansions, waited until the lift had risen, and then ran up the stairs. He had taken Slane's bunch of keys, and on the way had selected that which he knew would open the door. His first intention was to search the flat for everything that betrayed the man's association with his wife; but he heard the porter up above saying good night and, slamming the door, raced downstairs in time to be there when the man reached the ground floor.'

'We're not telling the police of this, of course?' said Manfred gravely.

Poiccart at the other end of the table burst into a loud guffaw.

'It's so good a story that the police would never believe it,' he said.

6

THE MARKED CHEQUE
(No record of prior magazine publication found)

The man who called at the little house in Curzon Street was in a rage, and anxious to say something that would hurt his late employer.

He had also a personal grievance against Mr Jens, the butler.

'Mr Storn took me on as a second footman, and it looked like being a good job, but I couldn't hit it off with the rest of the staff. But was it fair to chuck me out without a minute's warning because I happened to let drop a word in Arabic—?'

'Arabic?' asked Leon Gonsalez in surprise. 'Do you speak Arabic?'

Tenley, the dismissed footman, grinned.

'About a dozen words: I was with the Army in Egypt after the war, and I picked up a few phrases. I was polishing the silver salver in the hall, and I happened to say "That's good" in Arabic; and I heard Mr Storn's voice behind me.

'"You clear out," he said, and before I knew what had happened, I was walking away from the house with a month's salary.'

Gonsalez nodded.

'Very interesting,' he said, 'but why have you come to us?'

He had asked the same question many times of inconsequential people who had come to the House of the Silver Triangle, with their trifling grievances.

'Because there's a mystery there,' said the man vaguely. Perhaps he had cooled down a little by now, and was feeling rather uncomfortable. 'Why was I fired for my Arabic? What's the meaning of the picture in Storn's private room—the men being hung?'

Leon sat upright. 'Men being hanged? What is that?'

'It's a photograph. You can't get it, because it's in the panelling and you have to open one of the panels. But I went in one day and he'd left the panel ajar... Three men hanging from a sort of gibbet an' a lot of Turks looking on. That's a funny thing for a gentleman to have in his house.'

Leon was silent for a while.

'I don't know that that is an offence. It is certainly odd. Is there anything I can do for you?'

Apparently nothing. The man left a little sheepishly, and Leon carried the news to his partner. He remembered afterwards that he had heard nothing of the grievance against the butler.

'The only thing I learnt about Storn is that he is extraordinarily mean, that he runs his house in Park Lane with a minimum number of staff, that he pays those the smallest wages possible. He is of Armenian origin and made his money out of oilfields which he acquired by very dubious means.

'As to the three hanged men, that is rather gruesome, but it might be worse. I have seen photographs in the house of the idle rich that would make your hair stand on end, my dear Poiccart. At any rate, the morbid interest of a millionaire in a Turkish execution is not extraordinary.'

'If I were an Armenian,' said Manfred, 'they would be my chief hobby; I should have a whole gallery of 'em!'

And there ended the matter of the morbid millionaire who lived meanly and underpaid his servants.

Early in April, Leon read in the newspaper that Mr Storn had gone to Egypt for a short holiday.

By every test, Ferdinand Storn was a desirable acquaintance. He was immensely rich; he was personally attractive in a dark, long-nosed way; and to such people as met him intimately—and they were few—he could talk Art and Finance with equal facility. So far as was known, he had no enemies. He lived at Burson House, Park Lane, a small, handsome residence which he had purchased from the owner, Lord Burson, for £150,000. He spent most of his time either there or at Felfry Park, his beautiful country house in Sussex. The Persian and Oriental Oil Trust, of which he was the head, had its offices in a magnificent building in Moorgate Street, and here he was usually to be found between ten o'clock in the morning and three o'clock in the afternoon.

This Trust, despite its titled board, was a one-man affair, and conducted, amongst other things, the business of bankers. Storn held most of the shares, and was popularly supposed to derive an income of something like a quarter of a million a year. He had few personal friends, and was a bachelor.

It was just short of a month after Leon had read the news that a big car drew up at the door of the Triangle, and a stout, prosperous-looking man got out and rang the bell. He was a stranger to Leon, who interviewed him, and was apparently loth to state his business, for he hummed and hawed and questioned until Leon, a little impatiently, asked him point-blank who he was and what was his object.

'Well, I'll tell you, Mr Gonsalez,' said the stout man. 'I am the General Manager of the Persian and Oriental Oil—'

'Storn's company?' asked Leon, his interest awakened.

'Storn's company. I suppose I really ought to go to the police with my suspicions, but a friend of mine has such faith in you

THE MARKED CHEQUE

and what he calls the Three Just Men, that I thought I had better see you first.'

'Is it about Mr Storn?' asked Leon.

The gentleman, who proved to be Mr Hubert Grey, the Managing Director of the Trust, nodded.

'You see, Mr Gonsalez, I am in rather a peculiar position. Mr Storn is a very difficult man, and I should lose my job if I made him look ridiculous.'

'He's abroad, isn't he?' asked Leon.

'He's abroad,' agreed the other soberly. 'He went abroad, as a matter of fact, quite unexpectedly; that is to say, it was unexpected by the office. In fact he had an important Board meeting the day he left, which he should have attended, but on that morning I got a letter from him saying that he had to go to Egypt on a matter which affected his personal honour. He asked me not to communicate with him, or even to announce the fact that he had left London. Unfortunately, one of my clerks very foolishly told a reporter who had called that day that Mr Storn had left.

'A week after he had gone, he sent us a letter from an hotel in Rome, enclosing a cheque for eighty-three thousand pounds, and arranging that this cheque should be honoured when a gentleman called, which he did the next day.'

'An Englishman?' asked Leon.

Mr Grey shook his head. 'No, he was a foreigner of some kind; a rather dark-looking man. The money was paid over to him.

'A few days later we had another letter from Mr Storn, written from the Hotel de Russie, Rome. This letter told us that a further cheque had been sent to Mr Kraman, which was to be honoured. This was for one hundred and seven thousand pounds and a few odd shillings. He gave us instructions as to how the money was to be paid, and asked us to telegraph to him at an hotel in Alexandria the moment the cheque was honoured. This I did. The very next day there came a second letter written from the Hotel Mediterraneo in Naples—I will let you have copies of all these—telling us that a third cheque was to be paid without fail, but to a different man, a Mr Rezzio, who would call at the office. This was for one hundred and twelve thousand pounds, which very nearly exhausted Mr Storn's cash balance, although of course he has large reserves at the bank. I might say that Mr Storn is a man who is rather eccentric in the matter of large deposit reserves. Very little of his money is locked up in shares. Look here'—he took a note-case from his pocket and produced a cheque form—'this money has been paid, but I've brought you along the cheque to see.'

Leon took it in his hand. It was written in characteristic writing, and he examined the signature.

'There is no question of this being a forgery?'

'None whatever,' said Grey emphatically. 'The letter, too, was in his own handwriting. But what puzzled me about the cheque were the queer marks on the back.'

They were indistinguishable to Leon until he took them to the window, and then saw a line of faint pencil marks which ran along the bottom of the cheque.

'I suppose I can't keep this cheque for a day or two?' asked Leon.

'Certainly. The signature, as you see, has been cancelled out, and the money has been paid.'

Leon examined the cheque again. It was drawn on the Ottoman Oil Bank, which was apparently a private concern of Storn's.

'What do you imagine has happened?' he asked.

'I don't know, but I'm worried.'

Grey's troubled frown showed the extent of that worry.

'I don't know why I should be, but I've got an uncomfortable feeling at the back of my mind that there is a swindle somewhere.'

'Have you cabled to Alexandria?'

Mr Grey smiled. 'Naturally; and I have had a reply. It struck me that you might have agents in Egypt, in which case it might be a simple matter for you to discover whether there is anything wrong. The main point is that I don't wish Mr Storn to know that I've been making inquiries. I'll pay any reasonable expenditure you incur, and I'm quite sure that Mr Storn will agree that I have done the right thing.'

After the departure of his visitor, Leon interviewed Manfred.

'It may, of course, be a case of blackmail,' said George softly. 'But you will have to start at Storn's beginnings if you want to get under whatever mystery there is.'

'So I think,' said Gonsalez; and a few minutes afterwards went out of the house.

He did not return till midnight. He brought back an amazing amount of information about Mr Storn.

'About twelve years ago he was an operator in the service of the Turco Telegraph Company. He speaks eight Oriental languages, and was well-known in Istanbul. Does that tell you anything, George?'

Manfred shook his head.

'It tells me nothing yet, but I am waiting to be thrilled.'

'He was mixed up with the revolutionary crowd, the understrappers who pulled the strings in the days of Abdul Ahmid, and there is no doubt that he got his Concession through these fellows.'

'What Concession?' asked Manfred.

'Oil land, large tracts of it. When the new Government came into power, the Concession was formed, though I suspect our friend paid heavily for the privilege. His five partners, however, were less fortunate. Three of them were accused of treason against the Government, and were hanged.'

'The photograph,' nodded Manfred. 'What happened to the other two?'

'The other two were Italians, and they were sent to prison in Asia Minor for the rest of their lives. When Storn came to London, it was as sole proprietor of the Concession, which he floated with a profit of three million pounds.'

The next morning Leon left the house early, and at ten o'clock was ringing the bell at Burson House.

The heavy-jowled butler who opened the door regarded him with suspicion, but was otherwise deferential.

'Mr Storn is abroad, and won't be back for some weeks, sir.'

'May I see Mr Storn's secretary?' asked Leon in his blandest manner.

'Mr Storn never has a secretary at his house; you will find the young lady at the offices of the Persian Oil Trust.'

Leon felt in his pocket and produced a card.

'I am one of the Bursons,' he said, 'and as a matter of fact my father was born here. Some months ago when I was in London I asked Mr Storn if he would give me permission to look over the house.'

The card contained a scribbled line, signed 'Ferdinand Storn,' giving permission to the bearer to see the house at any hour 'when I am out of town.' It had taken Leon the greater part of an hour to forge that permit.

'I am afraid I cannot let you in, sir,' said the butler, barring the passage. 'Mr Storn told me before he went that I was to admit no strangers.'

'What is today?' asked Leon suddenly.

'Thursday, sir,' said the man.

Leon nodded. 'Cheese day,' he said.

Only for the fraction of a second was the man confused.

'I don't know what you mean, sir,' he said gruffly, and almost shut the door in the face of the caller.

Gonsalez made a circuit of the house. It stood with another upon an island site.

When he had finished, he went home, an amused and almost excited man, to give instructions to Raymond Poiccart who, amongst his other qualifications, had a very wide circle of criminal friends. There was not a big gangster in London that he did not know. He was acquainted with the public house in London where the confidence men and the safe smashers met: he could at any moment gather the gossip of the prisons, and was probably better acquainted with the secret news of the underworld than any man at Scotland Yard. Him Leon sent on a news-gathering mission, and in a small public house off Lambeth Walk, Poiccart learned of the dark philanthropist who had found employment for at least three ex-convicts.

Leon was sitting alone when he returned, examining with a powerful lens the odd marks on the back of the cheque.

Before Poiccart could retail his news, Leon reached for a telephone directory.

'Grey, of course, has left his office, but unless I am mistaken this is his private address,' he said, as his fingers stopped on one of the pages. A maid answered his call. Yes, Mr Grey was at home. Presently the Managing Director's voice came through.

'Mr Grey—who would handle the cheques which you have received from Storn; I mean who is the official?'

'The accountant,' was the reply.

'Who gave the accountant his job—you?'

A pause.

'No—Mr Storn. He used to be in the Eastern Telegraph Company—Mr Storn met him abroad.'

'And where is the accountant to be found?' asked Leon eagerly.

'He's on his holidays. He left before the last cheque came. But I can get him.'

Leon's laugh was one of sheer delight.

'You needn't worry—I knew he wasn't at the office,' he said, and hung up on the astonished manager.

'Now, my dear Poiccart, what did you find?'

He listened intently till his friend had finished, and then: 'Let us go to Park Lane—and bring a gun with you,' he said. 'We will call at Scotland Yard en route.'

It was ten o'clock when the butler opened the door. Before he could frame a question, a big detective gripped him and pulled him into the street.

The four plain-clothes officers who accompanied Leon flocked into the hall. A surly-faced footman was arrested before he could shout a warning. At the very top of the house, in a small windowless apartment that had once been used as a box-room, they found an emaciated man whom even his Managing Director, hastily summoned to the scene, failed to identify as the millionaire. The two Italians who kept guard on him and watched him through a hole broken through the wall from an adjoining room gave no trouble.

One of them, he who had carefully planted Burson House full of ex-convict servants, was very explicit.

'This man betrayed us, and we should have hanged like Hatim Effendi and Al Shiri and Maropulos the Greek, only we bribed witnesses,' he said. 'We were partners in the oilfields, and to rob us he manufactured evidence that we were conspiring against the Government. My friend and I broke prison and came back to London. I was determined he should pay us the money he owed us, and I knew that we could never get it from a Court of Law.'

'It was a very simple matter, and I really am ashamed of myself that I did not understand those marks at the back of the cheque at first glance,' explained Leon over the supper-table that night. 'Our Italian friend was one of the crowd that got the Concession: he had lived for years in London, and possibly it will be proved that he had criminal associates. At any rate, he had no difficulty in collecting a houseful of servants, playing as he did on his knowledge of Storn's character. All these men offered to serve Storn for sums at which the average servant would have turned up his nose. It has taken the better part of a year to fill our friend's establishment with these ex-convicts. You remember that the footman who came to us a few months ago said that he had been employed, not by the butler but by Storn himself. They would have taken the first opportunity of getting rid of him, only inadvertently he used an Arabic expression, and Storn, who was suspicious of spies and probably expected the men whom he had betrayed to return, sent him packing.

'On the day Storn was supposed to leave for Egypt, he was seized by the two Italians, locked up in a room and compelled to write such letters and sign such cheques as they dictated. But he remembered, rather late in the day, that the accountant was an old telegraphist, and so he put on the back of the cheque, in pencil marks, a Morse message in the old symbols which were employed when the needle machine was most commonly used.'

He produced the cheque and laid it on the table, running his finger along the pencil mark:

SOSPRSNRPRKLN

'In other words, "Prisoner in Park Lane." The accountant was on his holiday, so he did not read the message.'

Manfred took up the cheque, turned it and examined it.

'What handsome fee will this millionaire send you?' he asked ironically.

The answer did not come till a few days after the Old Bailey trial. It took the form of a cheque—for five guineas.

'Game to the last!' murmured Leon admiringly.

7

MR LEVINGROU'S DAUGHTER
(Reprinted in *The Scotland Yard Book of Edgar Wallace*, 1932)

Mr Levingrou took his long cigar from his mouth and shook his head sorrowfully. He was a fat man, thick-necked and heavy-cheeked, and he could not afford to spoil a good cigar.

'That is awful... that is brutal! Tch! It makes me seek... poor Jose!'

His companion snorted in sympathy.

For Jose Silva had fallen. An unemotional judge, who spoke rather precociously, had told Jose that certain crimes were very heinous in the eyes of the law. For example, women were held in special esteem, and to trade on their follies was regarded as being so dreadful that nothing but a very long term of imprisonment could vindicate the law's outraged majesty.

And Jose had offended beyond forgiveness. He ran the Latin-American Artists Agency to give young and pretty aspirants to the stage a quick and profitable engagement on South American stages. They went away full of joy and they never came back. Letters came from them to their relations, very correctly worded, nicely spelt. They were, they said, happy. They all wrote the same in almost identical language. You might imagine that they wrote to dictation, as indeed they did.

But the vice squad had got on Jose's tail. A pretty girl applied for a job and went to Buenos Aires, accompanied by her father and brother—they were both Scotland Yard men, and when they learnt all that they had to learn they came back with the girl, a rather shrewd detective herself, and Jose was arrested. And then they learnt more things about him, and the prison sentence was inevitable.

Nobody arrested Jules Levingrou and haled him from his beautiful little bijou house in Knightsbridge and sent him to a cold bleak prison. And nobody arrested Heinrich Luss, who was his partner. They had financed Jose and many other Joses, but they were clever.

'Jose was careless,' sighed Jules as he sucked at his cigar.

Heinrich sighed, too. He was as fat as, but looked fatter than, his companion, because he was a shorter man.

Jules looked round the pretty saloon with its cream and gold decorations, and presently his eyes stopped roving and fixed on a framed photograph that was on the mantelpiece. His big face creased in a smile as he rose with a grunt and, waddling across to the fireplace, took the frame in his hand. The picture was of an extremely pretty girl.

'You see?'

Heinrich took the picture and mumbled ecstatic praise.

'Not goot enough,' he said.

Mr Levingrou agreed. He had never yet seen a picture that quite did justice to the delicate beauty of this only daughter of his. He was a widower; his wife had died when Valerie was a baby. She would never know how many hearts were broken, how many souls destroyed, that she might be brought up in the luxury which surrounded her. This aspect of her upbringing never occurred to Mr Levingrou. He prided himself that he had no sentiment.

He was part proprietor of twenty-three cabarets and dance halls scattered up and down the Argentine and Brazil, and drew large profits from what he regarded as a perfectly legitimate business.

He put down the photograph and came back to the deep arm-chair.

'It is unfortunate about Jose; but these men come and go. This new man may or may not be good.'

'What is his name?' asked Heinrich.

Jules searched breathlessly in his pockets, found a letter and opened it, his thick fingers glittering in the light from the crystal chandelier, for he was a lover of rings.

'Leon Gonsalez—herr Gott!'

Heinrich was sitting upright in his chair, white as a sheet.

'Name of a pipe! What is the matter with you, Heinrich?'

'Leon Gonsalez!' repeated the other huskily. 'You think he is an applicant for the post... you do not know him?'

Jules shook his huge head.

'Why in God's name should I know him—he is a Spaniard, that is good enough for me. This is always the way, Heinrich. No sooner does one of our men make a fool of himself and get caught than another arises. Tomorrow I shall have twenty, thirty, fifty applicants—not to me but through the usual channel.'

Heinrich was looking at him hollow-eyed, and now in his agitation he spoke in German—that brand of German which is heard more frequently in Poland.

'Let me see the letter.' He took it in his hand and read it carefully.

'He asks for an appointment, that is all.'

'Have you ever heard of the Four Just Men?'

Jules frowned.

'They are dead, eh? I read something years ago.'

'They are alive,' said the other grimly; 'pardoned by the English Government. They have a bureau in Curzon Street.'

Rapidly he sketched the history of that strange organization which for years had terrorized the evil-doers who by their natural cunning had evaded the just processes of the law; and, as he spoke, the face of Jules Levingrou lengthened.

'But that—is preposterous!' he spluttered at last. 'How could these men know of me and of you... Besides, they dare not.'

Before Heinrich could reply there was a gentle knock at the door and a footman came in. There was a card on the salver he carried in his hand. Jules took it, adjusted his glasses and read, meditated a second, and then:

'Show him up,' he said.

'Leon Gonsalez,' almost whispered Heinrich as the door closed on the servant. 'Do you see a little silver triangle at the corner of the card? That is on the door of their house. It is he!'

'Pshaw!' scoffed his companion. 'He has come—why? To offer his services. You shall see!'

Leon Gonsalez, grey-haired and dapper, swung into the room, his keen, ascetic face tense, his fine eyes alive. A ready smiler was Leon. He was smiling now as he looked from one man to the other.

'You!' he said, and pointed to Jules.

Monsieur Levingrou started. There was almost an accusation in that finger thrust.

'You wish to see me?' He tried to recover some of his lost dignity.

'I did,' said Leon calmly. 'It is my misfortune that I have never seen you before. My friend Manfred, of whom you have heard, knows you very well by sight, and my very dear comrade Poiccart is so well acquainted with you that he could draw you feature by feature—and indeed did upon the table-cloth at dinner last night, much to the annoyance of our thrifty housekeeper!'

Levingrou was on his guard; there was something of the cold devil in those smiling eyes.

'To what am I indebted—' he began.

'I come in a perfectly friendly spirit,' Leon's smile broadened, his eyes were twinkling, as with suppressed laughter. 'You will forgive that lie. Monsieur Levingrou, for lie it is. I have come to warn you that your wicked little business must be destroyed, or you will be made very unhappy. The police do not know of the Cafe Espagnol and its peculiar attractions.'

He dived into his overcoat pocket and, with the quick, jerky motion which was characteristic of him, produced a sheet of notepaper and unfolded it.

'I have here a list of thirty-two girls who have gone to one or another of your establishments during the past two years,' he said. 'You may read it'—and thrust the paper into Jules' hand—'for I have a copy. You will be interested to know that that sheet of paper represents six months' inquiries.'

Jules did not so much as read a name. Instead, he shrugged, pushed the paper back to his visitor and, when Leon did not take it, dropped it on the floor.

'I am entirely in the dark,' he said. 'If you have no business with me you had better go—goodnight.'

'My friend'—Leon's voice was a little lower, and those eyes of his were piercing the very soul of the man who squatted like an ill-shaped toad in the luxurious deeps of silk and down—'you will send cables to your managers, ordering the release of those girls, the payment of adequate compensation, and first-class return ticket to London.'

Levingrou shrugged.

'I really don't know what you mean, my friend. It seems to me you've come upon a cock and bull story, that you have been deceived.'

M. Jules Levingrou reached out deliberately and pressed an ivory bell-push.

'I think you are mad, therefore I will take a very charitable view of what you say. Now, my friend, we have no more time to give to you.'

MR LEVINGROU'S DAUGHTER

But Leon Gonsalez was unperturbed.

'I can only imagine that you have no imagination. Monsieur Levingrou,' he said, a little curtly. 'That you do not realize the torture, the sorrow, the ghastly degradation into which you throw these sisters of ours.'

A gentle tap at the door and the footman entered. Mr Levingrou indicated his visitor with a wave of his hand.

'Show this gentleman to the door.'

If he expected an outburst he was pleasantly disappointed. Leon looked from one man to the other, that mocking smile of his still playing about the corners of his sensitive mouth then, without a word, turned, and the door closed on him.

'You heard—you heard?' Heinrich's voice was quivering with terror, his face the colour of dirty chalk. 'Herr Gott! you don't understand, Jules! I know of these men. A friend of mine...'

He told a story that would have impressed most men; but Levingrou smiled.

'You are scared, my poor friend. You have not my experience of threats. Let him prove what he can and go to the police.'

'You fool!' Heinrich almost howled the words. 'The police! Do I not tell you they want no proof? They punished—'

'Hush!' growled Jules.

He had heard the girl's step in the hall. She was going to the theatre, she said—her explanation stopped short at the sight of Heinrich's white face.

'Daddy,' she said reproachfully, 'you've been quarrelling with Uncle Heinrich.'

She stooped and kissed the forehead of her father and pulled his ear gently. The stout man imprisoned her in both his arms and chuckled.

'No quarrel, my darling. Heinrich is scared of a business deal. You wouldn't imagine he could be such a baby.'

A minute later she stood in front of the fireplace, using a lipstick skilfully. She paused in the operation to tell him an item of news.

'I met such a nice man today, Daddy, at Lady Athery's, a Mr Gordon—do you know him?'

'I know many Mr Gordons,' smiled Jules. And then, in sudden alarm: 'He didn't make love to you, did he?'

She laughed at this.

'My dear, he's almost as old as you. And he's a great artist and very amusing.'

Jules walked with her to the door and saw her go down the steps, cross the little flagged garden, and stood there until her Rolls had passed out of sight. Then he came back to his pretty saloon to argue out this matter of the Four Just Men.

It was a gay party of young people about her own age that Valerie joined. The box was crowded, and was hot and thick, for the theatre was one where smoking was allowed. She was relieved when an attendant tapped her on the shoulder and beckoned her out.

'A gentleman to see you, miss.'

'To see me?' she said in wonder, and came into the vestibule to find a handsome, middle-aged man in evening dress.

'Mr Gordon!' she exclaimed. 'I had no idea you were here!'

He seemed unusually grave.

'I have some rather bad news for you, Miss Levingrou,' he said, and she went pale.

'Not about Father?'

'In a sense it is. I am afraid that he is in rather bad trouble.'

She frowned at this.

'Trouble? What kind of trouble?'

'I can't explain here. Will you come with me to the police station?'

She stared at him incredulously, her mouth open.

'The police station?'

Gordon summoned a waiting attendant.

'Get Miss Levingrou's coat from the box,' he said authoritatively.

A few minutes later they passed out of the theatre together and into a waiting car.

Twelve o'clock was striking when Mr Levingrou rose from his chair stiffly and stretched himself. Heinrich had been gone nearly three hours. He had, indeed, left the house in time to catch the last train for the Continent, whither he fled without even packing so much as a pocket-handkerchief. Unaware of this desertion, Mr Levingrou was on the point of mounting the stairs to bed when a thundering rat-tat shook the house. He turned to the footman.

'See who that is,' he growled, and waited curiously.

When the door was opened he saw the stocky figure of a police inspector.

'Levingrou?' asked the visitor.

Mr Levingrou came forward.

'That is my name,' he said.

The inspector strolled into the hall.

'I want you to come with me to the police station.' His manner was brusque, indeed rude, and Levingrou felt for the first time in his life a qualm of fear.

'The police station? Why?'

'I'll explain that to you when you get there.'

'But this is monstrous!' exploded the stout man. I will telephone to my lawyers—'

'Are you going quietly?'

There was such a threat in the tone that Jules became instantly tractable.

'Very good, inspector, I will come. I think you have made a very great mistake and...'

He was hustled out of the hall, down the steps and into the waiting car.

It was not an ordinary taxi. The blinds were pulled down. Moreover, he discovered as soon as he entered the interior that it was well occupied. Two men sat on seats facing him, the inspector took his place by the prisoner's side.

He could not see where the car was going. Five minutes, ten minutes passed... there should be a police station somewhere nearer than that. He put a question.

'I can relieve your mind,' said a calm voice. 'You're not going to a police station.'

'Then where am I being taken?'

'That you will discover,' was the unsatisfactory answer.

Nearly an hour passed before the car drew up before a dark house and the authoritative 'inspector' ordered him curtly to alight. The house had the appearance of being untenanted; the hall was littered with refuse and dust. They led him down a flight of stone stairs to the cellar, unlocked a steel door and pushed him inside.

He had hardly entered before an electric light in the wall glowed dimly, and he saw that he was in what looked to be a concrete chamber, furnished with a bed. At the farther end was a small open doorway, innocent of door, which he was informed led to a washing place. But the revelation which came to Mr Levingrou, and which struck terror to his soul, was the fact that the two men who had brought him were heavily masked — the inspector had disappeared and, try as he did, Jules could not remember what he looked like.

'You will stay here and keep quiet, and you need not be afraid that anybody will be alarmed by your disappearance.'

'But... my daughter!' stammered Levingrou in terror.

'Your daughter? Your daughter leaves for the Argentine with a Mr Gordon tomorrow morning — as other men's daughters have left.'

Levingrou stared, took one step forward and fell fainting to the floor.

Sixteen days passed; sixteen days of unadulterated hell for the shrieking, half-demented man who paced the length of his cell for hours on end till, exhausted, he dropped almost lifeless on his bed. And every morning came a masked man to tell him of plans that had been made, to describe in detail the establishment in Antofagasta which was to be the destination of Valerie Levingrou; of a certain piestro... they showed him his photograph... who was the master of that hell broth.

'You devils! You devils!' shrieked Levingrou, striking wildly out, but the other caught him and flung him back on the bed.

'You mustn't blame Gordon,' he mocked. 'He has his living to earn... he is merely the agent of the man who owns the cabaret.'

Then one morning, the eighteenth, they came and told him, three masked men, that Valerie had arrived and was being initiated into her duties as a dancing girl...

Jules Levingrou spent the night shivering in a corner of his cell. They came to him at three in the morning and pricked him with a hypodermic needle. When he woke, he thought he was dreaming, for he was sitting in his own saloon, where these masked men had carried him in the dead of night.

A footman came in, and dropped the tray at the sight of him.

'Good God, sir!' he gasped. 'Where did you come from?'

Levingrou could not speak: he could only shake his head.

'We thought you was in Germany, sir.'

And then, clearing his dry throat, Jules asked harshly:

'Is there any news... Miss Valerie... ?'

'Miss Valerie, sir?' The footman was astonished. 'Why, yes sir, she's upstairs asleep. She was a bit worried the night she came back and found you weren't here, and then of course she got your letter saying you'd been called abroad.'

The footman was staring at him, an uncomfortable wonder in his gaze. Something peculiar had happened. Jules rose unsteadily to his feet and caught a glance of his face in the mirror. His hair and his beard were white.

He staggered rather than walked to his writing-table, jerked open a drawer and took out an overseas cable form. 'Ring for a messenger.' His voice was hoarse and quavering. 'I want to send fourteen cablegrams to South America.'

8

THE SHARE PUSHER
(First published in *John Bull's Christmas Annual*, 1927)

The man whom Raymond Poiccart ushered into the presence of Manfred was to all appearances a smart, military looking gentleman approaching the sixties. He was faultlessly dressed and had the carriage and presence of a soldier. A retired general, thought Manfred; but he saw something more than the outward personation of manner revealed. This man was broken. There was a certain imponderable expression in his face, a tense anguish which this, the shrewdest of the Three Just Men, instantly interpreted.

'My name is Pole—Major-General Sir Charles Pole,' said the visitor, as Poiccart placed a chair for him and discreetly withdrew.

'And you have come to see me about Mr Bonsor True,' said Manfred instantly, and when the other started nervously he laughed. 'No, I am not being very clever,' said Manfred gently. 'So many people have seen me about Mr Bonsor True. And I think I can anticipate your story. You have been investing in one of his oil concerns and you have lost a considerable sum of money. Was it oil?'

'Tin,' said the other. 'Inter-Nigerian Tin. You have heard about my misfortune?'

Manfred shook his head.

'I have heard about the misfortunes of so many people who have trusted Mr True. How much have you lost?'

The old man drew a long breath.

'Twenty-five thousand pounds,' he said, 'every penny I possess. I have consulted the police, but they say there is nothing they can do. The tin mine actually existed, and no misrepresentation was made by True in any letter he sent to me.'

Manfred nodded.

'Yours is a typical case, General,' he said. 'True never brings himself within the reach of the law. All his misrepresentations are made over a luncheon table, when there is no other witness, and I presume that in his letters to you he pointed out the speculative nature of your investment and warned you that you were not putting your money into gilt-edged securities.'

'It was at dinner,' said the General. 'I had some doubt on the matter and he asked me to dine with him at the Walkley Hotel. He told me that immense quantities of tin were in sight, and that while he could not, in justice to his partners, broadcast the exact amount of profit the company would make, he assured me that my money would be doubled in six months. I wouldn't mind so much,' the old man went on, as he raised his trembling hand to his lips, 'but, Mr Manfred, I have a daughter, a brilliant young girl who has, in my opinion, a wonderful future. If she had been a man she would have been a strategist. I hoped to have left her amply provided for, but this means ruin—ruin! Can nothing be done to bring this criminal to justice?'

Manfred did not reply immediately.

'I wonder if you realize. General, that you are the twelfth person who has come to us in the past three months. Mr True is so well protected by the law and by his letters that it is almost impossible to catch him. There was a time'—he smiled faintly—'when my friends and I would have taken the most dramatic steps to deal with the gentleman, and I think our method would have been effective; but now'—he shrugged his shoulders—'we are a little restricted. Who introduced you to this gentleman?'

'Mrs Calford Creen. I met the lady at a dinner of a mutual friend, and she asked me to dine with her at her flat in Hanover Mansions.'

Manfred nodded again. He was not at all surprised by this intelligence.

'I am afraid I can promise you very little,' he said. 'The only thing I would ask is that you should keep in touch with me. Where are you living?'

His visitor was at the moment living in a little house near Truro. Manfred noted the address, and a few minutes later was standing by the window watching the weary old man walking slowly down Curzon Street.

Poiccart came in.

'I know nothing of this gentleman's business,' he said, 'but I have a feeling that it concerns our friend True. George, we ought to be able to catch that man. Leon was saying at breakfast this morning that there is a deep pond in the New Forest, where a man suitably anchored by chains and weights might lie without discovery for a hundred years. Personally, I am never in favour of drowning—'

George Manfred laughed.

''Ware the law, my good friend,' he said. 'There will be no killing, though a man who has systematically robbed the new poor deserves something with boiling lead in it.'

Nor could Leon Gonsalez offer any solution when he was consulted that afternoon.

'The curious thing is that True has no monies in this country. He runs two bank accounts and is generally overdrawn on both. I should not be surprised if he had a cache somewhere, in which case the matter would be simple—I've been watching him for the greater part of a year, and he never goes abroad, and I have searched his modest Westminster flat so often that I could go blindfolded to the place where he keeps his dress ties.'

All this had occurred in the previous year and no further complaints came about this fraudulent share pusher. The Three were no nearer to a solution of their problem when came the rather remarkable disappearance of Margaret Lein.

Margaret Lein was not a very important person: she was by all social standards as unimportant a person as one would be likely to meet in a stroll through the West End of London. She occupied the position of maid to the Hon Mrs Calford Creen, and she had gone out one evening to the chemist to buy a bottle of smelling salts for her mistress, and had never come back.

She was pretty; her age was nineteen; she had no friends in London, being—so she said—an orphan; and, so far as was known, she had no attachments in the accepted sense of the word. But, as the police pointed out, it was extremely unlikely that a rather pretty maid, well spoken and with charming manners, in addition to her physical perfections, could spend a year in London without having acquired something in the shape of a 'follower.'

Mrs Calford Creen, not satisfied with the police inquiries, had called the Three Just Men to her aid. It was a week after the disappearance of Margaret Lein that a well-known lawyer crossed the polished dancing floor of the Leiter Club to greet the man who sat aloof and alone at a very small table near the floor's edge.

'Why, Mr Gonsalez!' he beamed. 'This is the last place in the world I should have expected to find you! In Limehouse, yes, prowling in the haunts of the underworld, yes, but at Letter's Club... Really, I have mistaken your character.'

Leon smiled faintly, poured a little more Rhine wine into his long-stemmed glass and sipped it.

'My dear Mr Thurles,' he drawled, 'this is my underworld. That fat gentleman puffing gallantly with that stout lady is Bill Sikes. It is true he does not break into houses nor carry a life-preserver, but he sells dud shares to thrifty and gullible widows, and has grown fat on the proceeds. Some day I shall take that gentleman and break his heart.'

The red-faced Thurles chuckled as he sat down by the other's side.

'That will be difficult. Mr Bonsor True is too rich a man to pull down, however much a blackguard he may be.'

Leon fixed a cigarette in a long amber tube and seemed wholly absorbed in the operation, which he performed with great care.

'Perhaps I oughtn't to have made that horrific threat,' he said. 'True is a friend of your client's, isn't he?'

'Mrs Creen?' Thurles was genuinely surprised. 'I wasn't aware of the fact.'

'I must have been mistaken,' said Leon, and changed the subject.

He knew right well that he was not mistaken. That stout share plugger had been the *tête-à-tête* guest of Mrs Creen on the night Margaret Lein had disappeared from human ken; and the curious circumstance was that neither to the police nor to the Triangle had Mrs Creen mentioned this interesting fact.

She lived in a modest flat near Hanover Court: a rather pretty, hard-faced young widow, whose source of income was believed to be a legacy left by her late husband. Leon, a very inquisitive man, had made the most careful inquiries without discovering either that she had had a husband or that he had died. All he knew of her was that she took frequent trips abroad, sometimes to out-of-the-way places like Roumania; that she was invariably accompanied by the missing Margaret; that she spent money, not freely but lavishly, gave magnificent entertainments in Paris, Rome, and once in Brussels, and seemed quite content to return from a life which must have cost her at least seven hundred and fifty pounds a week to the modest establishment near Hanover Court where her rent was seven hundred and fifty pounds per annum and her household bills did not exceed twenty pounds a week.

Leon watched the dancing for a little longer, beckoned a waiter and paid his bill. The lawyer had gone back to his party. He saw Mr Bonsor True, the centre of a gay table, and smiled to himself, and wondered whether the share plugger would be as cheerful if he knew that in the right hand inside pocket of Leon Gonsalez' coat was a copy of a marriage certificate that he had dug out that morning.

It had been an inspiration that had led Leon Gonsalez to Somerset House.

He glanced at his watch: late as the hour was, there was still a hope of finding Mrs Creen. His car was waiting in the park in Wellington Place, and ten minutes later he had stopped before the doors of Hanover Mansions. A lift carried him to the third floor. He pressed the bell of No 109. A light showed in the fanlight, and it was Mrs Creen herself who opened the door to him. Evidently she expected somebody else, for she was momentarily taken back.

'Oh, Mr Gonsalez!' And then, quickly: 'Have you had news of Margaret?'

'I am not quite sure whether I have or not,' said Leon. 'May I see you for a few minutes?'

Something in his tone must have warned her.

'It's rather late, isn't it?'

'It will save me a journey in the morning,' he almost pleaded and with some reluctance she admitted him.

It was not the first visit he had paid to her flat, and he had duly noted that, although her method of living was fairly humble, the flat itself was furnished regardless of expense.

She offered him a whisky and soda, which he accepted but did not drink.

'I want to ask you,' he said, when she had settled down, 'how long you have had Margaret in your employ?'

'Over a year,' she replied.

'A nice girl?'

'Very. But I told you about her. It has been a great shock to me.'

'Would you call her accomplished? Did she speak any foreign languages?'

Mrs Creen nodded.

'French and German perfectly—that was why she was such a treasure. She had been brought up with a family in Alsace, and was, I believe, half French.'

'Why did you send her out to the chemist for smelling salts?'

The woman moved impatiently.

'I have already told you, as I told the police, that I had a very bad headache, and Margaret herself suggested she should go to the chemist.'

'For no other reason? Couldn't Mr True have gone?'

She nearly jumped at this.

'Mr True? I don't know what you mean.'

'True was with you that night; you had been dining *tête-à-tête*. In fact, you were dining as one would expect a husband and wife to dine.'

The woman went white, was momentarily bereft of speech.

'I don't know why you're making such a mystery of your marriage, Mrs Creen, but I know that for five years past you have not only been married to True, but you have been his partner, in the sense that you have assisted him in his—er—financial operations. Now, Mrs True, I want you to put your cards on the table. When you went abroad you took this girl with you?'

She nodded dumbly.

'What was your object in going to Paris, Rome and Brussels? Had you any other object than to enjoy yourself? Was there any business reason for your move?'

He saw her lick her dry lips, but she did not reply.

'Let me put it more plainly. Have you in any of those cities a private safe at any of the banking corporations or safe deposits?'

She sprang to her feet, her mouth open in surprise.

'Who told you?' she asked quickly. 'What business is that of yours, anyway?'

As she spoke, came the gentle tinkle of a bell, and she half turned.

'Let me open it for you,' said Leon, and before she could move he was down the passage and had flung open the door.

An astonished financier was standing on the doormat. At the sight of Leon he gaped.

'Come inside, Mr True,' said Leon gently. 'I think I have some interesting news for you.'

'Who—who are you?' stammered the older man, peering at the visitor, and then of a sudden he recognized him. 'My God! One of the Four Just Men, eh? Well, have you found that girl?'

He realized at that moment that the question in itself was a blunder. He was not supposed to be interested in the missing maid.

'I haven't found her, and I think she's going to be rather difficult for any of us to find,' said Leon.

By this time Mrs Creen had recovered her self-possession.

'I'm awfully glad you came, Mr True. This gentleman has been making the most extraordinary statements about us. He is under the impression we are married. Did you ever hear anything so ridiculous?'

THE SHARE PUSHER

Leon did not attempt to refute the absurdity of his suggestion until they were back in the little drawing-room.

'Now, sir,' said Mr Bonsor True, his pompous self, 'whatever do you mean by making—'

Leon cut him short.

'I will tell you briefly what I have already told your wife,' he said; 'and as to your marriage, that is so indisputable a fact that I will not attempt to show you the marriage certificate which is in my pocket. I'm not here to reproach you, True, or this lady. The question of your treatment of the unfortunate people who have invested money with you is a matter for your own conscience. What I do wish to know is, whether it is a fact that in certain continental cities you have safes or deposits where you keep your wealth?'

The significance of the question was not lost upon the stout Mr True.

'There are certain deposits of mine on the Continent,' he said, 'but I don't quite understand—'

'Will you be perfectly frank with me, Mr True?' There was a hint of impatience in Leon's tone. 'Are there in Paris, Rome or Brussels safes of yours, and are you in the habit of carrying the keys of those safes?'

Mr Bonsor True smiled.

'No, sir; I have places of deposit, and they are in fact safes. But they have combinations—'

'Ah ha!' Leon's face lit. 'And do you by any chance carry the combination words in your pocket?'

For a second True hesitated, and then he took from his waistcoat pocket, fastened to a platinum chain, a small golden book about the size of a postage stamp.

'Yes, I carry them here—and why on earth I should be discussing my private business—'

'That's all I wanted to know.'

He stared at the visitor. Leon was laughing softly but heartily, rubbing his hands as at the best joke in the world.

'Now I think I understand,' he said. 'I also know why you sent Miss Margaret Lein to the chemist to get a little smelling salts. It was you they were for!'—his accusing finger pointed at the financier.

True's jaw dropped.

'That's true: I was taken suddenly ill.'

'Mr True fainted,' Mrs Creen broke in. 'I sent Margaret up to my room to get some smelling salts, but they weren't there. It was she who volunteered to buy them from the chemist.'

Leon wiped his eyes.

'That's a great joke,' he said; 'and now I can reconstruct the whole story. What time did you call on Mrs Creen that evening?'

True thought.

'About seven.'

'Are you in the habit of drinking cocktails, and are they usually waiting for you in the dining-room?'

'In the drawing-room,' corrected Mrs Creen.

'You took a cocktail,' Leon went on, 'and then you suddenly went out. In other words, somebody had doctored your drink with a knock-out drop. Mrs Creen was not, of course, in the room. When you fell, Margaret Lein examined your book and got the combination words she wanted. She had been abroad with Mrs Creen, so she knew this playful little method of yours of caching your ill-gotten gains.'

True's face went from livid red to ashy white.

'The combination word?' he said huskily. 'She got the combination word? Oh, my God!'

Without another word he flew from the room and they heard the front door thunder as he slammed it.

Leon went at greater leisure, but he arrived, in Curzon Street in time for supper.

'I'm not going to investigate any further,' he said, 'but it's any odds that those safes in Paris and Rome are empty by now, and that a very clever girl, who is certainly the daughter of one of Mr True's deluded clients, is now in a position to help her parents.'

'How do you know that she has parents?' asked Manfred.

'I don't know,' replied Leon frankly. 'But I am certain she had a father—I wired to General Pole last week to discover if his clever daughter was staying with him, and he wired back that "Margaret had been abroad finishing her education for the past year." And I suppose that acting as maid to the partner of a share crook is an education.'

9

THE MAN WHO SANG IN CHURCH
(First published in *20 Story Magazine,*
September 1927)

To Leon Gonsalez went most of the cases of blackmail which came the way of the Three Just Men.

And yet, from the views he had so consistently expressed, he was the last man in the world to whom such problems should have gone, for in that famous article of his entitled 'Justification,' which put up the sales of a quarterly magazine by some thousand per cent, he offered the following opinion:

'... as to blackmail, I see no adequate punishment but death in the case of habitual offenders. You cannot parley with the type of criminal who specialises in this loathsome form of livelihood. Obviously there can be no side of him to which appeal can be made: no system of reformation can effect him. He is dehumanised, and may be classified with the secret poisoner, the drug pusher and... '

He mentioned a trade as degrading.

Leon found less drastic means of dealing with these pests; yet we may suppose that the more violent means which distinguished the case of Miss Brown and the man who sang in church had his heartiest approval.

THE MAN WHO SANG IN CHURCH

There are so many types of beauty that even Leon Gonsalez, who had a passion for classification, gave up at the eighteenth sub-division of the thirty-third category of brunettes. By which time he had filled two large quarto notebooks.

If he had not wearied of his task before he met Miss Brown, he would assuredly have recognized its hopelessness, for she fell into no category, nor had he her peculiar attractions catalogued in any of his sub-sections. She was dark and slim and elegant. Leon hated the word, but he was compelled to admit this characteristic. The impression she left was one of delicate fragrance. Leon called her the Lavender Girl. She called herself Brown, which was obviously not her name; also, in the matter of simulations, she wore a closely-fitting hat which came down over her eyes and would make subsequent identification extremely difficult.

She timed her visit for the half-light of dusk—the cigarette hour that follows a good dinner, when men are inclined rather to think than to talk, and to doze than either.

Others had come at this hour to the little house in Curzon Street, where the silver triangle on the door marked the habitation of the Three Just Men, and when the bell rang George Manfred looked up at the clock.

'See who it is, Raymond: and before you go, I will tell you. It is a young lady in black, rather graceful of carriage, very nervous and in bad trouble.'

Leon grinned as Poiccart rose heavily from his chair and went out.

'Clairvoyance rather than deduction,' he said, 'and observation rather than either: from where you sit you can see the street. Why mystify our dear friend?'

George Manfred sent a ring of smoke to the ceiling. 'He is not mystified,' he said lazily. 'He has seen her also. If you hadn't been so absorbed in your newspaper you would have seen her, too. She has passed up and down the street three times on the other side. And on each occasion she has glanced toward this door. She is rather typical, and I have been wondering exactly what variety of blackmail has been practised on her.'

Here Raymond Poiccart came back.

'She wishes to see one of you,' he said. 'Her name is Miss Brown—but she doesn't look like a Miss Brown!'

Manfred nodded to Leon. 'It had better be you,' he said.

Gonsalez went to the little front drawing-room, and found the girl standing with her back to the window, her face in shadow. 'I would rather you didn't put on the light, please,' she said, in a calm, steady voice. 'I don't want to be recognized if you meet me again.'

Leon smiled.

'I had no intention of touching the switch,' he said. 'You see, Miss—' He waited expectantly.

'Brown,' she replied, so definitely that he would have known she desired anonymity even if she had not made her request in regard to the light. 'I told your friend my name.'

'You see, Miss Brown,' he went on, 'we have quite a number of callers who are particularly anxious not to be recognized when we meet them again. Will you sit down? I know that you have not much time, and that you are anxious to catch a train out of town.'

She was puzzled.

'How did you know that?' she asked.

Leon made one of his superb gestures.

'Otherwise you would have waited until it was quite dark before you made your appointment. You have, in point of fact, left it just as late as you could.'

She pulled a chair to the table and sat down slowly, turning her back to the window.

'Of course that is so,' she nodded. 'Yes, I have to leave in time, and I have cut it fine. Are you Mr Manfred?'

'Gonsalez,' he corrected her.

'I want your advice,' she said.

She spoke in an even, unemotional voice, her hands lightly clasped before her on the table. Even in the dark, and unfavourably placed as she was for observation, he could see that she was beautiful. He guessed from the maturity of her voice that she was in the region of twenty-four.

'I am being blackmailed. I suppose you will tell me I should go to the police, but I am afraid the police would be of no assistance, even if I were willing to risk an appearance in Court, which I am not. My father'—she hesitated—'is a Government official. It would break his heart if he knew. What a fool I've been!'

'Letters?' asked Leon, sympathetically.

'Letters and other things,' she said. 'About six years ago I was a medical student at St John's Hospital. I didn't take my final exam for reasons which you will understand. My surgical knowledge has not been of very much use to me, except... well, I once saved a man's life, though I doubt if it was worth saving. He seems to think it was, but that has nothing to do with the case. When I was at St John's I got to know a fellow-student, a man whose name will not interest you and, as girls of my age sometimes do, I fell desperately in love with him. I didn't know that he was married, although he told me this before our friendship reached a climax.

'For all that followed I was to blame. There were the usual letters—'

'And these are the basis of the blackmail?' asked Leon.

She nodded. 'I was worried ill about the... affair. I gave up my work and returned home; but that doesn't interest you, either.'

'Who is blackmailing you?' asked Leon.

She hesitated. 'The man. It's horrible isn't it? But he has gone down and down. I have money of my own—my mother left me two thousand pounds a year—and of course I've paid.'

'When did you see this man last?'

She was thinking of something else, and she did not answer him. As he repeated the question, she looked up quickly.

'Last Christmas Day—only for a moment. He wasn't staying with us—I mean it was at the end of...'

She had become suddenly panic-stricken, confused, and was almost breathless as she went on:

'I saw him by accident. Of course he didn't see me, but it was a great shock... It was his voice. He always had a wonderful tenor voice.'

'He was singing?' suggested Leon, when she paused, as he guessed, in an effort to recover her self-possession.

'Yes, in church,' she said desperately. 'That is where I saw him.'

She went on speaking with great rapidity, as though she were anxious not only to dismiss from her mind that chance encounter, but to make Leon also forget.

'It was two months after this that he wrote to me—he wrote to our old address in London. He said he was in desperate need of money, and wanted five hundred pounds. I'd already given him more than one thousand pounds, but I was sane enough to write and tell him I intended to do no more. It was then that he horrified me by sending a photograph of the letter—one of the letters—I had sent him. Mr Gonsalez, I have met another man, and... well, John had read the news of my engagement.'

'Your fiance knows nothing about this earlier affair?'

She shook her head.

'No, nothing, and he mustn't know. Otherwise everything would be simple. Do you imagine I would allow myself to be blackmailed any further but for that?'

Leon took a slip of paper from one pocket and a pencil from another.

'Will you tell me the name of this man? John—?'

'John Letheritt, 27, Lion Row, Whitechurch Street. It's a little room that he has rented, as an office, and a sleeping-place. I've already had inquiries made.'

Leon waited.

'What is the crisis—why have you come now?' he asked.

She took from her bag a letter, and he noted that it was in a clean envelope; evidently she had no intention that her real name and address should be known.

He read it, and found it a typical communication. The letter demanded £3,000 by the third of the month, failing which the writer intended putting 'papers' in 'certain hands.' There was just that little touch of melodrama which for some curious reason the average blackmailer adopts in his communiques.

'I'll see what I can do—how am I to get in touch with you?' asked Leon. 'I presume that you don't wish that either your real name or your address should be known even to me.'

She did not answer until she had taken from her bag a number of banknotes, which she laid on the table.

Leon smiled. 'I think we'll discuss the question of payment when we have succeeded. What is it you want me to do?'

'I want you to get the letters and, if it is possible, I want you so to frighten this man that he won't trouble me again. As to the money, I shall feel so much happier if you will let me pay you now!'

'It is against the rules of the firm!' said Leon cheerfully.

She gave him a street and a number which he guessed was an accommodation address.

'Please don't see me to the door,' she said, with a half-glance at the watch on her wrist.

He waited till the door closed behind her, and then went upstairs to his companions.

'I know so much about this lady that I could write a monograph on the subject,' he said.

'Tell us a little,' suggested Manfred. But Leon shook his head.

That evening he called at Whitechurch Street. Lion Row was a tiny, miserable thoroughfare, more like an alley than anything, and hardly deserved its grand designation. In one of those ancient houses which must have seen the decline of Alsatia, at the top of three rickety flights of stairs, he found a door, on which had been recently painted: 'J. LETHERITT, EXPORTER.'

His knock produced no response.

He knocked again more heavily, and heard the creaking of a bed, and a harsh voice on the other side asking who was there. It took some time before he could persuade the man to open the door, and then Leon found himself in a very long, narrow room, lighted by a shadeless electric table-lamp. The furniture consisted of a bed, an old washstand and a dingy desk piled high with unopened circulars.

He guessed the man who confronted him, dressed in a soiled shirt and trousers, to be somewhere in the region of thirty-five; he certainly looked older. His face was unshaven and there was in the room an acrid stink of opium.

'What do you want?' growled John Letheritt, glaring suspiciously at the visitor.

With one glance Leon had taken in the man—a weakling, he guessed—one who had found and would always take the easiest way. The little pipe on the table by the bed was a direction post not to be mistaken.

Before he could answer, Letheritt went on: 'If you have come for letters you won't find them here, my friend.' He shook a trembling hand in Leon's face. 'You can go back to dear Gwenda and tell her that you are no more successful than the last gentleman she sent!'

'A blackmailer, eh? You are the dirtiest little blackmailer I ever met,' mused Leon. 'I suppose you know the young lady intends to prosecute you?'

'Let her prosecute. Let her get a warrant and have me pinched! It won't be the first time I've been inside! Maybe she can get a search warrant, then she'll be able to have her letters read in Court. I'm saving you a lot of trouble. I'll save Gwenda trouble, too! Engaged, eh? You're not the prospective bridegroom?' he sneered.

'If I were, I should be wringing your neck,' said Leon calmly. 'If you are a wise man—'

'I'm not wise,' snarled the other. 'Do you think I'd be living in this pigsty if I were? Me... a man with a medical degree?'

Then, with a sudden rage, he pushed his visitor towards the door.

'Get out and stay out!'

Leon was so surprised by this onslaught that he was listening to the door being locked and bolted against him before he had realized what had happened.

From the man's manner, he was certain that the letters were in that room—there were a dozen places where they might be hidden: he could have overcome the degenerate with the greatest ease, bound him to the bed and searched the room, but in these days the Three Just Men were very law-abiding people.

Instead he came back to his friends late that night with the story of his partial failure.

'If he left the house occasionally, it would be easy—but he never goes out. I even think that Raymond and I could, without the slightest trouble, make a very thorough search of the place. Letheritt has a bottle of milk left every morning, and it shouldn't be difficult to put him to sleep if we reached the house a little after the milkman.'

Manfred shook his head.

'You'll have to find another way; it's hardly worth while antagonizing the police,' he said.

'Which is putting it mildly,' murmured Poiccart. 'Who's the lady?'

Leon repeated almost word for word the conversation he had had with Miss Brown.

'There are certain remarkable facts in her statement, and I am pretty sure they were facts, and that she was not trying to deceive me,' he said. 'Curious item Number One is that the lady heard this man singing in church last Christmas Day. Is Mr Letheritt the kind of person one would expect to hear exercising his vocal organs on Christmas carols? My brief acquaintance with him leads me to suppose that he isn't. Curious item Number Two was the words: "He wasn't staying with us," or something of that sort; and he was "nearing the end"—of what? Those three items are really remarkable!'

'Not particularly remarkable to me,' growled Poiccart. 'He was obviously a member of a house-party somewhere, and she didn't know he was staying in the neighbourhood, until she saw him in church. It was near the end of his visit.'

Leon shook his head.

'Letheritt has been falling for years. He hasn't reached his present state since Christmas; therefore he must have been as bad—or nearly as bad—nine months ago. I really have taken a violent dislike to him, and I must get those letters.'

Manfred looked at him thoughtfully.

'They would hardly be at his bankers, because he wouldn't have a banker; or at his lawyers, because I should imagine that he is the kind of person whose acquaintance with law begins and ends in the Criminal Courts. I think you are right, Leon; the papers are in his room.'

Leon lost no time. Early the next morning he was in Whitechurch Street, and watched the milkman ascend to the garret where Letheritt had his foul habitation. He waited till the milkman had come out and disappeared but, sharp as he was, he was hardly quick enough. By the time he had reached the top floor, the milk had been taken in, and the little phial of colourless fluid which might have acted as a preservative to the milk was unused.

The next morning he tried again, and again he failed.

On the fourth night, between the hours of one and two, he managed to gain an entry into the house, and crept noiselessly up the stairs. The door was locked from the inside, but he could reach the end of the key with a pair of narrow pliers he carried.

There was no sound from within, when he snapped back the lock and turned the handle softly. He had forgotten the bolts.

The next day he came again, and surveyed the house from the outside. It was possible to reach the window of the room, but he would need a very long ladder, and after a brief consultation with Manfred, he decided against the method.

Manfred made a suggestion.

'Why not send him a wire, asking him to meet your Miss Brown at Liverpool Street Station? You know her Christian name?'

Leon sighed wearily.

'I tried that on the second day, my dear chap, and had little Lew Leveson on hand to "whizz" him the moment he came into the street in case he was carrying the letters on him.'

'By "whizz" you mean to pick his pocket? I can't keep track of modern thief slang,' said Manfred. 'In the days when I was actively interested, we used to call it "dip".'

'You are out of date, George; "whizz" is the word. But of course the beggar didn't come out. If he owed rent I could get the brokers put in; but he does not owe rent. He is breaking no laws, and is living a fairly blameless life—except, of course, one could catch him for being in possession of opium. But that wouldn't be much use, because the police are rather chary of allowing us to work with them.' He shook his head. 'I'm afraid I shall have to give Miss Brown a very bad report.'

It was not until a few days later that he actually wrote to the agreed address, having first discovered that it was, as he suspected, a small stationer's shop where letters could be called for.

A week later Superintendent Meadows, who was friendly with the Three, came down to consult Manfred on a matter of a forged Spanish passport, and since Manfred was an authority on passport forgeries and had a fund of stories about Spanish criminals, it was long after midnight when the conference broke up.

Leon, who needed exercise, walked to Regent Street with Meadows, and the conversation turned to Mr John Letheritt.

'Oh, yes, I know him well. I took him two years ago on a false pretence charge, and got him eighteen months at the London Assizes. A real bad egg, that fellow, and a bit of a squeaker, too. He's the man who put away Joe Benthall, the cleverest cat burglar we've had for a generation. Joe got ten years, and I shouldn't like to be this fellow when he comes out!'

Suddenly Leon asked a question about Letheritt's imprisonment, and when the other had answered, his companion stood stock-still in the middle of the deserted Hanover Square and doubled up with silent laughter.

'I don't see the joke.'

'But I do,' chuckled Leon. 'What a fool I've been! And I thought I understood the case!'

'Do you want Letheritt for anything? I know where he lives,' said Meadows.

Leon shook his head.

'No, I don't want him: but I should very much like to have ten minutes in his room!'

Meadows looked serious.

'He's blackmailing, eh? I wondered where he was getting his money from.'

But Leon did not enlighten him. He went back to Curzon Street and began searching certain works of reference, and followed this by an inspection of a large scale map of the Home Counties. He was the last to go to bed, and the first to waken, for he slept in the front of the house and heard the knocking at the door.

THE MAN WHO SANG IN CHURCH

It was raining heavily as he pulled up the window and looked out; and in the dim light of dawn he thought he recognized Superintendent Meadows. A second later he was sure of his visitor's identity.

'Will you come down? I want to see you.'

Gonsalez slipped into his dressing-gown, ran downstairs and opened the door to the Superintendent.

'You remember we were talking about Letheritt last night?' said Meadows as Leon ushered him into the little waiting-room.

The superintendent's voice was distinctly unfriendly, and he was eyeing Leon keenly.

'Yes—I remember.'

'You didn't by any chance go out again last night?'

'No. Why?'

Again that look of suspicion.

'Only Letheritt was murdered at half past one this morning, and his room ransacked.'

Leon stared at him.

'Murdered? Have you got the murderer?' he asked at last.

'No, but we shall get him all right. He was seen coming down the rainpipe by a City policeman. Evidently he had got into Letheritt's room through the window, and it was this discovery by the constable which led to a search of the house. The City Police had to break in the door, and they found Letheritt dead on the bed. He had evidently been hit on the head with a jemmy, and ordinarily that injury would not have killed him, according to the police doctor; but in his state of health it was quite enough to put him out. A policeman went round the house to intercept the burglar, but somehow he must have escaped into one of the little alleys that abound in this part of the city, and he was next seen by a constable in Fleet Street, driving a small car, the number-plate of which had been covered with mud.'

'Was the man recognized?'

'He hasn't been—yet. What he did was to leave three fingerprints on the window, and as he was obviously an old hand at the game, that is as good as a direct identification. The City Detective Force called us in, but we haven't been able to help them except to give them particulars of Letheritt's past life. Incidentally, I supplied them with a copy of your fingerprints. I hope you don't mind.'

Leon grinned.

'Delighted!' he said.

After the officer had left, Leon went upstairs to give the news to his two friends.

But the most startling intelligence was to come when they were sitting at breakfast. Meadows arrived. They saw his car draw up and Poiccart went out to open the door to him. He strode into the little room, his eyes bulging with excitement.

'Here's a mystery which even you fellows will never be able to solve,' he said. 'Do you know that this is a day of great tragedy for Scotland Yard and for the identification system? It means the destruction of a method that has been laboriously built up...'

'What are you talking about?' asked Manfred quickly.

'The fingerprint system,' said Meadows, and Poiccart, to whom the fingerprint method was something God-like, gaped at him. 'We've found a duplicate,' said Meadows. 'The prints on the glass were undoubtedly the prints of Joe Benthall—and Joe Benthall is in Wilford County Gaol serving the first part of a ten years' sentence!'

Something made Manfred turn his head toward his friend. Leon's eyes were blazing, his thin face wreathed in one joyous smile.

'The man who sang in church!' he said softly. 'This is the prettiest case that I have ever dealt with. Now sit down, my

THE MAN WHO SANG IN CHURCH

dear Meadows, and eat! No, no: sit down. I want to hear about Benthall—is it possible for me to see him?'

Meadows stared at him.

'What use would that be? I tell you this is the biggest blow we've ever had. And what is more, when we showed the City policeman a photograph of Benthall, he recognized him as the man he had seen coming down the rainpipe! I thought Benthall had escaped, and phoned the prison. But he's there all right.'

'Can I see Benthall?'

Meadows hesitated.

'Yes—I think it could be managed. The Home Office is rather friendly with you, isn't it?'

Friendly enough, apparently. By noon, Leon Gonsalez was on his way to Wilford Prison and, to his satisfaction, he went alone.

Wilford Gaol is one of the smaller convict establishments, and was brought into use to house long-time convicts of good character who were acquainted with the bookbinding and printing trade. There are several 'trade' prisons in England—Maidstone is the 'printing' prison, Shepton Mallet the 'dyeing' prison—where prisoners may exercise their trades.

The chief warder, whom Leon interviewed, told him that Wilford was to be closed soon, and its inmates transferred to Maidstone. He spoke regretfully of this change.

'We've got a good lot of men here—they give us no trouble, and they have an easy time. We've had no cases of indiscipline for years. We only have one officer on night-duty—that will give you an idea how quiet we are.'

'Who was the officer last night?' asked Leon, and the unexpectedness of the question took the chief warder by surprise.

'Mr Bennett,' he said, 'he's gone sick today by the way—a bilious attack. Curious thing you should ask the question:

I've just been to see him. We had an inquiry about the man you've come to visit. Poor old Bennett is in bed with a terrible headache.'

'Can I see the Governor?' asked Leon.

The chief warder shook his head.

'He's gone to Dover with Miss Folian—his daughter. She's gone off to the Continent.'

'Miss Gwenda Folian?' and when the chief warder nodded: 'Is she the lady who was training to be a doctor?'

'She is a doctor,' said the other emphatically. 'Why, when Benthall nearly died from a heart attack, she saved his life—he works in the Governor's house, and I believe he'd cut off his right hand to serve the young lady. There's a lot of good in some of these fellows!'

They were standing in the main prison hall. Leon gazed along the grim vista of steel balconies and little doors.

'This is where the night-warder sits, I suppose?' he asked, as he laid his hand on the high desk near where they were standing: 'and the door leads—?'

'To the Governor's quarters.'

'And Miss Gwenda often slips through there with a cup of coffee and a sandwich for the night man, I suppose?' he added carelessly.

The chief warder was evasive.

'It would be against regulations if she did,' he said. 'Now you want to see Benthall?'

Leon shook his head.

'I don't think so,' he said quietly.

'Where could a blackguard like Letheritt be singing in church on Christmas Day?' asked Leon when he was giving the intimate history of the case to his companions. 'In only one place—a prison. Obviously our Miss Brown was in that prison: the Governor and his family invariably attend church. Letheritt was "not staying"—it was the end of his sentence, and he had been sent to Wilford for discharge. Poor Meadows! With all his faith in fingerprints gone astray because a released convict was true to his word and went out to get the letters that I missed, whilst the doped Mr Bennett slept at his desk and Miss Gwenda Folian took his place!'

10

THE LADY FROM BRAZIL
(First published in *20 Story Magazine*,
October 1927)

The journey had begun in a storm of rain and had continued in mist. There was a bumpiness over the land which was rather trying to airsick passengers. The pilot struck the Channel and dropped to less than two hundred feet.

Then came the steward with news that he bawled above the thunder of engines.

'We're landin' at Lympne... thick fog in London... coaches will take you to London...'

Manfred leaned forward to the lady who was sitting on the other side of the narrow gangway.

'Fortunate for you,' he said, tuning his voice so that it reached no other ear.

The Honourable Mrs Peversey raised her glasses and surveyed him cold-bloodedly.

'I beg your pardon?'

They made a perfect landing soon after, and as Manfred descended the steps leading from the Paris plane he offered his hand to assist the charming lady to alight.

'You were saying—?'

The slim, pretty woman regarded him with cold and open-eyed insolence.

'I was saying that it was rather fortunate for you that we landed here,' said Manfred. 'Your name is Kathleen Zieling, but you are known better as "Claro" May, and there are two detectives waiting for you in London to question you on the matter of a pearl necklace that was lost in London three months ago. I happen to understand French very well and I heard two gentlemen of the Surete discussing your future just before we left Le Bourget.'

The stare was no longer insolent, but it was not concerned. Apparently her scrutiny of the man who offered such alarming information satisfied her in the matter of his sincerity.

'Thank you,' she said easily, 'but I am not at all worried. Fenniker and Edmonds are the two men. I'll wire them to meet me at my hotel. You don't look like a "bull" but I suppose you are?'

'Not exactly,' smiled Manfred.

She looked at him oddly.

'You certainly look too honest for a copper. I'm OK, but thank you all the same.'

This was a dismissal, but Manfred stood his ground.

'If you get into any kind of trouble I'd be glad if you'd call me up.' He handed the woman a card, at which she did not even glance. 'And if you wonder why I am interested, I only want to tell you that a year ago a very dear friend of mine would have been killed by the Fouret gang which caught him unprepared on Montmartre, only you very kindly helped him.'

Now, with a start of surprise, she read the card and, reading, changed colour.

'Oh!' she said awkwardly. 'I didn't know that you were one of that bunch—Four Just Men? You folks give me the creeps! Leon something—a dago name...'

'Gonsalez,' suggested Manfred, and she nodded.

'That's right!'

She was looking at him now with a new interest.

'Honest there's no trouble coming about the pearls. And as to your friend, he saved me. He wouldn't have got into the gang fight, only he came out of the cabaret to help me.'

'Where are you staying in London?'

She told him her address, and at that moment came a Customs officer to break the conversation. Manfred did not see her again—she was not in the closed coach that carried him to London.

In truth he had no great wish to meet her again. Curiosity and a desire to assist one who had given great help to Leon Gonsalez—it was the occasion of Leon's spectacular unravelling of the Lyons forgeries—were behind his action.

Manfred neither sympathized with nor detested criminals. He knew May to be an international swindler on the grand scale, and was fairly well satisfied that she would be well looked after by the English police.

It was on the journey to London that he regretted that he had not asked her for information about Garry, though in all probability they had never met.

George Manfred, by common understanding the leading spirit of the Four Just Men, had in the course of his life removed three-and-twenty social excrescences from all human activities.

The war brought him and his companions a pardon for offences known and offences suspected. But in return the pardoning authorities had exacted from him a promise that he should keep the law in letter and in spirit, and this he had made, not only on his own behalf but on behalf of his companions. Only once did he express regret for having made this covenant, and that was when Garry Lexfield came under his observation.

THE LADY FROM BRAZIL

Garry lived on the outer edge of the law. He was a man of thirty, tall, frank of face, rather good looking. Women found him fascinating, to their cost, for he was of the ruthless kind; quite nice people invited him to their homes—he even reached the board of a well-known West End Company.

Manfred's first encounter with Garry was over a stupidly insignificant matter. Mr Lexfield was engaged in an argument at the corner of Curzon Street, where he had his flat. Manfred, returning late, saw a man and a woman talking, the man violently, the woman a little timidly. He passed them, thinking that it was one of those quarrels in which wise men are not interested, and then he heard the sound of a blow and a faint scream. He turned to see the woman crouching by the area railings of the house. Quickly he came back.

'Did you hit that woman?' he asked.

'It's none of your dam' business—'

Manfred swung him from his feet and dropped him over the area railings. When he looked round the woman had vanished.

'I might have killed him,' said Manfred penitently, and the spectacle of a penitent Manfred was too much for Leon Gonsalez.

'But you didn't—what happened?'

'When I saw him get up on his feet and knew nothing was broken I bolted,' confessed Manfred. 'I really must guard against these impulses. It must be my advancing years that has spoilt my judgment.'

If Poiccart had a very complete knowledge of the sordid underworld, Manfred was a living encyclopaedia on the swell mob; but for some reason Mr Lexfield was outside his knowledge. Leon made investigations and reported.

'He has been thrown out of India and Australia. He is only "wanted" in New Zealand if he attempts to go back there. His speciality is bigamous marriages into families which are too important to risk a scandal. The swell mob in London only know of him by hearsay. He has a real wife who has followed him to London and was probably the lady who was responsible for his visit to the area.'

Mr Garry Lexfield had 'touched' royally, and luck had been with him, since, unostentatiously and in an assumed name, he had stepped on to the Monrovia at Sydney. He had the charm and the attraction which are three-quarters of the good thief's assets. Certainly he charmed the greater part of three thousand pounds out of the pockets of two wealthy Australian land-owners, and attracted to himself the daughter of one who at any rate had the appearance of being another.

When he landed he was an engaged man: happily and mercifully, his bride-to-be was taken ill on the day of her arrival with a prosaic attack of appendicitis. Before she had left her nursing home, he learned that that bluff squatter, her father, so far from being a millionaire, was in very considerable financial difficulties.

But the luck held: a visit to Monte Carlo produced yet another small fortune—which was not gained at the public tables. Here he met and wooed Elsa Monarty, convent-trained and easily fascinated. A sister, her one relative, had sent her to San Remo—oddly enough, she also was convalescing from an illness—and, straying across the frontier, she met the handsome Mr Lexfield—which was not his name—in the big vestibule of the rooms. She wanted a ticket of admission—the gallant Garry was most obliging. She told him about her sister, who was the manager and part owner of a big dress-making establishment in the Rue de la Paix. Giving confidence for confidence, Garry told her of his rich and titled parents, and described a life which was equally mythical.

He came back to London alone and found himself most inconveniently dogged by the one woman in the world who was entitled to bear his name, which was Jackson—a pertinacious if handsome woman who had no particular affection for him, but was anxious to recover for the benefit of his two neglected children a little of the fortune he had dissipated.

And most pertinacious at a moment when, but for his inherent meanness, he would have gladly paid good money to be rid of her.

It was a week after he had had the shocking experience of finding himself hurled across fairly high railings into a providentially shallow area, and he was still inclined to limp, when Leon Gonsalez, who was investigating his case, came with the full story of the man's misdeeds.

'I would have dropped him a little more heavily if I had known,' said Manfred regretfully. 'The strange thing is that the moment I lifted him—it's a trick you have never quite succeeded in acquiring, Leon—I knew he was something pestilential. We shall have to keep an unfriendly eye on Mr Garry Lexfield. Where does he stay?'

'He has a sumptuous flat in Jermyn Street,' said Leon. 'Before you tell me that there are no sumptuous flats in Jermyn Street, I would like to say that it has the appearance of sumptuousness. I was so interested in this gentleman that I went round to the Yard and had a chat with Meadows. Meadows knows all about him, but he has no evidence to convict. The man's got plenty of money—has an account at the London and Southern, and bought a car this afternoon.'

Manfred nodded thoughtfully.

'A pretty bad man,' he said. 'Is there any chance of finding his wife? I suppose the unfortunate lady who was with him—'

'She lives in Little Titchfield Street—calls herself Mrs Jackson, which is probably our friend's name. Meadows is certain that it is.'

Mr Garry Lexfield was too wise a man not to be aware of the fact that he was under observation; but his was the type of crime which almost defies detection. His pleasant manner and his car, plus a well-organized accident to his punt on one of the upper reaches of the Thames, secured him introductions and honorary membership of a very exclusive river club; and from there was but a step to homes which ordinarily would have been barred to him.

He spent a profitable month initiating two wealthy stockbrokers into the mysteries of bushman poker, at which he was consistently unlucky for five successive nights, losing some £600 to his apologetic hosts. There was no necessity for their apologies as it turned out: on the sixth and seventh days, incredible as it may seem, he cleared the greater part of £5,000 and left his hosts with the impression of his regret that he had been the medium of their loss.

'Very interesting,' said Manfred when this was reported to him.

Then, one night when he was dining at the Ritz-Carlton with a young man to whom he had gained one of his quick introductions, he saw his supreme fortune.

'Do you know her?' he asked in an undertone of his companion.

'That lady? Oh, Lord, yes! I've known her for years. She used to stay with my people in Somerset—Madame Velasquez. She's the widow of a terribly rich chap, a Brazilian.'

Mr Lexfield looked again at the dark, beautiful woman at the next table. She was perhaps a little over-jewelled to please the fastidious. Swathes of diamond bracelets encircled her arm from the wrist up; an immense emerald glittered in a diamond setting on her breast. She was exquisitely dressed and her poise was regal.

'She's terribly rich,' prattled on his informant. 'My colonel, who knows her much better than I, told me her husband had left her six million pounds—it's wicked that people should have so much money.'

It was wicked, thought Garry Lexfield, that anybody should have so much money if he could not 'cut' his share.

'I'd like to meet her,' he said, and a minute later the introduction was made and Garry forgot his arrangement to trim the young guardsman that night in the thrill of confronting a bigger quarry.

He found her a remarkably attractive woman. Her English, though slightly broken, was good. She was obviously pleased to meet him. He danced with her a dozen times and asked to be allowed to call in the morning. But she was leaving for her country place in Seaton Deverel.

'That's rather strange,' he said, with his most dazzling smile. 'I'm driving through Seaton Deverel next Saturday.'

To his joy she bit the bait. At noon on the Saturday his car shot up the long drive to Hanford House.

A week later came Leon with startling news.

'This fellow's got himself engaged to a rich South American widow, George. We can't allow that to go any further. Let us have an orgy of lawlessness—kidnap the brigand and put him on a cattle boat. There's a man in the East India Dock Road who would do it for fifty pounds.'

Manfred shook his head.

'I'll see Meadows,' he said. 'I have an idea that we may catch this fellow.'

Mr Garry Lexfield was not in that seventh heaven of delight to which accepted lovers are supposed to ascend; but he was eminently satisfied with himself as he watched the final touches being made to the dinner table in his flat.

Madame Velasquez had taken a great deal of persuading, had shown an extraordinary suspicion, and asked him to introduce her to those parents of his who were at the moment conveniently attending to their large estates in Canada.

'It is a very serious step I take, Garry dear,' she said, shaking her pretty head dubiously. 'I love you very dearly, of course, but I am so fearful of men who desire only money and not love.'

'Darling, I don't want money,' he said vehemently. 'I have shown you my passbook: I have nine thousand pounds in the bank, apart from my estates.'

She shrugged this off. Madame was a lady of peculiar temperament, never in the same mood for longer than an hour.

She came to dinner and, to his annoyance, brought a chaperon—a girl who spoke no word of English. Mr Lexfield was a very patient man and concealed his anger.

She brought news that made him forget the inconvenience of a chaperon. It was while they were sipping coffee in his over-decorated little drawing-room that she told him:

'Such a nice man I meet today. He came to my house in the country.'

'He was not only nice, but lucky,' smiled Garry, who was really not feeling terribly happy.

'And he spoke about you,' she smiled.

Garry Lexfield became instantly attentive. Nobody in England knew him well enough to make him the subject of conversation. If they did, then the discussion had not been greatly to his advantage.

'Who was this?' he asked.

'He spoke such perfect Spanish, and he has a smile the most delightful! And he said so many funny things that I laughed.'

'A Brazilian?' he asked.

She shook her head.

'In Brazil we speak Portuguese,' she said. 'No, Senor Gonsalez—'

'Gonsalez?' he said quickly. 'Not Leon Gonsalez? One of those swi—men... the Three Just Men?'

She raised her eyebrows.

'Do you know them?'

He laughed.

'I have heard about them. Blackguards that should have been hanged years ago. They are murderers and thieves. They've got a nerve to come and see you. I suppose he said something pretty bad about me? The truth is, I've been an enemy of theirs for years...'

He went on to tell an imaginary story of an earlier encounter he had had with the Three, and she listened intently.

'How interesting!' she said at last. 'No, they simply said of you that you were a bad man, and that you wanted my money; that you had a bad—what is the word?—record. I was very angry really, especially when they told me that you had a wife, which I know is not true, because you would not deceive me. Tomorrow he comes again, this Senor Gonsalez—he really did amuse me when I was not angry. Shall I lunch with you and tell you what he said?'

Garry was annoyed: he was thoroughly alarmed. It had not been difficult to locate and identify the man who had taken such summary action with him; and, once located, he had decided to give a wide berth to the men who lived behind the Silver Triangle. He had sense enough to know they were not to be antagonized, and he had hoped most sincerely that they had been less acute in tracing him than he had been in identifying them.

He changed the conversation and became, in spite of the witness, the most ardent and tender of lovers. All his art and experience was called into play; for here was a prize which had been beyond his dreams.

His immediate objective was some £20,000 which had come to the lady in the shape of dividends. She had displayed a pretty helplessness in the matter of money, though he suspected her of being shrewd enough. Garry Lexfield could talk very glibly and fluently on the subject of the market. It was his pet study; it was likewise his continuous undoing. There never was a thief who did not pride himself on his shrewdness in money matters, and Garry had come in and out of the market from time to time in his short and discreditable life with disastrous results to himself.

He saw her and her silent companion to the car and went back, and in the solitude of his flat turned over the new and alarming threat represented by the interest which the Three Just Men were showing in his activities.

He rose late, as was his practice, and was in his pyjamas when the telephone-bell rang. The voice of the porter informed him that there was a trunk call for him and trunk calls these days meant the lovely Velasquez.

'I have seen Gonsalez,' said her urgent voice. 'He came when I was at breakfast. Tomorrow, he says, they will arrest you because of something you did in Australia. Also today he applies to stop your money coming from the bank.'

'Holding up my account?' said Garry quickly. 'Are you sure?'

'Certain I am sure! They will go to a judge in his rooms and get a paper. Shall I come to lunch?'

'Of course—one o'clock,' he said quickly. He glanced at the little clock on the mantelshelf: it was half-past eleven.

'And about your investments: I think I can fix everything today. Bring your cheque-book.'

He was impatient for her to finish the conversation, and at last rather abruptly he brought it to a termination, dashed down the receiver, and, flying into his bedroom, began to dress.

His bank was in Fleet Street, and the journey seemed interminable. Fleet Street was much too close to the Law Courts for his liking. The judge's order might already be effective.

He pushed his cheque under the brass grille of the tellers' counter and held his breath while the slip of paper was handed to the accountant for verification. And then, to his overwhelming relief, the teller opened his drawer, took out a pad of notes and counted out the amount written on the cheque.

'This leaves only a few pounds to your credit, Mr Lexfield,' he said.

'I know,' said Garry. 'I'm bringing in rather a big cheque after lunch, and I want you to get a special clearance.'

It was then he realized that by that time the judge's order would be in operation. He must find another way of dealing with Madame Velasquez's cheque.

The relief was so great that he could hardly speak calmly. With something short of £9,000 he hurried back to Jermyn Street and arrived simultaneously with Madame Velasquez.

'How funny that caballero was, to be sure!' she said in her staccato way. 'I thought I should have laughed in his face. He told me you would not be here tomorrow, which is so absurd!'

'It's blackmail,' said Garry easily. 'Don't you worry about Gonsalez. I have just been to Scotland Yard to report him. Now about these shares—'

They had ten minutes to wait before lunch was ready, and those ten minutes were occupied with many arguments. She had brought her cheque-book, but she was a little fearful. Perhaps, he thought, the visit of Gonsalez had really aroused her suspicions. She was not prepared to invest the whole of her £20,000. He produced the papers and balance sheets that he had intended showing her on the previous night and explained, as he could very readily explain, the sound financial position of the company—one of the most solid on the Rand—in which he wished her to invest.

'These shares,' he said impressively, 'will rise in the next twenty-four hours by at least ten per cent. in value. I've got a block held for you, but I must get them this afternoon. My idea is that immediately after lunch you should bring me an open cheque; I'll buy the shares and bring them back to you.'

'But why could not I go?' she asked innocently.

'This is a personal matter,' said Garry with great gravity. 'Sir John is allowing me to buy this stock as a great personal favour.'

To his joy she accepted this assurance—she actually wrote a cheque for £12,500 at the luncheon table, and he could scarcely summon patience to sit through the meal.

The proprietors of the flats in which he had his brief habitation did not cater on a generous scale, but the short time which elapsed before the dessert stage of the lunch arrived was a period of agony. She returned once to the question of her investment, seemed in doubt, referred again to Gonsalez and his warning.

'Perhaps I had better wait for a day—yes?'

'My dear girl, how absurd!' said Garry. 'I really believe you are being frightened by this fellow who called on you this morning! I'll make him sorry!'

He half rose from the table, but she put her hand on his arm.

'Please don't hurry,' she begged, and reluctantly he agreed. The bank did not close until three; there would be time to reach Dover by car and catch the five o'clock boat.

But the bank was situated in the City, and he must not cut his time too fine. He excused himself for a moment, went out in search of the valet he had acquired and gave him a few simple but urgent instructions. When he returned she was reading the balance sheet.

'I am so foolish about these matters,' she said, and suddenly lifted her head. 'What was that?' she asked, as the door slammed.

'My valet—I have sent him out on a little errand.

She laughed nervously.

'I am what you call on the jump,' she said, as she pushed his coffee towards him. 'Now tell me again, Garry, dear, what does ex-dividend mean?'

He explained at length, and she listened attentively. She was still listening when, with a sudden little choke of alarm, he half rose from his feet, only to fall back on the chair and thence to roll helplessly to the floor. Madame Velasquez took his half-empty cup of coffee, carried it at her leisure into the kitchen and emptied the contents into the sink. When he sent his valet out, Mr Garry Lexfield had saved her a great deal of trouble.

She rolled the unconscious man on to his back, and searched quickly and with a dexterous hand pocket after pocket until she found the fat envelope wherein Garry had placed his banknotes.

There was a knock at the outer door. Without hesitation she went out and opened it to the young guardsman who had so kindly introduced Mr Lexfield to her.

'It's all right, the servant's gone,' she said. 'Here's your two hundred, Tony, and thank you very much.'

Tony grinned.

'The grudge I've got against him is that he took me for a sucker. These Australian crooks—'

'Don't talk—get,' she said tersely.

She went back to the dining-room, removed Garry's collar and tie and, putting a pillow under his head, opened the window. In twenty minutes he would be more or less conscious, by which time his valet would have returned.

She found the cheque she had given to him, burnt it in the empty grate, and with a last look round took her departure.

Outside the airport a tall man was waiting. She saw him signal to the driver of the car to pull up.

'I got your message,' said Manfred sardonically. 'I trust you've had a good killing? I owe you five hundred pounds.'

She shook her head with a laugh. She was still the brown, beautiful Brazilian—it would take weeks before the stain would be removed.

'No, thank you, Mr Manfred. It was a labour of love, and I have been pretty well paid. And the furnished house I took in the country was really not a very expensive proposition— oh, very well, then.' She took the notes he handed to her and put them in her bag, one eye on the waiting plane. 'You see, Mr Manfred, Garry is an old acquaintance of mine—by hearsay. I sent my sister down to Monte Carlo for her health. She also found Garry.'

Manfred understood. He waited till the plane had passed through the haze out of sight, and then he went back to Curzon Street, well satisfied.

The evening newspapers had no account of the Jermyn Street robbery, which was easily understood. Mr Garry Lexfield had a sense of pride.

11

THE TYPIST WHO SAW THINGS
(First published in *20 Story Magazine*, November 1927)

About every six months Raymond Poiccart grew restless, and began prodding about in strange corners, opening deed boxes and trunks, and sorting over old documents. It was a few days before the incident of the Curzon Street 'murder' that he appeared in the dining room with an armful of old papers, and placed them on that portion of the table which had not been laid for dinner.

Leon Gonsalez looked and groaned.

George Manfred did not even smile, though he was laughing internally.

'I am indeed sorry to distress you, my dear friends,' said Poiccart apologetically; 'but these papers must be put in order. I have found a bundle of letters that go back five years, to the time when the agency was a child.'

'Burn 'em,' suggested Leon, returning to his book. 'You never do anything with them, anyway!'

Poiccart said nothing. He went religiously from paper to paper, read them in his short-sighted way, and put them aside so that as one pile diminished another pile grew.

'And I suppose when you've finished you'll put them back where you found them?' said Leon.

Poiccart did not answer. He was reading a letter.

'A strange communication, I don't remember reading this before,' he said.

'What is it, Raymond?' asked George Manfred. Raymond read:

'To the Silver Triangle. Private.

'Gentlemen:

'I have seen your names mentioned in a case as being reliable agents who can be trusted to work of a confidential character. I would be glad if you would make inquiries and find out for me the prospects of the Persian Oil Fields; also if you could negociate the sale of 967 shares held by me. The reason I do not approach an ordinary share-broker is because there are so many sharks in this profeccion. Also could you tell me whether there is a sale for Okama Biscuit shares (American)? Please let me know this.

'Yours faithfully,

'J Rock.'

'I recall that letter,' said Leon promptly. '"Negotiate" and "profession" were spelt with c's. Don't you remember, George, I suggested this fellow had stolen some shares and was anxious to make us the means by which he disposed of his stolen property?'

Manfred nodded.

'Rock,' said Leon softly. "No, I have never met Mr Rock. He wrote from Melbourne, didn't he, and gave a box number and a telegraphic address? Did we hear again from him? I think not.'

None of the three could recollect any further communication: the letter passed with the others and might have remained eternally buried, but for Leon's uncanny memory for numbers and spelling errors.

And then one night:

A police whistle squealed in Curzon Street. Gonsalez, who slept in the front of the house, heard the sound in his dreams, and was standing by the open window before he was awake. Again the whistle sounded, and then Gonsalez heard the sound of flying feet. A girl was racing along the sidewalk. She passed the house, stopped, and ran back, and again came to a standstill.

Leon went down the narrow stairs two at a time, unlocked the front door and flung it open. The fugitive stood immediately before him.

'In here—quickly!' said Leon.

She hesitated only a second; stepping backward through the doorway, she waited. Leon gripped her by the arm and pulled her into the passage.

'You needn't be frightened of me or my friends,' he said.

But he felt the arm in his hand strain for release. 'Let me go, please—I don't want to stay here!'

Leon pushed her into the back room and switched on the light.

'You saw a policeman running up toward you, that's why you came back,' he said, in his quiet, conversational way. 'Sit down and rest—you look all in!'

'I'm innocent... !' she began, in a trembling voice.

He patted her shoulder.

'Of course you are. I, on the contrary, am guilty, for whether you're innocent or not, I am undoubtedly helping a fugitive from justice.'

She was very young—scarcely more than a child. The pale, drawn face was pretty. She was well, but not expensively, dressed, and it struck Leon as a significant circumstance that on one finger was an emerald ring, which, if the stone were real, must have been worth hundreds of pounds. He glanced at the clock. A few minutes after two. There came to them the sound of heavy, hurrying feet.

'Did anybody see me come in?' she asked, fearfully.

'Nobody was in sight. Now what is the trouble?' Danger and fear had held her tense, almost capable. The reaction had come now: she was shaking. Shoulders, hands, body quivered pitiably. She was crying noiselessly, her lips trembled; for the time being she was inarticulate. Leon poured water into a glass and held it to her chattering teeth. If the others had heard him, they had no intention of coming down to investigate. The curiosity of Leon Gonsalez was a household proverb. Any midnight brawl would bring him out of bed and into the street.

After a while, she was calm enough to tell her story, and it was not the story he expected.

'My name is Farrer—Eileen Farrer. I am a typist attached to Miss Lewley's All-Night Typing Agenda. Usually there are two girls on duty, one a senior; but Miss Leah went home early. We call ourselves an all-night agency, but really we close down about one o'clock. Most of our work is theatrical. Often, after a first-night performance, certain changes have to be made in a script—and sometimes new contracts are arranged over supper, and we prepare the rough drafts. At other times it is just letter-work. I know all the big managers, and I've often gone to their offices quite late to do work for them. We never, of course, go to strange people and at the offices we have a porter who is also a messenger, to see that we are not annoyed. At twelve o'clock I had a phone message from Mr Grasleigh, of the Orpheum, asking me if I would do two letters for him. He sent his car for me, and I went to his flat in Curzon Street. We're not allowed to go to the private houses of our clients, but I knew Mr Grasleigh was a client, though I had never met him before.'

Leon Gonsalez had often seen Mr Jesse Grasleigh's bright yellow car. That eminent theatrical manager lived in some exclusive flats in Curzon Street, occupying the first floor, and paying—as Leon, who was insatiably curious, discovered—£3,000 a year. He had dawned on London three years before, had acquired the lease of the Orpheum, and had been interested in half a dozen productions, most of which had been failures.

'What time was this?' he asked.

'A quarter to one,' said the girl. 'I reached Curzon Street at about a quarter after. I had several things to do at the office before I left, besides which he told me there was no immediate hurry. I knocked at the door and Mr Grasleigh admitted me. He was in evening dress, and looked as if he had come from a party. He had a big white flower in the buttonhole of his tail coat. I saw no servants, and I know now there were none in the flat. He showed me into his study, which was a large room, and pulled up a chair to a little table by his desk. I don't know exactly what happened. I remember sitting down and taking my notebook out of my attache case and opening it, and I was stooping to find a pencil in the case when I heard a groan, and, looking up, I saw Mr Grasleigh lying back in his chair with a red mark on his white shirt-front—it was horrible!'

'You heard no other sound, no shot?' asked Leon.

She shook her head.

'I was so horrified I couldn't move. And then I heard somebody scream and, looking round, I saw a lady, very beautifully dressed, standing in the doorway. "What have you done to him?" she said. "You horrible woman, you've killed him!" I was so terrified that I couldn't speak, and then I must have got into a panic, for I ran past her and out of the front door—'

'It was open?' suggested Leon.

She frowned.

'Yes, it was open. I think the lady must have left it open. I heard somebody blow a police whistle, but I can't remember how I got down the stairs or into the street. You're not going to give me up, are you?' she asked wildly.

He leaned over and patted her hand.

'My young friend,' he said, gently, 'you have nothing whatever to fear. Stay down here while I dress, and then you and I will go down, to Scotland Yard and you will tell them all you know.'

'But I can't. They'll arrest me!'

She was on the verge of hysteria, and it was perhaps a mistake to attempt to argue with her.

'Oh, it's horrible. I hate London... I wish I'd never left Australia... First the dogs and then the black man and now this...'

Leon was startled, but this was not a moment to question her. The thing to do was to bring her to a calm understanding of the situation.

'Don't you realize that they won't blame you, and that your story is such that no police officer in the world would dream of suspecting it?'

'But I ran away—' she began.

'Of course you ran away,' he said soothingly. 'I should probably have run away too. Just wait here.'

He was half-way through dressing when he heard the front door slam and, running down the stairs, found that the girl had disappeared.

Manfred was awake when he went into his room and told him the story.

'No, I don't think it's a pity that you didn't call me earlier,' he interrupted Leon's apology. 'We couldn't very well have detained her in any circumstances. You know where she is employed. See if you can get Lewley's Agency on the telephone.'

Leon found the number in the book, but had no answer from his call.

When he was dressed he went into the street and made his way to Curzon House. To his surprise he found no policeman on guard at the door, though he saw one at the corner of the street, nor was there any evidence that there had been a tragedy. The front door of the flat was fastened, but inserted in the wall were a number of small bell-pushes, each evidently communicating with one of the flats, and after a while he discovered that which bore the name Grasleigh and was on the point of ringing when the policeman he had seen came silently across from the other side of the road. He evidently knew Leon.

'Good evening, Mr Gonsalez,' he said. 'It wasn't you blowing that police whistle, was it?'

'No—I heard it, though.'

'So did I and three or four of my mates,' said the policeman. 'We've been flying round these streets for a quarter of an hour, but we haven't found the man who blew it.'

'Probably I'll be able to help you.'

It was at that moment that he heard the door unlocked, and nearly dropped, for the man who opened the door to him he recognized as Grasleigh himself. He was in a dressing-gown; the half of a cigar was in the corner of his mouth.

'Hullo!' he said in surprise. 'What's the trouble?'

'Can I see you for a few minutes?' said Leon when he had recovered from his surprise.

'Certainly,' said the 'dead man', 'though it's hardly the time I like to receive callers. Come up.'

Wonderingly Leon followed him up the stairs to the first floor. He saw no servants, but there was not the slightest evidence to associate this place with the dramatic scene which the girl had described. Once they were in the big study, Leon told his story. When he had finished, Grasleigh shook his head.

'The girl's mad! It's perfectly true that I did telephone for her, and as a matter of fact I thought it was her when you rang the bell. I assure you she hasn't been here tonight... Yes, I heard the police whistle blow, but I never mix myself up in these midnight troubles.' He was looking at Leon keenly. 'You're one of the Triangle people, aren't you, Mr Gonsalez? What was this girl like?'

Leon described her, and again the theatrical manager shook his head.

'I've never heard of her,' he said. 'I'm afraid you've been the victim of a hoax, Mr Gonsalez.'

Leon went back to join his two friends, a very bewildered man.

The next morning he called at Lewles Agency, which he knew by repute as a well-conducted establishment of its kind, and interviewed its good-natured spinster-proprietress. He had to exercise a certain amount of caution: he was most anxious not to get the girl into trouble. Fortunately, he knew an important client of Miss Lewley's and he was able to use this unconscious man as a lever to extract the information he required.

'Miss Farrer is doing night duty this week, and she will not be in until this evening,' she explained. 'She has been with us about a month.'

'How long has Mr Grasleigh been a client of yours?'

'Exactly the same time,' she said with a smile. 'I rather think he likes Miss Farrer's work, because previous to that he sent all his work to Danton's Agency, where she was employed, and the moment she came to us he changed his agency.'

'Do you know anything about her?'

The woman hesitated.

'She is an Australian. I believe at one time her family were very wealthy. She's never told me anything about her troubles, but I have an idea that she will be entitled to a lot of money some day. One of the partners of Colgate's, the lawyers, came to see her once.'

Leon managed to get the girl's address, and then went on to the City to find Messrs. Colgate. Luck was with him, for Colgate's had employed the Three on several occasions, and at least one of their commissions had been of a most delicate character.

THE TYPIST WHO SAW THINGS

It was one of those old-fashioned firms that had its offices in the region of Bedford Row, and though it was generally known as 'Colgate's,' it consisted of seven partners, the names of all of whom were inscribed on the brass plate before the office.

Mr Colgate himself was a man of sixty, and at first rather uncommunicative. It was an inspiration for Leon to tell him of what had happened the night before. To his amazement, he saw the lawyer's face drop.

'That's very bad,' he said, 'very bad indeed. But I'm afraid I can tell you nothing more than you know.'

'Why is it so very bad?' asked Leon.

The lawyer pursed his lips thoughtfully.

'You understand that she is not our client, although we represent a firm of Melbourne solicitors who are acting for this young lady. Her father died in a mental home and left his affairs rather involved. During the past three years, however, some of his property has become very valuable, and there is no reason why this young lady should work at all, except, as I suspect, that she wishes to get away from the scene of this family trouble and has to work to occupy her mind. I happen to know that the taint of madness is a cause of real distress to the girl, and I believe it was on the advice of her only relative that she came to England, in the hope that the change of scene would put out of her mind this misfortune which has overshadowed her.'

'But she has been to see you?'

The lawyer shook his head.

'One of my clients called on her. Some property in Sydney which was overlooked in the settlement of her father's estate came into the market. He had a tenth share, it seems. We tried to get in touch with the executor, Mr Flane, but we were unsuccessful—he's travelling in the East—so we got the girl's signature to the transfer.'

'Flane?'

Mr Colgate was a busy man; he had intimated as much. He was now a little impatient.

'A cousin of the late Joseph Farrer—the only other relative. As a matter of fact, Farrer was staying in Western Australia on his cousin's station just before he went mad.'

Leon was blessed with an imagination, but even this, vivid as it was, could not quite bridge the gaps in what he suspected was an unusual story.

'My own impression,' said the lawyer, 'and I tell you this in the strictest confidence, is that the girl is not quite... ' He tapped his forehead. 'She told my clerk, a man who is skilled in gaining the confidence of young people, that she had been followed about for weeks by a black man, on another occasion had been followed about by a black retriever. Apparently, whenever she takes her Saturday stroll, this retriever has appeared and never leaves her. So far as I can discover, nobody else has seen either the black man or the dog. You don't need to be a doctor to know that this delusion of being followed is one of the commonest signs of an unbalanced mind.'

Leon knew something more than the average about police work. He knew that discovery is not a thing of a dramatic moment, but patiently accrued evidence, and he followed the same line of inquiry that a detective from Scotland Yard would follow.

Eileen Farrer lived in Landsbury Road, Clapham, and No 209 proved to be a house in a respectable terrace. The motherly-looking landlady who interviewed him in the hall was palpably relieved to see him when he stated the object of his visit.

'I'm so glad you've come,' she said. 'Are you a relation?'

Leon disclaimed that association.

'She's a very peculiar young lady,' the landlady went on, 'and I don't know what to make of her. She's been up all night walking about her room—she sleeps in the room above me—

and this morning she's taken no breakfast. I can't help feeling that there's something wrong—she's so strange.'

'You mean that she's not quite right in her head?' asked Leon brutally.

'Yes, that's what I mean. I thought of sending for my doctor, but she wouldn't hear of it. She told me she'd had a great shock. Do you know her?'

'I've met her,' said Leon. 'May I go upstairs?'

The landlady hesitated.

'I think I'd better tell her you're here. What name?'

'I think it would be better if I saw her without being announced,' said Leon, 'if you will show me the door. Where is she?'

Eileen Farrer was, he learnt, in her sitting-room—she could afford the luxury of an extra apartment Leon tapped at the door and a startled voice asked: 'Who is it?'

He did not answer but, turning the knob, entered the room. The girl was standing by the window, staring out; apparently the taxi that brought Leon had excited her apprehension.

'Oh!' she said in dismay, as she saw her visitor. 'You're the man... you haven't come to arrest me?'

Out of the corner of his eye he saw that the floor was strewn with papers. Evidently she had bought every available newspaper to discover tidings of the crime.

'No, I haven't come to arrest you,' said Leon in an even tone. 'I don't exactly know what you could be arrested for—Mr Grasleigh is not dead. He's not even hurt.'

She stared at him, wide-eyed.

'Not even hurt?' she repeated slowly.

'He was quite well when I saw him last night.'

She passed her hand over her eyes.

'I don't understand. I saw him—oh, it's terrible!'

'You saw him, as you thought, very badly hurt. I had the pleasure of meeting him a few minutes afterwards and he was quite uninjured; and, what is more'—he was watching her as he spoke—'he said that he had never seen you.'

Wonder, incredulity, terror were in her eyes.

'Now won't you sit down, Miss Farrer, and tell me all about yourself. You see, I know quite a lot. I know, for example, that your father died in an institution.'

She was staring at him as though unable to grasp his words. Leon became instantly practical.

'Now I want you to tell me. Miss Farrer, why your father went mad. Was there any other history of insanity in the family?'

Leon's calmness was of the dominant kind: under its influence she had recovered something of her self-possession.

'No, the cause was a fall from a horse; the full effect of it wasn't known for years afterwards.'

He nodded and smiled.

'I thought not. Where were you when he was taken away?'

'I was at school in Melbourne,' she said, 'or rather, just outside of Melbourne. I never saw my father from the time I was seven. He was a long time in that horrible place, and they wouldn't let me see him.'

'Now tell me this: who is Mr Flane? Do you know him?'

She shook her head.

'He was my father's cousin. The only thing I know about him is that Daddy used to lend him money, and he was staying on the farm when he became ill. I've had several letters from him about money. He paid my fare to England. It was he who suggested I should go home and try to forget all the troubles I'd had.'

'You never saw him?'

'Never,' she said. 'He came once to school, but I was away on a picnic.'

'You don't know what money your father left?'

She shook her head again.

'No, I've no idea.'

'Now tell me, Miss Farrer, about the black you have seen following you, and the dog.'

She had very little to tell except the bare fact. The persecution had begun two years before, and her doctor had once called to inquire the cause. Here Leon stopped her quickly.

'Did you send for the doctor?'

'No,' she said in surprise, 'but he must have heard from somebody, though who I can't think, because I told very few people.'

'Can you show me any of the letters that Mr Flane sent you?'

These she had in a drawer, and Leon examined them carefully. Their tone was rather unusual, not the tone one would have expected from a guardian or from one who had control of her destinies. In the main they were protestations of the difficulties the writer found in providing for her schooling, for her clothes, and eventually for the trip to England, and each letter insisted on the fact that her father had left very little money.

'And that was true,' she said. 'Poor Daddy was rather eccentric about money. He never kept his stocks at the bank but always carried them about with him in a big iron box. In fact, he was terribly secretive, and nobody knew exactly what money he had. I thought he was very rich, because he was a little'—she hesitated—'"near" is the word. I hate saying anything disparaging about the poor darling, but he was never generous with money, and when I found that he had only left a few hundred pounds and a very few shares, and those not of any particular value, I was astonished. And so, of course, was everybody in Melbourne—everybody who knew us, I mean. In fact, I always regarded myself as poor until a few months ago. We then discovered that father had a large interest in the West Australian Gold Mine, which nobody knew anything about. It came to light by accident. If all they say is true, I shall be very rich. The lawyers have been trying to get into touch with

Mr Flane, but they have only had a letter or two, one posted from China addressed to me, and another posted I think in Japan.'

'Have you got the letter addressed to you?'

She produced it. It was written on thick paper. Leon held it up to the light and saw the watermark.

'What shares did your father leave? I mean, what shares was he known to leave?'

She puzzled over this question.

'There were some absolutely valueless, I know. I remember them because of the number—967. What's the matter?'

Leon was laughing.

'I think I can promise you freedom from any further persecution, Miss Farrer, and my advice to you is that you get immediately in touch with the best firm of lawyers in London. I think I can give you their address. There's one thing I want to tell you'—there was a very kindly smile in Leon Gonsalez's eyes—'and it is that you are not mad, that you haven't imagined you were followed by blacks and by black dogs and that you didn't imagine you saw Mr Grasleigh murdered. There's one more question I want to ask you, and it's about Mr Flane. Do you know what he did for a living?'

'He had a small station—farm, you would call it,' she said. 'I think Daddy bought it for him and his wife. Before that I think he had the lease of a theatre in Adelaide, and he lost a lot of money.'

'Thank you,' said Leon. 'That is all I want to know.'

He drove straight back to the flats in Curzon Street, and met Mr Grasleigh as he was leaving his flat.

'Hullo! You've not come to tell me about another murder?' said that jovial man with a loud laugh.

'Worse than murder,' said Leon, and something in his tone struck the smile from Mr Grasleigh's lips.

Leon followed him into the study and himself closed the door.

'Mr Flane, I understand?' he said, and saw the colour fade from the man's face.

'I don't know what you mean,' blustered Grasleigh. 'My name is—'

'Your name is Flane,' said Leon very gently. 'A few years ago you got an inkling that the man you had robbed—Eileen Farrer's father—was richer than you thought, and you evolved a rather clumsy, and certainly a diabolical scheme to retain possession of Eileen Farrer's property. A shallow-brained man as you are, I have no doubt, would imagine that because the father was mad the daughter could also be driven into a mental asylum. I don't know where you got your black from or where you found your trained dog, but I know where you got the money to take the lease of the Orpheum. And, Mr Flane, I want to tell you something more, and you might pass the information on to your wife, who is, I gather, a fellow conspirator. "Negotiate" is spelt with a "t" and "profession" with an "s". Both words occur in the letters you wrote to Miss Farrer.'

The man was breathing loudly through his nose, and the hand that went up to take out the dead stump of his cigar was shaking.

'You've got to prove all this,' he blustered.

'Unfortunately I have,' said Leon sadly. 'In the old days when the Four Just Men were not quite so legally minded as they are today, you would not have been taken into a court of law: I rather imagine that my friends and I would have opened a manhole in Curzon Street and dropped you through.'

12

THE MYSTERY OF MR DRAKE
(First published in *20 Story Magazine*,
December 1927)

All events go in threes—that was the considered opinion of Leon Gonsalez. This, for example, was his second meeting with Cornelius Malan. The last time Mr Roos Malan, the bearded brother of Cornelius, had been a third party, but now Roos was dead—though of this fact Leon was at the moment unaware.

This alert and bright-eyed man had never had a driving accident. The fact that he was alive proved this, for he was never quite happy if the needle of the speedometer on his big sports car fell below the seventy mark. By an odd chance it was well below thirty when he skidded on the slush and snow of a lonely Oxford road and slithered a back wheel into a four-foot ditch. That the car did not overturn was a miracle.

Leon climbed out and looked round. The squat farmstead beyond the stone wall which flanked the road had a familiar appearance. He grinned as he leapt the wall and made his way across the rough surface of an uncultivated field towards the building. A dog barked gruffly, but he saw no human creature. And when he knocked at the door there was no answer. Leon was not surprised. Cornelius kept few servants, even in the summer—he was unlikely to have his house well staffed in the unprofitable days of late autumn.

He made a tour of the house, passed through an untidy and weed-grown garden, and still could find no sign of life. And then from the ground, not a dozen yards away, arose a big, broad-shouldered giant of a man. He came veritably from the ground. For a moment the observer was staggered, and then he realized that the man had come out of a well. The back of Cornelius Malan was turned to his uninvited guest. Leon saw him stoop, heard the clang of steel and the click of a lock fastened. Presently the big man dusted his knees and stretched himself and, turning, came straight towards where Leon was standing. At the sight of a stranger, the broad, red face of Cornelius went a shade redder.

'Hi, you!' he began wrathfully, and then recognized his visitor. 'Ah!' he said. 'The detective!'

He spoke with scarcely a trace of accent, unlike his dead brother, who could hardly speak English.

'What do you want, eh? Do more people think that poor Roos has swindled them? Well, he is dead, so you get nothing out of him.'

Leon was looking past him, and the man must have divined what was in his mind, for he said quickly: 'There is a bad well here, full of gas. I must have it filled up—'

'In the meantime you've had it sensibly fastened,' smiled Leon. 'I'm sorry to barge in upon your Arcadian pursuits, Mr Malan, but the fact is my car has ditched itself, and I wanted help to get it up.'

There had been a strange look of apprehension on the man's face, and this cleared away as Leon explained the object of his visit.

'I myself could pick a car out of any ditch,' he boasted. 'You shall see.'

As he walked across the field with Leon he was almost affable.

'I do not like you people from London, and you especially, Mr What's-your-name. You are like the lawyer who swindled me and my poor brother by Potchefstroom, so many years ago that I forget his name. Poor Roos! You and such people as you have hounded him into his grave! Inspectors of taxes and God knows what. And we are both poor men and have nothing to say to them.'

When they got to the car, he found that his strength was hardly sufficient, and they returned to the farm and from some mysterious place gathered two hungry-looking labourers, who, with planks and ropes, succeeded in hauling the Bentley to road level. By this time, Cornelius Malan was his old self.

'That will cost you one pound, my friend,' he said. 'I cannot afford to pay these men for extra work. I am poor, and now that Roos is dead, who knows that I may not have to take that lazy wench of our sister's...'

Very solemnly Leon produced a pound note, and handed it to the old miser.

When he got back to Curzon Street he related his experience.

'I'll bet you we're going to meet for the third time,' he said. 'It is odd, but it's a fact. One of these days I am going to write a book on the Law of Coincidence—I've any amount of data.'

'Add this,' said Poiccart briefly, as he tossed a letter across the table.

Leon smoothed it out: the first thing he read was an Oxfordshire address. He turned quickly to the end of the letter, and saw it was signed, 'Leonora Malan.'

Manfred was watching him with a smile in his eyes.

'There's a job after your own heart, Leon,' he said.

Leon read the letter.

'DEAR SIRS,

'Some time ago you came into town to see my uncle, who has now, I am sorry to say, passed over. Will you please grant me an interview on Wednesday morning in regard to my late uncle's money? I don't suppose you can help me, but there is just a chance.'

It was signed 'Leonora Malan,' and there was a postscript.

'Please do not let my Uncle Cornelius know I have written.'

Leon scratched his chin.

'Leon and Leonora,' murmured Manfred. 'That alone is sufficient basis for a chapter on coincidences.'

On Wednesday morning, rainy and gusty, Miss Malan called, and with her was the young man who was to be the fourth and the greatest coincidence of all.

A scrawny man of thirty, with irregular features and eyes that were never still, she introduced him as Mr Jones, the late manager of her dead uncle.

Leonora Malan was astonishingly pretty. That was the first impression Leon had of his visitor. He had expected something dumpy and plain—Leonora was a name to shy at. Malan was obviously Cape Dutch. He would have known this even if he had not been aware, from personal experience, of the nationality of her two uncles. He had had an encounter with the notorious Jappy, and the no less objectionable Roos—less objectionable now, since he had been gathered to his fathers. And he was agreeably surprised, for this slim, bright-eyed girl with the peach and rose complexion was a very happy upsetting of preconceived ideas.

She came with him into the bright little drawing-room which was also the office of the Three, and sat down in the chair which Poiccart pushed forward for her before, in his role of butler, he glided out, closing the door respectfully and noiselessly behind him.

She looked up at Leon, her eyes twinkling, and smiled.

'You can do nothing for me, Mr Gonsalez, but Mr Jones thought I ought to see you,' she said, with a trustful glance at her ill-favoured companion which appalled Gonsalez. 'That isn't a very promising beginning, is it? I suppose you'll wonder why I'm wasting your time if I believe that? But just now I'm clutching at straws, and—'

'I am a very substantial straw,' laughed Leon.

Mr Jones spoke. His voice was harsh and coarse.

'It's like this. Leonora is entitled to about eighty thousand pounds. I know it was there before the old boy died. Got the will, Leonora?'

She nodded quickly and sighed, half-opened her little hand-bag, reached mechanically for a battered silver case, but quickly withdrew her hand and snapped the bag tight. Leon reached for the cigarette box and passed it to her.

'You know my uncle?' she said, as she took a cigarette. 'Poor Uncle Roos often spoke about you—'

'Very uncomplimentarily, I am sure,' said Leon.

She nodded.

'Yes, he didn't like you. He was rather afraid of you, and you cost him money.'

Roos Malan had figured in one of Leon's more humdrum cases. Roos and his brother Cornelius had been prosperous farmers in South Africa. And then gold was discovered on their farm, and they became, of a sudden, very rich men; both came to England and settled on two desolate farms in Oxfordshire. It was Roos who had adopted his dead sister's baby with much grumbling and complaining for, like his brother, he was that rarest of misers who grudges every farthing spent even on himself. Yet both brothers were shrewd speculators; too shrewd sometimes. It was a case in which their cupidity had overrun their discretion, that had brought Leon into their orbit.

'Uncle Roos,' said the girl, 'was not so bad as you think. Of course, he was terribly mean about money, and even about the food that was eaten on the farm; and life was a little difficult with him. Sometimes he was kindness itself, and I feel a pig that I am bothering about his wretched money.'

THE MYSTERY OF MR DRAKE

'Don't worry about him,' began Jones impatiently.

'You find that there is no wretched money?' interrupted Leon, glancing again at the letter she had sent him.

She shook her head.

'I can't understand it,' she said.

'Show him the will,' Jones snapped.

She opened her bag again and took out a folded paper.

'Here is a copy.'

Leon took the paper and opened it. It was a short, handwritten document in Dutch. Beneath was the English translation. In a few lines the late Roos Malan had left 'all the property I possess to my niece Leonora Mary Malan.'

'Every penny,' said Jones, with satisfaction that he did not attempt to conceal. 'Leonora and I were going into business in London. Her money, my brains. See what I mean?'

Leon saw very clearly.

'When did he die?' he asked.

'Six months ago.' Leonora frowned as at an unpleasant memory. 'You'll think I am heartless, but really I had no love for him, though at times I was very fond of him.'

'And the property?' said Leon.

She frowned.

'All that is left seems to be the farm and the furniture. The valuers say that it's worth five thousand pounds, and it's mortgaged for four thousand. Uncle Cornelius holds the mortgage. Yet Roos Malan must have been very rich; he drew royalties from his property in South Africa, and I've seen the money in the house; it came every quarter and was always paid in banknotes.'

'I could explain the mortgage,' said Jones. 'Those two mean old skunks exchanged mortgages to protect one another in case the authorities ever tried to play tricks on 'em! The money's gone, mister—I've searched the house from top to bottom. There's a strongroom built in a corner of the cellar—we've had that door opened, but there's not a penny to be found. They're great for strongrooms, the Malans. I know where Cornelius keeps his too. He doesn't know it, but by God, if he doesn't play fair with this kid... !'

The girl seemed a little embarrassed by the championship of the man. The friendship was a little one-sided, he thought, and had the impression that Mr Jones' glib plans for 'going into business' were particularly his own.

Jones gave him one piece of news. Neither of the brothers had banking accounts. Though they speculated heavily and wisely in South African stocks, their dividends were paid or their stock was bought with ready money, and invariably cash payments were made in the same medium.

'Both these old blighters objected to paying taxation, and they used all sorts of dirty tricks to avoid payment. They suspected all banks, because they believed that banks tell the Government their clients' business.'

Leonora shook her head again despairingly.

'I don't think you can do anything, Mr Gonsalez, and I almost wish I hadn't written. The money isn't there; there's no record that it ever was there. I really don't mind very much, because I can work. Happily I took typing lessons and improved my speed at the farm. I did most of Uncle's correspondence.'

'During the last illness was Cornelius at the farm?'

She nodded.

'All the time?'

She nodded again.

'And he left—?'

'Immediately after poor Roos' death. I haven't seen him again, and the only communication I've had from him was a letter in which he told me that I ought to earn my living and that I couldn't depend on him. Now what can I do?'

Leon considered this problem for a long time.

THE MYSTERY OF MR DRAKE

'I'll be perfectly frank with you, Mr Gonsalez,' she went on. 'I am sure Uncle Cornelius collected what money there was in the house before he left. Mr Jones thinks that too.'

'Think it—I know it!' The hatchet-faced man was very emphatic. 'I saw him coming out of the cellar with a big Gladstone bag. Old Roos was in the habit of keeping his key of the strongroom under his pillow; when he died it wasn't there—I found it on the kitchen mantelpiece!'

When the man and the girl were leaving, Leon so manoeuvred the departure that she was the last to go.

'Who is Jones?' he asked, dropping his voice.

She was a little uncomfortable.

'He was Uncle's farm manager—he's been very nice... a little too nice.'

Leon nodded, and as he heard Mr Jones returning, asked her immediate plans. She was, she said, staying the week in London, making preparations to earn her own livelihood. After he had taken down her address and seen the party to the door, he walked thoughtfully back to the common room where his two companions were playing chess—an immoral occupation for eleven o'clock in the forenoon.

'She is very pretty,' said Poiccart, not looking up from the piece he was fingering, 'and she has come about her inheritance. And the man with her is no good.'

'You were listening at the door,' accused Leon.

'I have read the local newspapers and I know that Mr Roos Malan died penniless—not sufficient to meet the demands of the Inspector of Taxes,' said Poiccart as he checked Manfred's king. 'Both men were terrible misers, both are enormously rich, and both men have got Somerset House tearing their hair.'

'And naturally,' George Manfred went on, 'she came to you to recover her property. What did the man want?'

He sat back in his chair and sighed.

'We're fearfully respectable, aren't we? It was so easy ten, fifteen years ago. I know so many ways of making Cornelius disgorge.'

'And I know one,' interrupted Leon promptly. 'And if all my theories and views are correct—and I cannot imagine them being anything else—Mr Drake will make the recovery.'

'Mr Who?' Poiccart looked up with a heavy frown.

'Mr Drake,' said Leon glibly; 'an old enemy of mine. We have been at daggers drawn for ten years. He knows one of my most precious secrets, and I have lived in mortal terror of him, so much so that I contemplate removing him from his present sphere of activity.'

George looked at him thoughtfully; then a light dawned in his face.

'Oh, I think I know your mysterious Mr Drake. We used him before, didn't we?'

'We used him before,' agreed Leon gravely. 'But this time he dies the death of a dog!'

'Who is this Jones?' asked Poiccart. 'I've seen him at the Old Bailey—and he has a Dartmoor manner. You remember, George—an unpleasant case, eight-ten years ago. Not a fit companion for the pretty Leonora.'

Leon's car took him the next morning to a famous market town, ten miles from Mr Malan's farm. Here he sought and had an interview with the local inspector of taxes, producing the brief authorization which he had suggested Leonora should sign. The harassed official was both willing and anxious to give Leon all the information he required.

'I have the devil of a job with these people. We know their main income, which arrives from South Africa every quarter, but they've got a score of other South African interests which we're unable to trace. We knew that they are in the habit of receiving their money in cash. Both men have obviously been cheating the Revenue for years, but we could get no evidence against them. If Mr Malan keeps books, he also keeps them well out of sight! A few months ago we put a detective on to watch Cornelius, and we found his hiding place. It lies about twenty feet down a half-filled-in well in his garden.'

Leon nodded.

'And it's a solid rock chamber approached by a steel door. It sounds like a fairy tale, doesn't it? It's one of the many in which Charles II was reputedly hidden, and the existence of the rock chamber has been known for centuries. Cornelius had the steel door fitted, and as the well is right under his window and is fastened by an iron trapdoor and is, moreover, visible from the road, it's much more secure than any safe he could have in his house.'

'Then why not search the strong-room?' asked Leon.

The inspector shook his head.

'We've no authority to do that—the most difficult thing in the world to secure is a search warrant, and our department, unless it institutes criminal proceedings, has never applied for such an authority.'

Leon smiled broadly.

'Mr Drake will have to get it for you,' he said cryptically.

The puzzled official frowned.

'I don't quite get that.'

'You will get more than that,' said the mysterious Leon.

As Leon walked up the muddy cart-track, he became aware of the sound of voices, one deep and bellowing, one high and shrill. Their words, incoherent in themselves, were indistinguishable. He turned the corner of an untidy clump of bushes, and saw the two: Cornelius the giant, and the rat-faced Mr Jones, who was white with passion.

'I'm going to get you, you damned Dutch thief!' he cried shrilly. 'Robbing the orphan—that's what you're doing. You haven't heard the last of me.'

What Cornelius said was impossible to understand, for in his rage he had relapsed into Cape Dutch, which is one of the most expressive mediums of vituperation. He caught sight of Leon, and came striding towards him.

'You're a detective: take that man from here. He's a thief, a gaolbird. My brother gave him a job because he could get no other.'

The thin lips of Mr Jones curled in a sneer.

'A hell of a job! A stable to sleep in and stuff to eat that Dartmoor would turn up its nose at—not that I know anything about Dartmoor,' he added hastily. 'All that this man says is lies. He's a thief; he took the money from old Roos' safe—'

'And you come and say "Give me ten thousand and I'll tell Leonora not to trouble about the rest," eh?' snarled Cornelius.

Leon knew it was not the moment to tell the story of Mr Drake. That must come later. He made an excuse for his calling and then accompanied the man Jones back to the road.

'Don't you take any notice of what he said, mister, I mean about my trying to doublecross Leonora. She's a good girl; she trusts me, she does, and I'm going to do the right thing by her... Old Roos led her the life of a dog.'

Leon wondered what kind of life this ex-convict would lead Leonora Malan and was quite satisfied that, whatever happened, the girl should be saved from such an association.

'And when he says I was a convict—' began Jones again.

'I can save you a lot of trouble,' said Leon. 'I saw you sentenced.'

He mentioned the offence, and the man went red and then white.

'Now you can go back to London, and I'm warning you not to go near Miss Leonora Malan. If you do, there is going to be trouble.'

Jones opened his mouth as if to say something, changed his mind and lurched up the road. It was later in the evening when Leon returned to tell the story of Mr Drake.

He reached the farm of Mr Cornelius Malan at nine o'clock. It was pitch dark; rain and sleet were falling, and the house offered no promise that his discomfort would be relieved, for not so much as a candle gleam illuminated the dark windows. He knocked for some time, but had no reply. Then he heard the sound of laboured breathing: somebody was walking towards him in the darkness, and he spun round.

'Mr Cornelius Malan?' he asked, and heard the man grunt, and then: 'Who is it?'

'An old friend,' said Leon coolly, and though Cornelius could not see his face, he must have recognized him.

'What do you want?' His voice was shrill with anxiety.

'I want to see you. It's rather an important matter,' said Leon.

The man pushed past him, unlocked the door and led the way into the darkness. Leon waited in the doorway until he saw the yellow flame of a match and heard the tinkle of a lamp chimney being lifted.

The room was big and bare. Only the glow of a wood fire burnt in the hearth, yet this apparently was the farmer's livings and sleeping room, for his untidy bed was in one corner of the room. In the centre was a bare deal table, and on this Leon sat uninvited. The man stood at the far end of the table, scowling down at him; his face was pale and haggard. 'What do you want?' he asked again.

'It's about John Drake,' said Leon deliberately. 'He's an old enemy of mine; we have chased one another across three continents before now, and tonight, for the first time in ten years, we met.'

The man was puzzled, bewildered. 'What's this to do with me?'

Leon shrugged. 'Only tonight I killed him.'

He saw the man's jaw drop. 'Killed him?'—incredulously.

Leon nodded. 'I stabbed him with a long knife,' he said, with some relish. 'You've probably heard about the Three Just Men: they do such things. And I've concealed the body on your farm. For the first time in my life I am conscious that I have acted unfairly, and it is my intention to give myself up to the police.'

Cornelius looked down at him.

'On my farm?' he said dully. 'Where did you put the body?'

Not a muscle of Leon's face moved.

'I dropped it down the well.'

'That's a lie!' stormed the other. 'It is impossible that it was you who opened the cover!...'

Leon shrugged his shoulders.

'That you must tell the police. They at any rate will learn from me that I dropped him down that well. At the bottom I found a door which I succeeded in opening with a skeleton key, and inside that door is my unhappy victim.'

Malan's lips were quivering.

Suddenly he turned and rushed from the room.

Leon heard the shot and ran through the door into the night... the next second he sprawled over the dead body of Cornelius Roos.

Later, when the police came and forced the cover of the well, they found another dead man huddled at the bottom of the well, where Cornelius had thrown him.

'Jones must have been detected in the act of forcing the well, and been shot,' said Leon. 'Weird, isn't it... after my yarn about having buried a man there? I expected no more than that Cornelius would pay up rather than have the well searched.'

'Very weird,' said Manfred drily, 'and the weirdest thing is Jones' real name.'

'What is it?'

'Drake,' said Manfred. 'The police phoned it through half-an-hour before you came in.'

13

"THE ENGLISHMAN KONNOR"
(First published in *20 Story Magazine*, January 1928)

The Three Just Men sat longer over dinner than usual. Poiccart had been unusually talkative—and serious.

'The truth is, my dear George,' he appealed to the silent Manfred, 'we are fiddling with things. There are still offences for which the law does not touch a man; for which death is the only and logical punishment. We do a certain amount of good—yes. We right certain wrongs—yes. But could not any honest detective agency do as much?'

'Poiccart is a lawless man,' murmured Leon Gonsalez; 'he is going Fantee*—there is a murderous light in his eyes!'

Poiccart smiled good-humouredly.

'We know this is true, all of us. There are three men I know, every one of them worthy of destruction. They have wrecked lives, and are within the pale of the law... Now, my view is...'

They let him talk and talk, and to the eyes of Manfred came a vision of Merrell, the Fourth of the Four Just Men—he who

---

[* To go native. Cf. 'He was perpetually going Fantee among natives...'—Rudyard Kipling, 'Miss Youghal's Sais', *Plain Tales from the Hills*, 1888.]

died in Bordeaux and, in dying completed his purpose. Some day the story of Merrell the Fourth may be told. Manfred remembered a warm, still night, when Poiccart had spoken in just this strain. They were younger then: eager for justice, terribly swift to strike...

'We are respectable citizens,' said Leon, getting up, 'and you are trying to corrupt us, my friend. I refuse to be corrupted!'

Poiccart looked up at him from under his heavy eyelids.

'Who shall be the first to break back to the old way?' he asked significantly.

Leon did not answer.

This was a month before the appearance of the tablet. It came into the possession of the Four in a peculiar way. Poiccart was in Berlin, looking for a man who called himself Lefevre. One sunny afternoon, when he was lounging through Charlonenburg, he called in at an antique shop to buy some old Turkish pottery that was exhibited for sale. Two large blue vases were his purchase, and these he had packed and sent to the House with the Silver Triangle, in Curzon Street.

It was Manfred who found the gold badge. He had odd moments of domesticity, and one day decided to wash the pottery. There were all sorts of oddments at the bottom of the vases: one was stuffed with old pieces of Syrian newspaper for half its depth, and it needed a great deal of patience and groping with pieces of wire to bring these to light. Nearing the end of his task, he heard a metallic tinkle and, as he turned the jar upside down, there dropped into the kitchen sink a gold chain bracelet that held an oblong gold tablet, inscribed on both sides with minute Arabic writing.

Now it so happened that Mr Dorian of the Evening Herald was in the kitchen when this interesting find was made, and Mr Dorian, as everybody knows, is the greatest gossip-writer that ever went into Fleet Street. He is a youngish man of forty-something who looks twenty-something. You meet him at first nights and very select functions, at the unveiling of war memorials—he was a very good artilleryman during the war. Sometimes he called and stayed to dinner to talk over the old days on the *Megaphone*, but never before had he made professional profit out of his visits. 'Poiccart will be indifferent—but Leon will be delighted,' said Manfred as he examined the bracelet link by link. 'Gold, of course. Leon loves mysteries and usually makes his own. This will go into his little story box.'

The little story box was Leon's especial eccentricity. Disdaining safes and strong rooms, that battered steel deed-box reposed beneath his bed. It is true that it contained nothing of great value intrinsically: a jumble of odds and ends, from the torn tickets of bookmakers to two inches of the rope that should have hanged Manfred, each inconsiderable object had its attachment in the shape of a story.

The imagination of the journalist was fired. He took the bracelet in his hand and examined it.

'What is it?' he asked curiously.

Manfred was examining the inscription.

'Leon understands Arabic better than I—it rather looks like the identification disc of a Turkish officer. He must be, or must have been, rather an exquisite.'

'Curious,' mused Dorian aloud. Here in smoky London a jar or vase bought in Berlin, and out of it tumbles something of Eastern romance. He asked if he might muse in print to the same purpose, and George Manfred had no objection.

Leon came back that evening: he had been asked by the American Government to secure exact information about a certain general cargo which was being shipped from lighters in the port of London.

'Certain raw materials,' he reported, 'which could have caused a great deal of trouble for our friends in America.'

Manfred told him of his find.

'Dorian was here—I told him he could write about this if he liked.'

'H'm!' said Leon, reading the inscription. 'Did you tell him what this writing stood for? But you're not a whale at Arabic, are you? There's one word in Roman characters "Konnor"—did you see that? "Konnor?" Now what is "Konnor"?' He looked up at the ceiling. '"The Englishman Konnor"—that was the owner of this interesting exhibit. Konnor? I've got it—"Connor"!'

The next evening, under 'The Man in Town,' Mr Dorian's daily column, Leon read of the find, and was just a little irritated to discover that the thorough Mr Dorian had referred to the story box. If the truth be told, Leon was not proud of this little box of his; it stood for romance and sentiment, two qualities which he was pleased to believe were absent from his spiritual make-up.

'George, you're becoming a vulgar publicity agent,' he complained. 'The next thing that will happen will be that I shall receive fabulous offers from a Sunday newspaper for a series of ten articles on "Stories from my Story Box," and if I do I shall sulk for three days.'

Nevertheless, into the black box went the bracelet. What the writing was all about, and where 'the Englishman Konnor' came into it, Leon refused to say.

Yet it was clear to his two companions that Leon was pursuing some new inquiry in the days that followed. He haunted Fleet Street and Whitehall, and even paid a visit to Dublin. Once Manfred questioned him and Leon smiled amiably.

'The whole thing is rather amusing. Connor isn't even Irish. Probably isn't Connor, though it is certain that he bore that name. I found it on the roll of a very fine Irish regiment. He is most likely a Levantine. Stewarts, the Dublin photographers, have a picture of him in a regimental group. That is what I went to Ireland to see. There's a big bookmaker in Dublin who was an officer in the same regiment, and he says "Connor" spoke with a foreign accent.'

'But who is Connor?' asked Manfred.

Leon showed his even white teeth in a grin of delight.

'He is my story,' was all that he would say.

Three weeks later Leon Gonsalez found adventure.

He had something of the qualities of a cat; he slept noiselessly; the keenest ear must strain to hear him breathing; he woke noiselessly. He could pass from complete oblivion to complete wakefulness in a flash. As a cat opens her eyes and is instantly and cold-bloodedly alert, so was Leon.

He had the rare power of looking back into sleep and rediscovering causes, and he knew without remembering that what had wakened him was not the tap-tap of the blind cords for, the night being windy, this had been a normal accompaniment to sleep, but rather the sound of human movement.

His room was a large one for so small a house, but there could never be enough ventilation for Leon, so that, in addition to windows, the door was wedged open... He snuffled picturesquely, like a man in heavy sleep, grumbled drowsily, and turned in the bed; but when he had finished turning, his feet were on the floor and he was standing upright, tightening the cord of his pyjamas.

Manfred and Poiccart were away for the weekend, and he was alone in the house—a satisfactory state of affairs, since Leon preferred to deal with such situations as these single-handed.

Waiting, his head bent, he heard the sound again. It came at the end of a whining gust of wind that should have drowned the noise—a distinct creak. Now the stairs gave seven distinct creakings. This one came from the second tread. He lifted his dressing-gown and drew it on as his bare feet groped for his slippers. Then he slipped out on to the landing, and switched on the light.

There was a man on the landing; his yellow, uncleanly face was upraised to Leon's. Fear, surprise, hateful resentment were there.

'Keep your hand out of your pocket, or I'll shoot you through the stomach,' said Leon calmly. 'It will take you four days to die, and you'll regret every minute of it.'

The second man, half-way up the stairs, stood stock-still, paralysed with fright. He was small and slim. Leon waved the barrel of his Browning in his direction, and the smaller figure shrank against the wall and screamed.

Leon smiled. He had not met a lady burglar for years.

'Turn about, both of you, and walk downstairs,' he ordered; 'don't try to run—that would be fatal.'

They obeyed him, the man sullenly, the girl, he guessed, rather weak in the knees.

Presently they came to the ground floor.

'To the left,' said Leon.

He stepped swiftly up to the man, dropped the Browning against his spine, and put his hand into the jacket pocket. He took out a short-barrelled revolver, and slipped it into the pocket of his dressing-gown.

'Through the doorway—the light switch is on the left, turn it.' Following them into the little dining-room, he closed the door behind him. 'Now sit down—both of you.'

The man he could place: a typical prison man; irregular features, bad-complexioned: a creature of low mentality, who spent his short periods of liberty qualifying for further imprisonment.

His companion had not spoken, and until she spoke Leon could not place her into a category.

'I'm very sorry—I am entirely to blame.'

So she spoke, and Leon was enlightened.

It was an educated voice—the voice you might hear in Bond Street ordering the chauffeur to drive to the Ritz.

She was pretty, but then, most women were pretty to Leon; he had that amount of charity in his soul. Dark eyes, fine arches of eyebrows, rather full, red lips. The nervous fingers that twined in and out of one another were white, shapely, rather over-manicured. There was a small purple spot on the back of one finger, where a big ring had been.

'This man is not responsible,' she said, in a low voice. 'I hired him. A—a friend of mine used to help him, and he came to the house one night last week; and I asked him to do this for me. That's really true.'

'Asked him to burgle my house?'

She nodded. 'I wish you'd let him go—I could talk to you then... and feel more comfortable. It really isn't his fault. I'm entirely to blame.'

Leon pulled open the drawer of a small writing-table, and took out a sheet of paper and an inkpad. He put them on the table before the girl's unshaven companion.

'Put your finger and thumb on the pad—press 'em.'

'Whaffor?' The man was husky and suspicious.

'I want your finger-prints in case I have to come after you. Be slippy!'

Reluctantly, the burglar obeyed—first one hand and then the other. Leon examined the prints on the paper, and was satisfied.

'Step this way.'

He pushed his visitor to the street door, opened it, and walked out after him.

'You must not carry a gun,' he said. As he spoke his fist shot up and caught the man under the jaw, and the man went sprawling to the ground.

He got up whimpering.

'She made me carry it,' he whined.

'Then she earned you a punch on the jaw,' said Leon brightly, and closed the door on one who called himself, rather unimaginatively, 'John Smith.'

When he returned to the dining-room, the girl had loosened the heavy coat she wore, and was sitting back in her chair, rather white of face but perfectly calm.

'Has he gone? I'm so glad! You hit him, didn't you? I thought I heard you. What do you think of me?'

'I wouldn't have missed tonight for a thousand pounds!' said Leon, and he was telling the truth.

Only for a fraction of a second did she smile.

'Why do you think I did this mad, stupid thing?' she asked quietly. Leon shook his head.

'That is exactly what I can't think: we've no very important case on hand; the mysterious documents which figure in all sensation stories are entirely missing. I can only suppose that we've been rather unkind to some friend of yours—a lover, a father, a brother—'

He saw the ghost of a smile appear and disappear.

'No; it isn't revenge. You've done me no harm, directly or indirectly. And there are no secret documents.'

'Then it's not revenge and it's not robbery; I confess that I am beaten!'

Leon's smile was dazzling, and this time she responded without reservation.

'I suppose I'd better tell you everything,' she said, 'and I'd best start by telling you that my name is Lois Martin, my father is Sir Charles Martin, the surgeon, and I shall be married in three weeks' time to Major John Rutland, of the Cape Police. And that is why I burgled your house.'

Leon was amused.

'You were—er—looking for a wedding—present?' he asked, mildly sarcastic.

To his surprise, she nodded.

'That is just what I came for,' she said. 'I've been very silly. If I'd known you better, I should have come to you and asked for it.'

Her steady eyes were fixed upon Leon.

'Well?' he asked. 'What is this interesting object?'

She spoke very slowly.

'A gold chain bangle, with an identification disc...'

Leon was not surprised, except that she was speaking the truth. He jotted down the names she had given him. A gold bracelet,' he repeated, 'the property of—?'

She hesitated.

'I suppose you've got to know the whole story—I'm rather in your hands.'

He nodded.

'Very much in my hands,' he said pleasantly. 'It seems to me that you will get less discomfort in telling me now than in explaining the matter to a police magistrate.'

He was geniality itself yet she, womanlike, could detect a hardness in his tone that made her shiver a little.

'Major Rutland knows nothing about my coming here—he would be horrified if he knew I had taken this risk,' she began.

She told him, haltingly at first, how her older brother had been killed in Africa during the War.

'That's how I come to know Jack,' she said. 'He was in the desert, too. He wrote to me two years ago from Paris—said he had some papers belonging to poor Frank. He had taken them from his—from his body, after he was killed. Naturally, Daddy asked him to come over, and we became good friends, although Daddy isn't very keen on—our marriage.'

She was silent for a little while, and then went on quickly:

'Father doesn't like the marriage at all, and really the fact that we are getting married is a secret. You see, Mr Gonsalez, I am a comparatively rich woman: my mother left me a large sum of money. And John will be rich, too. During the War, when he was a prisoner, he located a big gold mine in Syria, and that is what the inscription is all about. John saved the life of an Arab, and in his gratitude he revealed to him where the mine was located, and had it all inscribed on a little gold tablet, in Arabic. John lost it at the end of the War, and he'd heard nothing more of it until he read in the Evening Herald about your discovery. Poor John was naturally terribly upset at the thought that he might be forestalled by somebody who could decipher the tablet, so I suggested he should call and see you and ask for the bracelet back; but he wouldn't hear of this. Instead, he's been getting more and more worried and upset and nervous, and at last I thought of this mad scheme. Jack has quite a number of acquaintances amongst the criminal classes — being a police officer he very naturally can deal with them; and he's done a lot to help them to keep straight. This man who came tonight was one of them. It was I who saw him, and suggested this idea of getting into the house and taking the bracelet. We knew that you kept it under your bed—'

'Are you sure it was you and not Major John Rutland who thought out this burglary?'

Again she hesitated.

'I think he did in fun suggest that the house should be burgled.'

'And that you should do the burgling?' asked Leon blandly.

She avoided his eyes.

'In fun... yes. He said nobody would hurt me, and I could always pretend it was a practical joke. It was very stupid, I know, Mr Gonsalez; if my father knew... '

'Exactly,' said Leon brusquely. 'You needn't tell me any more — about the burglary. How much money have you at the bank?'

She looked at him in surprise.

'Nearly forty thousand pounds,' she said. 'I've sold a lot of securities lately — they were not very productive—'

Leon smiled.

'And you've heard of a better investment?'

She was quick to see what he meant.

'You're altogether wrong, Mr Gonsalez,' she said coldly. 'John is only allowing me to put a thousand pounds into his exploration syndicate—he isn't quite sure whether it is a thousand or eight hundred he will require. He won't let me invest a penny more. He's going to Paris tomorrow night, to start these people on their way; and then he is coming back, and we are to be married and follow them.'

Leon looked at her thoughtfully.

'Tomorrow night—do you mean tonight?'

She glanced quickly at the clock, and laughed.

'Of course, tonight.'

Then she leaned across the table and spoke earnestly.

'Mr Gonsalez, I've heard so much about you and your friends, and I'm sure you wouldn't betray our secret. If I'd any sense I should have come to you yesterday and asked you for the tablet—I would even pay a good sum to relieve John's anxiety. Is it too late now?'

Leon nodded.

'Much too late. I am keeping that as a memento. The enterprising gentleman who wrote the paragraph told you that it is part of my story collection—and I never part with stories. By the way, when do you give your cheque?'

Her lips twitched at this.

'You still think John is a wicked swindler? I gave him the cheque yesterday.'

'A thousand or eight hundred?'

'That is for him to decide,' she said.

Leon nodded, and rose.

'I will not trouble you any further. Burglary, Miss Martin, is evidently not your speciality, and I should advise you to avoid that profession in the future.'

'You're not giving me in charge?' she smiled.

'Not yet,' said Leon.

He opened the door for her, and stood in his dressing-gown, watching her. He saw her cross the road to the taxi rank, and take the last vehicle available. Then he bolted the door and went back to bed.

His alarm clock called him at seven, and he arose cheerfully, having before him work which was after his own heart. In the morning he called at a tourist agency and bought a ticket to Paris—it seemed a waste of time to go to the office of the High Commissioner for South Africa and examine the available records of the Cape Police; but he was a conscientious man. The afternoon he spent idling near the Northern and Southern Bank in Threadneedle Street, and at a quarter to three his vigil was rewarded, for he saw Major John Rutland descend from a cab, go into the bank, and emerge a few minutes before the big doors closed. The Major looked very pleased with himself—a handsome fellow, rather slim, with a short-cropped military moustache.

Manfred came back in the afternoon, but Leon told him nothing of the burglary. After dinner he went up to his own room, took from a drawer an automatic, laid a few spots of oil in the sliding jacket, and loaded it carefully. From a small box he took a silencer, which he fixed to the muzzle. He put the apparatus into his overcoat pocket, found his suitcase, and came downstairs. George was standing in the hallway.

'Going out, Leon?'

'I shall be away a couple of days,' said Leon, and Manfred, who never asked questions, opened the door for him.

Leon was hunched up in a corner of a first-class carriage when he saw Major Rutland and the girl pass. Behind them, an unwanted third, was a tall, thin-faced man with grey hair, obviously the surgeon. Leon saw them from the corner of his eye, and as the train pulled out had another glimpse of the girl waving her hand to her departing lover.

"THE ENGLISHMAN KONNOR"

It was a dark, gusty night; the weather conditions chalked on a board at the railway station promised an unpleasant crossing, and when he stepped on to the boat at midnight he found it rolling uneasily, even in the comparatively calm waters of the harbour.

He made a quick scrutiny of the purser's list. Major Rutland had taken a cabin and this, after the boat began to move out of harbour, he located. It was the aft cabin *de luxe*—not a beautiful apartment, for the ship was an old one.

He waited till the assistant purser came along to collect his ticket, and then: 'I'm afraid I've lost my ticket,' he said, and paid.

His ticket from Dover to Calais was in his pocket, but Major Rutland had not taken the Calais but the Ostend boat. He watched the assistant purser go into the cabin de luxe, and peered through the window. The Major was lying on a sofa, his cap pulled down over his eyes.

After the assistant purser had taken his ticket and departed, Leon waited for another half-hour; then he saw the cabin go dark. He wandered round the ship: the last light of England showed glitteringly on the south-western horizon. There were no passengers on deck: the few that the ship carried had gone below, for she was tossing and rolling diabolically. Another quarter of an hour passed, and then Leon turned the handle of the stateroom door, stepped into the cabin and sent the light of his small torch round the room. Evidently the Major was travelling without a great deal of luggage: there were two small suitcases and nothing more.

These Leon took out on to the deck and, walking to the rail, dropped them into the water. The man's hat went the same way. He put the torch back into his pocket and, returning for the second time to the cabin, gently shook the sleeper.

'I want to speak to you, Konnor,' he said, in a voice little above a whisper.

The man was instantly awake. 'Who are you?'

'Come outside: I want to talk to you.'

'Major Rutland' followed on to the dim deck.

'Where are you going?' he asked.

The aft of the ship was reserved for second-class passengers, and this, too, was deserted. They made their way to the rail above the stern. They were in complete darkness.

'You know who I am?'

'Haven't the slightest idea,' was the cool reply.

'My name is Gonsalez. Yours, of course, is Eugene Konnor—or Bergstoft,' said Leon. 'You were at one time an officer in the—' He mentioned the regiment. 'In the desert you went over to the enemy by arrangements made through an agency in Cairo. You were reported killed, but in reality you were employed by the enemy as a spy. You were responsible for the disaster at El Masjid—don't try to draw that gun or your life will be shorter.'

'Well,' said the man, a little breathlessly, 'what do you want?'

'I want first of all the money you drew from the bank this afternoon. I've an idea that Miss Martin gave you a blank cheque, and I've a stronger idea that you filled that almost to the limit of her balance, as she will discover tomorrow morning.'

'A hold-up, eh?' Konnor laughed harshly.

'That money, and quick!' said Leon, between his teeth.

Konnor felt the point of the gun against his stomach, and obeyed. Leon took the thick pad of notes from the man, and slipped it into his pocket.

'I suppose you realize, Mr Leon Gonsalez, that you're going to get into very serious trouble?' began Konnor. 'I thought you'd probably decipher the pass—'

'I deciphered the pass without any trouble at all, if you're referring to the gold tablet,' said Leon. 'It said that "the Englishman Konnor is permitted to enter our lines at any moment of the day or night and is to be afforded every assistance," and it was signed by the Commander of the Third Army. Yes, I know all about that.'

'When I get back to England—' began the man.

'You've no intention of going back to England. You're married. You were married in Dublin—and that was probably not your first bigamy. How much money is there here?'

'Thirty or forty thousand—you needn't think that Miss Martin will prosecute me.'

'Nobody is going to prosecute you,' said Leon, in a low voice.

He took one quick glance around: the decks were empty.

'You're a traitor to your country—if you have a country; a man who has sent thousands of the men who were his comrades to their death. That is all.'

There was a flash of fire from his hand, a guttural 'plop!' Konnor's knees went under him, but before he reached the ground Leon Gonsalez caught him under the arms, threw the pistol into the water, lifted the man without an effort and heaved him into the dark sea...

When Ostend harbour came into sight, and the steward went to collect Major Rutland's luggage, he found it had gone, and with it the owner. Passengers are very often mean, and carry their own luggage on to the deck in order to save porterage. The steward shrugged his shoulders and thought no more of the matter.

As for Leon Gonsalez, he stayed in Brussels one day, posted without comment the £34,000 in notes to Miss Lois Martin, caught the train to Calais and was back in London that night. Manfred glanced up as his friend strode into the dining-room.

'Had a good time, Leon?' he asked.

'Most interesting,' said Leon.

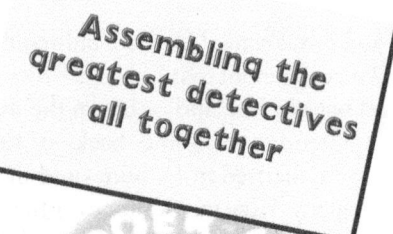
Assembling the greatest detectives all together

Covering the full range and history of detective fiction.
From Zadig, *The Moonstone*, and Dupin through Sherlock Holmes, Loveday Brooke, Montague Egg, Lord Peter Wimsey, *The Thinking Machine*, Father Brown down to Solar Pons.

Voltaire/ Beckford ZADIG AND VATHEK	**Wilkie Collins** THE MOONSTONE	**Edgar Allan Poe** THE COMPLETE DUPIN	**Catherine Pirkis** THE EXPERIENCES OF LOVEDAY BROOKE, LADY DETECTIVE	**G.K. Chesterton** THE COMPLETE FATHER BROWN
Jacques Futrelle THE COMPLETE THINKING MACHINE VOLUME 1	**Dorothy L. Sayers** THE COMPLETE MONTAGUE EGG	**Baroness Orczy** LADY MOLLY OF SCOTLAND YARD	**Dorothy L. Sayers** A PETER WIMSEY OMNIBUS	**August Derleth** THE MEMOIRS OF SOLAR PONS
Sax Rohmer THE FU MANCHU OMNIBUS	**Edgar Wallace** THE COMPLETE J. G. REEDER STORIES	**Émile Gaboriau** MONSIEUR LECOQ	**Ernest Bramah** THE COMPLETE MAX CARRADOS VOLUME 1	**Freeman Wills Crofts** INSPECTOR FRENCH'S GREATEST CASE

For more details and a full list of titles:
visit https://www.hachetteindia.com/home/yellowbacks